For Barry and Josh.

And for everybody trying to
figure out who they really are.

BEAUTY QUEENS

LIBBA BRAY

SCHOLASTIC INC.
New York Toronto London Auckland
Sydney Mexico City New Delhi Hong Kong

ISBN 978-0-439-89598-9

12 11 10 9 8 7 6 5 4 3 2   13 14 15 16 17/0

Printed in the U.S.A.   40
First paperback printing, June 2012

The text was set in Adobe Garamond with Helvetica Neue.
Book design by Elizabeth B. Parisi

A WORD FROM YOUR SPONSOR

This book begins with a plane crash. We do not want you to worry about this. According to the U.S. Department of Unnecessary Statistics, your chances of dying in a plane crash are one in half a million. Whereas your chances of losing your bathing suit bottoms to a strong tide are two to one. So, all in all, it's safer to fly than to go to the beach. As we said, this book begins with a plane crash. But there are survivors. You see? Already it's a happy tale. They are all beauty queen contestants. You do not need to know their names here. But you will get to know them. They are all such nice girls. Yes, they are nice, happy, shining, patriotic girls who happen to have interests in baton twirling, sign language, AIDS prevention in the animal population, the ancient preparation of popadam, feminine firearms, interpretive dance, and sequins. Such a happy story. And shiny, too.

This story is brought to you by The Corporation: Because Your Life Can Always Be Better™. We at The Corporation would like you to enjoy this story, but please be vigilant while reading. If you should happen to notice anything suspicious in the coming pages, do alert the proper authorities. Remember, it could be anything at all — a subversive phrase, an improper thought or feeling let out of its genie bottle of repression, an idea that challenges the status quo, the suggestion that life may not be what it appears to be and that all you've taken for granted (malls, shopping, the relentless pursuit of an elusive happiness, prescription drug ads, those annoying perfume samples in magazines that make your eyes water, the way anchormen and women shift easily from the jovial laughter of a story about a dog that hula-hoops to a grave report on a bus crash that has left five teenagers dead) may be no more consequential than the tattered hem of a dream, leaving you with a bottomless, free-fall feeling.

This is the sort of thing we are warning you about.

But let's not worry, shall we? There's nothing to worry about. Though there is the threat of a war, it happens in the background, in snippets on the nightly news between ads for sinus medicines. It's none of our concern. This is a happy story.

Now, our story begins, as so many happy stories do, with a blue, blue sky. A blue, blue sky punctuated by thick white clouds; they drift across the expanse like semicolons, reminding us that there is more to come. The pilot, a man in his forties who once stayed on a mechanical bull for a full eight seconds, has just turned off the FAS-TEN SEAT BELTS sign. The flight is on its way to a remote tropical paradise where the girls will compete against one another for the title of Miss Teen Dream.

Oh, dear. *Compete* is a rather ugly word, isn't it? After all, these are such lovely girls, pure of heart and high of spirits. Let's say that they will be "drawing on their personal best," and some girls will "proceed on a path of Miss Teen Dreamdom" while others will "have the option to explore other pageant opportunities elsewhere at an unspecified future time." Ah. There. That's much better, isn't it?

The pilot and copilot, whose names are not important to our tale, are trading stories with each other, as they may be wont to do in those mysterious quarters beyond the galley. We cannot truly know. We do know that in just a few moments, they will struggle valiantly to land the plane on a small scrub of island in the middle of the ocean. They will be partly successful.

On the other side of the cockpit door, fifty girls smile and preen and pose for the cameras. One girl confesses this is her first plane ride as she stares out the window, her mouth open in awe, her mind completely unbothered by thoughts of who will live and who will "have her living options curtailed."[1]

In the cabin, the pilot notes the red light and abandons his story. Flames erupt from the right engine. The turbine breaks into useless slivers. Vibrations shake the plane, causing it to pitch and wobble. The view from the right is now marred by a billowing plume of black smoke.

And so our tale begins with a sudden fall from blue skies, with screams and prayers and a camera crew bravely recording every bit of the turbulence and drama: What a lucky break for their show! How the producers will crow! Ratings will skyrocket! Suddenly terse flight attendants rush through the aisles barking orders, securing latches on the agitating overhead bins. One girl leads the others in a song about Jesus being her copilot, which makes them feel better, as if, even as they assume crash-landing positions with their arms over their heads, a bearded man in white robes and sandals is strapping on a headset and grabbing the controls.

The right engine quits entirely, and there is a brief period of absolute silence. In the pressurized air of the cabin, a hopeful, euphoric feeling swells behind the lacy underwires guarding the chests of these girls — the thought that perhaps there was nothing to be frightened about after all, that they've escaped a grisly fate and are now being given a second chance. Through the left-side windows, they can see the strange, verdant land taking shape, growing bigger as they descend. It's beautiful. They will land safely, no matter the sudden near-vertical descent. They're sure of it. After all, these are can-do girls from a nation built upon dreams. And what is the ear-splitting scream of metal against metal, the choking smoke, the sensation of falling through a surprisingly uncaring sky, against such unshakable dreams?

---

[1] You look worried. Really, you should relax. Reading is a pleasurable activity and worrying is bad for your heart.

CHAPTER ONE

"Are you all right?"

The voice was tinny in Adina's ears. Her head ached, and she was wet. She remembered the plane pitching and falling, the smoke and screams, the panic, and then nothing.

"Am I dead?" she asked the face looming over hers. The face had apple cheeks and was framed by a halo of glossy black curls.

"No."

"Are *you* dead?" Adina asked warily.

The face above her shook from side to side, and then burst into tears. Adina relaxed, reasoning that she had to be alive, unless the afterlife was a lot more bipolar than she'd been led to believe. She pulled herself to a sitting position and waited for the wooziness to subside. A gash on her knee was caked in dried blood. Another on her arm still seeped. Her dress was ripped and slightly scorched and she wore only one shoe. It was one half of her best pair, and in her state of shock, finding the other became important. "Can you help me find my shoe?"

"Sure. I saw some in the water. I hope they're not leather," the other girl said in an accent flat as a just-plowed field. She had huge, blue, anime-worthy eyes. "I'm Miss Nebraska, Mary Lou Novak."

"Adina Greenberg. Miss New Hampshire." Adina cupped her hands over her eyes, looking out toward the sea. "I don't see it."

"That's a shame. It's a real nice shoe."

"Roland Me'sognie[2]," Adina said, and she honestly couldn't figure out why. She didn't care about the stupid brand. That was her mother's influence. Shock. It had to be the shock.

"If I can find my suitcase, I've got an extra pair of sneakers in there. I'm a size eight."

"Thanks."

"You're welcome. I like to be helpful. It's sort of a Nebraska thing. My pageant sponsor says I've got a real good chance at Miss Congeniality this year."

"Miss Congeniality represents the true heart of the pageant," Adina found herself repeating from the Miss Teen Dream manual. She vaguely remembered that she used to make a gagging motion at that, but she was too dazed for snarkiness just now. Dazed because, yes, when she'd been looking for her shoe, she'd seen bodies in the water. Lifeless bodies.

"Miss Congeniality is an ambassador of smiles," Mary Lou said in a choked voice.

"It'll be okay," Adina said, even though she was pretty sure that this was the textbook definition of *so not okay*. "I think we should find everybody else."

Mary Lou wiped her nose on the torn chiffon of her sleeve and followed Adina along the crescent of beach. The air smelled of smoke. A blackened metal wing lay on the sand. Sparkly evening gowns floated on the tide like jellyfish skin, the shininess attracting

---

[2] Roland Me'sognie, the notoriously fat-phobic French designer whose tourniquet-tight fashions adorn the paper cut–thin bodies of models, starlets, socialites, and reality TV stars. In fact, when the svelte pinup Bananas Foster, famous for starring in a series of medical side-effect commercials, was arrested in a Vegas club for snorting cholesterol-lowering drugs while wearing a Roland jumpsuit, he pronounced her "too fat to steal my oxygen. I die to see her misuse my genius. The earth weeps with me." Sales rose 88% that week. The House of Roland was the first to introduce sizing lower than 0 — the -1. "We make the woman disappear and the fashion appear!"

the curiosity of the seagulls who swooped over them in a repeated figure eight. Girls in various states of bedraggled dotted the sand like exotic, off-course birds. The contents of opened suitcases and flung purses were strewn across the beach. A red-white-and-blue, fringed baton-twirler's dress hung from a tree. A soggy beauty whose sash identified her as Miss Ohio stumbled out of the surf and sank to her knees, coughing up water and bile.

"Oh my God," Adina muttered. She knew she should do something here; she just couldn't remember what. The Corporation's Miss Teen Dream plane had been flying them to Paradise Cove for the Forty-first Annual Miss Teen Dream Pageant. They were to film some fun-in-the-sun promotional pieces, ride the waterslides, and practice their performance numbers. They had all just arrived in Florida the night before, and that morning, at ten A.M., fifty beaming girls in outfits adorned with something emblematic of their states had boarded the plane. Adina had wanted to put New Hampshire's famous poet Robert Frost on her outfit, but her mother and Alan had said there were no poets among the judges, and now her dress had an image of the White Mountains that ranged disastrously across her 36DDs. She'd sat on the plane, her arms folded over her chest, hating that she'd been talked into wearing it. Then came the bang and the smoke, the screams, the falling, the exit doors opening, the sensation of tumbling through the air and landing in a mound of warm sand. How many had made it out? What had happened to the pilots, the chaperones, the Corporation film crew? Where were they now?

A voice with a strong twang rang out. "All right, Miss Teen Dreamers! Yoo-hoo! Over here! I'm wigglin' my fingers for y'all's attention! Could y'all come on over here, please?"

The waving goddess stood outlined by the smoking metal wing as if she were a model in a showroom of plane wreckage. She was tall and tanned, her long blond hair framing her gorgeous face in messy waves. Her teeth were dazzlingly white. Across the midriff of her dress was a sheer mesh inset of a Lone Star Flag. The girls wandered over, drawn to the command her beauty bestowed.

"Y'all come on down and gather round, horseshoe formation — thank you. Some of y'all can fill in here in front where there are gaps."

The girls did as they were told, happy that someone had taken the reins.

"Hi. I'm Taylor Rene Krystal Hawkins, and I'm Miss Teen Dream Texas, the state where dreams are bigger and better — nothing against y'all's states. I'm a senior at George Walker Bush High School and I hope to pursue a career as a motivational speaker."

There was polite, automatic applause. A dazed girl beside Adina said, "I want to pursue a career in the exciting world of weight-management broadcast journalism. And help kids not have cancer and stuff."

Miss Texas spoke again: "Okay, Miss Teen Dreamers, I know we're all real flustered and everything. But we're alive. And I think before anything else we need to pray to the one we love."

A girl raised her hand. "J. T. Woodland[3]?"

"I'm talkin' about my personal copilot, Jesus Christ."

"Someone should tell her personal copilot that His landings suck," Miss Michigan muttered. She was a lithe redhead with the panther-like carriage of a professional athlete.

"Dear Jesus," Taylor started. The girls bowed their heads, except for Adina.

"Don't you want to pray?" Mary Lou whispered.

"I'm Jewish. Not big on the Jesus."

"Oh. I didn't know they had any Jewish people in New Hampshire. You should make that one of your Fun Facts About Me!"

Adina opened her mouth but couldn't think of anything to say.

"Ahem. *Dear Jesus*," Taylor intoned more fervently. "We just want to thank you for gettin' us here safe —"

---

[3] J. T. Woodland, known as "the cute one" in The Corporation's seventh-grade boy band, Boyz Will B Boyz. Due to the success of their triple-platinum hit, "Let Me Shave Your Legs Tonight, Girl," Boyz Will B Boyz ruled the charts for a solid eleven months before hitting puberty and losing ground to Hot Vampire Boyz. Five years later, Boyz Will B Boyz is nothing more than a trivia question.

There was a loud, gurgling groan. Somebody shouted, "Oh my gosh! Miss Delaware just died!"

"— for gettin' some of us here safe," Taylor continued. "And we pray that, as we are fine, upstandin', law-abidin' girls who represent the best of the best, you will protect us from harm and keep us safe until we are rescued and can tell our story to *People* magazine. Amen."

"Amen," the girls echoed, then fell into noisy chatter. Where were they? What would happen to them? Would they be rescued? Where were the adults? Was this something to do with the war?

"Teen Dream Misses!" Taylor singsonged above the din, smiling. "My stars. It's gettin' kinda noisy. Now. My daddy is a general, and I know what he'd say if he were here: We need to do a recon mission, see if there are any more survivors, and tend to the wounded."

"My head kinda hurts," Miss New Mexico said. Several of the girls gasped. Half of an airline serving tray was lodged in her forehead, forming a small blue canopy over her eyes.

"What is it?" Miss New Mexico checked to make sure her bra straps weren't showing.

"N-nothing." Miss Ohio managed an awkward smile.

"First things first," Taylor said. "Any of y'all have first-aid training?"

Miss Alabama's hand shot up at the same time as Miss Mississippi's. They were both artificially tanned and bleach-blond, with the same expertly layered long hair. If not for the ragged state sashes they still wore, it would be hard to tell them apart.

"Names?" Taylor prompted.

"I'm Tiara with an *A*," said Miss Mississippi.

"I'm Brittani with an *I*," said Miss Alabama. "I got my Scouting Badge in First Aid."

"Ohmigosh, me, too!" Tiara threw her arms around Brittani. "You're so nice. If it's not me, I hope you win."

"No, I hope YOU win!"

"Ladies, this part is not a competition," Taylor said. "Okay. Miss

Alabama and Miss Mississippi are on first-aid duty. Anybody have a phone that survived?"

Two of the girls brought forward phones. One was water damaged. The other could not get a signal.

Adina spoke up. "Maybe we should have a roll call, see who's here and who's missing."

Missing settled over the girls like a sudden coat of snow shaken loose from an awning, and they moved forward on autopilot, dazed smiles in place, and stated their names and representative states. Occasionally, one would divulge that she was an honors student or a cheerleader or a volunteer at a soup kitchen, as if, in this moment of collective horror, they could not divorce themselves from who they had been before, when such information was required, when it got them from one pageant to the next, all the way to the big one. Of the fifty states, only twelve girl representatives were accounted for, including Miss California, Shanti Singh; Miss Michigan, Jennifer Huberman; and Miss Rhode Island, Petra West, who, ironically, was the biggest girl in the pageant at nearly six feet. Some girls argued over whether the death of Miss Massachusetts — favored by bookies to win the whole thing — meant that the competition would never feel entirely fair.

"Thank you, ladies. I'm guessing that's where the rest of the plane is." Taylor pointed to the thick black smoke spiraling up from the jungle. "There might be more of us in there. We need to organize a search party. A Miss Teen Dream Recon Machine. Any volunteers?"

As a unit, the girls turned to gaze at the forbidding expanse of jungle. No one raised her hand. Taylor clicked her tongue. "Well, I guess there aren't any Ladybird Hopes[4] in this crowd. My stars, I'm glad she's

---

[4] Ladybird Hope, the most famous Miss Teen Dream who ever lived, making her name as a bikini-clad meteorologist, small-town talk show host, lobbyist, mayor, and Corporation businesswoman with her own clothing line. Rumored to be running for president.

not here to see this. I bet she'd vomit in her mouth with disappointment. And then, like a pro, she'd swallow it down and keep smiling."

Taylor took a pink gloss from a hidden pocket and slicked the glittery wand over her lips. "You remember that The Corporation almost canceled the Miss Teen Dream Pageant last year due to low ratings, and they were gonna replace it with that show about Amish girls who share a house with strippers, *Girls Gone Rumspringa*? And then, just like a shining angel, Ladybird Hope stepped in and said she would personally secure the advertisers for the pageant. I have lived my whole life according to Ladybird and her platform — Being Perfect in Every Way — and I'm not about to let her down now. If I have to, I will go into that jungle by myself. I'll bet those Corporation camera crews will be real happy to see me."

"I'll go!" Shanti's hand shot up.

"Me, too!" Petra yelled.

Mary Lou nudged Adina. "I guess it wouldn't be very congenial of me not to go. Will you come, too? I want to have one friend."

Adina didn't know what they'd find in the jungle, but journalists always went where the story was, and Adina was the best journalist at New Castle High School. It was what had gotten her into this mess. She raised her hand to volunteer.

Two teams were organized and, after much debate, names were chosen: The Sparkle Ponies would stay on the beach, tend to the wounded, and try to salvage whatever they could from the wreckage. The Lost Girls would soldier into the jungle in the hopes of finding survivors.

Shanti gave instructions to the girls heading into the surf toward the mangled half plane, which was taking on water quickly. "We need to remember to bring out anything we can — first-aid kits, blankets, pillows, seat cushions, clothes, and especially food and water."

"But why?" Tiara asked. "They'll be coming to rescue us real soon."

"We don't know how long that will be. We've got to survive till then."

"Ohmigosh. No food at all." Tiara sank down on the sand as if the full weight of their predicament had finally hit her. She blinked back tears. And then that megawatt smile that belonged on cereal boxes across the nation reappeared. "I am going to be so superskinny by pageant time!"

CHAPTER TWO

The Lost Girls set off down the beach. Taylor led the way. Adina, Shanti, Petra, Mary Lou, and Tiara followed. Above them, the sun was a jaundiced eye. To the right, the vast turquoise ocean bit at the shoreline, gobbling small mouthfuls of sand. The sand itself, white as desert-bleached animal bones, stretched for miles, in one direction yielding to jungle growth and, farther on, green mountains and lava-formed cliffs, which created an almost turretlike wall running the length of the island. Just behind those cliffs a volcano rose, vanishing into heavy cloud cover. Its rumble could be heard on the beach, like a giant groaning in its sleep.

Shanti pointed to the volcano. "I hope that's not active," she said in a slightly British Indian–inflected voice.

The girls walked in the direction of the smoke and possible survivors, chaperones or handlers who might take charge and make everything better. They trekked through the inhospitable growth, breathing in gelatin-thick humidity mixed with soot and smoke. The jungle sounds were what they noticed first: Thick. Percussive. A thrumming heartbeat of danger wrapped in a muscular green. Sweat beaded across their upper lips and matted their sashes to their bodies. A bird shrieked from a nearby tree, making all the girls except Taylor jump.

"The smoke's comin' from over there, Miss Teen Dreamers," Taylor said. She veered to the right, and the girls followed.

The jungle gave way to a small clearing.

"Holy moly . . ." Mary Lou said.

Enormous totems rose next to the trees. With their angry mouths, jagged teeth, and bloodred, pupilless eyes, they were clearly meant to frighten. But who had built them and what were they supposed to frighten away? The girls huddled closer together, alert and terrified.

"You think there might be cannibals here?" Mary Lou whispered.

"Maybe these have been here for centuries and the people who built them are long gone," Adina said without conviction.

Shanti put up a hand. "Wait. Did you hear that?"

"Hear what?" Petra said.

"It came from over there!" Shanti pointed to a copse just beyond the ring of totems. The sound came again: a grunting. Something was moving through the bushes.

"Grab whatever you can," Taylor instructed. She yanked a heavy switch from a tree. "Follow my lead."

Shanti, Mary Lou, Tiara, and Petra picked up handfuls of rocks. Adina could find nothing but a measly stick. Taylor held up three fingers, counting down to one. "Now!"

The girls launched the rocks and sticks at the jungle. From behind a bush came a hiss of pain.

"Lost Girls, hold your fire," Taylor instructed.

A willowy girl wrapped in a singed navy blanket stepped out into the open, moaning. Her skin was the same deep brown as the carved figures.

"I'll try to communicate," Taylor said. She spoke slowly and deliberately. "Hello! We need help. Is your village close?"

"My village is Denver. And I think it's a long way from here. I'm Nicole Ade. Miss Colorado."

"We have a Colorado where we're from, too!" Tiara said. She swiveled her hips, spread her arms wide, then brought her hands together prayer-style and bowed. "Kipa aloha."

Nicole stared. "I speak *English*. I'm *American*. Also, did you learn those moves from Barbie's *Hawaiian Vacation* DVD?"

"Ohmigosh, yes! Do your people have that, too?"

Petra stepped forward. "Hi. I'm Petra West. Miss Rhode Island. Are you okay?"

"Yeah. I'm fine. A little sore and scratched up from where I got thrown into some bushes, but no contusions or signs of internal bleeding." Nicole allowed a small smile. "I'm pre-pre-med."

Shanti frowned. She'd hoped to have the ethnic thing sewn up. Having a black pre-pre-med contestant wasn't going to help her. She covered her unease with a wide smile. "It's good we found you."

Taylor sheathed her makeshift club. "We're trying to find survivors. Did you see anybody else out here?"

Nicole shook her head. "Just a lot of dead chaperones and camera crew. I was scared I was the only one left alive. Are *we* the only ones?"

Tiara shook her head. "We left the Sparkle Ponies on the beach to tend to the wounded. We're the Lost Girls. Oh, but you can choose to be a Sparkle Pony if you want. You don't have to be a Lost Girl."

For a second, Nicole wasn't sure that she should go with these white girls. They sounded like they'd gone straight-up crazy, and the only other brown girl was giving her an eyeful of attitude. Nicole did what she'd been taught since she was little and her parents had moved into an all-white neighborhood: She smiled and made herself seem as friendly and nonthreatening as possible. It's what she did when she met the parents of her friends. There was always that split second — something almost felt rather than seen — when the parents' faces would register a tiny shock, a palpable discomfort with Nicole's "otherness." And Nicole would smile wide and say how nice it was to come over. She would call the parents Mr. or Mrs., never by their first names. Their suspicion would ebb away, replaced by an unspoken but nonetheless palpable pride in her "good breeding," for which they should take no credit but did anyway. Nicole could never quite relax in these homes. She'd spend the evening perched on the edge of the couch, ready to make a quick getaway. By the time she left, she'd have bitten her nails and cuticles ragged, and her mother would shake her head and say she was going to make her wear gloves.

"I'm glad to see you." Nicole smiled right on cue and watched the other girls relax. She fought the urge to put her fingernails in her mouth.

"Daylight's wasting, Miss Teen Dreamers. Let's not stand here jibber-jabbering," Taylor said and set off in the direction of the smoke.

On the trail, Shanti hurried to walk alongside Nicole. "Hello. I'm Shanti. Miss California. I can make popadam as my mother and grandmother taught me in honor of our heritage."

"Oh. Cool," Nicole said.

"Do you have any traditions like that?"

Nicole shrugged. "We go to my Auntie Abeo's house on Thanksgiving. That's about it."

Shanti smiled. *Bingo.* "Sounds fun."

"Yeah. It's pretty fun, I guess," Nicole said, trying to seem extra friendly. "She's Nigerian, and it's all about teaching me traditional Igbo drumming. Sort of boring. But it comes in handy for the talent portion."

Shanti's smile faltered. "You do traditional Nigerian drumming as your talent?"

"Mmm-hmm. What's your talent?"

"Traditional Indian dancing."

"Oh. Cool," Nicole said.

"Yes. You, too."

A low-lying branch almost caught Shanti in the nose, but her reflexes had been honed through years of synchronized Tae Kwon Do, and she whapped it away at the last moment. She glanced sideways at Nicole, sizing her up. Pre-pre-med. Traditional Nigerian drumming. Great legs. The degree of difficulty had just gone up, but Shanti hadn't spent two years under the tutelage of her handler, Mrs. Mirabov, for nothing. It was just another challenge to be met, another challenge to win.

"Go ahead," Nicole said, letting Shanti pass.

"No. After you," Shanti said. After all, it was the last time Nicole would get ahead of her.

They reached the smoking wreckage of the plane's cabin. The front still burned. Debris was spread out in a wide circle. Inside, Adina could make out the charred bodies of the pilot and copilot still strapped to their seats, hands stuck to the gears. There were other bodies burned beyond recognition.

"Oh, Jesus, Mary, and Joseph," Mary Lou whispered.

They spread out, searching for anyone who might have survived, but there was no one. And the plane was too hot for them to go inside. They called, but no one answered.

"We better go back and see what the Sparkle Ponies have found," Taylor said.

Mary Lou squealed and the girls rushed to her side. The body of a flight attendant lay in the bushes about ten feet away, her arms reaching forward as if she had tried to escape by crawling into the jungle. Her dark blue uniform was only slightly singed.

"So sad," said Mary Lou.

"Miss Teen Dreamers, we can't leave this body here. It will attract predators," Taylor said.

"You mean like those guys who NetChat you and pretend they're a hot German pop star named Hans but who turn out to be some old fat guy in a house in Kansas?" Tiara shook her head. "My mom was so pissed."

"She means like tigers or bears," Petra said.

"Oh my."

Mary Lou made a face. "What . . . what should we do?"

Taylor thought for a minute. "Put her in the fire."

Shanti swallowed hard. "Way harsh. I mean, it's terrible."

"Yes, it is. But sometimes a lady has to do what's necessary," Taylor said. "From Ladybird Hope's *I'm Perfect and You Can Be, Too*, Chapter Three: 'A lady's quick thinking can save a bad situation.'

She was talking about putting nail polish on a runner in your hose, but I think the same rule applies here."

The girls set about their grisly task. They dragged the body to the front of the plane, where the fire raged, and hoisted the flight attendant into it.

"Oh God," Mary Lou said, and threw up in a bush.

In her head, Adina said a mourner's prayer for the flight attendant, and for everyone else who'd died. It was true that the situation was dire and Adina had hardly known these people. But their deaths still deserved the dignity of a prayer here in the wilderness.

Petra stared at the dead woman another long minute. In her head, she did the math of survival. Seven days of medication. That was all she'd brought with her — and that was if she could find her overnight case.

"What do we do now?" Mary Lou asked through fresh tears. She rubbed the St. Agnes medal at her throat.

"They'll be looking for us," Nicole assured her. "Right? I mean, they have to be looking for us."

"There's probably a search plane on its way right now," Mary Lou said.

The jungle answered with unknown screeches and a low, murmuring hiss. No one moved. They watched what was left burn.

"We should get back and let the others know," Taylor said at last. "It's just us. We're the only survivors. We're on our own."

CHAPTER THREE

By the time the Lost Girls returned to the beach, the sky was the color of wet slate and an army of angry clouds massed along the horizon, awaiting further instruction.

Taylor convened the girls in the same spot as before. "All right, Miss Teen Dreamers. If y'all could settle into our horseshoe all nice and orderly, please? Miss Montana? Is that the way a Miss Teen Dream sits, all slutty like that with her hoo-hoo showing?"

Miss Montana knocked her knees together and yanked down the hem of her skirt.

"Thank you." Taylor addressed the crowd. Her expression was calm. "I've got a little bit of bad news: Everybody else is dead."

A great gasp went up. A few girls cried and some simply stared, unable to process the information.

Miss Ohio raised her hand. "What about the film crew?"

"Gone," Petra confirmed. She'd added a rescued shawl to her ensemble, tying it in an elaborate bow beneath her chin. In times of stress, she relied on her skills at accessorizing to calm her.

"That's terrible," Brittani wailed. "They seemed so nice."

"One of the camera guys told me I was just like Lorrie Connor on *The Shills*[5]," Tiara said.

---

[5] *The Shills*, The Corporation's wildly popular program about product placement and the teens who love it. Currently, it ranks #3 among the coveted 13–18 demographic, just behind *What Would You Do to Be Famous?* and *My Drama So Tops Your Drama!*

"OMG, I love that show!"

The girls fell into excited chatter. "Did you see the one where Lorrie and Chad broke up and she gave him back the Frou-Frou handbag he bought her after she agreed to fake marry him to promote his new beer line? I totally cried."

"That was awesome TV. I heard she's gonna hire a ghostwriter to write a book about that episode."

Taylor's sharp clap echoed on the beach. "Teen Dreamers! We need to focus like it's the final interview round and the questions are all about anorexia and current events. Now, I know y'all are upset. This is just plain awful. But God doesn't make mistakes. Is this is a setback, Teen Dreamers?"

"Totally," wailed Miss Arkansas. Her left arm was broken. It had been bandaged into a ninety-degree angle as if she were perpetually waving to an unseen crowd.

"No, ma'am. No, it is not. I know what Ladybird Hope would say. She would say that this is an opportunity for growth and the establishment of your personal brand. Everybody loves a survivor. And everybody loves a Miss Teen Dream contestant. When you put those two together, you have a lot of hope. And big endorsement opportunities when we get back. Let's get a woo-hoo goin'!"

A halfhearted chorus of "woo-hoo" rippled through the horseshoe-shaped cluster of exhausted, hungry girls.

Taylor shouted, "Now, I *know* y'all can be louder than that!"

"WOO-HOO!"

"That's the Miss Teen Dream spirit. Sparkle Ponies, report: What did y'all salvage from the plane?"

The girls listed off their bounty: four hot roller sets, two straightening irons, a few teeth-bleaching trays, five seat cushions, three waterlogged beauty magazines, a notebook, laxatives, diet pills, a few suitcases filled with clothes, evening gowns, a collection of mismatched bathing suit tops and bottoms, various shoes, bags of pretzels, and bottles of water.

"Good work, Sparkle Ponies," Taylor commended. "We are going to stay here and build a fire that any passing ships can see so we can be rescued. And I think for now we should keep our sashes on so we can identify one another easily, especially in the dark. And, of course, we need to keep up our pageant skills."

"Pageant skills? You're kidding, right?" Adina hadn't meant to blurt it out.

Taylor narrowed her eyes. "I never kid about Miss Teen Dream."

"Reality check: We're stuck on a freaking island with only a few bags of pretzels to eat and God only knows what kinds of dangerous animals or mega-zombie-insects out there, and you want us to keep working on our pageant skills?"

Taylor glossed her lips again and smacked them together. "Correct."

"Don't be so negative," Miss Ohio said. "I'll bet the coast guard is on its way to rescue us right now."

Adina shook her head. "What we need is a team leader."

"I accept," Taylor said.

"Um, not to be rude or anything, but usually you put it to a vote. It's a democracy, right?" Adina laughed uncomfortably.

Taylor gave her a sharp look that was not softened in the least by a new smile. "Anybody else want to run for leader?"

No one spoke.

"Okay. Well, looks like —"

"I do," Adina said quickly.

"What are your leadership qualifications?" Taylor asked.

"I won awards for my work on the school newspaper. And I'm a member of the National Honor Society."

"No offense," Taylor said, "but this is a little different from running the school newspaper."

Adina had gone to state twice with the Quarry Quarrelers debate team. Her argument in favor of having a contraception fund-raiser for the junior prom had been rock solid — her debate captain, Mr. El-Shabaz, had said so — and it wasn't her fault that the administration was so sexist and backward-thinking. At times, Adina's whole life felt like one giant push against a paint-stuck door. But there was no way she was going down to this overgrown Babez Doll[6] with misplaced priorities. These birdbrained beauty freaks needed her. Squaring her shoulders as she'd been taught to do on those afternoons in the portable building where the debate team practiced, she faced her audience.

"Hello. I am Adina Greenberg, Miss New Hampshire, and I would like to be your team leader. Point A: We need to think realistically. It could be weeks before we're rescued. I submit that our goal should not be the continuation of the pageant, but survival. We need to find food and potable water. Also, out here in the open we're totally defenseless. I think we should find some kind of shelter; a cave or something."

"I don't want to do that! What if there's, like, a creature living in the cave?" Tiara said. "Seriously, I saw this show once where these people were stranded on an island and there were these other people who were sort of crazy-slash-bad and there was this polar bear creature running around."

"What happened?" Miss Ohio asked.

"I don't know. My parents got divorced in the middle of season two and we lost our TiVo."

"In conclusion," Adina shouted, "I am great at organizing a team and making things happen. I am willing to make tough decisions even if it means people won't like me. In short, I would make an excellent team leader. Thank you."

The girls glanced around awkwardly. Mary Lou clapped; it was followed by halfhearted applause by the others. Taylor moved forward. She tossed her already tousled hair and beamed. "Judges ready? Hi, y'all. I am Taylor Rene Krystal Hawkins, Miss Texas."

---

[6] Babez Dolls, the most popular toy for girls ages 4–10. Known for their oversize heads and fabulous accessories, including the Babez Peacock-Feather Sports Bra and the Babez Rockin' Doc Cubic Zirconia Stethoscope/Microphone and Peel-away Lab Coat. Total sales annually: one billion.

"In the history of the pageant, there's never not been a Miss Texas in the Top Ten," Petra whispered.

Adina rolled her eyes. "So? You do need a few more qualifications than that to be a leader."

"Like what?" Tiara asked.

Taylor stood in a perfect three-quarters stance, arms hanging easily at her sides. "I have been class president three years in a row, homecoming queen, a National Merit Scholar, and a member of the National Honor Society, and I am a proud, card-carrying member of FAF — Femmes and Firearms. I can shoot a thirty-aught-six as well as a nine-millimeter and a Pink Lady paint gun. Last year, I took down my first buck, which I cleaned, filleted, and vacuum sealed, and with my taxidermy skills, I stuffed the head and used the antlers as a supercute jewelry tree, which I plan to market for the Armchair Shopping Network in the spring. That is American ingenuity. It's what makes this country great, and if elected, I would be proud to serve. Thank you."

For a moment, the roar of applause drowned out the rough surf. Adina's stomach clenched. It was just like fifth grade all over again, when she lost hall monitor to Ryan Berry, who couldn't even spell *hall monitor* but who did a rap routine about lining up in an orderly fashion for his in-class presentation and totally killed.

Taylor flashed Adina a wolfish smile. "All righty, then. Let's put it to a vote! All y'all who want to elect Adina team leader, raise your hands."

Three hands were held up: Mary Lou, Jennifer, and Miss Arkansas, who couldn't lower her hand due to the bandaging.

"All y'all who want to vote for me, Taylor Rene Krystal Hawkins of the Lone Star State, raise your hands." A sea of fingers waved in the breeze. "Looks like I'm the winner. But you're first runner-up, Adina. And you know what they say — if anything should happen, you'd assume the responsibility and the privilege. Now. When we get rescued and get to Paradise Cove, America's gonna be wantin' to see a pageant. And I do not intend to let them down. So. Starting tomorrow, we'll be back to working on our dance numbers and our walking, talent, swimsuit, and evening gown presentations, just like nothing ever happened."

"What about this?" Miss New Mexico pointed to the tray lodged in her forehead.

Taylor looked to Tiara and Brittani, who shrugged in unison.

"We can't take it out. Not without surgery. I know my head wounds," Nicole confirmed. She smiled and gave a small wave. "Hi. Nicole Ade. Miss Colorado, the Centennial State."

Miss New Mexico broke into a full-blown wail. The girls tried to comfort her, to no avail.

"You know what would be cute on you?" Petra said with new authority. "Bangs. So 1960s chic. You'd hardly notice the, um, the . . . addition."

"Love bangs!" Mary Lou said.

"Miss Florida was the only one who had bangs and she's de — um, she's no longer participating in the pageant system. So you'd really stand out."

Miss New Mexico stared, dumbfounded. "Stand out? Stand out! *I have a freaking tray stuck in my forehead!*" She broke into fresh sobs.

Taylor clapped for attention. "Miss New Mexico, let's not get all down in the bummer basement where the creepy things live. There are people in heathen China who don't even have airline trays. We have a lot to be grateful for."

"And a few things to worry about. Look at those clouds." Nicole nodded toward the darkening sky. "Tropical climate. Trade winds. This place probably has a monsoon season. We should scout out some higher ground just in case of flash floods."

Taylor beamed. "Excellent advice, Miss Colorado. Y'all hear that? That's real Miss Teen Dream–thinking."

"Meteorology was another one of my extracurriculars," Nicole said.

"Awesome," Shanti murmured.

"What were your well-roundeds?" Nicole asked, using the pageant terminology for the skills that gave a Miss Teen Dream an edge.

"Oh, nothing much," Shanti said with practiced humility. "Opera. Botany. Chemistry. Fencing. Cello. Synchronized Tae Kwon Do. Indian dance. And, of course, I can make popadam as my mother and grandmother taught me. Family tradition is important, and my family is lucky enough to celebrate both our Indian heritage and the customs of this great country."

She smiled right at Nicole, who immediately chewed on her pinkie nail.

"My family traditions are alcoholism and dysfunction," Jennifer said. "Oh, and anything you can make from government cheese."

Taylor clapped again for attention. "All right, ladies. This is your new team leader talking. Right now, we are not competitors. We are all one team. Let's find a place to camp and look for firewood. Tonight, we'll keep watch in shifts. When we're rescued, The Corporation will be so proud of us, they'll probably give us a summer variety show. 'In the pageant of life, a girl picks up fallen sequins and turns them into a brand-new dress of awesome.' Ladybird Hope's *How to Be Perfect in Every Way*, page forty-two. Let's build us a fire, Teen Dreamers!"

CHAPTER FOUR

"Gee, that went well," Adina snarked to Mary Lou as they searched for anything remotely flammable.

"Mmm."

Adina stopped. "What's that *mmm* mean?"

"Nothing," Mary Lou said quickly. "I mean, I don't want to make you feel bad or anything."

"Mary Lou, I've just survived a plane crash, and now I'm stuck on a hostile island with no food and no way off. Trust me, you're not going to make me feel any worse."

"It was talking about how good you are at your school newspaper that turned everybody off."

"What do you mean?"

Mary Lou picked up a dried frond and added it to the meager pile in her arms. "I don't know, maybe it's a Midwestern thing, but where I'm from, you're not supposed to brag about yourself. That's what my mom says. She says you should wait for people to recognize your good qualities. And then you should say, like, 'Oh, no. I'm not really that great at whatever-it-is. I'm just okay.' And then they'll say, 'No, really. You're great.' And you say, 'I'm really not, but thanks anyway for saying so.' And they'll say, 'Yes, you are. You so are!' And you say, 'Gee, do you really think so?' And they'll say, 'Totally!' And then people think you're good at whatever it is you're good at, but they don't think you're braggy about it 'cause that makes you seem like a real tool. Plus, it's unladylike."

Adina stared. "That is quite literally the most ludicrous thing I have ever heard."

"Thank you. I'm not really that ludicrous, but thanks anyway for saying so. See? That's how it works." Mary Lou gave a shy smile. "Um, that was a joke, by the way. I do know what ludicrous means."

"Thank God."

Out in the ocean, waves crashed over broken fists of treacherous-looking black rock.

Mary Lou played nonstop with a silver ring on her left ring finger.

"Pretty," Adina said. "Special?"

"This? Yeah. It's, um, a purity ring?"

"Oh. The old patriarchal chastity belt. Now in convenient ring form," Adina snarled.

"It's not like that," Mary Lou said, blushing. "It's a symbol. It shows that you've made a pledge to bring your purity into the marriage. It's the ultimate gift to your husband."

"Really? Like you can't just give him a gift card to GameStop or something?"

Mary Lou stopped smiling. "You don't have to make fun of me."

"I'm sorry," Adina said.

"Some girls need protection," Mary Lou mumbled.

"What?" Adina asked.

"Nothing. Jeez, I hope that thing isn't active," Mary Lou said, pointing to the volcano.

"No kidding. That's all we need. Think we've got enough to make a fire?"

"Worth a shot," Mary Lou answered.

Back on the beach, the girls built a signal fire from sticks, palm leaves, and paper from their morals clause contracts, rescued from their official "Welcome, Miss Teen Dream" folders. Taylor lit it with a book of matches that had survived the crash. Night crouched around them, a hungry, patient animal. The girls lay in the sand, exhausted. Some cried themselves to sleep.

"You're on first watch, Miss New Hampshire. Don't let us down," Taylor said. She performed a few high kicks, stretched her long limbs, then settled under a tree to get her beauty sleep.

MISS TEEN DREAM FUN FACTS PAGE!

Please fill in the following information and return to Jessie Jane, Miss Teen Dream Pageant administrative assistant, before Monday. Remember, this is a chance for the judges and the audience to get to know YOU. So make it interesting and fun, but please be appropriate. And don't forget to mention something you love about our sponsor, The Corporation!

Name: Adina Greenberg
State: New Hampshire
Age: 17
Height: I resent this question.
Weight: I really resent this question.
Hair: Brown. Obviously.
Eyes: Also brown. Also obviously.
Best Feature: My intellect

Fun Facts About Me:

- I hate high heels. Walking in high heels for eight hours a day should be forbidden by the Geneva Convention.
- I am applying to Brown, Yale, Harvard, and Columbia.
- I was voted Most Likely to Figure Out Who Really Killed JFK.
- My mom is married to Alan, aka, Stepfather #5. He is a complete tool. No, you have no idea.
- My favorite Corporation TV show is the news. If you can call it that.
- My platform is Identifying Misogyny in American Culture. It's all about helping girls ID the objectification of women when they see it. You know, like when girls are asked to parade around in bathing suits and heels and get scored on that.

- The thing that scares me most is falling in love with some jerkwad and ending up without an identity at all, just like my mom.
- I intend to bring this pageant down.
- You will never see this.

CHAPTER FIVE

Alone on the dark beach, Adina had to laugh at her lousy luck. Unlike the others, she'd entered this cheesy pageant as a revolutionary act. She hated the Miss Teen Dream Pageant. Hated everything it stood for. Mostly, she hated how much her mother loved it. Ever since she was four, Adina and her mother had watched Miss Teen Dream. It had seemed to Adina then to be a TV fairy tale: All those pretty girls smiling and waving and showing off their tumbling skills. And the gowns! Such sparkles and movement!

"Those girls will never have trouble getting husbands. They'll have their pick," her mother had said dreamily.

Adina's mom had had her pick, too. She'd gone from one guy to the next, in an act of downward husband mobility, until she'd married Alan the Tool. Alan, who ran self-improvement seminars for business leaders. Alan, who spoke in blowhard aphorisms like "A bird in the hand can still poop in your palm" and "If you want to beat a snake at its game, you have to think like a snake and not like a duck."

It was both Adina's mom and Alan who encouraged her to enter the Miss Teen Dream Pageant to show that "just because you're smart doesn't mean you can't also be pretty." They told her if she placed in Miss New Hampshire, they'd buy her a bass for her all-girl punk band, Drink My Sweat. They figured once she got wrapped up in the pageant work, she'd forget all about the bass and the band and her journalistic aspirations.

Adina had entered . . . but for her own secret reasons. She would smile and pose, and when the time was right, she would show everyone what a joke this was — what a joke her mom's life was. How stupid the girls in her high school were for believing in this beauty and happily-ever-after crap. She would use the money from the publication of her exposé to buy that drum kit herself. Maybe she'd even write a song about the whole experience. "Artificial Girl." Or "Teen Dream Armageddon." Yeah. Adina liked the sound of that. She would be a beauty pageant Che Guevara[7].

A thick fogbank had rolled in at dusk, and now, between the intense dark and the fog, it was impossible to see much of anything except for the volcano outlined by the moon. A small tickle ran up her neck. Adina had the feeling she was being watched. It was silly — they hadn't found any other survivors and they hadn't seen any other signs of life. Still, a shiver passed over her, and she forced herself to concentrate on the soothing sound of the waves coming in, going out. Soon, her eyelids flickered with fatigue.

A quick flash of lights near the volcano startled her awake. She stood up quickly, gasping as she got too close to the fire's warmth. She looked again. Nothing. But she had seen them: short blasts, like signals. Or were the night and the events of the day getting the best of her? In the watery moonlight, the island's volcano was a formless monster wearing a halo of thin gray clouds. Adina saw no repeat of the mysterious lights, but she hunched closer to the fire, grateful for its light like some primitive ancestor. The jungle nipped at her confidence with each sudden screech or low growl. She'd managed the heels. The swimsuit trauma. The endless interviews with steel-eyed judges asking if she'd ever sent naked pictures of herself to a boyfriend or anything else that could cast a shadow of scandal over the pageant. She'd thrown herself into each challenge with total commitment, thinking only

[7] Che Guevara, the Argentine Marxist revolutionary who later became a best-selling T-shirt icon.

about the endgame — taking down Miss Teen Dream for good. With each victory, she felt emboldened and determined. Giddy, almost.

Now, for the first time since she'd started this crazy project, she felt afraid.

Sheltered by the dark, the agent watched the girls sleeping on the beach and shook his head. This was not good, not at all. They were six weeks away from Operation Peacock, and this was a serious wrench in the monkey works. The Boss wasn't going to like this. Better deliver the bad news now and get it over with.

The agent crept back to the catamaran stashed behind the rocks and paddled through rough surf to the far side of the island. As he walked onto the beach, a sudden hiss-growl came from the right. A nearly extinct breed of giant snake particular to the island leapt onto the sand, blocking the path. It puffed out its Elizabethan ruff of colorful neck webbing in warning, and with a terrifying hiss-screech, it lunged. In an instant, the bullet tore through the colorful neck. As it fell, the snake's expression was one of surprise, as if it had shown up to work only to find someone else sitting in its desk and using its stapler. And then it was dead.

The agent lowered the silencer. Damn snakes. They had no manners. They were tasty, though. Just like chicken. But there were more important things to tend to, and so the agent rolled the creature's corpse out into the surf, watching it go under. Then, whistling the jaunty Miss Teen Dream theme song about a world of pretty, the agent turned and disappeared into the jungle, covering any trace of his tracks.

Armed guards in black shirts nodded as the agent passed through security and into the secret compound. He punched in four digits on a keypad and the door hidden in the rock facade slid open. The elevator shot him down five floors. He took the hallway to the conference room and used the red phone. There was a beep and the agent said two words: "Operation Peacock." He put the phone back on its base and waited. In a moment, the large screen on the wall crackled to life.

"This better be good," the sleepy voice said from the screen.

The agent cleared his throat. "We've got a problem," he said before giving a full status on the plane crash and the surviving girls. The person on the screen listened intently as the agent spoke.

"Agent Jones, in six weeks, Operation Peacock is a go. Nothing can interfere. Nothing. A rescue mission to the island will mean attention. We don't want attention."

"I understand. What about the girls?"

"Six weeks is a long time, Agent. And it's a hostile island. They'll be lucky to last two days," the Boss answered. "Brief everyone in the morning. The official word is that there were no survivors. Operation Peacock goes on as scheduled."

COMMERCIAL BREAK

INT. BEDROOM — MORNING
(A PERKY MOM carrying a laundry basket enters her TEEN DAUGHTER'S bedroom. The girl lies on the bed, upset. The mother's face registers concern. She sits beside her daughter.)

MOM
What's the matter, honey? Why aren't you ready for school?

DAUGHTER
I'm not going to school today, Mom!

MOM
Not go to school? But you love school. You're a high achiever who fulfills my narcissistic need to outshine the other mothers on the block.

DAUGHTER
I know, Mom, but I can't go! Not with this unsightly lip hair.

MOM
(Smiling smugly, Mom pulls a large white plastic vat from her laundry basket.)
Oh, honey. You just need some of this. New Lady 'Stache Off with triple beauty action™.

DAUGHTER
Lady 'Stache Off. Isn't that what you use to sanitize our toilets?

MOM
(laughing) It does both! And now, with new Lady 'Stache Off's triple beauty action™, you can *moisturize* and *self-tan* while you rip that unsightly hair from every pore.

DAUGHTER

Wow! (biting lip) Does new Lady 'Stache Off with triple beauty action™ hurt?

MOM

Oh, honey, of course it hurts! Beauty is pain. But you don't want to look like a troll, do you?

DAUGHTER

Mom!

MOM

It's more than that, sweetheart. Every time you use new Lady 'Stache Off with triple beauty action™, you're contributing to our economy, our way of life. Don't you want to be a contributor to our economy? Don't you want to make sure we can have bikinis, cable, and porn? What are you, a communist?

DAUGHTER

Mo-o-om!

MOM

(Smiling and hugging)

Of course not! You're my eager-to-please teenage daughter with a hair maintenance problem, and I am your sympathetic mom here to help you. In addition to new Lady 'Stache Off with triple beauty action™, there's also Lady 'Stache Off Organic with bonus buffing pad.

DAUGHTER

There's an organic hair remover?

MOM

No. Not really. But don't you love the package? Look, it has butterflies.

DAUGHTER

(holding out hand)

INT. CAR — LATER

(Teen daughter emerges with a freshly plucked upper lip. She also has porcelain teeth veneers, hair extensions, and a body-hugging school uniform. Her skin is artificially tan and shiny.)

MOM

Wow! Look at you! You're looking great!

DAUGHTER

Thanks to you — and new Lady 'Stache Off with triple beauty action™.

MOM

Lady 'Stache Off. Because there's nothing wrong with you . . . that can't be fixed.

MISS TEEN DREAM FUN FACTS PAGE!

Please fill in the following information and return to Jessie Jane, Miss Teen Dream Pageant administrative assistant, before Monday. Remember, this is a chance for the judges and the audience to get to know YOU. So make it interesting and fun, but please be appropriate. And don't forget to mention something you love about our sponsor, The Corporation!

Name: Petra West
State: Rhode Island
Age: 16 1/2
Height: 5' 11"
Weight: A lady never tells
Hair: Caramel blond
Eyes: Topaz
Best Feature: My mouth

Fun Facts About Me:

- I love old Hollywood glamour, and my dream role would be to play Marlene Dietrich's role in *The Blue Angel*.
- My mom is a seamstress and artist. She taught me to sew, bead, knit, smock, and just about everything else. I make all my own costumes.
- My favorite novel is *Orlando*, by Virginia Woolf. I've read it four times.*
- The Corporation product I couldn't live without is Lady 'Stache Off. It leaves my legs silky smooth for days.

*Pageant official says I should change this to something more "relatable," like *I Love You So Much I Forgot to Have a Real Life*. But that book makes me want to yak.

Sometimes it gives me a bad rash first, but that's the price of beauty, right?**

- I can do all the moves from the video for "You're My Only Girl, Girl" by Boyz Will B Boyz. But only if you beg.
- I believe in mystery and old-school modesty, so I wear a sarong in the bathing suit competition.
- The thing that scares me most is not being myself.

** Pageant official also says not to mention rash.

CHAPTER SIX

Petra woke before the others and began the search for her overnight case and the necessary medication hidden inside the lining. The tide had delivered a few more of their belongings in the night — random shoes, clothing, beaded headdresses, gloves — and Petra's heart beat with new hope as she moved up the beach toward a skull-shaped rock and its tongue of a jetty where a few colorful garments floated, stopped by the natural barrier.

Silently, she cursed herself for entering the pageant in the first place. It was a foolish, desperate move, and now here she was, stuck on an island with only a week's worth of pills. Once that ran out . . . well, she wouldn't think about it. Stay positive. That was the thing.

The salt spray kissed her skin, and Petra thought back to the first time she'd played dress-up when she was eight. Sitting at her mother's makeup table, she'd felt a giddy joy as she'd applied the eye shadow — blue and too heavy — the pink blusher, the powder, and finally, a coat of red lipstick. When Petra had looked at herself in the mirror, she'd felt pretty for the first time, a fairy-tale frog transformed into a princess.

So enamored was Petra of her new self that she didn't hear her mother come up from her art studio in the basement. Her mother's lips were parted slightly, as if she were calculating the answer to a math problem that had been in her head a long time but she had only just come upon the answer. She kissed Petra's cheek and said, "Through playing?"

Petra wasn't through playing, not by a long shot, but she nodded, and her mother helped her wash her face and then treated her to a special moisturizing mask, which was cold and green and made them both giggle.

"Will I be beautiful like you someday?" Petra asked her mother.

"You already are beautiful," her mother answered.

"No. Like you," Petra repeated, and her mother's expression was unreadable.

"I guess we'll have to see."

A bikini-clad Taylor emerged through the skeletal rock's mouth like a beauty from a Loch Lomond[8] movie. Watching Taylor, sun-kissed and bronzed and effortless, Petra felt jealous and more than a little out of her league. What was she doing here? What did she hope to prove? That she, Petra West, had just as much right to the Miss Teen Dream crown as all these other girls? That there was beauty in her, too? She could still drop out, she supposed. Give it all up. After all, she'd been in the spotlight before, and while it had been exhilarating in some ways, it had been a nightmare in others. Would she handle it any differently this time? Or would it implode as it had before?

During her mother's chemo, Petra had promised she would go after her dreams. "Life is too short not to be who you are, honey," her mom had told her. She thought of her mom back home in her art studio in Providence, scarred and shorn and still beautiful, full of fierce belief in the rightness of her daughter. And Petra knew she would see it through.

"Good morning!" she called as politely as possible.

"Good morning, Miss Rhode Island. Oh, Miss New Hampshire!" Taylor called out. "How was first watch? Anything to report?"

Adina trudged over sleepily and plopped down onto the sand with a groan. "Yeah. I have five humongous bug bites on my legs

[8]Loch Lomond, the sexy and manly spy in a series of popular Scottish crime capers. Known for his fancy gadgets, fast cars, beautiful women who often end up dead, and his trademark phrase, "I'll have the haggis — boiled, not fried."

and arms, my butt crack has been thoroughly exfoliated with sand, I'm hungry, exhausted, and I haven't seen a ship anywhere."

"Don't you have anything positive to say?" Taylor chided.

Adina glared. "There's still a possibility this is all a very bad dream."

"My goodness. Somebody needs to learn resilience. It's a miracle you've gotten this far in the pageant system, Miss New Hampshire. I myself slept just fine."

"Did you see a green overnight case with an Audrey Hepburn decal on top?" Petra asked. She bit nervously at a fingernail, thought better of it, and hid her hands behind her back.

"Nuh-uh. I did see some weird lights up near the volcano, though. Flashes, like signals or something. At least, I thought I did. I don't know. I was really tired."

"Battle fatigue, my daddy calls it," Taylor said with assurance. She rubbed at the stains on her minidress with seawater.

Adina ignored Taylor. With a stick, she wrote *This sucks* in the sand. "I had this weird feeling that we were being watched last night."

"Watched by what?" Petra asked.

"I don't know. But it gave me the total creeps."

"Sounds like Most Holy Name Academy," Mary Lou said, joining them. Damaged spangles hung from her dress on hair-thin threads like some molting bird. "When those nuns say they have eyes everywhere, they are not kidding. I didn't pee at school for the first two years. I wore a pee pad."

Petra put a hand on Mary Lou's shoulder. "TMI."

"I think we should go check it out," Adina said.

Mary Lou glanced at the great lava wall protecting the heart of the jungle. "You mean go *in there*?"

"Yes. As a journalist, I am compelled to know the answers."

"As a girl, I am compelled to protect what's left of my manicure," Petra said.

"But what if the rescuers are looking for us there and not here?

What if . . ." Adina swallowed hard. "What if there's somebody else on this island with us?"

"Somebody with food?" Mary Lou asked weakly.

"Or somebody who wants to make *us* into food," Adina said.

Mary Lou's eyes widened. "Oh, Jesus, Mary, and Joseph."

Taylor smoothed the wrinkles from her wet dress and wiped her hands on her knees. "I am team captain. And I say we're doing our pageant prep first, according to plan. Priorities."

"Shouldn't our priorities be food, shelter, and rescue?"

"Miss New Hampshire, I appreciate your concerns. But I am eighteen. This is my last year to compete. I do not intend to lose my edge. Besides, I'm sure the rescue team will be here today. And we want them to find us at our best. Miss Teen Dreamers! Let's get to it!" Taylor clapped in a cheerleader rhythm for attention and began to give the day's structure. Adina cupped a hand over her eyes and squinted in the direction of the volcano. The top disappeared into mist. It seemed unassailable and uninhabitable. She'd probably imagined the lights.

After a breakfast of rationed airline pretzels and four sips each from the rescued water bottles, the girls worked on their opening dance number. Each girl had received a DVD of the dance steps in her prep packet, but they'd never had a chance to rehearse it as a unit. That's what this week before the pageant was supposed to be about. Now, without the choreographer, it wasn't coming together smoothly. Somebody would inevitably high-kick when it was time for spirit fingers, the timing was off on the contagion, and the whole thing was such a disaster that Petra pronounced it "so dinner theater on Mars." After an hour of work in the hot island sun, Taylor called a break.

Nicole tapped Adina. "Taylor wants you to play Fabio Testosterone[9] and ask all the questions."

---

[9] Fabio Testosterone, former teen star of the nighttime soap *Study Hall*, where he spent ninety percent of his time shirtless, and host of this year's Miss Teen Dream Pageant, where he will wear a rip-away tux.

"Why me?"

Nicole faltered. "Um, I guess because you're smart and good at questions and . . ."

"Because you pissed her off," Petra said, dabbing self-consciously at the sweat on her upper lip. "Count me out. I already know where to find Iran on a map and I have to look for my overnight bag."

Nicole whistled. "That won't make Taylor happy."

"Tell her I'll keep a watch out for a rescue ship. That I'm taking one for the team."

"Tell her I'm doing that, too," Adina seconded.

"I got there first," Petra said.

Nicole patted Adina's shoulder. "Sorry. Guess you better go round everybody else up, Fabio."

Ten minutes later, the girls lined up as they had in every pageant. It was a relief to know this part. All they had to do was be charming and answer the questions with confidence.

"Remember, don't show fear," Taylor called. Over the firewood, she struck two rocks together, trying to catch a spark. "Judges are like dogs: They'll smell it. If you don't know the answer, answer it like you do anyway."

"Can I get started?" Adina snapped. The heat was making her bug bites itch and she hadn't had a decent meal since yesterday. "Our first contestant is Brittani Slocum, Miss Mississippi."

"I'm Miss Alabama," Brittani corrected.

At the end of the line, Tiara raised her hand. "I'm Miss Mississippi."

Adina looked from one tan, blond southern goddess to the other. They both cocked their heads to the left and smiled in a practiced, patient way.

"Whatever," Adina grumbled. "So, Miss Alabama, Tiara —"

"Brittani!"

"Brittani Slocum. First question. The pageant has come under fire for perpetuating an unrealistic image of superthin girls as beautiful, and many people feel this is harmful to girls' self-esteem. What do you say to these critics? And what do you personally feel about these narrow standards of beauty?"

Brittani's smile remained Vaseline smooth, but her eyes showed fear. "Um, what does *perpetuate* mean?"

"Keep something going."

"Keep what going?"

"No, *perpetuate* means *to keep something going*." *Like I am perpetuating your stupidity*, Adina thought.

"Oh. Um, well, I would say that being skinny and stuff is good because you can, like, fit into supercute jeans, unlike my friend Lisa? She totally ballooned up to a size six and none of her pants fit, and she had, like, three-hundred-dollar Sandeces[10] jeans!"

In the line, several girls gasped.

"Seriously! And she got all depressed and stuff? And she wouldn't come out of her room or do cheerleading anymore because her uniform wasn't fitting right and her parents had to do, like, a li'l benefit concert to raise the money to send her to fat camp, and when she came back from fat camp, she was super, super angry and started piercing things. She took a nail gun and nailed all her old Barbies to the wall in a cross pattern just like little Barbie Jesuses. It was so, so freaky. And we had, like, nothing in common anymore, and before she got fat we used to go shopping *every weekend* and watch all our favorite Corporation shows. It was super, super tragic, and so, like, I know the pain of this because I lost my best friend in the whole world over it and stuff, so, yeah, it's bad and, um, what was the question again?"

Adina stared, openmouthed. "I have no idea."

"My turn!" Miss Ohio walked the makeshift runway. She stopped beside Adina, her body turned in a perfect three-quarter pose,

[10] Sandeces, a denim line sewn by small Peruvian children and adorned with the face of one's celebrity avatar on the back pockets. Each pair is blessed by droplets of local holy water said to ward off unhappiness.

which her handler said made her look thinner. She gave Adina a flirtatious, fingertips-only wave.

"What was that about?"

"It's my flirty wave so I can get Fabio's attention and we can establish a joking patter and maybe end up as a clip on ViralVideo. See, you have to do something to stand out. I'm going to be the naughty one."

"The naughty ones don't win Miss Teen Dream," Taylor called. She'd started a small fire. Now she fanned the flames by performing military dance exercises.

"I don't need to win. I just need to get noticed. So for now, I'm pretending you're Fabio Testosterone." Miss Ohio waved again and winked.

"Well, I'm not, so don't." Adina slapped at a mosquito on her arm. "Miss Ohio, what are your life goals?"

Chin held high, Miss Ohio beamed at an imagined crowd. "I want to be a motivational speaker."

"What are you going to motivate people to do?"

Smile still in place, she cut her eyes at Adina. "You know. Motivational . . . stuff."

"Well, are you going to motivate people to bring peace to war-torn nations, or are you going to motivate people to join a cult and drink the Kool-Aid?"

"The first one."

Adina sighed. "Nice. You might want to take the gum out of your mouth next time."

The sun was hot. It burned holes in the fog cover and wilted the girls' spirits. Periodically, they scanned the horizon for signs of a ship or plane, but there was nothing but those same darkening clouds in the distance. Only Taylor seemed unbothered by the heat, the bugs, the fear.

"Again!" she called from her perch on the rock as the girls marched forward one by one addressing an imaginary audience:

"I'm from Ohio, birthplace of seven U.S. presidents, and I hope you elect me to be your next Miss Teen Dream!"

"Hello from New Mexico, Land of Enchantment. We're the forty-seventh state, but I want to be number one in your hearts tonight!"

"Hi. I'm from Arkansas, the cantaloupe state. And tonight, I hope you will hold my melons close to your heart and vote me your Miss Teen Dream."

Adina cocked her head. "Umm . . ."

"What?"

"Nothing. Miss Colorado?"

"Oh. Sorry!" Nicole sprinted to the sandy runway and walked it carefully, making sure to wave to the crowd with her elbows against her sides as she'd been taught. That way you didn't get jiggle. She took her place beside Adina, towering over her, all legs.

"Hello. I am Nicole Ade from the heart of the Rockies, the great state of Colorado!" She beamed.

Adina slapped a fly on her cheek. She missed the fly, but now her cheek stung. "Miss Colorado, how do you feel about being the only African-American girl in the pageant?"

"What do you mean?" Nicole shifted on her legs like a flight-less bird.

"You're the only black contestant out of fifty states."

"It's . . . it's an honor to represent the great state of Colorado."

"I didn't even know they had black people in Colorado," Tiara said. "You never see them in the ski brochures we get at church."

Adina kept her focus on Nicole. A journalist was relentless in her questioning. "You don't think the pageant's a little racist? I mean, in the whole history of the pageant, an African-American girl has only won once — Sherry Sparks."

Nicole knew about Sherry Sparks and the scandal. Everybody did. In the forty-year history of the Miss Teen Dream Pageant, she was the only African-American winner — until it was revealed that

Sherry had once shoplifted an eye shadow from an Easy Rx store and she was drummed out in shame. It didn't matter that in the years since then, two white contestants had been disqualified for sexy phone photos, or that last year's winner, Miss Florida, had been forced to apologize when it was discovered that she had gotten drunk at a frat party and a video surfaced of her sloppily twirling batons in her underwear and bra. No, it was still Sherry Sparks they talked about.

"Well, you know how they are," Nicole had overheard a pageant mom say to a hairdresser backstage once, and the hairstylist had nodded knowingly, as if they were discussing rambunctious toddlers or shelter dogs, things hard to train.

Nicole hated that she could never quite feel like she was just herself, just Nicole, but that she was somehow representing an entire race. That's how they saw her, as a "they" and not a "she." She knew how to deflect this question, and she did so now with a boxer's dodging grace. "The amazing thing about Miss Teen Dream is that it's all about girls coming together — different races, creeds, ethnicities," she said, looking from girl to girl with a reassuring smile. "There is no race in Miss Teen Dream. You are only judged on the strength of your character."

"Absolutely," Shanti chimed in quickly. "Just like I'm Indian, but nobody's judging me on that."

"You're Indian?" Miss Arkansas brightened. "Oh my gosh, I bought the cutest Indian beaded bag at a gift shop in the Best Western outside Sedona."

"I'm not that kind of Indian," Shanti said, her practiced smile never leaving her face, though it faltered just a bit, and in that slight wobble was something hard and angry, something that looked like centuries of colonial oppression boiling up into an I'm-going-to-kick-your-ass-in-this-pageant-and-then-take-over-all-your-beauty-outsourcing-needs hatred.

"So you don't think racism plays a role at all, Miss Colorado?" Adina prompted.

"No," Nicole continued. "Miss Teen Dream represents the melting pot of American girls. I mean, just four years ago, a Latino girl took first runner-up. Before that, Miss California was first runner-up, and she was half Japanese. And that Filipino girl made first runner-up, too."

"You know what they say — the first runner-up is important in case anything should happen to Miss Teen Dream," Shanti called.

Nicole cut a glance at the Indian girl trying to horn in on her show. "Exactly. First runner-up is important."

"Very important," Shanti echoed.

"I said that," Nicole muttered. She chewed at her finger.

"Thank you, Miss Colorado. Who's next?"

"Me!" Shanti strode forward with a dazzling smile. She locked her position like a gymnast after a dismount, never wavering. "Hello. I am Shanti Singh, Miss California, and as an Indian-American, I represent the rich immigrant tradition of this great country. Though I am as American as apple pie, I can also make popadam as my mother and grandmother taught me. Bollywood meets Hollywood," she said, attempting a joke.

Jennifer raised an eyebrow. "She's using her multicultural grandma? Man, she's good."

Shanti adopted her earnest face, the one she'd practiced in the bathroom mirror every day for weeks. "My parents immigrated to this country for a better way of life. I am so grateful to this country that allows me to be whatever I want to be, whether it's a television anchorwoman, a contestant on *America Sings!*, or the future Miss Teen Dream. Thank you."

The girls sat in the sand, sapped of all energy. Two contestants had salvaged pieces of metal from the downed plane and were using them as tanning reflectors.

Taylor jogged in place on the beach, punching the air in a series of dancey boxing moves. "Let's go, go, go, ladies! Miss Michigan, you're up! Miss New Hampshire, you're doin' great. I almost believe you're Fabio himself."

"I almost believe you're not a colossal jerk," Adina muttered under her breath. She was hot and tired and thirsty. Her words were like gunshots. "Miss Michigan! Yo! Front and center!"

"I don't think Fabio would say, 'Yo!'" one girl complained, and Adina had to resist the urge to strangle the girl with her own hair extensions.

Miss Michigan, Jennifer Huberman, sauntered over. Unlike the others, she looked like she enjoyed the occasional cheeseburger. She had real curves and a pantherlike walk. "Yeah. Hi. Jennifer Huberman, Miss Michigan. Go, Blue! I'm from Flint, the smaller Motor City. Well, before they went bankrupt. Now, I'm from Repossessed City. Sorry. Little gallows humor there."

"Great. Swell. Why don't you tell us about your platform?"

Jennifer gave Adina a shove. "Yeah? Why don't you tell me about your platform, Homeroom?"

"Whoa. Chill."

"Why don't you chill?"

"What pageant did you enter, Miss Orange Jumpsuit? What's with the hostility?"

"Maybe I don't like people asking so many questions."

"Okaaaay. That's kind of an important part of the competition."

"It counts for forty percent of your overall," Tiara said as she practiced a circle turn in place.

Jennifer relaxed. "Sorry. I don't mean to get all up in your face. I'm just not used to this beauty stuff."

"You aren't?"

"No. First time. My guidance counselor got me into it. Some new program they're trying out for at-risk girls." Jennifer rolled her eyes. "Like this isn't a gang. Please. It's the freakiest gang ever."

"Just curious: How did you manage to win Miss Michigan?"

"I didn't. I was second runner-up."

"What happened to the winner?" Adina asked.

"She tripped."

"And the first runner-up?"

Miss Michigan cracked her knuckles. "She tripped, too."

Adina swallowed hard. "Right. So, Miss Michigan, can you tell us about your platform? Please. I mean, if you're okay with that."

"Oh. Sure. My platform's called Don't Even Think About It. I go into schools and I say, 'Whatever bad thing it is you're thinking of doing, don't even think about it. 'Cause I can see into your soul, and I will hide in your closet and come for you in the night, and the last sound you ever hear will be my sharp teeth popping through the flesh of my gums, ready to eat you.' Their eyes get all big. It's awesome. I love little kids, man. They're the cutest."

"Next!" Adina practically shouted. "Tiara, Miss Mississippi, right?"

Tiara stared. "Is that my question?"

"It is *a* question. I just wanted to make sure I got your name right."

"Oh. Hi, y'all! I'm Tiara Destiny Swan from Jackson, Mississippi, which is spelled M-I-double-S-I . . . um . . . shoot."

Adina looked to Taylor to end this travesty, but Taylor was trying to keep the signal fire going. The ominous clouds had moved closer to the island, and a strong wind came up, blowing sand and promising rain. "Tiara . . ." Adina had lost all steam. "What's your favorite color?"

Tiara's eyes darted left and right in fear and her smile was strained. "Um. Thank you, Fabio. I personally believe that we have a duty such as . . . as Americans . . . to help other people who are not Americans such as the peoples of the China and the Alaska and the freedoms we enjoy in our great nation and such and that is my opinion which I personally believe will make us a stronger nation. Thank you."

Adina squeezed her hands against her head. "What are you even saying? You just made my brain die a little. You know, people, just being beautiful isn't enough."

Tiara looked confused. "But . . . it always has been."

Petra gave a sudden cry, startling the others. "There it is!" She barreled down the beach in the direction of the skull-shaped rock and its long tongue of a jetty.

The cry went up. "Oh my God! Is it a ship? It must be a ship! Ship! Ship!"

The girls stumbled over one another on their way after Petra.

Nicole cupped her hand over her eyes. "Where? I don't see anything but some nasty-looking clouds out there."

Petra waded into the chest-high water, fighting the heavy surf, and grabbed at a small, green leather satchel. "Oh, Holly Go-Overnightly — thank God you showed up!" Grinning, she held the luggage aloft. "My overnight case — I found it!"

"Are you kidding me?" Shanti complained.

The wind rose, blowing sand into the girls' faces. The cloud army advanced. It began to rain hard, then harder. The strip of beach seemed to vanish within seconds, and the girls were calf-deep in the sea.

Nicole pointed out at the horizon. "Um, does that ocean look kind of high to you?"

"How can the ocean get high? It can't inhale. I know a lot about it. My platform is called Don't Do Drugs Because They Make You Dumb," Brittani explained.

"And I thought it was just inbreeding," Petra quipped.

Nicole began to back away from the beach. "Hey, y'all, I don't like the looks of that wave out there."

The back of the sea curled up and fanned out, blocking the sky, threatening to bear down on the island.

Taylor gave three short, attention-focusing claps. "Miss Teen Dreamers! This is your team captain speaking. It is time to get our Rumpelstiltskins in gear and run for higher ground. Ready? Okay!"

Taylor tried to lead the way, but many of the girls ran scattershot for the forbidding jungle, scrambling over brambles, scraping their tender flesh against the prickly trunks of the palms. They were nearly up the first hill when the wave hit full force, upending girls like bowling pins, the fast-moving current carrying them down, out, under.

Tiara, Shanti, and Nicole had managed to climb into the branches of an ornately limbed tree. Below them, Petra held tight to a low-lying branch with a precarious crack in it. The water tugged at her overnight case, bending the tree dangerously close to the raging waters and threatening to bring them all down.

"You have to let go!" Shanti yelled.

"I can't!" Petra shouted. If she let go, her pageant dreams and her secret, more important dream would wash away with it.

"Let it go!" Shanti tried to kick the case loose. The strain broke the tree's limb, and the four girls plummeted into the water and were borne along by the fast-moving current. They bobbed up and down like a wet Whack-A-Mole game, their screams cut off only when they disappeared for a few seconds before fighting their way back to the surface. They barely even noticed the falls as they slipped over them.

Jennifer had been the first one away from the beach. She broke right, running hard and fast toward the volcano and the mist-shrouded circle of mountains that bordered it. The water caught her like a giant Slip 'N Slide, spinning her through trees, making her dizzy.

"Holy f — !" she managed before going under again, as if the water sensed that young ladies of such beauty and promise should never curse.

"Move, move, move!" Taylor shouted to her crew as the angry sea chased them relentlessly. "Go higher, Teen Dreamers!"

The girls clambered over the steep terrain. The growth was thick here, and the ground turned to mud as if by an alchemist's touch, but they managed to reach the top of the mountain.

Taylor addressed the soaking, exhausted survivors. "Ladybird Hope says a lady's true colors come out in times of crisis. These circumstances are not as big as you are! We are bright, shining lights in the darkness, and nothing can extinguish the fierce light of a Miss Teen Dream's true heart."

"That's mixing your metaphors!" Adina spat out bits of mud and grass.

"Don't be a hater, Miss New Hampshire," Taylor scolded.

"I hate everything about this! It's the beauty pageant from hell! I didn't even want to be a Miss Teen Dream! Do you know why I'm here? I'm an investigative reporter for the New Castle Knights school paper. I embedded myself so I could expose the pageant from the inside."

"That explains the budget weave," Miss Ohio said.

Adina whipped around. "This is my own hair."

Miss Ohio put her hands up in a "whatever" gesture.

"Why did you want to do that?" Mary Lou asked.

"Because it's wrong! It exploits women. We're parading around in bathing suits and evening gowns, letting people judge us for the way we look. No wonder the world doesn't take us seriously."

"What's wrong with wanting to look pretty?" Brittani asked.

Taylor's face was as hard as the lava cliffs jutting up from the island green. "I am shocked, Miss New Hampshire. You are a real Judas. When we get back, I intend to make a full report to the pageant officials and have you replaced with your state's first runner-up."

Adina threw her hands in the air and laughed bitterly. "Fine. You do that. IF we ever get back, Little Miss Perfect!"

"For your information, I have not held the title of Little Miss Perfect since I was six. We *will* be rescued, Miss Teen Dreamers. I have absolute faith in that. And *you*, Miss New Hampshire, will be reported."

"Cripes, you guys. Let's not fight. At least we're safe here," Mary Lou said.

The muddy ground shook. Adina's eyes widened. "Oh sh —"

The earth beneath them gave way suddenly, and the girls were swept down the mountainside in a spiral of mud and sequins and screams.

LIVE ON *BARRY REX LIVE*

BARRY REX: Ladybird Hope, thank you for joining us tonight.

LADYBIRD HOPE: You betcha, Barry. I just want to assure everybody out there in our great nation that we're doing everything we can to make sure we bring these girls home safe. You know, Barry, it just makes my heart kinda sick when I think of all the bad girls whose planes could have gone down. It's such a tragedy that these sweet girls who follow the rules set down for women through the ages while also learning to walk in bathing suits and heels are the ones who are now missing. Some of those bathing suits are from my own Ladybird Hope, Pageant Princess swimwear line, which is America's bestselling teen swimwear line, by the way.

BARRY REX: The plane was a Corporation plane, which have been rumored to have navigation troubles. The Corporation has been accused of cutting costs on its airlines. Do you think that could have something to do with this? Does this reflect badly on The Corporation?

LADYBIRD HOPE: I like your suit, Barry.

BARRY REX: Can you answer the question, please?

LADYBIRD HOPE: Barry, my opponents will stop at nothing to smear me just because I'm a straight talker who loves her country and her pageant. I can't talk too much about it, but there's evidence, Barry, that the plane was shot down by hostile forces. That this was a terrorist attack on this country's best and brightest. The sort of scenario I warned about in my new book, *Get Scared, America!*

BARRY REX: What are you saying, Ladybird?

LADYBIRD HOPE: I'm saying that if I were president, this wouldn't have happened. Not on my watch.

BARRY REX: The call-board is lighting up like a Christmas tree over here!

LADYBIRD HOPE: Well, it's no coincidence that Christmas is Jesus's holiday, Barry.

BARRY REX: We'll take your calls in a moment. But first, Ladybird, you've come under fire recently for your promotion of a pageant that some see as antiquated. That the system rewards girls for being pretty and it values compliance and conformity rather than the boldness and rule-breaking that we pride in our boys and which often help them feel entitled to success, to getting ahead in life.

LADYBIRD HOPE: Well, frankly, that's the sort of stuff I expect my critics to say, because they want to turn all women into sluts who can get an abortion at the drive-through while they're off at college gettin' indoctrinated with folk-singin', patchouli-wearin', hairy-armpit-advocatin' feminism, which is just one step away from terrorism, and we should all be afraid of that.

BARRY REX: I'm not sure I —

LADYBIRD HOPE: Barry, let me give you a history lesson, Ladybird Hope–style. When the Vietnamese got kids hooked on drugs and we had to fight a war to stop it, did we give in?

BARRY REX: Uh . . .

LADYBIRD HOPE: No! We said "Crack is wack!" and we made sure everybody could have guns instead of drugs. Back before the British were our friends, and they had a mean king who made us pay too much tax instead of just having hot princes who go to nightclubs, they wanted to keep us from bringing freedom to the people of Mexico and making it a state, and George Washington had to chop down a cherry tree and write the "Star-Spangled Banner," and that's the reason we fought World War II, and why we keep fighting, because those freedom-hating people out there want to take away our right to be rich and good-lookin' and have gated communities and designer sweatpants like the ones from my Ladybird Hope Don't Sweat It line, and they want us all to learn to speak Muslim and let the lawyers stop us from teaching about Adam and Eve and that will be the day that *every* child gets left behind. Our country needs something to believe in, Barry. They need us to be that shining beacon on the hill, and that shining beacon will not have all these complications and tough questions about who we are, 'cause that's hard, and nobody wants to think about that when you already have to decide whether you want Original Recipe or Extra Crispy and that little box is squawkin' at ya. And let me tell you something, Barry, that shining beacon will have a talent portion and pretty girls, because if we don't come out and twirl those batons and model our evening gowns and answer questions about geography, then the terrorists have won.

BARRY REX: Your Don't Sweat It line is made in China.

LADYBIRD HOPE: Well, I can find China on my map, Barry, and these days, it looks a lot like America. All I can say is, these brave girls represent the very best of us, in both evening wear and talent, and I sure hope they're okay. But if this is a terrorist attack, we will go after these evildoers, so help me, God.

BARRY REX: Anything else you'd like to add?

LADYBIRD HOPE: I think at this point all we can do is pray.

MISS TEEN DREAM FUN FACTS PAGE!

Please fill in the following information and return to Jessie Jane, Miss Teen Dream Pageant administrative assistant, before Monday. Remember, this is a chance for the judges and the audience to get to know YOU. So make it interesting and fun, but please be appropriate. And don't forget to mention something you love about our sponsor, The Corporation!

Name: Jennifer Huberman
State: Michigan
Age: 17
Height: 5' 5"
Weight: Super featherweight
Hair: Auburn
Eyes: Brown
Best Feature: My razor-sharp retractable claws. Kidding. That's an X-Men joke. Gotta say my guns. Check 'em out.

Fun Facts About Me:

- I'm pretty mechanical. My mom worked in the auto industry and I can ~~pimp your ride~~ rebuild an engine in a hot minute.
- I'm a total comics fiend, and my favorite shop is Galaxy Comics in Flint. Shout-out to Mohammed and Akilah!*
- My favorite Corporation show is *Patriot Daughters*.[11]

---

*Pageant officials think this makes me sound Muslim. Want to know if we can change it to "Shout-out to Mo and Alice."

[11] *Patriot Daughters* (Tuesdays, 9:00 P.M. EST), The Corporation's drama chronicling the lives of three teen girls during the Revolutionary War as they fight the British, farm the land, and take off their clothes to secure America's freedom.

- I came to Miss Teen Dream via a new program for at-risk girls that takes them from juvie to pageants, or, as I like to call it, from one correctional facility to another.**
- My personal motto is: WWWWD?: What Would Wonder Woman Do?

**Pageant officials didn't think this was funny. Pageant officials not big on the jokes.

CHAPTER SEVEN

When the muddy waters receded, Jennifer found herself in a part of the jungle where nothing was familiar anymore. Far overhead was a small clearing of blue sky bordered by the wizened branches of thick-trunked trees whose gnarled roots clutched the earth like the talons of some primeval bird frozen midgrip by a sorcerer's curse. She called out for the others, but there was no response.

Being alone didn't scare Jennifer. She'd been alone since she was ten, when she begged her mom to stop sending her to stay with Grandma Huberman, the religious nut, who told her God could see into her wicked, wicked heart. While saying this, she'd waved the copy of *Women's Basketball Weekly* she'd found under Jen's bed, the one in which Jen had drawn a heart around the picture of star point guard Monica Mathers.

"God doesn't like lesbians," Grandma Huberman hissed, throwing the magazine in the trash.

Jennifer knew what lesbian meant, and she knew she probably was one. But she couldn't understand why God would hold that against her or against Monica Mathers, who'd never started a war or killed anybody, and whose deadeye three-pointers were straight-up amazing. After all, hadn't God made both of them? But people were like that, she'd noticed. They'd invoke Godly privilege at the weirdest of times and for the most stupid of reasons. Jen decided that if God wasn't putting any faith in her, she wasn't putting her faith in Him. And so, now, alone in the jungle, she did not call out for special favors. As far as she was concerned, that would be cheating. Jennifer played rough sometimes, but she always played fair.

A long rope of root formed an almost-bench above the mossy ground, and after testing its solidity, she sat on it to think. It was only moments later that she heard off-key humming and saw a girl marching between the trees, a spear in one hand. The girl had a strawberry blond bob and an impish face. The remnants of her sash read *Miss Illin*, and for a moment, Jennifer thought of her as being from a very cool hip-hop state.

"Hi. Uh, hello," Jennifer said. "I'm Jennifer Huberman. Miss Michigan."

The girl didn't respond.

"Hey!" Jennifer waved her arms. "Over here!"

The girl looked up. Startled, she dropped the spear, which stuck fast in a fat tree root. A flock of shrieking black birds spiraled skyward as the giant, gnarled tree seemed to uncoil, and Jennifer saw that it was not a mass of roots looped about the trunk but a freakishly big snake the length of a custom RV.

Jennifer leapt to her feet. "Holy {bleep bleep}[12]! Get your {bleep}[13] out of the way!"

Too late, the girl looked up just as the snake opened wide and swallowed her down in a giant gulp.

"{Bleeeeeeeeeeeeeeeeeeeeeeeeeeeep}[14]!" Jennifer said many, many times.

The snake, with its girl-size, midthroat bulge, turned to Jennifer with a strangled hiss.

They say in near-death experiences that one's life plays out before one's eyes. Jennifer's brain went to scan, flitting from one random

---

[12] These words have been sanitized for your protection. An adjective and a noun, respectively.

[13] A part of the body. Not the knee or the nostril.

[14] A spectacular cursing display. Really, an absolute ten. And the dismount was spot-on.

image to the next: her mom coming home from the factory, bone-weary, angry, and utterly defeated, the bills sitting untouched on the chipped, Rent-A-Racket dinette set. Tommy, her little brother, riding around the crappy, one-bedroom apartment on a dumpster-dive Big Wheel till Jennifer thought she would scream from the constant whine of it. The days of ditching school to hang out at Galaxy Comics and talk mutants and *Watchmen* with Mohammed and Akilah, who ran the place and sometimes paid her in old comics if she'd help them stock. Getting busted for stealing a pack of Ho Hos from a Gas-It-N-Go and landing in juvie. The counselor who saw Jen as the perfect do-gooder project on her resume, offering her a chance at beauty pageant redemption meant to save them both. The crash. The island. The snake.

The snake. It seesawed its way toward her in an ungainly, almost blind fashion, tongue lashing wildly, mouth pulled back slightly to reveal double rows of grungy, bladelike teeth and puffy, bleeding gums. This was how she was going to die? After the years of crushing poverty, the dismissal by her teachers and schoolmates, the way that most people looked through girls like Jennifer as if they were too inconsequential to acknowledge with a glance? She was going to go down as kibble for some giant snake alcoholic? This was utter bullshit[15].

"What Would Wonder Woman Do?" she said, like a prayer.

And then, as if in answer, Jennifer raced for the spear, which had been thrown free when the girl was swallowed. But the snake's undulating tail knocked it just out of reach.

"You scaly bitch[16]!" Jen gasped.

The snake lunged. With a loud screech, Jennifer leapt up and grabbed hold of a tree limb, hoping that it was, in fact, a tree limb, and not some other freaky form of island life intent on eating her. Inside the snake's throat, the girl pushed with her hands and feet,

[15] This is not cursing. This is delineating.
[16] This is also not cursing. This is . . . oh, all right. It totally is.

forming a blockade with her body. She wasn't going down easy, and it gave Jen new courage.

A quick drop to the ground and she snatched the spear in her right hand. With a loud "GAAAAAHHHHHHHH!!!!!" she hopped onto the snake's back and jabbed the sharp end into the creature's head. It thrashed wildly and Jennifer was thrown clear. Now it was truly pissed. But it wasn't from Jen's assault. From inside the snake, the swallowed girl had managed to crawl up. She positioned what looked like a smallish white tub between the snake's back teeth. It allowed just enough room for her to slide out on a tide of heavy saliva. Without thinking, Jennifer pulled the girl to safety behind a fat, broken tree.

The snake bit down on the large jar between its teeth and exploded. The girls were coated in snake insides.

"Yes!" Jennifer screamed. She pumped her fist. "How ya like me now, Snake Parts?"

Beside her, the rescued girl coughed and hacked. Her eyes widened as she hacked up a mouthful of slime on Jennifer's shoulder.

"Ew."

"Sorry," the girl said in a voice that sounded slightly broken and a little loud. "I was choking. I'm Sosie Simmons. Miss Illinois."

"Jennifer Huberman, Miss Michigan. Oh my God. I thought that you were a total goner, man. But you were all, 'Feel my fists of fury, Amphibian Bitch,' and I was all, 'Let's settle this, X-Men-style,' and you were all, 'Aaaaaaahhhhhh jar action!' and I was all, 'Kayaaaaaaaa spear time!' and, oh my God, that was flippin' amazing. Wasn't that amazing? I haven't felt so good since I punched Dennis Anastasias during sixth grade recess when he called me thunder thighs 'cause, I'm sorry, that little punk had it coming." Laughing maniacally, Jennifer combed her hands through her snake-slimed, muddy hair and looked up at the doily of sky far above, and even though she had just nearly met her demise with a gigantic snake on a deserted island far from home, somehow this moment was glorious.

Sosie stared at Jennifer's mouth, trying hard to make out the words that rushed over her lips in a formless torrent. "Um, sorry. I didn't get that. I lost my hearing aid inside that thing. I'm hearing impaired."

Jennifer was forced to really look at Sosie. What she saw was a face with large, green eyes and a light dusting of freckles across a small nose. And for a moment, she was more undone by this girl's beauty than by the carnivorous snake.

"Oh. Sorry," she said slowly.

Sosie smiled. "That's okay. Even though I have a disability, it doesn't stop me from realizing my aspiration of representing my country as Miss Teen Dream."

"No. Of course —"

Sosie placed a hand over the left side of her chest. "They said that because I could not hear the music, I would not be able to dance, but I refused to be limited. I chose to listen to the music of my soul. With the help of my teachers, I organized a dance troupe of non-hearing kids called Helen Keller-bration! And we travel America, showing that nothing can stop you if *you* don't stop believing."

Jennifer looked around. "Who are you talking to?"

Sosie squinted at Jen's mouth. "Oh! My handler said you should act like the cameras are on you at all times and always be at your best."

"There are no cameras. The crew, the handlers, they're all dead."

"What?"

Jennifer mimed a finger across her throat.

"Oh. *Oh!*"

Slowly, with great care, Jennifer explained about the storm, how she lost the others, that she didn't know if they had survived.

Sosie took it all in, nodding. "After the crash, I was so scared. I found this place. It was really weird. There were all these jars of Lady 'Stache Off."

"Maybe they fell when the plane crashed?"

"That's what I thought at first. But one of the jars — the one the snake just had for breakfast — had this weird, almost-battery-looking thing in it. The jars were all in a box. And that's not all. Come on, I'll show you."

She offered her hand to Jennifer, and Jennifer took it, marveling at the softness of the girl's fingers.

"Sorry. I stink like snake insides."

"Don't worry about it."

"What?"

"It's okay," Jennifer shouted, feeling like an idiot because wasn't that what people always did with the deaf? Talked louder, as if that would help?

Sosie positioned Jennifer's fingers in her own, nudging them gently into new forms. "O . . . kay," she said.

"Okay," Jen repeated, putting her fingers through the motions again.

Sosie smiled. "Very good. If you want, I can teach you to sign."

Jennifer blushed. She wanted. She wanted very much.

Sosie inched closer to the snake corpse. She poked it with a stick. It didn't move. Feeling braver, she and Jennifer examined it and saw that it had been sick. Its long body was covered in disgusting sores and tumors. Its scales were mostly gone. The few that remained were an iridescent greenish blue that dazzled. It had probably once been a glorious creature, and Jen was reminded of the old, tough-as-algebra barflies in her neighborhood, the ones with the long, permed hair who still clung to the leopard-print dresses they'd put on thirty years ago and refused to retire.

"Poor thing," Sosie said.

"That poor thing tried to eat us," Jennifer said.

Sosie nodded. "Poor bitch." She grabbed a shard of the plastic Lady 'Stache Off jar. "I wonder what made the snake explode? You think it was that battery thingie?"

Jennifer wiped her hands with the edge of her dress. "Don't know. It looked pretty sick anyway."

"What?"

"The snake. Looked sick," Jennifer repeated, and Sosie showed her the sign for *sick*.

"I want to show you something."

Sosie led the way through ruined trees and denuded earth. Off to the right were a series of weathered totems. Clearly, this had once been somebody's home, but whoever they were, they were gone now, and the land around here didn't look like it could support so much as a carrot patch, let alone people. At last they came to the ruins of an ancient temple carved into the side of a mountain. Veiny tree roots closed around it protectively, as if saving it from the destruction their brothers and sisters had faced.

Sosie motioned for Jennifer to follow. The temple wasn't too dark inside, thanks to a hole in the top where a family of birds had built a nest. There were also seat cushions from the plane, a blanket, a kerosene lantern, and an old ham radio.

"Dude! A radio!" Jennifer grabbed for it and hugged it to her chest.

"Doesn't work," Sosie said.

Jennifer twisted the knobs and dials. Nothing. She opened the back of the radio. The wires were a jumble of color. She let out a low whistle. "Man. That is a mess. Still. I might be able to get it up and running. I'm pretty mechanical. I wonder where all this stuff came from."

"What?" Sosie said, and Jen said it more slowly, letting Sosie read her lips. "That's not all. Look." Sosie showed Jennifer what appeared to be a military ration kit. Inside were chocolates, water, and protein bars. There was also a machete, two knives, and a wooden crate packed for shipment with the lid pried loose. Sosie removed the lid. Inside were moldy packing peanuts stuffed around several jars of Lady 'Stache Off.

"It's so strange. What's this stuff doing on this island?"

Jennifer ignored Sosie's question and pointed instead to the ration kit. She made a puppy begging face, which made Sosie grin. Together, they sat on the weed-choked temple floor and shared a chocolate bar, which tasted better than anything Jen could remember. She'd never had a meal in silence before. At home, there was her little brother yakking it up, Jen and her mom arguing. At school, at juvie, at the pageant training center, someone was always instructing, advising, reprimanding, and Jen had learned her only defense was to talk, loudly and a lot, in order to keep the needling "helpful" words of others at bay. Now, there was just the food, the company, and the quiet.

She kind of liked it.

MISS TEEN DREAM FUN FACTS PAGE!

Please fill in the following information and return to Jessie Jane, Miss Teen Dream Pageant administrative assistant, before Monday. Remember, this is a chance for the judges and the audience to get to know YOU. So make it interesting and fun, but please be appropriate. And don't forget to mention something you love about our sponsor, The Corporation!

> **Name:** Shanti Singh
> **State:** California
> **Age:** 17
> **Height:** 5' 3"
> **Weight:** ~~128 lbs. A lot of it is muscle.~~ 116 lbs
> **Hair:** Black
> **Eyes:** Brown
> **Best Feature:** My hair. People say it is glossy. I use an old Indian treatment.

Fun Facts About Me:

- I have studied botany, fencing, synchronized Tae Kwon Do, gymnastics, classical piano, cello, Bollywood dancing, and Indian cinema.
- I can make popadam as my mother and grandmother taught me.
- My favorite class is chemistry.
- I hope to be the head of my own Fortune 500 company.
- My platform is called First Generation Health. It helps kids in immigrant populations get the health care they need.
- My proudest accomplishment was hearing my handler, Mrs. Mirabov, tell me that my evening gown walk only made her want to put out one eye. Trust me — that's a compliment.
- The thing that scares me most is failure.

CHAPTER EIGHT

The river had carried Nicole, Shanti, Petra, and Tiara through the mountains and deposited them in a steaming spring surrounded by blackened rock that looked like burned-over cake batter.

"Wh-where are we?" Tiara asked.

"Some kind of lava fields, it looks like," Shanti answered. Algae clung to her scalp. She'd lost her sash in the raging waters. They all had. They were covered in mud till all that could be seen were their eyes and mouths.

"I hate this place," Tiara whimpered. "It's super creepy. Like a haunted Chuck E. Cheese's where the games all want to kill you and you never get your pizza."

Shanti glared at Petra. She struggled to keep her tone even, but it was difficult. "Why didn't you let go of that case? If you had just let go, we could have held on to the tree, and we wouldn't be out here in the middle of some lava field with no idea how to get back to the beach."

"I'm sorry," Petra said. "It . . . the case was — is — important to me."

"What do you have in there — a vintage Bermes scarf[17]?" Nicole struggled to her feet and offered Petra a hand.

"My medicine."

---

[17] Bermes scarf, a highly coveted status symbol. When the Pope chided pop star Magdalene for her collection by saying she could feed a village for a year for the cost of it, she responded, "Yes, but I can't wear a village around my neck."

"Bipolar Bears[18]," Tiara said sympathetically. "My mom put me on those as soon as I turned thirteen. She couldn't deal."

"It's not that," Petra said. "I have a medical condition."

"What kind of medical condition?" Nicole asked.

"It's a hormonal thing," Petra answered nervously.

Tiara's hands flew to her mouth. "In health class, they told us there's an *or* in *whore* because you always have the choice to respect your body and say no. You've got one of those STPs now, don't you?"

Petra stared. "STP is a motor oil."

"Oh. My. Gosh. We didn't even learn about that one. It must be really bad!" Tiara gestured solemnly to her crotch. "Protect the citadel. Protect the citadel."

Petra looked to the others. "Help."

Nicole shook her head. "Public school Sex Non-Ed. When I'm surgeon general, I am so fixing that." On the walk, she explained *hormonal,* and Tiara nodded, smiling.

"Ooh. It's okay, Petra. When I get my monthlies, I need a handful of Advil and a chocolate donut. I'd give anything for a chocolate donut right now. I'm so hungry. Even hungrier than when my mom put me on that grapefruit and hot sauce diet before the Miss Tupelo pageant last year."

"I've done that diet," Nicole said.

Shanti nodded. "Me, too. Except without the grapefruit."

Tiara's eyes filled with tears. "All those years of starving myself and now I'm really starving."

"All those pageants — local, city, state. The car rides with my hair in rollers," Shanti echoed.

"Straighteners and extensions," Nicole said.

---

[18] Bipolar Bears, The Corporation's cuddly combination vitamin and mood-leveling drug marketed to tween and teen girls. Bipolar Bears banish bad moods and keep you beauty-queen perfect. Sold in a variety of signature bottles. Collect them all!

"Teeth bleaching," Tiara added. "Eyebrow shaping. Tanning booths. Bikini waxes. Lipo."

"Pills. Injections," Petra mumbled.

"What?"

"Nothing."

"Feels like we've been in training for the wrong pageant," Nicole said with a sigh.

"What are we going to do?" Tiara asked.

Their bellies ached with hunger, and the earlier thrill of losing a few pounds before pageant time had been replaced with a terrible, desperate longing for food. To make matters worse, the rain had started again. It pounded wet fists against them.

"Let's move on," Shanti said. "I think if we follow the stream it'll lead back to the beach and the others."

They marched alongside the stream as it fattened into a river, alert all the while to the constant sound track of caws, shrieks, growls, and croaks. Birds flew suddenly from treetops, the slapping of their wings like gunshots. Things slithered, hissed, and cackled in the great unknown. Petra sang a Boyz Will B Boyz song softly to herself to drown out the noise.

"You have a really nice voice," Tiara said. "Almost as good as the record."

"Thanks," Petra mumbled and blushed. "I was a big Boyz Will B Boyz fan."

"Who wasn't?" Nicole laughed. "When I was eleven, I had their posters all over my room."

"Me, too!" Tiara said, smiling. "Who was your favorite?"

"Mmm, maybe Joey."

Petra let out a loud "Ha!"

"What's wrong with Joey?"

"Nothing, if you like boys who tan like it's an Olympic sport."

"He *was* pretty orangey," Nicole agreed. "J. T. Woodland was the best, anyway. He was so cute, with those big eyes and those curls.

He was the most talented one, I think. I wonder why they kicked him out?"

"I'll bet it was drugs." Tiara batted away a dragonfly.

"It wasn't drugs," Petra said.

"How can you be sure?" Tiara asked.

"He just didn't seem like the drugs type to me."

"Boy band loyalty." Nicole nodded. "I feel you."

"Can we keep going please?" Shanti called back.

The girls picked up their pace. On the other side of the river, orange-and-pink birds waded on stalklike legs. Shafts of sun broke through the heavy trees. They lit patches of ground like the reflections from some tropical disco ball.

"What was your favorite song of theirs?" Tiara asked.

"'Let Me Shave Your Legs Tonight, Girl,'" Petra blurted out.

"Ohmigosh, I LOVE that one!" Tiara said, clapping. "How about 'I Only Want to Be with You' or 'I Just Need to Be Yours' or 'You, You, You'?"

Nicole chimed in. "'I Gave Up My Hobbies So I Could Spend More Time with You.' 'I Love You Like a Stalker!' Or — ooh, I know: 'Safe Tween Crush'?"

"That one is so awesome!" Tiara began to sing. "*Wanna rock you, girl, with a butterfly tunic. / No, I'm not gay, I'm just your emo eunuch. / Gonna smile real shy, won't cop a feel, / 'cause I'm your virgin crush, your supersafe deal. / Let those other guys keep sexing. / You and me, we be texting / 'bout unicorns and rainbows and our perfect love. / Girl, we fit together like a hand in a glove. / Now I don't mean that nasty, tell your mom don't get mad. / I even wrote 'You're awesome' on your maxi pads.*" Tiara sighed. "My mom let me use that song for my Christian pole dancing routine."

Petra sputtered. "Christian pole dancing?"

"Yeah. It was my talent for a while. I was a virgin bride on her wedding day — kinda like in that TiffanyJeanTiffany video? I wore this mini wedding dress and these white stockings with garters and some pretty silver handcuffs. It was a real fun routine." She sighed. "But once I turned ten, my mom said I needed something new."

"That is total crazytown," Petra said.

"I know! I think I could have done it till I was at least twelve."

Petra rolled her eyes and sang, *"Let me shave your legs tonight, girl. Let me show you how it feels when your man . . ."*

"Your man!" the girls sang.

"Can't stand . . ."

"Can't stand!"

"The stub-ble inside your heart, oh!"

Annoyed, Shanti walked a good ten paces ahead of the others. She liked being in the lead, and as she walked, she practiced.

"Hello," she said, practicing her intonation, because tone was everything. "I am Shanti Singh, Miss California, land of opportunity! I am a junior at Valley High School, where I currently maintain a 4.0 GPA. My parents immigrated to America just before I was born, and I am so grateful to this country for giving me so many great opportunities. I hope to show my gratitude one day by becoming the first Indian-American president. And I also hope to work with children," she added hastily. "And, um, animals."

Shanti cursed her verbal clumsiness. *Um*s were deadly. Hadn't her handler, Mrs. Mirabov, told her so? Keeping it together under pressure was what separated the winners from the losers. Shanti had been setting goals since she was four and won her preschool's finger painting contest. By the time she hit middle school, she'd won just about everything there was to win — science fair, debate team, gymnastics, soccer, synchronized Tae Kwon Do. Winning was easy and addictive; the more she won, the more she felt she couldn't risk failing. It was as if she were in constant competition with herself.

But she couldn't control everything.

She looked back at Nicole — friendly, easygoing Nicole — with envy and unease. She knew the Top Five would not hold both a black and a brown contestant. No matter what they claimed, the pageants were not multicultural-friendly. It was funny to Shanti how her white classmates could distinguish between several white faces but would get confused when confronted with, say, two Asians, frequently mistaking one for the other as if looking at a spot-the-difference kids' magazine puzzle and feeling stumped.

To win Miss Teen Dream, Shanti knew she would have to work twice as hard as the other girls. That's why she'd hired Mrs. Mirabov, whose record was superb and whose drive matched her own. It was Mrs. Mirabov who'd evaluated Shanti through narrowed, steel-gray eyes and made her pronouncement: "Your problem, Comrade Singh, is a lack of likeability. No one wants to be your friend. You are efficient and ambitious, which is good for KGB agent; not so much for teen beauty queen. We must humanize you."

Shanti had flinched slightly at Mrs. Mirabov's assessment, as if she'd told Shanti that her personality made her look fat. "Tell me what you can do," Mrs. Mirabov demanded. And Shanti dutifully recited all her talents. "No, no, no. Not what you can do like trained dog. What you love. What you have special passion for?"

Shanti had stared blankly, feeling a sense of panic as if she were in a dream in which she had forgotten to study for a test. There was one thing Shanti loved, but it was not the sort of achievement that wowed judges. It was a secret passion, and that's what it would remain: secret.

"No," Shanti had answered. "Nothing."

"Well, then. We will have to try on personalities until we find one that fits."

They tried everything: telling jokes, country and western songs, a ventriloquist act with a lovable fuzzy sidekick, photo ops with terminally ill children. But Shanti wasn't natural with the kids, whose wary expressions seemed to suggest she'd actually given them cancer. Finally, during a painful roller boogie version of "The Midnight Ride of Paul Revere" that was supposed to make Shanti appear "quirky, but cute and patriotic," Mrs. Mirabov had moaned in Russian and begged her to stop. After a long pause, she raised her perfectly coiffed gray head. There was a new gleam in those eyes.

"You know, Comrade Singh, there is one thing I learned during my defection: Everybody loves a happy assimilation story."

An American underdog was born.

Shanti delighted the judges with the *Parents, what-can-you-do?* anecdote about her dad putting out the life-size, blow-up lawn Santa on the Fourth of July. She charmed them with heartwarming tales of making popadam in her grandmother's kitchen while simultaneously introducing the old woman to the joys of hip-hop. At regionals, she dazzled the crowd during her Bollywood dance routine. Her likeability scores came back in the high nines. Representing the marriage of old-world traditions with the apple-pie aspirations of the new country, she took crown after crown. It made everyone feel warm and hopeful, and they moved Shanti forward as if reaffirming their beliefs in all they stood for. It was great for everyone. It just wasn't true. And Shanti wondered if her actual talent was fraud.

Shanti stopped to catch her breath. She had never been so tired. More than anything, she wanted to stop and rest. That was what her grandmother used to say to her all the time. "You work too hard. You should relax and enjoy your life. Maybe play Ragnaroknroll[19], like your nani. I made an avatar of myself — I'm Super-Kali-Fragilicious! I just laid waste to the Dungeon Master of Carpathia. It was fun."

"I can't go another step," Nicole said, panting.

Shanti was relieved that somebody else had said it first. The rains had stopped. They'd reached a wide plain sheltered by tall rock walls. In the distance, the rock yielded to more jungle.

"All right," Shanti said. "We'll rest."

The girls stretched out on the carpet of green and fell asleep.

When Shanti woke again, the island sky had sneaked toward dusk, and she noticed that Tiara was missing. Quickly, she shook

[19] Ragnaroknroll, an online gaming community whose members meet once a year at a Holiday Inn in Brainerd where they eat reconstituted eggs and stage mock battles. Soon to be a major motion picture with merchandising opportunities out the wazoo.

the others awake, and they searched the surrounding area, shouting Tiara's name. An almost ecstatic moan led them to a large bush adorned with a haphazard assortment of red, star-shaped fruit. Tiara was sprawled beside it, her mouth and hands stained with red juice.

"Tiara, did you eat this fruit?" Nicole asked, frightened.

"Uh-huh. Don't tell my mom. She'll make me go for a run."

"How many did you eat?"

"I don't know. Four or twelve."

"Which one was it — four or twelve?"

"I don't know. I'm not good at math. They're really yummy. They taste kinda like gummi bears, but with dirt on them."

Shanti whispered to the others, "Those could be poisonous."

"Tiara, do you feel okay?" Nicole asked.

"I feel . . . full," Tiara said, tasting the word, which seemed as delicious as the fruit. "I can't remember the last time I felt full. It's awesome."

"It's getting dark. We should get going," Shanti said.

"So tired," Tiara muttered. Her eyelids fluttered.

"I think we should wait to see if Tiara's okay," Nicole whispered.

"It's her fault she ate that fruit, not mine."

"Harsh much? I thought you were all about family and togetherness."

Shanti's cheeks colored. "No one in my family would do something that stupid."

"She was hungry! Look, we'll just watch her for a while. If she's fine, then we know that fruit is safe to eat. We might have found a food source, okay?"

"It beats cannibalism," Petra said. "Plus, do you really want to be walking through the jungle at night? At least this place seems open."

"Remember that big zit I had on my chin this morning? It's all gone," Tiara said, rubbing her thumb over her chin. Tiara's skin was, in fact, perfectly clear and dewy.

"Wow. It looks like you just had a rock dust facial," Petra said.

"Are those good?" Nicole asked. "I've always wanted to try one."

Shanti examined Tiara's face and looked more closely at the small fruit. She wished she had her botany book. "I'll bet these have special properties that cause cell turnover in your skin — I did a science project on free radicals. I'll bet I could turn this into my own skincare line and be Fortune 500 before I'm twenty-five. I'd call them Shanti Berries™."

"You can if there are any left." Petra grabbed a handful and gobbled them down.

"What are you doing?" Nicole asked.

"Tiara ate those hours ago and she's fine *and* her skin looks great. If I'm going to die, I'd rather go out with a full stomach and amazing skin." Petra smacked her lips, tasting. "Oh wow. These really *are* good!"

"Told you," Tiara said sleepily.

"Okay. Here goes nothing." Nicole crossed herself and bit into one, squirting juice. "Mmm. Oh wow."

Shanti was weak from hunger, but she didn't like going into situations in which she was not one hundred percent in charge. The fruit was an unknown. What if it were poisonous? She knew what Mrs. Mirabov would say: "Comrade Singh, you must train yourself to be without. Being beauty queen is like being marine, only harder. Marines do not fight in four-inch heels." Still, the fruit was so inviting, and Tiara seemed fine. In the end, her hunger was stronger. She allowed herself three small pieces of fruit, marveling at their sweetness.

The sun's light retreated. Sated and tired, the girls stretched out in the soft grass and watched the pale rind of moon grow more pronounced.

It began as a slight tingling in her fingers, and then Shanti was aware that her vision was more acute and that the edges of the jungle were unfolding, showing her more and more, like one of those accordion birthday cards.

"Anybody else feel . . . strange?" she asked, trying to keep the panic at bay.

Petra sang another old Boyz Will B Boyz tune to herself and mimed dance steps. Nicole giggled. Tiara stared up at the sky. From the corner of her eye, Shanti caught a colorful bird skating above the bushes. It looked at her and trilled one word: *fraud*.

"Oh my God."

"What's the matter, Bollywood?" Nicole asked, and laughed at the nickname.

"Don't call me Bollywood," Shanti snapped, but it only made Nicole giggle more. "What's happening? I don't understand — Tiara was fine after she ate that fruit. You didn't see or hear anything strange, right?"

Tiara's fingers tried to grab hold of an invisible ladder. "No. Well, the trees were singing funny camp songs to me and I think I saw a big rabbit surfing through the air. But that was all."

"Oh my God!" Shanti cried, her words floating out in front of her in strings of black type.

"You sound funny, Bollywood. Like a Valley girl." Nicole giggled anew.

Shanti clapped a hand over her mouth and fought to regain her composure. Carefully, she lifted her fingers, which no longer felt like her fingers but like butterflies, light and free. "Why didn't you tell us, Tiara?"

"I didn't want to bother you."

Shanti blinked desperately, fighting the plant's power. She liked to be in control — it was her safety net — and she could feel that net being ripped away from her by the star-shaped fruit.

Petra tried to calm her. "It's kind of like Burning Man without the patchouli."

"Do you think they'll give us a pee test when we get back?" Tiara asked.

"Back where? What's back?" Petra asked, and Tiara nodded.

Shanti fought with everything she had — synchronized Tae Kwon Do moves and circle turns. She shifted through her Bollywood talent routine, but soon her fingers forgot the language. Her head was an overgrown garden, and she was lost inside. She no longer knew where or who she was. Finally, she stretched out beside the others, and the jungle came to embrace her.

"I will search for berries as my ancestors did upon the plains before hunting the buffalo," Shanti said dreamily.

Nicole rolled her head toward Shanti. At least, she thought she rolled her head. It was getting hard to tell what was what. "You're not that kind of Indian, Bollywood."

"Whatever," Shanti replied. "Hey. Did you just see a purple dinosaur? He was wearing a boater hat."

"Nice. I love a stylish dinosaur," Petra murmured.

"I had a dinosaur when I was little. A stuffed dinosaur named Mr. Wiggles," Tiara said. "One night, I found him under the covers, down, you know, there." She lowered her voice to a whisper. "I think he did the nasty to me."

Nicole patted her mouth. "My lips are spongy. Anybody else's lips spongy?"

Tiara grabbed Petra's arm. Her voice was low and urgent. "Mr. Wiggles. I put him in the back of the closet. I couldn't look at him after that. He was a bad, bad dinosaur. What if he finds me? What if he finds me here?"

Petra held Tiara's face in her large hands. "You're safe. Ride the wave, my Mississippi flower. You're on a smooth, pretty wave, just floating."

"Okay," Tiara said, settling back. "Okay."

"Isn't that nice?"

"Yeah."

"Do you see the stars up there? Can you make out any shapes?"

"Yeah. I can."

"What do you see?"

Tiara began to whimper. "A pervy dinosaur." She leapt up and made a serpentine run for the jungle.

"Should we go after her?" Petra asked.

"Go after who?" Nicole asked.

Petra tried to remember, but her mind would not stay on task. "I don't know."

Shanti felt the blades of grass petting her ears. "I'm not sure what kind of Indian I am. I'm not really sure what I am at all anymore."

"We're not just sashes and states," Nicole said on a sigh.

"Or gender," Petra murmured. "Or bodies."

"I'm sort of everything all at once," Nicole whispered.

And then they were silent, lost to dreaming.

Shanti was a kite flying high in the sky. She'd never felt so weightless. At first, it was terrifying — where would she go? How would she get back? What if she were to drift away unnoticed? But soon she found she liked the feeling of not knowing. She was in control of her thoughts, and that was all she really needed. A strong tug brought her back.

Down below, Mrs. Mirabov held her string. "Comrade Singh, you are disgrace. Come down at once. We have work to do if you are not to be total failure like high-waisted, acid-wash jeans."

"But I don't want to. I like it up here."

"You will fail, Shanti Singh. You need the winning. As yourself, you are not enough."

Shanti the Kite wobbled and dipped. She feared that the wind might upend her and she would crash to earth and break into a million small splinters. Everyone would see. In a frightened voice, she called to Mrs. Mirabov. "Hold me up!"

"Only if you do as I tell you."

"Okay," Shanti agreed.

Mrs. Mirabov tightened her hold on both the string and the kite's tail, and the kite went taut. Shanti felt it as a stabbing pain between her shoulder blades.

"I'm going to break," Shanti gasped out.

"Nonsense. You are only as good as what you can do. Remember that you are not likeable, Comrade Singh," Mrs. Mirabov called.

"I know." The pain in Shanti's back sharpened. It was unbearable.

"It is important for girls to be likeable."

"But why?" Shanti asked.

If Mrs. Mirabov had an answer, she wasn't sharing. "Come down this instant and we work on interview portion. You can tell story of how much you wish to be mother someday. People like to hear about your future plans for ovaries."

Carefully, Shanti inched her way down, but the wind resisted. "Let go," it whispered.

"I can't. I'll crash," she said.

"Everybody crashes sometime."

"Not me."

"Comrade Singh, there are other girls who would not keep me waiting. Other girls who want it more."

"She's the best," Shanti tried to explain.

The wind was warm. It caressed Shanti's skin. It wanted to play. "We will hold you for a while."

And for a moment, Shanti wondered why she needed Mrs. Mirabov when she already had the wind.

"I'm sorry," she called down. "But I have to do this on my own. Thank you. And good-bye."

"You will fail, Comrade Singh!" With a scowl and a blast of Russian, Mrs. Mirabov let go of the string connecting them. As Shanti soared higher, her handler shouted, "You are on your own! A girl without a tribe is no one. No one!"

"No one," the wind said, laughing. "No one," it sang like a round. "No one," it repeated until it sounded like the ringing of a temple bell signaling something sacred, some great happiness, a moment freed from attachment. "No one," it chanted, and all Shanti heard was *Om*.

Petra sat by the river's edge listening to the night sounds and watching a frog hopping along the marshy, muddy bank. When Petra was little, her mother used to tell her a bedtime story. Now she found herself inside the story, which went as follows:

Once upon a time, when magic was not questioned and the miraculous showed itself in every dewdrop and moon shadow, there lived a frog. The frog had fine, strong legs and a wonderful, full-throated croak and was the pride of its mother and father. They loved the frog's jolly temper, its warm greeting to the sun each morning, and did not mind at all that the frog thought itself a princess.

When the frog said, "Once I am grown, I shall have the most beautiful golden hair," they said only, "To match your beautiful heart." When the frog asked, "When shall I become a princess?" they answered, "When you are ready."

And so it went, the frog cheerfully insisting to all in the meadow that it was a princess-in-waiting, until one day, a real princess strutted into the meadow, proud and vain.

"Hello, sister princess," said the frog happily, for it was certain this was a sign that the time for its transformation had come.

"Why do you call me sister, little frog?"

"I'm not a frog," the little green creature laughed (and Petra felt it deep in her belly). "I'm a princess, like you."

"You?" laughed the girl. "You've no long golden hair like I. You've no alabaster arms and delicate feet with toenails painted a sweet pink. You've no honey-sweet laugh like mine. You're just a lowly, croaking, ugly frog."

"You're wrong," the frog said.

"I will show you," the princess said. She led the little frog to the clearest part of the river. "See for yourself. You are a frog. And I am a princess. And nothing, nothing on this earth, will ever change that."

The frog gazed at itself in the cursed water as if seeing for the first time and saw that what the princess said was true, and its sadness was beyond measure. In her dream, Petra felt warm tears on her cheeks.

Before sleep each night, the frog prayed to the four winds, to the great fish, to the sun above, and to the goddess moon that when it woke, it would be a princess. Yet each morning, the frog opened its eyes to find it was still only a frog. How could nature be so wrong about something so important? The frog grew bitter and lonely. It despaired. The frog's parents became terribly frightened.

"We must do something," croaked the mother.

"What can we do?" croaked the father.

They sat with their little frog and said, "We wish you only happiness. If you are meant to be a princess, then so be it. We will love you no matter what. Perhaps you should visit the Wise Witch of the Woods. She will know what to do."

It was a daring plan, for the woods were full of many dangers, but the little frog was determined. After kissing its mother and father good-bye, it traveled far and wide in search of the mysterious, elusive Wise Witch of the Woods. For years it searched without luck. The frog feared it would never become a princess.

"Don't give up," Petra whispered in her dream, and as if the story-frog heard her, it came upon a large acorn covered in vines. The half-buried acorn was easy to miss, but the frog saw straightaway that the acorn was a false shell hiding something inside.

"Hello? Is there anyone there?" the frog croaked out.

"Yes! I am the Wise Witch of the Woods. I've been trapped inside this acorn by a terrible spell," came the response. "If you can release me, I will grant you your heart's desire."

The frog didn't know how it could possibly save a witch from so great a spell. But it sat for a while and it thought and eventually it came up with a plan. It summoned up all its courage and let loose a mighty croak, which cracked the acorn to bits and freed the witch.

The Wise Witch was very grateful to the little frog. She kept her promise. "What is your heart's desire?" she asked.

But the frog had almost given up on its wish. It didn't know if such a wish were possible. "Well," it said softly, afraid, "I have always wanted to be a princess. But I have seen myself in the river. And it has shown me that I am a frog."

The witch smiled. "The river does not know everything. Look again."

Together, they traveled to another part of the river. It was hard to see anything here, but the witch said, "If you are brave and your heart is true, make your wish and jump."

The frog dove into the water, and soon its legs began to lengthen. Its three spindly fingers became five slender ones with jeweled rings on each. And when the frog broke the surface, its long golden hair shone in the sun.

"I am a princess!" said the frog in a voice soft and sweet as first spring clover.

"Princess," Petra repeated.

The frog on the bank croaked in response and leapt into the moon-dappled river. On the water's surface, a bright orange fish swam through Petra's reflection, blurring all definition.

Nicole could not sit still, and so she went for a walk in the glistening green of the jungle. To her surprise, she came upon a gingerbread house that smelled of cinnamon and cloves. Smoke pumped from its chimney.

"I wonder where I am?" she said.

A beautiful café au lait teen stuck her head out of one of the windows. She wore a pointed princess hat with a #1 on it. "You're on the corner of stupid and clueless."

Canned laughter echoed in the trees. It sounded like the laugh track on all those teen TV shows Nicole had seen a million times.

"I'm sorry?" Nicole said.

Another comely sister stuck her head out a window. There was a #2 on her hat. "You a couple snaps short of a gingersnap, aren't you?"

"I beg your —"

A third girl in a hat marked #3 shoved her hand out the window, palm first. "Talk to the hand."

The laugh track roared and subsided again. The house, the trees, and the sidekicks cast tall shadows that reminded Nicole of an art exhibit she'd seen by an African-American artist. The exhibit was a series of silhouettes of slaves and minstrels. It was very controversial and pissed off a lot of people. But Nicole had found it powerful; it had made her angry and afraid in equal measure.

"Excuse me," Nicole said as she ran into the house, where she found her mother sitting at her vanity, putting more and more powder on her face. The vanity held a collection of hair relaxers, skin brighteners, oils, and flattening irons. Hanging from a department store rack was a sleek, sparkly dress in a doll's size.

"There's my baby now," her mother said to the mirror. She frowned. "Oh, you look so rough, sugar. Have you been using your grease?"

"Mom, my plane crashed on this island and we had no food and people died and —"

"Don't you worry, baby. We'll get you fixed up in no time." Her mother reached over and patted a collage taped to the wall. The glossy pictures had all been torn from magazines, a collection of pale, blond, hipless women with aquiline noses, bony legs, blank eyes, and thin, wan smiles. The body parts had been taped together like a series of lines, more Bauhaus building than woman. Sighing, Nicole's mom ran a hand over the thickness of her thighs, the roundness of her bottom, and it was as if Nicole could feel the shame in her own body. "It won't do, baby. It won't do at all."

"What should we do?" Nicole asked.

Nicole's mother turned to her. It was hard to see her features under so much cover. Only her eyes shone out, wide and afraid. "The giant's coming," she whispered. "We don't have much time to get you ready, Ne-Ne."

"Ready for what?"

Her mother clapped and the sidekicks danced into the room. One did the moonwalk. They struck their poses, hips cocked, lips pursed, palms out in a talk-to-the-hand motion.

"I know you," Nicole said to them. "You did pageants before you went to Hollywood. Now you're on TV."

"That's right. We're the sassy black sidekicks."

"You know, the best friend of the main character."

"The comic relief."

"The ones who can put you down and tell you off."

"I've been working on my head swivel. Wanna see my head swivel?"

"What happened to you?" Nicole said, going down the line. "You used to play Bach on the viola and work at a nonprofit after school. *You* wanted to go to London and start that cool underground theater and you never, ever moonwalked. And *you* . . . you were Episcopalian."

Number 3 swiveled her head perfectly. "Not no more, sugar."

"Why are you talking like that? What's with the double negatives?"

"I'm about to double negative your head in a minute!" She snapped twice, and the laugh track erupted again. In it, Nicole heard barks and screams.

The ground shook. Nicole's mother gasped and the girls went into their head-swiveling, finger-snapping minstrel show at a frenzied pace.

"What's happening?"

Number 1 offered Nicole's mother a large pair of garden shears. Her mother looked balefully to the collage. "It's the only way, baby."

Nicole understood and she felt frightened. She didn't want to cut herself down. The jungle shook with a giant's footsteps.

"Quick!" Nicole's mother lunged at her with the scissors and Nicole ran out of the house and into the menacing shelter of the jungle. Behind her, footsteps thundered. Trees cracked and fell. The jungle was losing color, becoming a silhouette. The white space nipped at Nicole's heels, tugged at her hair. She could not outrun it, and then she was lost inside, a feathery black cutout in the background, her hand still reaching for safety.

Inside the volcano, the elevator's thick steel doors whisked open. Agent Jones entered the control room. Glowing green maps flickered on wall-size screens. The constant hum of work filled the cavernous space — the clicking of fingers on keyboards. This base had existed for some time, privately financed by interested parties. Unregulated by the government, it had operated without rules or oversight, almost as its own country, and it had done as it pleased. But now, the island's resources were nearly tapped out. Something new was needed. That's why there was Operation Peacock.

The agent poured himself a cup of free trade coffee from the wheezing pot, took a sip, and frowned. French Roast. Was it so hard for these guys to get Hazelnut like he'd asked? Every month, he filled out coffee requisition forms in triplicate. To date, they'd received Arabica, French Vanilla, House Blend, Viennese, even Kona. But no Hazelnut. The agent sighed in irritation.

"Yo, Agent Jones, my main man!" An Ivy Leaguer in a Lakers T-shirt popped his head above the cubicle partition. Harris Buffington Ewell Davis III, aka the Dweeb, was the son of The Corporation's former CEO. The kid had never held a job in his life and was spending his summer break from the Ivy League here, ostensibly to get training. Mostly he played covert games of Pong and annoyed the hell out of Agent Jones. "What's going on?" Harris raised his hand for a slap.

Agent Jones left the kid's hand kissing air. "Hello, Harris. How's production going?"

"Okay. No love for the hand. Production's good. See?" The Dweeb flipped a switch and the factory floor came up on the monitor in grainy black and white. Agents in black shirts stood guard while scientists in lab coats busied themselves over a stainless steel table filled with jars. "Who knew hair remover could also make a cool explosive?"

"Miracles never cease."

"Oh, hey, wanna see something megacool? I rigged the compound's override system to respond only to PowerPoint." Harris cackled.

Agent Jones was stone-faced. "So, in the event of a self-destruct initiation, the only way to stop the sequencing is by making and uploading a full PowerPoint presentation?

"Yeah. Isn't that awesome?"

"No. Not awesome. Change it back."

Harris glowered. "Well, I think it's awesome. I took Advanced PowerPoint last semester. You guys are always misunderestimating me. I'm totally ready to handle the big stuff."

"The word is *underestimate*. And when you've got a few more years under your belt, then we'll talk big stuff, Harris." Agent Jones forced a smile that he hoped passed for benevolent. His performance reviews all praised his skills but said he lacked warmth. He was not someone anyone wanted to have a beer with.

Harris made a face. "Did you just cut one? 'Cause you're making a face like you did."

Agent Jones stopped trying to smile. "Briefing in the conference room in five."

The fortresslike conference room was an interior room with concrete walls, fluorescent lighting, and ergonomically correct leather chairs that cost five thousand a pop. Agent Jones resented the chairs as much as the lack of Hazelnut coffee. Back before the agency had been bought by The Corporation and privatized, they'd had adequate seating but great benefits. Now, they were lucky to get dental.

The room filled with the private security detail — the black shirts, as they were called. The Dweeb took a seat and put his sneakered feet on the Brazilian cherry oblong table.

Agent Jones took a sip of his disappointing coffee. "Kill the lights."

A black shirt took out his gun.

"Not literally, Agent. I meant turn them off."

The room dimmed to a hazy gray. Agent Jones pulled down a white screen and plugged in his twenty-five-year-old slide projector. Despite the high-techery available, he preferred the old wheezing machine. He clicked the remote. The fan whirred. On the projection screen was the faded-color image of a short man in a militarized black jumpsuit and huge, blue suede platforms. The man sported oversize sunglasses and a long, fat mustache. He wore an obvious wig, which bore a resemblance to Elvis Presley's famous pompadour.

"MoMo B. ChaCha, aka The Peacock. Dictator of the Republic of ChaCha and a very creative dresser. Thief. Murderer. Racked up more human rights violations than Genghis Khan[20]."

"Who?" the Dweeb asked.

"I thought you went to Yale."

"I study business, not Chinese." Harris snorted.

Agent Jones exhaled loudly and clicked to a new slide. "The Republic of ChaCha, or the ROC, is one of the richest countries in the world. Incredible natural resources. But we can't get to those resources because a) our government has levied sanctions against the ROC, so all Corporation interests would be in violation of the Trading with the Enemy Act and b) MoMo B. ChaCha is certifiably insane. This is a man who is so paranoid, his most trusted advisor is a taxidermied former pet named General Good Times."

The carousel clicked to a new slide. MoMo B. ChaCha in full military colors inspected his army from a Jeep. Beside him was a stuffed lemur in sunglasses and a general's hat.

[20] Genghis Khan, thirteenth-century Mongolian ruler. Genocidal maniac. Wearer of very smart hats.

"But didn't we put MoMo in power in the first place when the ROC elected a socialist president?" one of the black shirts asked.

Agent Jones glared at the man until he began to play with his pencil. "In a few weeks, MoMo B. ChaCha will travel to this very island to make an arms deal with The Corporation. As you know, MoMo is not a fan of our country."

Agent Jones switched to the big screen and a grainy video of MoMo sitting at his enormous desk, a swivel-hipped Elvis clock ticking behind his bewigged head. "Death to the capitalist pigs! Death to your cinnamon bun–smelling malls! Death to your power walking and automatic car windows and *I'm With Stupid* T-shirts! The Republic of ChaCha will never bend to your side-of-fries-drive-through-please-oh-would-you-like-ketchup-with-that corruption! MoMo B. ChaCha defies you and all you stand for, and one day, you will crumble into the sea and we will pick up the pieces and make them into sand art."

"So why is he doing a deal with us if he hates us so much?" someone asked.

"MoMo's been trying to tamp down an insurgency in the ROC. Needs some firepower. We sell him arms; he lets The Corporation set up shop in his country. Covertly, of course."

"How're you going to get those weapons into the country?"

Agent Jones held up a small, white jar of Lady 'Stache Off.

"Lady hair remover?" a black shirt asked.

"Looks like it. Actually, it's a powerful explosive. Dr. Du'Bious?"

"We found that if you change one compound in Lady 'Stache Off, it becomes highly unstable. All it needs is a charge of some kind and you've got incredible shock-and-awe capabilities," the scientist explained excitedly.

"And it leaves your legs baby smooth." Agent Jones attempted another smile. No one laughed. Agent Jones cleared his throat. "So. We sell MoMo his weapons. And The Corporation gets a foothold in the Republic of ChaCha."

A new slide whirred into place. It showed an artist's colorful rendering of the new ROC, with huge shopping complexes, smiling people in sunglasses toting oversize shopping bags, a Corporation oil rig shining from the blue water in the background. "Violà. The Republic of The Corporation. God bless America."

There was a round of applause.

CHAPTER NINE

Under Taylor's direction, her group of girls found their way back to the damaged beach, which resembled a dorm room after an island-themed kegger gone wrong. Broken trees and fractured palm leaves littered the sand. Belongings were strewn about. But the sea was now calm and the sky forgiving. The girls fell into the sand, exhausted and groaning.

"How long have we been stranded here?" someone asked.

"About three days," Miss Ohio answered.

Mary Lou looked at the hair on her legs. "Four."

"All right, Miss Teen Dreamers. Let's get this place a little cleaned up and get us a signal fire going. Tomorrow morning at sunrise sharp we'll practice the opening number. Just lettin' y'all know, we might have to make a few more adjustments to the choreography if the other girls don't make it back."

"I'm so hungry," Mary Lou mumbled. "So, so hungry."

"I can't move," Miss Arkansas cried. "I'm too tired."

Taylor had already begun clearing plant debris into a tidy pile for burning. "This is not the Miss Teen Dream spirit, ladies."

Miss New Mexico tried scooping a handful of sand into her mouth, but Adina stopped her.

"We need food!" Miss Ohio cried, and the others moaned in agreement.

"Miss Teen Dreamers. It is time to get ahold of ourselves. Miss Alabama, I did not mean that literally. That is gross. Stop it." Taylor scooped up seawater in a large shell and poured it over the ends of her hair, rinsing out the mud. "Remember: We are Miss Teen Dreamers. We are not victims. We are not cowards. We are bright shining stars, beacons of hope to all who arrive on the shores of our beauty."

Mary Lou pointed to the surf. "There's an ocean full of fish out there if we could find some way to catch them."

"I hope there's salmon," Brittani said. "Salmon has a lot of omega-3. My consultant, Tricia, says it's really good for your skin and nails."

"Right. Because I'm really worried about my FUCKING NAILS AT THIS POINT!" Adina screamed.

"Language, Miss New Hampshire. You owe me twenty-five cents for that potty mouth." Taylor took the lip gloss from her zippered pocket and slicked it over her mouth. "Let's ignore those who would bring us down and *affirm*, Teen Dreamers: How are we gonna get us some fish?"

Everyone shouted at once. "We could try grabbing them!" "Fishing pole." "Laser gun!" "Think positive thoughts!"

"We could spear them," Mary Lou offered.

"With what?" Miss Ohio asked.

Mary Lou blushed. "Um, with a . . . spear?"

"Oh my gosh! My bad. How could I have forgotten to pack my spear for my beauty pageant?" Miss New Mexico snapped. The tray in her forehead shook.

"Because you probably left it in your competition's back," Miss Ohio snarked. Miss Montana high-fived her.

"Well, your evening gown looks like it was put together in the dark by a bunch of dyslexic sweatshop workers!" Miss Arkansas gave Miss Montana a small shove.

Miss Montana shoved back. "Oh really? Says the girl with flotation device boobs."

"These are one hundred percent real!"

"So's Santa."

"At least my talent isn't totally lame," sniffed Miss Ohio.

Miss Arkansas laughed a loud *HA!* "Your talent? Are they letting people perform oral sex in these pageants now?"

Taylor clapped three times for attention. "Ladies! Ladies! My stars! That's enough. Now. We all know Miss Arkansas's girls are fake, Miss Ohio's easier than making cereal, and Miss Montana's dress is something my blind meemaw would wear to bingo night. And Miss New Mexico — aren't you from the chill-out state? Maybe you can channel up some new-age-Whole-Foods-incense calm right about now, because we have a big job ahead called staying alive."

"What do we do?" Brittani asked. She lay in the sand with her arm over her forehead.

"We need something we can use to turn these sticks into spears."

"A knife!"

"A rock!"

"Two rocks!"

"Adina's tongue."

"Thanks. Thanks a lot," Adina snapped.

Mary Lou pulled something from one of the suitcases. It was egg-shaped and shiny. "Pumice stone?"

Taylor examined the palm-size foot grater. "Good work, Nebraska. Sparkle Ponies and Lost Girls, start buffing and polishing those sticks into fish-killing machines."

"But that could take forever. I'm starving *now*," Miss Ohio cried.

"Fine. Desperate times call for desperate measures." Taylor grabbed a shell and gouged the sand, going deeper and deeper. She reached into the sand and brought up a white, cylindrical bug. It wiggled lazily in her palm. "Who wants to eat first?"

"What's that?" Miss Montana asked with obvious distaste.

"It's a grub and it's packed with protein. My daddy said his unit had to survive on these for a whole month once. Who's going first?"

Collectively, the girls took a step back.

"My stars, I thought y'all were hungry and wanted to survive."

No one made a move.

"Well, then. I guess as team leader I will just have to draft some-one as a volunteer." Taylor looked over the girls like a general inspecting the ranks of new recruits. She stopped at Adina. "Miss New Hampshire. Congratulations. You're the winner."

"If you're so keen on it, why don't you go first?" Adina asked.

"Because y'all know I'll do it," Taylor answered. "This is about building trust. Take one for the team, New Hampshire."

Adina had a memory of Alan and the ridiculous trust-building exercises he conducted for business retreats full of blowhard execs who apparently liked wasting money on glorified corporate camp. Once, Alan had asked her to fall backward with the assurance that he would catch her and that she would see she could trust him. But Adina balked. The only person she trusted was herself. She was not ending up on the floor with a concussion, and she was not, absolutely not, eating that filthy bug in Taylor's hand just so she could prove her mettle and get a round of high fives from the beauty queen set.

She crossed her arms over her chest. "No. Sorry. Not doing it."

"I'll do it," Miss Arkansas volunteered.

"No. This is about Miss New Hampshire. We are the Miss Teen Dream team. We are only as strong as our weakest link. There is no *I* in *team*."

"There's no *U* in *asshole*, either, and yet . . ." Adina muttered.

"I'm dockin' you another twenty-five cents for your potty mouth and bad attitude, Miss New Hampshire."

"Fine. Let me just go to the JUNGLE ATM TO GET A WITHDRAWAL!"

Taylor leveled her gaze at Adina. "Do you know what your prob-lem is, Miss New Hampshire?"

"You mean, besides the fact that my plane crashed on a hostile island, we haven't eaten in days, you want me to chug a bug, and you keep calling me New Hampshire?"

"Your problem is not having any trust. You expect the world to fail you, so it does. And then you get all pouty-pants about it. How's that workin' out for you, New Hampshire?"

Adina's cheeks reddened. "Well, you're the one who wanted to practice that pageant crap instead of trying to find a way off this island! We should have been looking for food and shelter days ago, trying to build a boat — something other than practicing our goddamned canned responses to stupid questions about our life goals thought up by clueless adults who need their own life goals!"

Taylor pursed her lips. "Well, like Ladybird Hope says: There's two ways to look at things — crowns and pimples. For instance, right now, I am coated in a sweater set of sand. I could complain about that nonstop — *pimples*. Or I could see this as an exciting exfoliation opportunity that will give me the smoothest skin of my life — *crowns*. And you owe me another twenty-five cents for taking our Lord's name in vain."

"You are truly Satan's sequined spawn."

Taylor held the pale, wriggling grub up to Adina's face. "So what's it going to be, New Hampshire?"

"Adina . . . Adina . . . Adina . . ." the girls chanted.

Taylor dropped the larva into Adina's open palm.

"Adina . . . Adina . . . Adina . . ."

Adina felt the slimy wetness of the bug in her hand. Her stomach lurched. The chants of her name grew louder. It was like falling, waiting for untested hands to catch her.

"Oh God . . ." Adina whimpered. In one quick gulp, she downed the white larva, then fell to her hands and knees, gagging like a cat with a hairball. The girls backed away, giving her space. Finally, Adina staggered to her feet and wiped her mouth. For a moment under the hot sun, she thought she might faint. Or hurl. Or both.

"Adina?" Mary Lou whispered. "You okay?"

Adina gave a thumbs-up, and the girls grabbed her in a group hug. They cheered. *For me*, Adina thought. They were cheering *her*, and she was hit with a sense of pride and camaraderie she would have found cheesy back home.

"You're so brave," Mary Lou said, hugging her.

"How was it?" Brittani asked.

"Not totally awful. It kind of reminded me of French kissing Jake Weinstein and his spelunker tongue."

Taylor appraised Adina coolly. "Let's all give some snaps to New Hampshire." Taylor clicked her fingers like castanets and the others followed till it sounded like Cinco de Mayo night at the senior home. "All right, Teen Dreamers — start digging for worms. It's what's for lunch."

Tiara heard singing, and for a moment she thought she was in her room back home listening to Boyz Will B Boyz and waiting for her mom to wake her for her daily weigh-in. Instinctively, she tried to shove her secret snack cake wrappers under the imaginary mattress, only to feel a caterpillar crawling across her hand, startling her awake. Nicole and Shanti were still passed out, and she definitely heard singing. She walked in the direction of the song, following it till she found a small, bucolic waterfall that fed into a turquoise pond. On the bank lay Petra's mud-caked clothes.

Petra stood in the pond, her lithe back to Tiara. She was as skinny as a boy or a supermodel, or a boy supermodel, and Tiara felt a pang of envy that Petra would never have to endure daily weigh-ins or go on juice fasts. She felt bad for spying, though. It wasn't very nice. Should she make a noise? What if she scared Petra? She was trying to decide the best way to announce herself when Petra, still oblivious to Tiara's presence, turned and rose from the water, and Tiara made the only sound she could. She screamed.

"Oh. My. God," Nicole said.

"You're a . . . you're not even . . ." Shanti stammered. "You're really J. T. Woodland? From Boyz Will B Boyz?"

Nicole raised an eyebrow. "Not anymore."

"I had your poster in my room when I was ten!" Tiara blubbered.

"I wrote to your fan club. You sent me a bandanna with your autograph."

"I hated those bandannas. They were so cheesy." Petra pulled her knees close and rested her chin on them.

"I think you're missing the salient point here," Shanti said. "Miss Teen Dream is a girls' pageant. You are not a girl. Ergo, you are disqualified."

"Who says I'm not a girl?"

"You have a wang-dang-doodle!" Tiara squeaked.

"Is that all that makes a guy a guy? What makes a girl a girl?"

And the girls found they could not answer. For they'd never been asked that question in the pageant prep.

Tiara's expression was pained. "I don't mean to offend you, Petra or J. T. or whatever, but my mom says that's against nature and God."

"Maybe you should ask God and nature why they put a girl inside a boy's body?" Petra shouted to the uncaring sky. "And while you're at it, maybe you should ask your mom why she thinks it's not against God and nature to dress her little girl up in garters, spackle her face with makeup, and let her pole dance."

"It's *Christian* pole dancing," Tiara said softly.

"It's abuse," Petra said. "Making your third grader go for a spray tan instead of playing in the park just so Mom can outsource her failed dreams to her kid? So wrong."

Tiara's eyes filled with tears. "She only wants what's best for me. She knows I love the pageants."

"Do you, really?" Petra challenged, and Tiara was silent.

"Why did you enter Miss Teen Dream?" Nicole asked Petra. "I mean, that's, like, suicidal."

Petra let out a long exhale. "My parents always wanted me to be able to have the surgery. I got the therapist, had the electrolysis, went on the hormones and the androgen blockers. I did almost everything. But then my mom got cancer. The chemo was expensive and the insurance wouldn't pay. Said it was a preexisting condition."

"Breast cancer?"

"Breasts," Petra said bitterly. "Long story short, we were massively in debt. So long, sex reassignment surgery."

"What about all that money you made with Boyz Will B Boyz?" Nicole asked.

"Embezzled by our manager."

"Harsh. Wow, I'm really sorry," Nicole said. "So how'd you decide on Miss Teen Dream?"

Petra rocked back, still holding tightly to her knees. "It wasn't my idea. Through my support group, I met these political activists from a transgender rights group called Trans Am."

"Trans Am?" Shanti made a face. "Your transgender rights group named themselves after a cheesy 1980s car and you aligned yourself with them? That's like picking a plastic surgeon out of the grocery circular."

"Okay. The name's stupid. But they wanted to make a statement. They got me my hormones and promised to pay for the surgery if I'd go through Miss Teen Dream, the ultimate female pageant, as a contestant. All I had to do was place and then reveal myself at a press conference afterward and people would have to question everything they think about transgender people and about gender itself."

"So you're making fun of us?" Tiara asked.

"No! Not at all," Petra said.

"Why not do one of those drag pageants, win money that way?" Nicole asked.

Petra kicked the tree. "Because I'm not in drag! This is who I am. That's why I want to make a statement, so people understand. It's a stand against discrimination. Look, I don't need to win. I just need to place and do the press conference, and then I'll have enough for the operation. Can you just not say anything? Please?"

The girls exchanged glances. It was Shanti who spoke. "I'm sorry. You broke the rules. I have to turn you in."

"He — she might not even place," Nicole tried.

"And if he does, that's taking away a spot that could go to you or me. It's not like the pageant just loves women of color, you know."

Tiara looked up. "I thought you said the pageant wasn't racist."

"Bitch, please," Shanti and Nicole said in unison.

"Besides, the pageant's already on shaky ground," Shanti argued. "All we need is another scandal, and then it's over and none of us gets scholarship money. I'm sorry. But I'm a rules girl. I have to turn you in, Petra. We should get moving while there's daylight."

Nicole was torn. She liked Petra and she understood what it was to be discriminated against. But this was different, wasn't it? Petra had deceived them, and Nicole didn't like being lied to. She honestly didn't know what to do.

"Maybe there's another way to get the money." She patted Petra's shoulder and fell in behind Shanti.

Petra turned to Tiara. "I guess you hate me, too."

Tiara tried not to look at Petra. Her eyes kept slipping down to her non-girl region. "I'm so confused. I don't know if you're a girl or a boy."

"I'm a girl who just happened to get the wrong body."

"My mom says people like you are wrong."

"I can't speak for your mom."

"I don't know. I have to think about it," Tiara said, and she hurried to join the other girls on the trail.

CHAPTER TEN

By day's end, everyone had made it back to the camp on the beach. Jennifer introduced Sosie to the group and told everyone about their misadventure with (and eventual victory over) the giant snake, about the Lady 'Stache Off jars and the old ration kit. The girls took it as a sign that the island was known and there would be an eventual rescue, especially if Jennifer could get the radio up and running.

"I'll give it a shot. I learned a lot when my mom used to work at the plant," Jennifer said.

Taylor convened a meeting. The girls settled into their horseshoe formation. Taylor raised a baton whose ignitable ends had been reduced to stubs.

"Whoever needs to talk can ask for the baton. Parliamentary procedure will be followed."

"Parliamentary procedure? Did you go to girls' state? Because I did," Adina interjected.

Taylor frowned and waggled the baton. "You're out of order, Miss New Hampshire. I have the baton. As I was saying, if you need to say something, you raise your hand and ask for permission to speak. The speaker will recognize you and hand over the baton. If you speak out of turn, you're gonna be hit with penalties. So," Taylor said as she wiped a small spot of dirt off the baton's glittery stick. "Now that we're all back together, we need to talk about getting rescued and resuming our pageant practice."

Adina's hand went up like a missile. "Permission to speak!"

Taylor rolled her eyes. "Granted, Miss New Hampshire. Please try to keep it clean. Not all of us were raised in a traveling RV of foul-mouthed circus folk."

She handed the baton to Adina, who started to say something in response, then thought better of it. "For as long as we're here, we need to survive. You know, build some shelter, find reliable food and drinking water. We need to organize."

Taylor's hand shot up. "Taylor Rene Krystal Hawkins of the great state of Texas! Permission to speak!"

"What fresh hell is this?" Adina muttered. "Granted."

Taylor took back the baton. "Miss New Hampshire is right."

"You're agreeing with me?" Adina blurted out. "What are the other signs of the apocalypse?"

"You're out of order, Miss New Hampshire. I'll issue a warning. Next time it's a penalty." Taylor stood and paced with the baton cradled in her arms like a winner's bouquet. "You know what I'm thinkin', Miss Teen Dreamers?"

"What?" Mary Lou asked.

"That was rhetorical, Miss Nebraska. I'm thinkin' that when we do finally get rescued, we want them to find us at our best. And what could be better and more in line with the Miss Teen Dream mission statement than having them find that we have tamed and beautified this island? It's like extra credit. And you know how the judges love extra credit."

Shanti raised her hand and received the baton. "I wrote my junior AP science thesis on micro farming and sustainable agriculture. I could come up with some plans for planting a garden and constructing an irrigation system. And I know how to make a system for drinking water."

"But can you also make popadam as your grandmother taught you?"

"Out of order, Montana," Taylor tutted.

Miss New Mexico raised her hand. "My sophomore year, I took set design when I couldn't get into interpretive dance. I'm pretty good at building things."

"You are now the building committee, Miss New Mexico. What else do we need?"

The baton passed from girl to girl as ideas were discussed: Huts. Fishing lines. Rain-catching tarp. Zip lines. Tanning booth. By the time the baton came to Taylor again, the girls had a renewed sense of hope. After all, they were the best of the best. They had lived through the pageant circuit, which was no place for wimps.

"When they come to rescue us, they will find us with clean, jungle-forward, fashionable huts and a self-sustaining ecosystem. We will be the Miss Teen Dreamers they write about in history books," Taylor said.

"Nobody writes about Miss Teen Dreamers in history books," Adina scoffed.

"They will now, Miss New Hampshire. We will be the best ever. This is my new goal. And I am very goal-oriented. Also, penalty: You're on first watch tonight. Is there anything else?" Taylor asked. It was quiet. "Then I'll call this meeting —"

"Permission to speak?" Shanti raised her hand and glanced nervously at Petra. "I have something I need to tell everyone."

"Shanti, don't," Nicole whispered.

"Miss Colorado? Were you speaking out of turn?"

"No. Just clearing my throat."

"Then you have the runway, Miss California. Take your promenade." Taylor passed her the baton.

"Well, we didn't really get a chance to know one another before we left. And it's just that some of us might not be who we pretend to be."

Taylor gripped one end of the baton, sharing it with Shanti. "What are you saying, Miss California?"

"I'm saying —"

"That we should have a cutest hut contest!" Nicole interrupted.

"Miss Colorado, it was not your turn on the runway," Taylor admonished. "Tomorrow, you will bring coconuts back from the jungle."

"Sure," Nicole continued. "It's just that I'm sure what Shanti is *trying* to say is that it's really hard when you've grown up feeling discriminated against, you know, because of your race or religion or because you just happened to be born a certain way. . . ."

"Like really pretty," Miss Ohio said.

Miss New Mexico nodded. "Or naturally thin."

"Or you have a third nipple," Brittani said, shaking her head.

"Excuse me, I have the runway," Shanti reminded everyone. "You need to know that Petra has been lying to us all this time. Nicole and Tiara can back me up."

In her head, Nicole heard her mother's voice, the million-and-one times she'd turned to Nicole with an "Isn't that right, baby?" or "Nicole agrees with her mama, don't you?" She heard her mother's voice and she gave the response she'd always wanted to give. "I don't know what you're talking about."

Shanti turned to Tiara. "Tell everybody the truth."

Tiara looked from Petra to Shanti to Nicole and back to Petra again.

"Miss Mississippi?" Taylor asked.

"Well . . . um . . . I . . . I . . ."

Petra stood. "Stop badgering her! Fine. You want to know the secret. I'll tell you. Permission to speak."

"Granted," Taylor said.

Shanti raised the baton. "But I'm the only one who can grant permission."

"Miss California. Don't be such a douche nozzle. Miss Rhode Island?"

"I wasn't . . . I haven't always . . ." Petra took a deep breath. The baton trembled in her hands. She'd wanted her chance to compete like any other girl, to make a statement to the world that there was nothing wrong with her, that she was beautiful, through and through. But the hiding was too hard — harder than learning group dance steps or finding size-eleven heels that didn't look like total ass. "I'm not technically a girl. Yet."

Thirteen pairs of eyes stared back at Petra. The only sounds were the crackle of the fire and the whoosh of surf. Finally, Taylor raised her hand and Petra recognized her.

"Did you get hit on the head out there, Miss Rhode Island? Because I am a National Merit Scholar, and I know a girl when I see one."

"Well, thanks for that." Petra gave a wan smile. "I'm transitioning. Male to female. I was born a boy, but I always knew that on the inside, I am a girl. I've been taking the hormones — that's what was in my overnight case and why I was so desperate to get it back."

"She used to be J. T. Woodland from Boyz Will B Boyz," Tiara said. "Sorry. Permission to speak before what I just said. No takebacks!"

Again, there was silence. Miss Ohio raised her hand and was granted permission. "Really? You used to be J. T. Woodland?"

Petra nodded.

"What is Billy Merrell really like? Does he like blondes? Do you think he'd like me?"

Taylor wrenched the baton away from her. "Miss Ohio! This is not about you sleeping your way up the pathetic ladder of D-list celebrity. We have a situation here." She paced the narrow strip of sand. "The rules of Miss Teen Dream state, quite clearly, that it is a pageant open to girls between the ages of fourteen and eighteen. The rules also state that any Miss Teen Dream contestant caught with a boy who is not a blood relative in her room will be disqualified."

"So we're all disqualified?"

"You do not have the baton, Miss Ohio. Latrine duty tomorrow."

"Balls," Miss Ohio whispered.

"No. We didn't know. We were duped. But now that we do know, we can't continue to fraternize with Miss Rhode Island. It's against the rules."

Adina was on her feet. "What? That's ridiculous! We're on a deserted island, for chrissakes! We're way beyond the rules of some stupid pageant here!"

"Rules are rules, Miss New Hampshire. They exist for a reason. For taking the Lord's name in vain, you owe me another quarter. You also spoke without the baton. Latrine duty for you, too."

"Yes!" Miss Ohio mouthed while making a small fist pump.

Adina's hand shot up. "Permission to speak!" She wiggled her fingers.

Taylor let them hang there.

"Permission to speak," Mary Lou said.

"Recognizing Miss Nebraska." Taylor handed Mary Lou the baton, casting a triumphant glance at Adina.

"Well, um, I just want to say that I've read the rule book cover to cover and there's no specific rule *against* a transgender contestant," Mary Lou said in a halting voice. "Not a single one. So, technically, we're not breaking the rules."

"But . . . she's a he! A guy!" Shanti growled.

"Says who? What makes a girl a girl? What makes a guy a guy?" Petra asked. Her eyes blazed in the firelight. Quickly, Mary Lou shoved the baton at her. "Do you have to be what they want you to be? Or do you stop and listen to that voice inside you? I know who I am. I'm Petra West. And I'm a girl. You want me to sleep somewhere else, fine. Whatever. But I'm not going to pretend to be somebody I'm not. I've done enough of that."

Adina stood and linked arms with Petra. "If Petra goes, so do I."

Nicole jumped up. "Me, too."

"Word," said Jennifer. "And I'll be taking the radio."

Taylor reached a hand out for the baton and Petra relinquished it. "I think this is a matter for the pageant officials to decide. But since there's no specific rule against Miss Rhode Island being with us as dictated by the official Miss Teen Dream handbook, I move that we all stay together for the time being. All those in favor say *aye*."

The ayes were strong.

"All those opposed."

A few nays straggled in.

"Motion carries. Miss Rhode Island bunks with us. Let's get some sleep, Miss Teen Dreamers. Tomorrow's going to be a real busy day. And I, for one, do not intend to have puffy eyes. Miss New Hampshire, you're on first watch."

The girls filed out. Nicole and Adina gave Shanti dirty looks on the way past, and Shanti felt shamed and unfairly picked on.

"Look, I wasn't trying to ostracize anybody. It's just that she — he lied about who he was."

Petra turned to her. "Everybody lies about who they are. Name one person here who isn't doing that and I will drop out right now!"

Shanti felt that snake of truth coil around her legs, threatening to squeeze.

"I didn't mean . . ."

"No one ever does," Petra said, shoving the baton back at Shanti.

CLASSIFIED
THE REPUBLIC OF CHACHA
18:00 HOURS

MoMo B. ChaCha was not happy. His favorite pajamas were not yet back from the cleaners. When MoMo was unhappy, everyone was unhappy. With a sigh, he settled on a pair of cotton pj's. In the morning, he would have the cleaners assassinated.

MoMo removed his custom Elvis-with-sideburns hairpiece and placed it carefully on the plaster of Paris wig form made to look just like MoMo, complete with long, fat mustache and oversize sunglasses. Without the wig, the dictator's head was like a smooth pond covered by thin strands of brown floss, strands that had grown thinner during the fifteen years, four months, three days, and twenty-two hours he had been absolute ruler of the Republic of ChaCha. It was a small country, but rich in natural resources of the type that made other countries bend over backward to accommodate it. For this reason only, MoMo had a seat in the UN where, on more than one occasion, he had stood on the table in his platform shoes and ermine-trimmed bell-bottoms and danced out his protest against U.S. sanctions. He hated everything about the country of the Miss Teen Dream Pageant, except for three things: Elvis Presley, the greatest entertainer who ever lived; reality TV, especially the raucous *Captains Bodacious*; and Ladybird Hope.

For this reason, every night after dinner and executions, he would retire to his secret bedroom on his private yacht, which had been wallpapered ceiling to floor in photos of Ladybird Hope. He would don his Elvis Comeback Special black jumpsuit pajamas, crawl into his heart-shaped bed, and pretend that Ladybird was beside him, as if they were a couple on an American sitcom.

"Ladybird, why do we not have the sex? A little less conversation and a little more action, please."

"You are so fresh, Peacock!" MoMo answered himself in a high, Ladybird Hope voice. "Let us to watch episodes of *Captains Bodacious* now, and in the morning, we kill defenseless animals with our big guns."

"As you wish, Ladybird. Dreams come true in Blue Hawaii."

With a sigh, MoMo settled into the enormous bed and watched the state-sanctioned news, which told of the army's resounding defeat of the mountainside rebels. This was not entirely true. The rebels were a constant annoyance, an unlanced bunion on the foot of the country. But soon he would take care of that problem. Soon, he would travel by yacht to The Corporation's private island, away from prying government eyes. The arms deal would be made with no trouble. He reached over and opened the desk drawer that housed the secret DVD he had made, his insurance policy that everything would go according to MoMo's plans.

MoMo cackled. "Oh, sometimes, General Good Times, I am to make myself so happy with my scheming. It is like I am Elvis Presley in *Roustabout* and those college boys are in for a surprise karate chop. Oh. But you have not touched your food, my friend."

General Good Times, the stuffed lemur, sat in the leather desk chair. He had been dressed in his special ninja pajamas with the words *Silent Killah* stitched over the breast pocket.

MoMo flicked on the TV to watch *Captains Bodacious*. It was a rerun, but he didn't mind. He liked those rock-star pirates. His favorite was the one called "Casanova of the Sea," who kept a blog about his romantic conquests. Maybe one day, he would meet them all, tour their ship, see the gangplank and the cannons for himself, wear the white, poufy shirt of the captain, shake hands with Casanova. Maybe he would kill one of them for fun. Maybe not. Mood was everything.

"I like these pirates, Ladybird. They bring the giggles," MoMo said to his imaginary fiancée. "When we are married, let the cameras to follow us always, even when we make the pee-pee. Let us never to live in private. Private is for small people, yes?"

"Yes," he answered in his high Ladybird voice. "We are not small people. We are stars."

"Soon, we will have our weapons. I will release the videotape, and we will be famous on American TV. Sing along, General Good Times."

General Good Times did not respond.

The scientist sneaked from the compound to the abandoned temple where he had secreted tubs of Lady 'Stache Off and an old radio he'd outfitted with some new wiring. It only needed to be assembled to make contact. Benny's stocks had taken a real header during the last crash. By his calculations, he wouldn't be able to retire before he turned ninety-eight. Corporate espionage was the answer. Another company would pay highly for his weaponized jars of Lady 'Stache Off. That's why he had hidden a case of them and the radio in the old temple. Now all he had to do was rewire the radio, send a message, and wait for his contact to arrive.

Once inside the temple, he was surprised to discover that his weaponized jars of Lady 'Stache Off were no longer there. Nor was the radio or his ration kit. Instead, he was looking at the business end of a gun.

"Going somewhere, Benny?"

Benny held up his hands and backed away. "I-I just needed some fresh air."

"That's a good idea. I think we need some fresh air in the department, Benny." The laugh echoed in the ruins. A flock of birds scurried through the broken roof as if sensing trouble. "That was a good line. You gotta admit."

Benny tripped over a gnarled vine and fell hard to the ground, his hands still up in a defensive gesture. "Please . . ."

"Who's your contact, Benny?"

"I'll tell you! It's . . ."

The gun, a Corporation Git R Done 447, went off, killing Benny instantly. He lay sprawled against the rocks. The top of his head was missing.

"Oh, dammit!" Harris said. "Thought they fixed that." Harris kicked Benny's inert body and sighed. He hadn't gotten the information he needed, which was a real bummer. It was going to take a lot of Pong to make him feel better.

COMMERCIAL BREAK

(Images of Americana scroll across the screen: Fourth of July picnic. Loving families. A suburban neighborhood. Playground.)

WARM, REASSURING VOICEOVER
Dear Valued Customer: We know you want to protect what matters to you most. That's why we manufactured the Git R Done 447 Personal Safety® handgun with honor and pride, so that you can go to sleep each night with the knowledge that the outside world stays outside, and if it tries to come inside, you can shoot it dead.

However, it has come to our attention that there is a small safety "glitch" with the Git R Done 447, which might cause it too fire too soon or even randomly, accidentally killing someone you love. Awkward, we know. That's why we are issuing a voluntary recall of the Git R Done 447 Personal Safety® handgun. Issuing this voluntary recall shows how much we care, and it is hard to dislike or take legal action against those who really care.

CUT TO: Image of the Git R Done 447 with a red circle and line through it.

VO, CONT'D
If you purchased a Git R Done 447, please do not fire the weapon. Do not exhale or laugh within a five-foot radius of the 447. Instead, go to our online fulfillment center at www .thecorporation.com/gitrdone. Type in code OHCRAP447 and you will receive a discount on the purchase of The Corporation's Home Weapon Containment Robot. Once the Robot has successfully disassembled the Git R Done 447, simply mail it to The Corporation and you will receive Corporation credit

coupons, which you may use for ordering any of our many fine products.

CUT TO: Shot of Corporation employees waving

VO, CONT'D

As always, we at The Corporation are committed to making your lives better, safer, and happier. You're welcome, and have a nice day.

CHAPTER ELEVEN

"All right, Teen Dreamers. Let's take stock of everything we have." Taylor marched before the line of sleepy beauty queens, inspecting them drill sergeant–style. "Miss Nebraska, what are the island's natural resources, please? Report."

Mary Lou scratched at a bite on her leg with the toes of her other foot, holding on to Adina for balance. "Um, trees. Plants. Grubs. Fish. Coconuts. Water. Mud. That's all I can think of right now."

"Very good. Miss New Mexico, what salvaged materials do we have from the plane?"

Miss New Mexico listed things off, using her fingers to keep count. "Some teeth-bleaching trays, padded bras, three safety razors, bobby pins, thongs, the jars of Lady 'Stache Off and the radio Jennifer and Sosie found, the hot roller sets, two straightening irons, bathing suits, assorted shoes, some makeup, and a few evening gowns, including that unholy beaded green thing over there."

"That was Miss Massachusetts's, I think," Brittani said.

Petra smirked. "Maybe it wasn't the plane crash that killed her. Maybe she actually saw herself in that dress."

"Let's not speak ill of the dead, no matter how hideous their fashion sense," Taylor instructed. "All right, Teen Dreamers. These are our tools. Starting today, we are adding a new survival skills portion to our pageant. I want you to treat this with the seriousness you would your other duties, like tanning and exfoliation. You need to wow the judges. Think about what you can make with what we've got."

"It's like an episode of *Design This!*[21] All we need is Roger Piston to come in and say, 'Do your magic!'" Miss Montana said.

"I'm turning our program over to Miss California and Miss Colorado. Please give them the same attention you would the makeup artist showing you how to contour your nose and make your lips look bigger under the lights, which I never have to do as my lips are in perfect proportion to my face."

Shanti and Nicole stood side by side, but they'd left plenty of space between them. Nicole's arms were crossed.

Shanti cleared her throat. "The first thing —"

"Who said you were first?" Nicole interrupted.

"Do you want to go first?"

"No. But it's nice to be asked. Go ahead."

"The first thing we really need to do is make sure we have drinking water."

"I forgot — why can't we just drink the ocean water?" Tiara asked.

"Because people pee in there all the time," Brittani explained with assurance.

"Also, the bloat," Miss Ohio chimed in. "I retain like crazy."

"No," Shanti said. "It's because if you drink salt water, you'll get sick. Drink enough and you'll die."

Tiara raised her hand. "But will you still be bloated?"

Shanti ignored her. "It's a tropical climate, so we get some rain every day. We can make a tarp out of Miss Massachusetts's ugly evening gown to collect that rainwater to drink."

Miss Montana made a face. "Ew. That is so hurl."

"Actually, so hurl is the way you look when you die of dehydration."

[21] *Design This!*, a popular interior design show in which maligned teen contestants get to overhaul the bedroom of the person they hate most using only what they can find in the house. On hiatus after one contestant decorated her rival's room in cat poo.

Shanti explained the mechanics of the plan and the girls set to work. It was an intricate system of weights and counterweights. But the engineering was best-case scenario, and their meager resources were worst-case. Nothing was working and the girls soon grew frustrated.

"It's too complicated," Nicole said. "We need to simplify."

"It's not too complicated. You're just not getting it!"

"Whatever!" Miss New Mexico said. Her face dripped with sweat. "Do you want drinking water or not?"

"That's the whole point."

"Then we need to try it another way."

Shanti crossed her arms. "Like what?"

"Excuse me?" Tiara raised her hand. "One summer when I was about nine, my dad went off to rehab for his dryer sheet addiction. He used to huff 'em down in the basement, box after box. Then he'd come upstairs and start making these dioramas out of old cake mix boxes right on the kitchen floor and tell us that we should leave him alone because he was a serious artist and needed space for his work but that it was okay because the Fluffy Soft™ Laundry Puppy[22] would look after us. I always wondered why he smelled like Spring Freesia."

Adina dropped down into the sand. "Does this story have a point?"

"Anyway, after my mom flipped out, my dad went off to rehab to heal his wounded chi and he got this spirit guide named Astral, who was kind of annoying because my dad would be all, 'Let's ask Astral about that,' even if it was just about whether or not to have Hamburger Helper for dinner, and my mom said she would personally kick his Astral to the curb if he didn't shut up, and so he went to Jesus rehab instead, and my mom sent me to sleepaway camp for the rest of the summer. I loved it in the woods. But there were no toilets or anything, so we had to build a latrine."

[22] Fluffy Soft™ Laundry Puppy: The laundry detergent mascot that became a plush toy and multimillion-dollar product line. "Your friend in the laundry room. Cuddle up to new Fluffy Soft™ and see just how soft life can be!"

"'Kay. I'm now officially scared of where this story's going," Adina said.

Tiara's cheeks reddened. "I let you talk."

"Sorry, Tiara," Adina said.

"Anyway, it was probably a dumb idea."

"No. Tell it. I want to hear it. Go on." Petra silenced the others with a glare.

"Well, I was just thinking that if we dig out the sand like a latrine and stretch the dress across it and hold it down with some rocks or something, maybe the water would catch in there?"

"How's that going to help?" Miss Ohio asked.

"Hold on." Shanti pulled the dress taut. She surveyed the sand around it. "That could work."

"Yeah?" Nicole asked.

"Yes."

Tiara brightened. "I said a smarty?"

"You definitely said a smarty."

The girls used coconut shells to dig a deep trench. They packed sand around the edge into a high wall, stretched the evening gown, which they had ripped open to make it bigger, across the hole, and weighted the dress's edges with rocks. Beneath the dress, they placed anything that could collect whatever rainwater fell through the fabric's pores: empty coconut shells, high heels, and a jewelry cleaning unit they'd rinsed four times with seawater.

"Not bad," Shanti said, inspecting it. "Not bad at all. Now we just have to wait for the afternoon rain shower."

"I can't believe we're gonna drink out of a ground toilet!" Tiara trilled.

Adina put a hand on her arm. "Please never say that again."

Right on cue, the skies opened up. Normally, the girls cursed the rain that soaked them and brought the bugs out after. But now, they cheered it. They do-si-doed around the dress like an offering dance and cheered as it filled up with water and tipped down to pour into the waiting coconuts.

"Bottoms up!" Petra said, and guzzled from the half shell of fresh rainwater. Her eyes grew large. She grabbed at her throat. The girls backed away. Petra grinned. "Needs a slice of lemon, but otherwise, it's really good," she said, and drained the shell of the last few drops.

By the end of the week, the girls had managed to erect eight huts, and Taylor announced that there would be a Miss Teen Dream cutest hut contest. The girls went about the business of survival, collecting rainwater, identifying and gathering edible plant life, catching small fish with their straightening irons. Miss Montana, who turned out to be from a family of fishermen and women, showed them how to plait seaweed and vines to construct loose fishing lines, which had netted them a decent catch in addition to the straightening iron haul. The whole thing had come to resemble a giant science fair, with teams of girls proudly showing off their various projects.

"Hey, you guys, over here, please!" Miss Ohio called. The girls lined up to see what Miss Ohio had put together. She'd shoved two sticks into the sand and rigged a piece of metal plane wreckage between them so that it caught the sun's light.

"Careful," she warned Nicole, who'd gotten close. "It's really hot."

"Now watch." With a flourish, Miss Ohio dropped a fish on the metal's steaming hot surface. It sizzled and popped.

"It's a solar hibachi," Miss Ohio explained, serving up a perfectly done fillet. "I used a safety razor to descale the fish, rinsed it in a little of the freshwater, and now . . ." Using the handle of a hairbrush, she scooped up the fish and dropped it onto a mound of clean rocks. "Miss New Mexico?"

Miss New Mexico took a bite and rolled her eyes in bliss. "OMG, this is so good, I'm not even going to make myself barf it back up."

"Tiara and I caught the fish with these!" Brittani said, brandishing a pair of straightening irons.

"Awesome!" Mary Lou high-fived them.

"This is so cool. How did you come up with this?" Adina asked.

"Hello!" Miss Ohio rolled her eyes. "I'm from the Buckeye State. We are serious about our tailgating parties. I can turn *anything* into a grill."

Petra sat surrounded by fabric strips. That morning, she'd ripped apart swimsuits and dance costumes. She'd fashioned a needle from a fish bone and stripped plant roots down to a stiff, thin thread. From a dead girl's evening gown, she'd harvested sequins; from another girl's jewelry pouch, she'd taken rhinestone earrings. These elements she sewed into a colorful banner with sparkles to catch the sun. When she was finished, they would stretch the banner between two trees in the hope that it would draw the attention of a passing plane or ship. Petra had been hunched over in the same position for hours. Her fingers ached. At last she finished, smiling at the message she'd sewn into the center. If that didn't get somebody's attention, they were lost for sure.

Mary Lou and Sosie gathered rocks and pebbles from the beach and spelled out the word *HELP* along the shore so that it might be seen from a passing plane. At the end of the word, Sosie made an exclamation mark with a smiley face at the bottom.

"That way, they'll know we're friendly," she reasoned.

Jennifer took off the back cover of the radio and examined the tangled inner workings. It was a mess and more complicated than anything she'd worked on before. Why had she been so quick to volunteer? To promise the girls that she could get it up and running? What if she couldn't? They were counting on her. That in and of itself was an odd feeling. Nobody counted on her. Back home, she'd been written off so many times and by so many people, she'd begun to feel like a comic book character who'd died but wouldn't stay down. She knew what they thought when they saw her: Trash. Wrong side of the tracks. Dyke. Juvenile delinquent. Rehabilitation project.

When Jennifer had stepped in to take over for Miss Michigan after the first girl broke her leg skiing and the second had to go to anorexia camp, she knew no one expected much from her. "Just do your best," her social worker had said, giving her a lame thumbs-up. Nobody expected anything from girls like Jennifer, except for them to drop out, get pregnant, fuck up. She stared hopelessly at the tangle of red, blue, green, and white wires. If she were like her comic book alter ego, the Flint Avenger, she'd have this up in a nanosecond. But she wasn't. She was Jennifer, and she was utterly baffled.

"Can you fix it?" Sosie asked. She made the sign for *fix* and Jennifer repeated it. Sosie bit her lip, waiting for an answer.

Jennifer gave her a thumbs-up. Sosie hugged her and Jennifer closed her eyes, inhaling the slightly salty smell of her hair. She watched her go, then turned her attentions back to the radio and the strange, beautiful mystery of wires.

Adina and Mary Lou stood thigh-deep in the cool, clear lagoon where Adina tried her luck and her new, pumice-sharpened spear on the fish. So far, the fish had proved wilier than they'd imagined. Each time, Adina missed and the spear struck the muddy bottom, sending little tornadoes of sand swirling.

"I see one!" Mary Lou shouted.

Adina turned left and right. "Where?"

Mary Lou pointed. "There — by that rock. Oh. Not anymore. Boy, they're fast."

"Why didn't you just spear it instead of telling me?" Adina said with some annoyance.

"I'm a vegetarian."

"They have vegetarians in Nebraska?"

"Well." Mary Lou thought for a moment. "There's me."

"If you're a vegetarian, why did you volunteer to come fishing with me?"

Mary Lou shrugged. "So you'd have a friend with you."

"Oh." Adina hadn't had a close friend since Roxie Black in fourth grade, who let Adina borrow her headband. Adina and Roxie both got lice and Roxie's mom didn't let her come over much anymore. "Well, thanks."

"No problem. Still hoping for Miss Congeniality when we get back. Oh, there's another one!"

Adina made a stab, but the golden fish was too swift. "You'll never evolve!" she shouted as it swished away. "Just like Ray Marshall."

Mary Lou laughed. "Okay. No love for Ray Marshall. Ex-boyfriend or something?"

"What? God, no. He's this idiot in my Adolescent Issues class who spends the whole time putting things in his nose. I don't have a boyfriend. I don't need a man to be complete."

"Oh. Sure."

"Plus, there is the small problem of none of the guys in my high school being interested. My teachers say that when I get to college I'll meet guys who aren't intimidated by a smart, confident girl." With a grunt, Adina stabbed again and again at the water, coming up empty. "What about you? Do you have a boyfriend?"

"No. I used to. Sort of," Mary Lou said, playing with her purity ring. Her fingers were thinner, and it fit loosely now.

"A sort-of boyfriend? Is it like a time-share and you get him for a couple of weeks in May and November?"

Mary Lou fashioned a chain from grasses, carefully knotting them together, end to end. "We were dating. And then we weren't."

"Okaaaay," Adina said. "That's not cryptic. What happened?"

In her mind, Mary Lou saw Billy's horrified face, heard him say, *"What's wrong with you?"*

"He didn't really like me," Mary Lou said softly.

"What? What the hell was the matter with him?"

Mary Lou allowed a small smile. "I think we might have more luck over there."

The girls waded through the shallows into deeper water. It was a beautiful blue, and they could see tiny neon-bright fish darting about. What they needed was a big one, and they waited.

"Have you ever been in love?" Mary Lou asked after a period of quiet.

"Me? No. Not really. The closest I got was when I dated Matt Jacobs for one summer. He was smart enough. And nice. Too nice. He stared at me all moony-eyed a lot."

"Sounds romantic to me," Mary Lou said.

"It was irritating. Too much devotion feels like an obligation. Anyway, I think Matt and I were doomed from the start because of our musical disconnect. I mean, he burned me a CD with Feast for the Fishermen[23] on it. Feast for the Fishermen! Such a sex killer."

Mary Lou thought back to that night in the back of Billy's station wagon. How close they'd come. Her heart beating so quickly, every sense sharpened. She had wanted to throw away all the rules and eat up the world. Even her skin had been full of want. And that want had been her undoing. Billy's eyes wide with alarm. *What's wrong with you?* Mary Lou had run off into the night, hiding in the sheltering stalks of the cornfields until it was safe to face the world again. Her mother had taken one look at her when she came through the door at dawn and she had known. They had the ring made the next day.

"Are you okay?" Adina was looking at her strangely.

"Yeah!" Mary Lou said quickly.

"You don't have to do this if it makes you queasy."

"No. I'm okay. Oh, hey, bulrush." Mary Lou pointed to the tall stalks bordering the pond.

"What's a bulrush?" Adina asked.

[23] Feast for the Fishermen, the ultimate emo band. Said to be sold with a complimentary prescription for antidepressants and a free flatiron.

"This funny little plant. They grow wild on my uncle's farm. You can eat the roots and this white part of the stem. It's pretty tasty. And the tougher stems are really strong — we used them to make sit-upons in Girl Scouts. These'll be good for tonight." Mary Lou yanked one up by the roots. "So do you think you'll ever meet The One and get married and have kids?"

"'The One?'" Adina snorted. "My mom has had five husbands, and every single time, it was 'The One,' and every single time, it was like I lost her. Like she shape-shifted into whatever form the guy wanted till I couldn't recognize her anymore. I'm never letting some guy come in and change me."

"But don't you think . . ." Mary Lou stopped to regroup her thoughts. "Love has to change you some, right?"

Adina shrugged. "I guess. But all those romances they feed us are wrong. They make us think it's just supposed to be hearts and wind machines and boys who slay dragons for you."

"But . . . is it wrong to want a guy to slay a dragon for you? Not that I would want a guy to slay a dragon, because I'm a vegetarian. But maybe he just needs a little encouragement. He'd do right by you if you could just see past his faults, like in *Beauty and the Beast*."

"Riiiiight." Adina swept a hand dramatically to her brow. "And only your love can heal him."

"Well . . . yeah."

"That's how they get you, my friend."

"Can I ask you something?"

"Sure. Unless it's about spearing fish, because apparently I suck at that."

"Do you think people can be cursed?"

"I believe Taylor is cursed to be a pain in the ass." Adina craned her neck. "I should be careful. I'm sure she has supersonic hearing, too."

"I mean really cursed." Mary Lou turned her ring.

"What do you mean?" Adina gave Mary Lou a quizzical look.

"Forget it. It's silly. I still believe in true love, though. You're wrong about that."

"You know what you are, Mary Lou? You are a hopeless romantic."

"*I'm* not the one who's hopeless, Adina."

Adina gave a little shriek. "That fish just swam past my leg! Creepy! Where did it go?"

"To your right! Two o'clock! Get it!"

"You are officially the most bloodthirsty vegetarian ever." Adina stabbed hard and yelled in triumph. A fat fish wriggled on the end of her spear. "OMG. That was harder than the SATs."

Mary Lou liked Adina. She liked her directness. In school, they would tell you that life wouldn't come to you; you had to go out and make it your own. But when it came to love, the message for girls seemed to be this: Don't. Don't go after what you want. Wait. Wait to be chosen, as if only in the eye of another could one truly find value. The message was confusing and infuriating. It was a shell game with no actual pea under the rapidly moving cups. Mary Lou knew this firsthand, and she wished she could ask Adina more questions. But that would mean telling her everything, and she just couldn't risk that. Like the bulrush shoots, shame and fear could be woven into a plaiting of surprising strength.

Taylor led the girls deeper into the jungle to a basin surrounded by hills. An enormous cave cut into one of the hills.

"Sparkle Ponies and Lost Girls, we already know that Miss Illinois and Miss Michigan had to take down a giant snake. We don't know what other hostiles we might run into while we're waiting for the rescue ship. As you know, I am a card-carrying member of Femmes and Firearms, just like my spiritual leader, Ladybird Hope. And if we're gonna protect ourselves, we need to build us some weapons. The Glitz Attack. Everything we need is here. We just have to be resourceful. And there are bonuses," Taylor said. She held out a makeup bag.

Unconsciously, the girls took a step forward. "Before we left home, I took the liberty of having a makeover at every counter in every mall in town. I racked up quite a few free gifts with purchase." She jiggled the bag. "There is some very nice conditioner in this bag. Teen Dreamers, it's time to represent. Your platform is Personal Arsenal. Miss Montana, Miss Ohio, Miss California. Are you ready?"

The three girls moved to a mound of palm fronds, carefully removing them to reveal a rickety wooden trebuchet made of bamboo and counterweighted with coconuts. "This is our new Teen Dream missile launcher. As you can see, it's a catapult. You can thank Miss Montana, Miss Ohio, and Miss California for that."

"We rock physics." Miss Montana beamed. "Made one of these for ninth grade science. And Shanti makes them for fun in her spare time."

Tiara raised her hand. "I thought Catapult was a spring break city in Mexico."

"That's Acapulco," Mary Lou said.

"Next up: geography skills," Adina muttered.

"Eyes up here, ladies," Miss Montana continued. "You'll note back here is a net thingy. Well, technically it's a pair of DiscomfortWear™."[24]

"Shapes you and makes an awesome launch pad," Miss Ohio joked as she thumped the taut fabric attached to the long arm like an exotic underwear lacrosse stick. "If you put something in here — Miss California, will you do the honors, please?"

Shanti brandished a pastel pump for everyone to see before placing it in the nude-fabric basket.

"And cut the vine — oh, y'all might want to step back."

The girls moved to the side. With one swift move, Shanti cut the vine. The coconut hit the ground and the trebuchet arm swung up,

---

[24] DiscomfortWear™, shapewear designed to eliminate rolls, ripples, and muffin tops. In some cases known to eliminate circulation and breathing. If you're not uncomfortable, it's not DiscomfortWear™.

launching the pump through the air with a ferocious zip. It stuck, heel-first, into the bark of a small tree with such force, it split the tree in two.

"Holy stiletto, Batman," Jennifer said.

"We used a shoe, but you can use anything, really."

Taylor balanced herself on the bottom beams of the catapult like MacArthur in the South Pacific. "Beauty is pain. And in this case, it's somebody else's pain. Miss Ohio, Miss Montana, Miss California, you have each earned yourself something from the goody bag. Reach in."

"Oh my God, microfiber mascara!" Miss Ohio clutched the tube to her chest.

Shanti smiled. "Body glitter!"

"Coral Frost All-Day lip quench," Miss Montana said. She didn't seem as excited. But Taylor had moved on.

"Miss Colorado and Miss Alabama, what do you have for us?"

Nicole held up a thin, hollowed-out tube of bamboo. "This is the makeup splat gun. You pour a small amount of foundation in the end like so," she said, letting Brittani demonstrate. "And then . . ." Nicole blew hard into the tube and the makeup splattered the ground. "It's hypoallergenic and noncomedogenic, but you still wouldn't want it in your eyes."

"Excellent work, ladies. Goodies?"

Nicole took her swag. "Cocoa butter! Thank you, universe!"

Brittani rooted around, eyes closed, mouth moving as if making a wish. She pulled out a small plastic bottle of bubble bath.

Taylor made her way down the line, inspecting each girl's work. The girls had worked in teams, and they beamed with pride at their inventive defense systems.

"Miss Michigan?" Taylor asked.

"Well, I melted down some of our jewelry and made arrows," Jennifer said, holding up the thin, homemade metal shafts.

Petra admired one. "Wow. That's cool. How'd you know how to do that?"

"I took a smelting class at the Y one time. Well, it was between that and water aerobics with my grandmother, so I took the smelting class. It took me a few tries but I think these turned out pretty well. And Ohio gave us some of that tree sap nail polish to stick them to the wood. What up, O-hi-o!"

Miss Ohio did a little dance.

"Very nice," Taylor said. "Do we have bows?"

Jennifer nodded to Sosie, who held up a curved bow of tree limb strung with seaweed. "We steamed the wood. The first one burned to a crisp. So did the second one. The third one fell in the fire. The fourth one sucked ass. The fifth one I wouldn't wish on my math teacher, Mr. Buttons, and he is a total chancroid. This is the sixth one." Sosie held it high overhead like an ancient warrior. "Just like Green Lantern!"

Jennifer put a hand over her heart. "They grow up so quickly."

"Claim your prizes, Miss Michigan, Miss Illinois." Taylor offered the makeup bag.

"Sparkle-blue nail polish!" Sosie danced around with the bottle. "Oh yeah! Uh-huh!"

"Butterfly barrettes," Jennifer said.

"I'll trade you!" Miss Montana offered the lipstick.

Jennifer clutched the barrettes to her chest. "No way. I love butterflies."

"Damn," Miss Montana said.

"Okay, last but not least, Miss New Hampshire, Miss Rhode Island, and Miss Nebraska. You're up."

Taylor peeled a banana and waited for their demonstration.

"We've got ground defense," Adina said. "If some big animal runs through here and catches a paw, it'll be hoisted up into the air in a big hammock."

"But it will not be harmed," Mary Lou assured everyone. "It's a humane containment system."

"We've also dug a pit over here — watch your step!" Petra cautioned. She removed a covering of leaves. Below was a pit about eight feet deep. "Anything running after us can crash right through here and *kaboom!*"

"It was a lot of digging. But check out my arms!" Mary Lou's bicep curved with new muscle.

"We should totally make that into a workout video when we get back," Shanti said.

"Good idea, Miss California," Taylor agreed. "Goodies."

The girls stepped up to claim their prizes.

"Blotting sheets," Petra said.

"Hand lotion!" Mary Lou squealed.

"Miss New Hampshire?" Taylor offered the bag again.

Adina reached in. "Oh, look! It's a boat with a GPS set for home — awesome!"

"Trade you," Miss Montana said.

"I was kidding about the boat. It's bronzer."

"Ooh!" the girls squealed at once.

"You got the best one," Miss Ohio lamented.

"Here. Merry Christmas. I come from sallow people. I accept my fate." Adina handed the bronzer to Miss Montana, who singsonged "Awesome!" and promised to share with her teammates as long as they didn't all use the brush and get it bacterified, which would give them pimples.

"Teen Dreamers, I am very proud of us. You've given us the Department of Teen Dreamland Security. Personally, I know I will sleep better tonight knowing this is here. If anything tries to mess with us, we will show it that Miss Teen Dreamers mean business."

"What's your weapon?" Adina pressed.

Taylor cocked her head as if she had just asked the stupidest question in the world. "I am my own weapon, Miss New Hampshire."

"Ready!" Petra shouted.

The girls stopped what they were doing and went to help Petra with the banner she'd been sewing for many days. "All right, Miss

Teen Dreamers. Let's get that banner a-wavin' proud like the red, white, and blue!" Shanti balanced on Jennifer's shoulders, and Adina sat on Nicole's. They tied the corners to the limbs of two scraggly trees.

"How does it look?" Shanti called down.

Petra's needlework was evident in the carefully crafted letters: *IT'S MISS TEEN DREAM, BITCHES!*

Petra stepped back to examine it. She smiled. "Perfect."

COMMERCIAL BREAK

VOICEOVER
This Tuesday, on PATRIOT DAUGHTERS!

(A group of British soldiers bursts into the home of BETSY ROSS, surrounding her and her reading circle of comely young women.)

VO, CONT'D.
Has time finally run out for Betsy and her revolutionary band of sisters?

BRITISH COMMANDER
Miss Ross, we are to arrest you for treason. You give these rebels a symbol through your sewing, I hear. What say you to these charges?

(Betsy sheds her dressing gown. Underneath, she wears stockings and a skimpy undershirt. The other women follow suit.)

BETSY ROSS
How could I make a flag, sir, when I seem to have run out of thread?

VO, CONT'D.
She gave it all for her country — and then she gave just a little more.

Watch the show critics say "makes American history totally hot. . . . It takes some of the most important women of the Revolutionary War and turns them into hellcats who fight the British with everything they've got — and then some."

Followed by the season premiere of CAPTAINS BODACIOUS IV:
BADDER AND MORE BODACIOUSER.

(Several hunky, shirtless young men in breeches, earrings, and
very little else stand on a large ship. There seems to be a feeling
of mutiny in the air.)

PIRATE CHU
Cor blimey, Cap'n Sinjin! We ran away from prep school for this?

CAPTAIN SINJIN
Might I remind you that we witnessed a murder and were forced
to go on the run? Believe me, I'd rather be studying for my chem
final than running from barmy terrorist blokes who want to kill us
just because we know too much.

PIRATE AHMED
Captain! Starboard — look!

(Captain Sinjin puts a small telescope to his eye. When he pulls
it away, his expression is one of teen heartthrob alarm. His hair
is still perfect.)

CAPTAIN SINJIN
Gentlemen, we may get a battle yet.

FIRST MATE GEORGE
Should we oil our pecs, sir, so that we'll look fantastic during the
fight scenes?

CAPTAIN SINJIN
Indeed. Gentlemen! Glisten up those pecs! And if you've got
any hair gel for making tousled waves, now's the time to use

it! We stand and fight. But we stand and fight with hotness on
our side.

VOICEOVER

PATRIOT DAUGHTERS. Tuesdays at 8. CAPTAINS BODACIOUS IV:
BADDER AND MORE BODACIOUSER at 9. Followed by a
special encore performance of CAPTAINS BODACIOUS III: THE
CALL OF BOOTY at 10. Only on The Corporation Network:
Giving you what you don't even know you want.

MISS TEEN DREAM FUN FACTS PAGE!

Please fill in the following information and return to Jessie Jane, Miss Teen Dream Pageant administrative assistant, before Monday. Remember, this is a chance for the judges and the audience to get to know YOU. So make it interesting and fun, but please be appropriate. And don't forget to mention something you love about our sponsor, The Corporation!

Name: Sosie Simmons
State: Miss Illinois
Age: 16
Height: 5' 6"
Weight: 118 lbs
Hair: Strawberry blond
Eyes: Green
Best Feature: My hands

Fun Facts About Me:

- I am hearing impaired but that doesn't stop me! I hear with my heart. Well, not really. Because, as anybody who is not a complete and total moron knows, the heart does not have ears. This is the kind of s**t they make disabled people say all the time so everybody's all "okay" with us. Soooo annoying.
- I perform with the non-hearing dance troupe Helen Keller-bration! And by "non-hearing" I mean deaf. Again, people, get over yourselves.
- My dream is to have my own dance troupe and work with kids. For real.
- Once, I saved my family from an earthquake because I could sense the seismic activity.

- My favorite Corporation TV show is the makeover show, *Pimp My Face (Ugly Stepsister)*. I love to watch the girls get all new faces and clothes. I love that part after all the bruising and swelling and stitches and pain when they see themselves in the mirror for the first time and they just cry and cry. It's really sweet.
- The thing that scares me most is being left out.
- The thing I want most is a best friend.

CHAPTER TWELVE

Sosie wasn't afraid of the jungle. Her ears didn't register the screeches and growls that so unnerved the others. She heard only her heartbeat, which ticked in rhythm with the swaying leaves of a tree, the tiny ripples in the stream, the flutter of feathers on the wild bird roughly ten paces ahead of her. Her pumiced spear at the ready, Sosie crouched behind the bush to watch and wait. The bird pecked at seeds on the ground. It probably cooed or gobbled or some shit like that, but she couldn't hear it. Maybe it was complaining about the quality of the seeds: "Really? Seeds again? I thought Wednesdays were taco day!" *That's right, birdie. Life's unfair*, Sosie thought as she poised her stick to strike. *Go out squawking.*

When the virus stole most of Sosie's hearing, it also stole her right to complain. She figured out early that nobody liked an angry disabled person. It messed with their sympathy, with the story in their head about people overcoming adversity to be shining lights in the world. People wanted to think you were *so okay* with it all so they wouldn't have to expend any energy feeling guilty. Sosie had played her part, being the smiling, plucky, don't-worry-about-me, lip-reading Pollyanna. If she was angry about how unfair life could be, she never let on. Not like Fawnda Toussaint. Fawnda was fat and in a wheelchair due to cerebral palsy. She had not gotten the memo about how disabled people were supposed to be happy and noble all the time in order to make people without disabilities feel okay about being lucky bastards.

Sosie was in sixth grade when her teacher had wheeled Fawnda over to her at recess. "SOSIE," she shouted with a smile. "THIS IS FAWNDA. SHE MIGHT NEED A FRIEND HERE AT BRIGHT PROMISES ELEMENTARY. I'LL LET YOU TWO GET ACQUAINTED."

Sosie had only heard about every third word, but she understood completely that Mrs. Brewer thought she could pair disabled kids like socks. Still, she played along.

"Hi. I'm Sosie. I may be disabled but that doesn't stop me from —"

Fawnda glared. "Stop."

"Excuse me?"

"I said, Stop. With. The. Bullshit," Fawnda enunciated clearly.

Sosie's cheeks grew hot. "It's not, um, what you said. I choose to have a positive attitude. I don't let my hearing loss get me down. I can do anything a hearing person can do."

Fawnda's eyes went flinty. She grabbed a notebook from the purse dangling from her chair and scribbled with hard strokes. Then she held up the notebook for Sosie to read: *Yeah? Anything? Like hear?* While Sosie digested the shock of it, Fawnda flipped the notebook closed, placed it back in the purse, and stared out at the kids racing around screaming on the blacktop.

"Why are you being so mean?" Sosie asked.

Fawnda answered with a mangled shrug. "I'm not here to make anybody feel better," she enunciated. Then she wheeled herself off.

Fawnda stuck to her guns. Her seventh grade essay was entitled "The Cerebral Palsy Wheelchair Olympics Blues." Her eighth grade poetry unit featured the poems "Reasons I Hate You," "Hope You Enjoy Those Legs, Cheerleader Beyotch," and "Dear Well-Meaning Church Groups: Please Ask Jesus to Stop Dicking Around and Get Me Out of This Chair. Sincerely, Fawnda." Those had landed her a visit from the guidance counselor, who'd suggested that Fawnda might try an art therapy group to help heal her inner tantruming child. Fawnda suggested the guidance counselor might try something that started with "F" and ended in "Off." After that, Fawnda was sent to a special school for the differently abled — out of sight, out of mind, as if she had never existed.

Fawnda might not have been likeable. She might not even have been a nice person. But she had something: anger. It gave her a reason to wake up in the morning. And she wasn't giving it up just to make some guidance counselor or church group feel okay. Deep down, Sosie had admired her. Because what had she herself done? Rolled over and showed her belly. *Like me and I won't be any trouble at all.*

But things were different out here in the jungle. It was as if the wheels were coming off the old Sosie. She wasn't interested in being everybody's good sport anymore. The sweet deaf girl mascot. Fuck that.

Bye, Bye, Birdie, she thought and let the spear fly. It veered to the right, missing the bird and bouncing into the bushes. With a panicked rustle of feathers and probably a lot of squawking, the bird flapped its wings and scuttled away.

"Damn," Sosie said. There was a tap on her shoulder and Sosie whipped around, ready to fight.

Jennifer put her hand up. "Whoa! Peace!"

"Sorry," she signed. She retrieved the spear from the bushes.

"Cool. Very B-A-D-A-S-S," Jennifer answered and finger-spelled. Her signing had gotten pretty good. "Want to go for a swim?"

"Nah. Wanna bag the bird. Sick of fish."

"Okay. Let's . . ." Jennifer stopped. "What's the sign for *hunt*?" she asked. Sosie showed her and Jennifer repeated it. "This is cool. Like having a secret code."

Sosie glared and Jennifer's stomach tensed. "What did I say?"

"It's not code. It's how I talk." She both said and signed it, her fingers moving sharply.

"I-I didn't mean . . ."

"I just need you to know that it's not some cute code. It's a language. My language."

Jennifer nodded. "What's the sign for *asshole*?"

Sosie grinned. "Did you see which way it went?"

Jennifer shook her head.

"Crap." Sosie stuck her spear into the ground. "Hey! I've been working on a new dance based on girl superheroes. Wanna see what I've got so far?"

Jennifer nodded enthusiastically. Without hesitation, Sosie launched into her sequence, a modern dance full of grace and power and vulnerability. When she was dancing, Sosie felt as powerful as any superhero. Her body did what she wanted it to without her having to say a word. With every flex of her foot or contraction of her muscles, she came wondrously alive, blood pumping, emotions playing across her face. Once, while dancing a piece from *Swan Lake*, she'd cried, so overcome by the beauty of it that she felt as if she really were the dying swan. But this dance was not about wounded bird girls, and Sosie reveled in unleashing the full power of her body.

Jennifer watched, awestruck, at Sosie's grace and power and utter lack of self-consciousness. For most of her life, Jennifer had learned to hold her emotions in check. But it was obvious that Sosie had full access to hers, and Jennifer felt envious of her ease. She wondered why she'd held so tightly to her feelings for so long, and if it might be possible to give them some slack.

Sosie stopped, breathing heavily. "That's all I've got so far."

Jennifer clapped enthusiastically. She made the sign for *awesome*. "Yeah?"

Jennifer nodded.

Sosie grinned and reached out to her friend. "Come dance with me."

"Oh, no!" Jennifer waved her off.

"I'll teach you! It's easy." Sosie pulled on Jennifer's arm, but Jen resisted.

"I can't dance," Jennifer signed.

Sosie scoffed. "Everybody can dance. It's about passion. It's like kissing. If you can kiss, you can dance." Sosie looked her square in the eyes. "*Can* you kiss?"

Jennifer blushed hard. "Well, yeah, but —"

Sosie brightened. "Then you can dance!"

Jennifer folded her arms across her chest and shook her head.

There were few things Sosie loved more than a direct challenge. If she had to pick a personal motto, it would be "Bring it!" Her grin was a dare. "Gonna make you." Laughing, Sosie made another grab for Jennifer's arms, but Jen, also laughing, broke away.

"You're not the boss of me!" Jen yelled and adopted a fake ninja pose.

"I can make you. . . ." Sosie taunted. She snapped her fingers across her body like one of the Jets in *West Side Story*.

"Stop!"

Sosie stretched out her arm as if wielding some invisible energy source. "I have a secret weapon. A secret weapon . . . of dance!"

"Ooh!" Jennifer mock shuddered.

"You will be powerless against it."

Jennifer dropped to the ground and sat, arms crossed, a defiantly amused expression playing across her face.

"Okaaay . . ." Sosie said in warning. She stood perfectly still, her hands held stiffly before her chest, her head tipped to one side, a blank expression on her doll-like face. With startling precision, Sosie's feet began to move one way while her torso inched the other direction. Her hands jerked up and down like pistons. "Dance, earthling, dance."

Jennifer's mouth twitched toward a smile. "Are you doing . . . *the robot*?" She spelled out robot. "Oh. My. God."

Sosie frowned. "Robot. Is. Sad. Because silly bitch. Will. Not. Dance."

With that, Sosie dropped quickly to her knees and backed up, moving with tremendous skill. It was as if she were made of liquid and elastic. Her arms worked independently of her shoulders, and her neck swiveled back and forth like a pendulum. Somehow, she incorporated a mechanical beauty queen wave, which exploded into a motion where she seemed to pull herself up by an invisible string. It was ridiculous — and amazing.

"Sad. Sad. Sad." Sosie lurched toward Jennifer, who laughed.

"That is messed up! Get away!"

"Dance, silly bitch," Sosie intoned.

She made a strange whirring sound and watched wide-eyed as her arm shot out, machinelike, toward Jennifer's. She pulled Jennifer to her feet, and this time Jen didn't object. Sosie snaked an arm around Jennifer's waist and bent her side to side as if they were a robot couple taking a turn around some factory dance floor.

"Robot. Getting. Happy. Robot. Like. Girl. Who. Can't. Dance."

"Hey!" Jennifer said, but she couldn't stop laughing.

"Robot girl give rhythm chip for disability," Sosie said, starting to lose it. "Do not let bad-dancing disability define you, bad-dancing girl. We will have benefit concert to help you. *Can't-Dance-For-Shit-A-Thon.*"

Both girls laughed uncontrollably — full, body-shaking guffaws. In the laughter, the girls' feet became entangled and they fell to the ground, Sosie on top of Jennifer, their faces separated by no more than an inch of warm jungle air. Jennifer looked into Sosie's eyes. A small, involuntary sigh escaped. Sosie felt the breath soft and warm on her face and something fluttered deep inside her. A dance she did not yet know had begun.

Sosie tensed and jumped to her feet. "Robot leave girl alone now."

"Thank God," Jennifer said, but she didn't mean it.

They glanced nervously at each other.

"Maybe you could teach me?" Jennifer signed.

Sosie smiled. "Sure," she signed back.

The bird scrabbled into view. Seeing the girls, it squawked and darted into the dense jungle growth. With a war cry, Sosie grabbed her spear, and she and Jennifer ran after it, full-bore, without second-guessing.

CHAPTER THIRTEEN

Brittani raced into Petra's hut, her voice full of alarm. "Petra, come quick! Tiara's freaking out!"

A crowd had gathered around the hut Tiara shared with Brittani.

"What's going on?" Petra asked.

"Tiara grabbed the machete and started going all women's prison movie on her hair," Miss Ohio informed her. "She said something about sparkle hips and pretty feet and princess hair."

"She won't let anybody in. She keeps waving the machete around," Brittani said. "And the earrings I wanted to wear are in there."

"Why me?" Petra asked.

"She likes you," Brittani answered.

"She thinks I'm a freak of nature."

"I know. She says she's a freak, too, and you're the only one who would understand."

Petra went inside. Tiara sat on a rock, sawing through a section of hair with the machete. Her hair was a mix of short and long pieces. She pointed the machete at Petra.

"Whoa! Whoa, there. Can't a friend just drop in and say hi?"

Tiara blinked. She gave a vague smile. "Oh, hi, Petra. Come on in."

"So. Going for a new 'do?"

"Yeah. Something new," she said in an empty voice. A clump of hair hit the sand. "My parents are gonna be so pissed, though."

"Your parents aren't here. Can I have the machete?"

"Huh-uh." Tiara pulled a long piece of hair in front of her face and examined it. "Split ends. Guess I'll have to get some princess hair when I get back."

"Princess hair?"

"That's what my mom calls the hairpieces we use. Princess hair. They cost a lot, about five or six hundred dollars."

Petra made a whistling sound.

"The dresses, too. And you need new dresses for each pageant."

Petra did the math in her head. "You could start a business on that. Or pay for college. Well, state college."

Tiara hacked off another bit of hair.

"Hey, could I see that awesome knife for a sec? It's so cool!"

"No, thank you. I like the knife." More hair hit the sand.

Petra needed to distract Tiara. She glanced around the hut for something that might help and noticed that Tiara had bobby pinned fat, blue flowers to the walls. It was crazy-cool and very adorable. "Wow, you did this?"

Tiara looked up for a moment and gave a weak smile. "Mmm-hmm. I wanted to give my hut a jungle theme."

"Tiara, I think they've all got a jungle theme," Petra said. "But yours is definitely the most creative. And hella cute."

"You think?" Tiara seemed to come alive. The knife stopped its mutilations. "Can I tell you something? I kinda always wanted to be an interior decorator."

"You'd be great at it."

The empty stare returned to Tiara's eyes. She flicked the blade against her arm, drawing blood.

"Hey. Don't do that. Please."

"My parents want me to do the Miss USA pageant after I'm too old for this one," she said.

Petra sidled up next to her. "Is that what you want to do?"

Tiara gave the smallest of shrugs. "It's all I know how to do. I did my first pageant when I was two weeks old."

"Two weeks!" Petra sputtered.

"Mmm-hmm. But my parents said I really, really wanted to do it. They could tell by the way I was crying."

"Babies cry. That's pretty much their job description."

"Everything they did, they did for me. Because I loved doing it," Tiara whispered. She sliced a jagged arc across a new section of hair.

"How do you know?"

"They told me. They said I was always perfect and happy and so good. Except for once. Only once."

"What happened?" Petra kept her eyes on the knife in Tiara's hands.

"It was at a Mega-Glamour Pageant. We'd just come off a Glitter Pageant and before that a Miss Pizzazz Pageant. I was really tired. And when it was almost my time, I threw myself down on the carpet at the Holiday Inn and pitched a fit. I just didn't want all those people looking at me. It was like, the more they looked at me, the less I felt like anybody really saw me. Does that sound stupid?"

"No," Petra said. "Not at all."

"My mom was all, 'Come on now, pretty girl. It's time to do your sparkle hips. You know the judges love your sparkle hips. Don't you want to be Mommy's good little girl and blow kisses and get a crown?' Then my dad told me I was his special princess and he'd buy me a big pink teddy bear if I'd go onstage and show everybody how good I could dance to 'Mama's Gotta Go-Go.' I still wouldn't get up."

"So what happened?"

Tiara dug her big toe into the sand. "My mom said I was embarrassing her. That she guessed the other girls just wanted it a little more than me. My dad said those dresses cost a lot of money and that's why he was working two jobs. They both said they were doing this for me and not them and they'd sacrificed a lot for my dream."

"Wow. Guilt trip much?" Petra said. "And did you get up?"

"No. I kept pitching a fit."

"Good for you."

Tiara sniffled as a tear rolled down her cheek and plopped into the sand. "That's when my mom told me that I was being a bad little girl and nobody loved bad little girls. So I'd better straighten up, stop crying, be quiet, and get my best smile on, or she was gonna sell all my crowns and trophies." Tiara sniffled again. She wiped her eyes so quickly it was like it didn't happen. "I stopped crying. Mama hurried me off to get my spray tan and this lady named Mirabella put on my eyelashes and makeup. My mom gave me my princess hair and sprayed it up high. Daddy put the flipper back over my teeth so my smile would be all perfect. And I went out in my big, blue, fluffy petticoat dress, and swished my sparkle hips, and blew kisses to the judges with a wink. That night, I won Miss Grand Supreme."

"Does that come with fries?"

"My daddy bought me that pink teddy bear but I never liked it. I used to beat it up." Tiara wiped her nose on her arm. She looked up at Petra through a broken curtain of hair. "You sure you want to be a girl? It's a lot of work."

"Yeah. I know."

"Don't tell anybody, but sometimes, I just don't want to sparkle."

"That's okay."

"This is all I know how to do."

"That's not true." Petra gestured to the flower-bedazzled hut.

Tiara smiled a little. "Do you really think my hut is cute?"

"Are you kidding me? It's awesome."

"Thank you." Tiara reached over and took one of the flowers from the wall. It was a deep blue tinged with black around the petals. She pinned it to Petra's hair like an old-fashioned movie star. "You look pretty."

"Thanks."

Tiara closed her eyes and blew out five sharp exhales. Then she opened her eyes again. "I'm a winner, I'm a winner, I'm a winner," she intoned. She fingered a section of freshly hacked hair. "I guess I really messed up my hair, huh?"

"Well, you could start a whole new career as a deranged Muppet. Okay. Not funny. Sorry."

Tiara bit her bottom lip. "Can you fix it? I don't care what you do. I just want something different."

Tiara swung the machete around and Petra jumped back. "Let's be careful with the sharp objects, okay?"

"Sorry."

Petra wielded the machete with surprising grace. Chunks of bleach-blond hair hit the sand. Tiara's hair was darker underneath and there were bits that had been kissed by the sun. At last, Petra stood back and wiped the sweat from her forehead. "All done."

Tiara's 'do was short and spiky with a longer strip sticking up in the middle, warrior-style. Petra held the machete sideways. Tiara gazed at her reflection in it. She ran her hands across her scalp, over and back, examining her head from left and right, and Petra braced herself for sobbing. Instead, she smiled and her face opened like a blossom.

"I guess this isn't princess hair," Tiara said.

"Sure it is. It's warrior princess hair."

And Petra tucked a flower above Tiara's ear.

That night, the girls cooked up a dinner of slightly burned fish, grubs, and bulrushes. For dessert, they scooped the sweetmeat from coconut shells, licking the juice from their fingers. The fire sent up wispy smoke messengers that vanished before they cleared the treetops. The girls were taking turns with the pumice stone, scraping it along the ends of sticks to make spears. The air was warm, the sound of the waves soothing. And they fell into contented conversation, as if they'd been lucky enough to con all their parents into letting them have a colossal sleepover with no supervision.

Jennifer pretended her hand was a microphone. "Miss New Mexico, can you tell the audience about your day?"

Miss New Mexico adopted a fake-cheery voice and an artificially wide smile. "Well, Fabio, judges, I spent my day digging for grubs in the most disgusting mud you can possibly imagine. Then I helped build a desalination still. Oh, and my shoes are by Cheri of Paris."

"I made a hut out of mud, palm fronds, and ripped-up swimwear. And walking in the sand is toning my calves while I work!" said Miss Arkansas.

"I used seaweed to reinforce the walls on my lean-to," Miss Montana chimed in. "And worked on my tan."

"I peed in the ocean," Brittani said.

Miss Arkansas made a face. "Which part?"

Brittani looked confused. "All of it."

"I know this is going to sound weird, but this is kind of fun," Nicole said, grinning. She stuck a piece of fish on the end of her stick and turned it in the fire.

"All we need now is a scary movie to watch," Mary Lou said.

Miss Ohio snapped her fingers. "Ooh, like that one about the crazy stalker guy who hunts girls down and kills them off one by one."

"Which one?" Adina snarked.

"I think it was called *I See Your Naked Blood Naked*." Miss Ohio tossed bark peels into the fire. "The main girl has to strip down to her underwear to get away from the killer."

"You're thinking of *Sorority House Bloodbath*," Miss Montana said.

"No," Shanti piped up. "*Sorority House Bloodbath* is the one with Verity Bootay[25] where she tricks the psycho killer into watching her do a sexy striptease before she nabs him through the eye with her stiletto."

"Verity Bootay is kind of hot," Jennifer said.

"What about *Shop to Kill*? I love that one!" Brittani said.

---

[25] Verity Bootay, curvaceous former lead singer of the stripper-nurse pop group Nymphet.

"Is that where the killer straps the girl to a dentist's chair and uses a drill on her, but first he says, 'Now, this might sting a little. . . .'?"

"Huh-uh," Nicole said. "That's *Dentist of the Damned*, and the dentist lures ugly girls to his office with a promise to make them pretty, then he tortures and kills them. The sexy girl who's only going there to ask about cosmetic dentistry for her little sister who was born with a mouth defect is the one who survives. But only after she accidentally has sex with him."

"Hold up. How do you *accidentally* have sex with somebody?" Adina scoffed. "Is she all, 'Oh, I'm so sorry, I didn't see your penis there'?"

Tiara squealed and waved her hands. "Don't say that word!"

"What? *Accidentally?* Sorry? *Penis?*"

"Gah!" Tiara put her fingers in her ears.

"What about *phallic?*" Petra teased. "Like, 'Yon volcano is quite phallic, Lady Tiara.'" Tiara looked confused. "*Phallic* means penis-like," Petra explained.

"Ooh," Tiara said.

"Right! I remember," Miss Arkansas said. "*Shop to Kill* is the one where the girls are trapped in the department store and the killer hunts them down in every department and, like, strangles one with a thong and kills another one with a makeup brush through the head and there's, like, the most *shut up* clothes ever!"

"The ribbon vest?"

"Shut. Up."

"So shut up."

"I thought there was a shower scene."

"There's always a shower scene."

"I miss showers."

"And shopping."

"Movies."

"Pizza."

"School." Everyone stared at Shanti. "What? I like school."

"Me, too," Nicole said and gave Shanti a fist bump, which Shanti fumbled. "You sure you're not white, Bollywood?"

"I miss getting in my car and just driving without anybody telling me what to do or how loud I can play the radio or asking if I've practiced piano."

"I miss practicing piano!"

"I miss my friends."

"I miss my playlists I spent two days making and posting to UConnect[26]."

"I miss my bed."

"Flip-flops."

"Books."

"Basketball."

"Shopping."

"My laptop."

"Frozen yogurt."

"Guys."

"I so miss guys."

"Yeah," Jennifer said dreamily. "Sometimes they have nice trucks."

"I wouldn't want any guys to see me now. My pits are totally tragic."

"My legs are, like, man-hairy."

"No joke. I thought you'd put on kneesocks."

"You think that's bad, you should see my —"

"Stop."

The girls screamed with laughter. It was the first time some of them had laughed in days, and it felt good.

---

[26] UConnect, a social networking site perfect for wasting time posting quizzes and party pics, until you discover that your mom and dad are on there reconnecting with old high school friends and leaving you hideously cutesy messages on your wall.

"You guys don't know about hair trauma. I am a black woman without her grease. My weave is all kinds of messed up right now," Nicole said.

"I like it natural," Petra said.

"My mom would freak out. I got my first relaxer at five."

"Harsh."

"She wanted me to blend in," Nicole said with a sigh. "Have you ever been to Colorado? I think there are ten black people in the whole state. I don't miss people looking at me funny."

The wind caught the fire and it flared. Somewhere in the jungle, an unidentified bird trilled, cawed, and fell silent.

"I don't miss the baton twirling," Brittani said softly. "Or the teeth bleaching."

"I don't miss having my dad yell at me for messing up during my talent program. If I make one little mistake, he gets real upset and says I don't appreciate what he and my mom have sacrificed for me so I can do this," Tiara said.

"What *they've* sacrificed," Petra scoffed.

"That sounds like *my* mom," Miss Arkansas said. "She's all, 'Sparkle, sparkle, sparkle!' Sometimes I want to say, 'If you like this so much, why don't you put down the donuts and get up here and sparkle yourself?'"

Miss Montana stared into the fire. "Sometimes I just want to go in a room and break things and scream. Like, it's so much pressure all the time and if you get upset or angry, people say, 'Are you on the rag or something?' And it's like I want to say, 'No. I'm just pissed off right now. Can't I just be pissed off? How come that's not okay for me?' Like my dad will say, 'I can't talk to you when you're hysterical.' And I'm totally not being hysterical! I'm just mad. And he's the one losing it. But then I feel embarrassed anyway. So I slap on that smile and pretend everything's okay even though it's not. Anyway." Miss Montana pasted on an embarrassed half smile. "Sorry for the rant."

"Why do you have to be sorry?" Nicole asked.

"Well . . . I don't know."

"Why do girls always feel like they have to apologize for giving an opinion or taking up space in the world? Have you ever noticed that?" Nicole asked. "You go on websites and some girl leaves a post and if it's longer than three sentences or she's expressing her thoughts about some topic, she usually ends with, 'Sorry for the rant' or 'That may be dumb, but that's what I think.'"

"I say *sorry* all the time. The other day, this lady bumped into me with her grocery cart, and *I* said I was sorry," Mary Lou said, shaking her head.

Shanti raised her hand. "I move we officially ban the word *sorry* from our vocabularies while we're here."

"I second that, if that's okay," Petra said, grinning. "If not, *sorry.*"

"I third it. *Sorry.*"

"I just scratched my nose. *Sorry.*"

"I just scratched my ass. *Sorry.*"

"I'm getting up to stretch my legs. *Sorry.*"

"Sometimes I just want to burn down all the rules and start over," Mary Lou said. Everyone waited for the punch line of "sorry," but it never came.

"What would you really like to say up there to that studio audience?" Adina asked.

Petra pretended her fist was a microphone. "Well, Fabio. I'm glad you asked."

"Don't you dare call me Fabio," Adina said, giggling.

"Would you rather be Fabiana? 'Cause you know I'm flexible. I'd say . . ." Petra crossed her legs, tucked a wayward strand of hair behind her ear. "I'd say, I am too fucking fabulous for one gender. Oh, and can we please get rid of the cheesy dance numbers? It's like torture by step-ball-change."

"I'd say I am not a race. I am an individual," Nicole said.

Brittani hugged her. "You're so nice, Nicole. It's like you're not even mad at me for being white."

Nicole cut her eye at Brittani, then looked over to Shanti, who rolled her eyes.

Sosie moved her fingers gracefully, but no one understood. She waited for a moment. "I would say, learn to hear me in my own voice. I'm hearing impaired, not invisible."

"I feel invisible sometimes, too," Tiara said softly.

"What would you say, Bollywood?" Nicole asked.

Shanti had been telling her story at pageant after pageant: How her parents came to this country — the land of dreams and opportunity — from India. How they had opened a business, a restaurant, and taught their daughter that with hard work, she could be anything she wanted to be. How they taught her to honor where she was from but to love and embrace the customs of the new country. Shanti had told her story so many times, she had even started to believe it. She'd built herself into something perfect and unassailable. Now, under the clear night sky, she wondered if it might be the time to break it all down like some elaborate pageant set the day after the show. But what to put on the bare stage that remained?

"I'd say I need more fish!" She reached for what was left on Miss Ohio's plate.

"Hey!" Miss Ohio protested, but she let her eat it anyway.

"You know, instead of some old, backassward pageant competition, we should have a con. A Girl Con! How awesome would that be?" Adina said.

"What would we do at Girl Con?" Jennifer said, giving the words a cheesy announcer's voice.

"We could have some wicked cool workshops — writing, film, science, music, consciousness-raising. . . ."

"Comic Nerds with Ovaries!" Jennifer shouted. "I will lead that one. And a seminar on DIY zine production."

"My platform is about climate change," Miss Montana said. "It's so beautiful in Montana. I really do want to save our environment."

"Miss Montana is down for a Save the Environment panel," Adina said. "Who else?"

Miss New Mexico raised her hand. "I always wanted to make films. I love French New Wave. Godard. Truffaut. I made a short about my school cafeteria called *Meatloaf, Tu Es La Morte à Moi*."

"I work at a center for LGBT kids. I was thinking of starting my own nonprofit LGBT center in college," Petra said.

"Love it!" Adina yelled. She lay sprawled in the sand, her head resting on a tree limb.

"Can we also . . . sorry! Was I interrupting?" Brittani winced.

"Thou shalt not say sorry!" Mary Lou chided in a deep voice.

Brittani smiled. "Right. I forgot. Sor — I mean, can we do makeovers at Girl Con?"

"Do we have to?" Adina said with a sigh. "How is that empowering?"

"Things don't have to be empowering all the time. It can just be fun. Way to cut a fart in the middle of the party, New Hampshire," Jennifer said.

"And I *like* makeovers," Tiara said.

Petra gave her a high five. "So do I."

"And me," Shanti added. "If I only had ten minutes left to live, I would spend it at the makeup counter at the Nordstrom in the Galleria."

"Really?" Adina made a face.

Shanti shrugged. "If you find me in that jungle dead of a rare spider bite, make sure you put my eyeliner on."

Miss Ohio flailed with excitement. "Makeovers are so fun! It's like the Superman phone booth of girl."

Adina sat up. "It's denigrating and objectifying."

"No. It's eye shadow and lipstick and sex and mystery and magic and transformation and fun. And nobody's taking that away from me. You will pry my Petal Power lip gloss out of my cold, dead hands," Shanti insisted.

Adina rolled her eyes. "Okay. Democracy rules. Makeover panel, too."

Tiara clapped. "Yay!"

"Dancing," Sosie called out defiantly.

"Sex Monkey!" Petra shouted.

Miss Montana sputtered. "Sex Monkey? What's that?"

"I don't know. I just really want to go to a workshop called Sex Monkey."

"Honoring Your Inner Wild Girl," Mary Lou said softly.

"Wow. Great title," Adina said.

"You calling us wild, Nebraska?"

"Huh? No! It's . . . nothing. Sorry."

"SORRY!" the girls yelled as one before dissolving into laughter. Mary Lou didn't laugh. Somebody passed around half a coconut and everyone took a small bit.

Nicole chewed on a piece of bulrush. "We could take the world by storm, you know? It'll be like we proved ourselves, like all those heroes' journey stories about boys, only we're girls."

"Damn straight." Adina high-fived her.

Taylor emerged from the shadows. The firelight deepened the planes of her face till she seemed an X-ray of a girl. "You know, ladies, I've been listenin' to y'all over here talkin' while I work out because I am a very good multitasker. This is not about Girl Cons and Sex Monkey workshops, which, frankly, makes my mouth feel soiled just sayin' it. This is about Miss Teen Dream! The pinnacle of teen girl perfection."

Adina stacked pieces of fish on her stick and twirled it over the fire to cook them, as she'd learned to do. "Taylor, I think we're kind of beyond Miss Teen Dream now. I mean, look at us — look what we've built here in the past however long we've been here."

"Beyond Miss Teen Dream?" Taylor sat on a log and stared at the girls, dumbfounded. "Miss Teen Dream is all I ever wanted from the time I was six years old. This is the big one. The one that matters. Don't y'all remember why we're here?"

The girls looked at one another.

"Maybe that's where I started, but I'm not sure now," Miss New Mexico said. "Doesn't seem like enough anymore."

"Well, you can be a quitter if you like, Miss New Mexico. I'm in it to win it. And as team leader, I say that we need to get back to practicin' and beautifyin' if we're gonna be ready to go when we get back. Once they rescue us."

"But what if they don't rescue us?" Nicole asked.

"They will."

"But what if they don't?" Nicole said. "I just think maybe we should think about trying to rescue ourselves. Sorry, it's just what I think. I mean, no, I'm not sorry. It's what I think."

Taylor fell into her three-quarters pose, a reflex, a battle stance. "Miss Teen Dream is the ideal of young womanhood."

"The ideal? What ideal?" Sosie asked. "Says who? All they do is keep raising the bar, adding things we have to do or prettify or fix to be accepted. And we take the bait. We do it. That's what Miss Teen Dream represents. Well, not me. I'm out. I mean, Taylor, what are you going to do when your pageant years are over?"

"Over?" Taylor repeated. "They're never over. Life is a pageant, Miss Illinois. Everything I've learned will help me on my path."

A bloodcurdling scream interrupted the standoff. "My ring! It's gone!" Mary Lou held up her ring finger. All that remained was a band of pale skin where the ring had been. "You have to help me look for it! Please!"

"Okay, okay, calm down," Petra said. "Is it a family heirloom or something?"

"No, it's just — it's very important," Mary Lou said, near tears. She crawled in the sand.

"It keeps her purity vacuum-sealed to preserve its freshness for her future husband," Adina sniped.

Petra glared. "Just because you're funny doesn't mean you get to be cruel," she said in a low voice.

Adina swallowed hard. She got down on her knees and patted the ground, searching for a glint of silver. The girls lit torches and combed the immediate area, but the ring was nowhere to be found, and it wasn't safe to go any farther.

"Sorry, Mary Lou," Tiara said. "I know we're not saying sorry anymore, but I'm still sorry we didn't find your ring."

"Thanks," Mary Lou said. She sat on a rock staring out at the ocean, her face full of misery.

"Hey. Don't worry. We'll find it tomorrow." Adina put an arm around her friend. She hated everything the ring stood for, but it mattered to Mary Lou and so it mattered to Adina. "It'll be okay."

Mary Lou shook her head and placed a shaking hand against her St. Agnes medal. "You don't understand. You don't understand at all."

MISS TEEN DREAM FUN FACTS PAGE!

Please fill in the following information and return to Jessie Jane, Miss Teen Dream Pageant administrative assistant, before Monday. Remember, this is a chance for the judges and the audience to get to know YOU. So make it interesting and fun, but please be appropriate. And don't forget to mention something you love about our sponsor, The Corporation!

Name: Mary Lou Novak
State: Nebraska
Age: 17
Height: 5' 4"
Weight: 135 lbs. A lot of it is muscle.
Hair: Curly black
Eyes: Dark blue?
Best Feature: My smile. I guess.

Fun Facts About Me:

- I grew up on a farm in a town of only a thousand people.
- My platform is called Animals Are Awwww-some. We find foster homes for older pets.
- For obvious reasons, I am a vegetarian.
- I've never been to a water park! I can't wait to go on the slides.
- The most important quality in a friend is to be yourself. Unless you're not a very nice person. Then you should try to be somebody else.
- My favorite Corporation show is *Captains Bodacious*. I've always thought it would be cool to be a pirate. My sister, Annie, and I used to pretend we were pirate queens. We always thought one day we'd get a boat and sail the seas,

find buried treasure, fight villains and monsters, and live outside the rules. We'd have total command of our ship.*

- The thing that scares me most is letting go.

*The Corporation suggests changing this to something more feminine, like
this: "My favorite Corporation show is *Captains Bodacious*. I think the pirates
are supercute, and I'd love to find my true pirate love, get married, and sail
away with him into the sunset and live happily ever after. With treasure!"

CHAPTER FOURTEEN

The dream had been about a sexy pirate captain, and when Mary Lou woke, panting and undone, the sensual moon lay back like a lover against the soft bed of night, and her palms itched. Shaking off sleep, she touched her bare finger, remembering with panic that her ring was missing. The itching intensified. It always started with the itch, and the beauty queen stifled a small cry. This was what she had feared, and now she was defenseless against the change.

She remembered the first time it happened. She was twelve and watching the original *Captains Bodacious* on TV. All those handsome men parading around shirtless. She'd watched the show before and had felt nothing but an embarrassed gigglyness. But that night, something new and dangerous stirred within her. "Let's watch something else," her mother had said suddenly, and she'd changed the channel to a show about quilting. The exciting feeling inside Mary Lou had passed.

Later, as she lay in bed thinking of pirates, fantasizing about them in their formfitting breeches, her hand wandered beneath the sheets. Her breathing grew rapid. Her blood quickened. Warmth suffused her cheeks. An intense pleasure rippled through her. How alive she felt! How good and right it was that her body could do this!

The backs of her hands began to prickle, faintly at first, then insistently. No scratch would ease it. Terrified, she stole into the bathroom, locking herself in. In the mirror, she saw that her pupils were enormous. Her teeth seemed longer and sharper, her lips full as cabbage roses and just as red. Her hair was a corona of curls. A light growl-purr clawed its way out of her mouth from somewhere deep within, startling Mary Lou with its insistence. She stepped into a cold shower, letting the unpleasantness of the icy water pelt her until her skin was red but normal again.

In the morning, her mother appraised her over the orange juice. "Are you okay?"

"Yes," Mary Lou said with irritation. Inside, her heart pounded. She wondered if some trace of last night's episode remained.

Then there was the time with Billy. She was fourteen and he was sixteen and so sexy. Lying there beneath him, his shirt opened to reveal the broad expanse of his chest, the ripples of muscle across his stomach, she wanted him. The wanting was a physical ache. She'd pushed him onto his back and straddled him, her thighs squeezing gently against his sides. It started softly: She licked his neck. His smell undid her. She wanted more. She licked again.

"Hey, that's usually the guy's job," he said as if he were joking, but she could tell there was a scold in it. Like when she took an extra helping at the dinner table and her uncle would tease, "Putting on your winter coat there?"

A minute ago, he had been doing much the same to her. Why couldn't she answer in kind? She pressed her lips to his, tasting, enjoying, wanting. The itching in her palms began. But this time, it spread fast as a brush fire on a windy day. Her hunger was uncontrollable.

Billy's eyes widened at the sight of her in her wild state. "What's wrong with you?"

And Mary Lou had run away — from Billy, from the passion surging through her. She hid all night in the cornfields, crying softly in shame. When her body finally settled, somewhere around dawn, she returned home. Her mother sat at the kitchen table with a cold cup of coffee, worry etched into the lines of her face, and when she looked up to see her daughter at the kitchen door, an expression of sad understanding softened her eyes.

"It's hard to be a woman," she said, and poured Mary Lou a glass of milk in a Princess Pony glass. Her mother waited until Mary Lou's tears stopped and she'd finished her snack, and as dawn's first light pinkened the claustrophobic kitchen, she told Mary Lou about the curse that had plagued the women in her family for generations. Wild girls, they were called. Temptresses. Witches. Girls of fearless sexual appetite, who needed to run wild under the moon. The world feared them. They had to hide their desires behind a veneer of respectability.

"But I feel *so much* — it's like I want to eat up the world," Mary Lou warbled through the snot-slick tears on her upper lip. "Why is that wrong?"

Her mother cradled her softly then. "You learn to hold it back, to numb yourself to it," she said in a bitter voice. "Until one day, the world forgets to look at you. And then it doesn't matter anymore."

The next morning, they'd gone to see about the ring that could contain her curse. She had taken the vows that were supposed to keep her safe from her own impulses, her own desires. Mary Lou learned to be afraid of her own body. What if it betrayed her again? Already, Billy avoided her, and hurtful gossip spread about "that wild Mary Lou." Stinging slaps of names bit at her skin in the school hallways: *Whore. Slut. Nympho. Easy. Trashy. Trampy. Not the girl you bring home to Mother.* But Mary Lou didn't really want to go home to someone's mother. She already had one of those and, frankly, one was more than enough.

Mary Lou wore the ring faithfully. She studied the coy girls, the ones who pretended not to get the dirty joke that made Mary Lou stifle a laugh. The ones who practiced the shy, downward glance, who pretended giggly outrage when a boy made a suggestive remark, who waited to be seen and never made the first move. The ones who called other girls sluts and judged with ease. The good girls.

Occasionally, from the school bus windows, she would see other wild girls on the edges of the cornfields, running without shoes, hair unkempt. Their short skirts rode up, flashing warning lights of flesh: backs of knees, the curve of a calf, a smooth plain of thigh.

Sometimes, it was a girl just waiting for a bus, but in her eyes Mary Lou recognized the feral quality. That was a girl who wanted to race trains under the moon, a girl who liked the feel of silk stockings against her skin, the whisper promise of a boy's neck under her lips, who did not want to wait for life to choose her but wished to do the choosing herself. It made Mary Lou ache with everything she held back.

Over a dinner of leftover veggie meatloaf, she asked her mother about these girls on the edges of life. Had they been cursed, too? They seemed okay. And their clothes were bitchin'.

"I'm not their mother," she answered, as if that settled it.

Mary Lou's sister, Annie, walked in then, her eyes haunted, her shirt covered in spit-up formula. Her mother gave a small nod as if to say, "You see what happens?"

"Don't forget your vitamin," her mother said.

"I never do," Annie answered in a rag-thin voice.

Annie had been a wild girl, too. Together, the sisters had sailed out over the creek on a tire swing tied to a fat tree limb by a knotted fist of rope. They took turns flinging their heads back in defiance of gravity, letting the ends of their hair trail along the water's surface, reveling in the feeling of weightlessness. Later, they made tiny tattoos on their skin with a blue Sharpie.

"I'll be a sorceress," Annie said, inking a star into her palm.

"I'll be a pirate queen named Josephine," Mary Lou said. She'd chosen an ancient Celtic design she'd seen in a book from the library.

"I'll turn your ship into a dragon."

"I'll tame the dragon and ride it to the ends of the world."

"That's a very good plan. Let's be pirate queens together and roam the seas like we own them," Annie said. "We could ride motorbikes across the Indian countryside and watch the sun turn the land the color of saffron. It does that, you know. Or we could go to Prague and put our hands on the crumbling stones of the churches and imagine all the other hands that have touched there." Annie read from a copy of *On the Road* she'd checked out of the library. "'The only people for me are the mad ones, the ones who are mad to live, mad to talk, mad to be saved, desirous of everything at the same time.'"

Annie shimmied out of her dress and Mary Lou saw that her sister's body had ripened over the year. She was sixteen, and her breasts were full and firm. Her hips curved like treble clefs, notations in a music Mary Lou had yet to hear.

Annie passed her hands up those curves. Her eyes had a dreamy quality. "I feel like I'm too much for one body to hold. Do you ever feel like that?"

"No," Mary Lou answered. She was twelve.

"You will, Pirate Queen."

With a fierce yell, Annie cannonballed into the cold, clear water, making as much of a splash as possible, soaking Mary Lou in her wake. For the first time she could remember, Mary Lou had the sense that her sister stood apart from her, that though she could jump in after, they would not share exactly the same water. She tried not to be afraid.

One Thursday in March, the circus had come through Humble, Nebraska, like a rogue spring wind, the kind that kicks pollen into the air and sends the shoots up too early. Annie bent toward the sun of that circus like a March daffodil, blooming full. She especially loved the daring acrobats, and one in particular, a dark-eyed, ruddy-cheeked boy named Jacques-Paul. He had a crooked front tooth that reminded Mary Lou of a lady crossing her legs, and when he smiled, there was something slightly naughty in it. Annie felt the pull of that circus in her bones. She spent her afternoons with the lion tamers and clowns. The bearded lady taught her to play the mandolin, and the snake charmer said she was a natural. But she always ended up in the big tent, her eyes trained on Jacques-Paul as he defied the odds, grabbing through thin air at nothing, finding temporary safety in the bar at the last minute.

"Climb," he commanded and extended a hand.

Annie shed her shoes and stockings and scaled the ladder. On the platform, she closed her eyes and put out her hands. And then she was screaming and laughing far above the net, his arm around her waist like the surest harness.

It was during lunch period that Mary Lou saw Annie standing by the chain-link fence that guarded the middle school's muddy running track. Her battered, butter-plaid suitcase was at her feet. She'd stopped wearing her hair in pigtails, and now it ranged about her shoulders like kudzu, untamed, uncontainable.

"I can't live in a cage," she told Mary Lou without tears. "I'm leaving with the circus." Jacques-Paul leaned against the hood of a beat-up blue Impala playing with a yo-yo.

Mary Lou wanted to ask her sister about the plans they'd made, about being pirate queens who played by their own rules. "What will you do?" she asked instead.

"I'll see the world's biggest ball of yarn and play my mandolin outside diners. We're going to take pictures at the Dinosaur Pit. Jacques-Paul's going to teach me to be an acrobat. He says I can do it. I think he might be a little wild, like us."

Mary Lou wasn't certain. He didn't smell right. She glanced at Jacques-Paul's hands to see if they were sure enough to bear a wild girl's weight. She guessed it was hard to tell just by looking. Mary Lou closed one eye and tried to imagine Annie singing from the passenger seat of that Impala as they traveled the asphalt arteries of the nation. Behind them, the circus wagons were loaded up and ready to roll. All those traps in the back of the bear wagon made Mary Lou nervous.

"You better write," Mary Lou said at last.

The first postcard arrived on a Thursday. It had pictures like an old Technicolor movie and was from somewhere called Peoria, Illinois. Other postcards followed: Topeka, Kansas. St. Cloud, Minnesota. Marfa, Texas. Norman, Oklahoma. Sometimes, pictures arrived in long, flat brown envelopes. Annie posing with a whip beside the striped circus tent. A bear in a fez on a unicycle. Moss-laden trees you'd never find in Nebraska. The world's largest pile of shoes. No note would accompany these. Annie would simply write a caption on the back. "Miss Novak admonishes the tent for its fashion faux pas." "Bear on Unicycle, Series 12." "World's largest pile of air fresheners next stop." For a time, there were no pictures or postcards. And then there was a strip from a photo booth. In these stacked blocks of portraiture, Annie stared at the camera, unchanged from frame to frame. Her face was pale and her eyes, haunted. She'd written nothing on the back.

Annie returned to them in the fall with a belly too swollen for flying in the big tent. Jacques-Paul sulked about the house, sullen and cramped, till even his shadow grew small. Sometimes Annie stood at the back screen door listening to the night howl, her hands pressed against the metal webbing that left indentations in the pads of her fingers. One afternoon, Mary Lou heard raised voices and crying and door slamming. She came out to see Jacques-Paul packing his tights, harnesses, and yo-yo into the trunk.

"I am a performer," he croaked. "You knew that when you met me."

"You're some performer, all right!" Annie screamed and hurled the rattle she'd gotten at the baby shower given by the Lutheran Ladies' Auxiliary. The rattle was made of pure silver and had come wrapped in tissue paper from a store in Kearney. It landed with a thud near Jacques-Paul's feet.

He looked down at the toy and his shoulders sagged under some invisible, impossible weight. "You'll figure it out. You always do," he said, climbing into the car. The Impala kicked up dust as it squealed out.

"He didn't smell right. Even Mary Lou could tell," Annie cried, her eyes red-lined.

"Cursed," her mother nearly spat. "Cursed," she said, softer this time.

Mary Lou rescued the rattle. In the kitchen sink, she washed off the dirt and wrapped it again in the crumpled tissue paper. It didn't look the same, so she put it in her mother's closet among the handbags and summer blankets.

Mary Lou found the pictures of her mother in an old shoe box on the high shelf. In the photos, her mother was young, a girl of seventeen or so, and her face was not so tired. She wore a red dress with big brass buttons down the front. The photographer had caught her midlaugh, and the defiance of her bared teeth and wide lips gave her face a hint of mischief and forthrightness. The girl in this photograph bet the house. Mary Lou could sense the wildness beneath her mother's skin.

Mary Lou marched in and slapped the picture down by her mother's knitting. She folded her arms and waited for a response. Her mother squinted at the girl in the photo as if she were a distant relation whose name she struggled to remember. Without dropping a stitch, she nodded at the day's paper. "There's a pageant tryout in Omaha this weekend. Thought we could go see what all the fuss is about."

Mary Lou had never been to Omaha.

This was the reason, then, that she had entered the pageants. Her mother wasn't having Mary Lou turn out like Annie. The pageants got Mary Lou out of town, plus they were closely chaperoned and the girls were kept constantly busy. Far from any influence that might whisper unwanted thoughts and feelings to her too-weak soul, she was safe from the change. But here on the island, with the warm breeze tickling its fingers over her bare skin, the ever-present threat to survival keeping her body in a state of fight-or-flight, without the chaperones and routines and control — without the ring! — she was at the mercy of her body.

Closing her eyes tightly, she tried to head it off by thinking of terrible things. This is what her mother and the nuns had said to do when the curse came on. But she was too tired to fight it tonight. Her teeth grew sharper; her senses heightened; her skin tickled and warmed till she was forced to shuck her clothes. The wind caressed her nakedness, and she gasped at the unwelcome, but not unwanted, joy of it. Under the moon's besotted gaze, she ran deep into the jungle, her body strong, her every sense heightened. That was the shameful part — how good it felt to command her body in this way. How erotic the thrill of it! Like a caged beast finally allowed to hunt. Her mother called it a curse, and she understood that it was, that she had to control her urges. But somewhere deep down, she loved the sheer heady freedom of it. In this state, she was not afraid of the jungle, but part of it.

"I'm weightless, Annie," she whispered into the syrup-thick air.

At the cliff's top she saw the small campfire and the man in the sleeping bag. He was sheltered by the ledge. Her breath caught. He was gorgeous. She crept closer. Firelight sent shadow fingers to caress his tattooed face as Mary Lou wished she could. Nobody looked like that in Nebraska. Nearby was a backpack with his name: *Tane Ngata. Department of Ornithology.*

She wanted to wake him and ask if he knew a way off the island, but she couldn't let him see her like this. She was no patient princess waiting to be plucked and taken off to a castle. No. She was naked. Exposed. Her body full of want and need. Desire. He was like the sleeping prince in a fairy tale, and she had the urge to kiss him. But the prince would never want a cursed girl like her. Still, in her wild-girl state, she could not resist the smell of him, and so she inched carefully forward, put her face to his neck and inhaled.

The prince startled awake. Frightened, Mary Lou scampered back into the jungle. Her foot came down on a rope. With a sharp jerk, the net trap scooped her up and slammed her against the side of a tree. Her shoulder burned with pain and she cried out.

"Hello?" someone called. The prince with the backpack approached. He carried a kerosene lamp.

Mary Lou tried to remain silent, but her shoulder hurt and a small hiss escaped. The prince looked up to see her still swinging from the tree.

"Got yourself caught up there, eh?"

She said nothing in response.

"No worries. I'll get you down."

He put the lamp on the ground, and with a knife in his teeth, he shimmied up the tree till he was just above her. Another acrobat. What was it with her family and flying men? She shivered a bit at the sight of the knife.

"Give me your hand," he said. She was too afraid to touch him. "All right. That's cool. Try to relax everything in case I drop the rope."

Mary Lou felt a surge of panic. She thrust her hand at him. He held on to her, and with his other hand, he cut through the rope. There was a drop and Mary Lou dangled above the ground.

"It's all right, mate. I've got you," the prince said.

His hand was sure, but Mary Lou was afraid. With a thump, she dropped to the ground, wincing in pain, then scurried to hide her nakedness behind a bush.

The prince climbed down. He looked worried. "You okay?" He waited for a response. "Don't suppose you've seen a big bird, wing-span of a small plane, likes shiny things?"

Mary Lou held her breath and counted her heartbeats.

"Yeah, me neither. That's a taro plant, that big, elephant-eared thing you're crouching behind. If you cook it, it's delicious. If you eat it raw, it'll kill you. Kind of a dodgy plant when you think about it, yeah?"

He laughed, and it warmed her. "By the way, it's about three o'clock. If you were wondering." Pause. "Probably not. I like these hours. Feels like you could live inside your dreams, have a walk-about. You know?" Pause. "Yeah. All right, mate. I'm gonna get some sleep. Big day tomorrow. Taking my boat round the north side —"

"You have a boat? Are you a pirate?" Mary Lou started to step out, remembered her state, and ducked back behind the taro plant.

"Yeah. I mean, no. I mean, yeah, got a boat — well, it's a dinghy, light craft. And no, I'm not a pirate. I'm an ornithologist. Student, really. At university, second year. I'm looking for a rare bird, the *Venusian raptorus*. Are *you* a pirate?"

"I might be," Mary Lou said. A new confidence surged in her. She liked this funny prince.

"Cool. Say something piratey."

"Like what?"

"Don't know. You're the possible pirate, aren't you, mate?"

Back at the swimming hole in Nebraska, Mary Lou had pretended that she was a pirate queen. Now, she wished she were one. She wished she were anything but a cursed wild girl, a beast. How she wanted to thank this prince with a kiss. But he would see the way she was, her carnality and need, and he would shrink back in disgust like Billy. It would never work out.

"You sure you're okay?"

She didn't answer him, and he looked disappointed. Mary Lou bit her lip. "Be safe. Be good," her mother had said. But she didn't want to follow her mother's advice and sleepwalk through the days. Was it really so terrible to be a wild girl? Could it be any worse than lying about yourself?

She peeked her head above the top of the plant. "I'm not a pirate. I'm a wild girl from a cursed line of women. I paw at the ground and run under the moon. I like the feel of my own body. I'm not a slut or a nympho or someone who's just asking for it. And if I talk too loud it's just that I'm trying to be heard."

She stood panting. Her nose ran. She wiped it on her arm.

"Okay," the prince said.

Mary Lou pushed aside the leaves and stuck her head out a bit farther. "Did — did you say *okay*?"

"Yeah."

He smiled.

"You're not scared of me? You don't think I'm some kind of unnatural girl, a beast?"

He gave her the smallest smile. "Nah. Well, I mean, all the best people have a little beast in them. I'm Tane, by the way."

Mary Lou could taste desire in the back of her mouth like a sugary caramel. "Josephine," she said, using her old name from the days before she knew of her curse, when she was weightless. "Queen of the Wild Girls."

"How'd you get here?" he asked.

Mary Lou was jolted back to her predicament — the plane crash, the survivors, the need for rescue. But she felt less in danger at this moment than she ever had. It was like being inside a living dream that she could control. Later, she would tell him. Yes, there would be time for that later. She just wanted to stay with this moment a bit longer.

"I'm not really here. You're just dreaming," she answered and stepped out from behind the covering of the plant. He registered her nakedness with a small intake of breath, followed by the lightest of sighs, and this pleased her. She gave his neck another sniff. He smelled of fire smoke, salt breezes, and man. "And since this is a dream, I'm going to kiss you now."

"Fair enough," he said.

She bestowed the blessing of a wild girl's lips.

CHAPTER FIFTEEN

In the morning, Adina offered to help Mary Lou find her ring.

"Oh, that old thing. Don't need it. Thanks anyway," Mary Lou said with a smile, and watched Adina shake her head in confusion.

The next night around three, Mary Lou ran through the jungle full-bore, relishing the freedom. It did not feel like a jolt of panic anymore, this change in her body, but like a part of her was being integrated into all the other parts. She was full.

She came to Tane, waking him with a kiss, and they swam in the cool waters of a lagoon. She told him about the plane crash and all they'd done to survive. They talked about what it might be like to sail around the world for a year. How hard it was to be yourself in the world. Tane told Mary Lou about the wing structures of birds and evolution, and the time he had to pee on his little brother's jelly-fish bite to stop the sting. Mary Lou told Tane about the family curse, about Billy and the Dinosaur Pit, the world's largest pile of shoes, and Annie and Jacques-Paul's ill-fated romance.

"I knew he wasn't the one. He didn't smell right, and his hands were weak. He said he liked the wildness in her, but I don't think he really did. I think he was sort of threatened by it. And she wanted so much to make him happy that she forgot how to make herself happy," Mary Lou said, resting her head against Tane's chest.

"That's not happiness. That's a kind of murder, yeah?"

"Yeah," Mary Lou said.

"There's something I need to tell you, too. I had to be sure I could trust you first," Tane said. His voice was no longer playful.

"What is it?"

"I'm not just looking for birds. I'm an eco-warrior. This island used to belong to my people before The Corporation pushed them out and took it over."

"But this island is deserted. We've been here for weeks. I swear, there's nobody here."

"They *were* here. My people talk about it still. How they came to drill and mine. They violated the land and tested products on the animals. Made them very sick, killed a lot of them. They say the Venus bird was so sad, she flew away and was never seen again. The great volcano goddess was silenced, her fire extinguished by her tears."

"That's awful." Mary Lou had rolled onto her stomach so that she could see Tane's face.

"A few years ago, my people lost all contact with the island. The Corporation closed us out. Whatever they're doing here is top secret. And the authorities are all paid off. So I decided to come on my own, see what they're up to. Tomorrow I have to go to the other side, near the volcano. Might be gone a bit. Then I'll go get help, get you off this island. I'll be back — I promise."

Mary Lou pictured Jacques-Paul climbing into his Impala and kicking up dust as he pulled away forever. "Don't promise."

He lifted her chin with his finger. "I promise. I'll even leave my bedroll and lantern here."

Mary Lou didn't want to cry. Pirate queens were not weepy. They lived and died by their own code. "Look at that moon. Pretty happening tonight."

"Yeah. Impressive," Tane said, but he was not looking at the moon. "Tomorrow it'll be even bigger."

"You never know about tomorrow," Mary Lou said. She pulled Tane to her for a deep kiss.

Under a three o'clock sky, they explored each other with their mouths. He slid down along the curve of her stomach until she could no longer see his face and her hands were in his hair. It was exquisite, this thing he was doing to her, and she closed her eyes tightly and cried out, and it joined with the shrieking of birds who took to the unfettered skies with the powerful push of their wings. When this happened, she was sure that all those things she'd been taught about feeling shame were wrong. It was not a curse to fully inhabit your body. You were only as cursed as you allowed yourself to be.

After, when they were a sweaty tangle of limbs, she told him, "I'm not ready for the other things yet." He was quiet and she wondered if this would drive a wedge between them. "What are you thinking?"

"I'm thinking that I'm starving and I have a candy bar in my bag. You want half?"

It was caramel and nougat, her favorite. She licked the chocolate from his fingers, which led to more kissing and exploring, and when the moon paled against the dawn, Mary Lou tucked her St. Agnes medal into Tane's pocket. She inhaled the scent of him so that she'd have it with her no matter what.

"You have really good hands, Tane Ngata," she said and kissed the sleeping prince good-bye.

Mary Lou was not the only girl awake under a three o'clock sky. The sound of rain had woken Jennifer. She rubbed sleep from her eyes and remembered fragments of a dream in which she was Wonder Woman and Sosie was Hippolyta, Queen of the Amazons. From under her pillow — a wadded-up evening dress — she brought out her pen and notepad and began to draw. Her style was rough; her people had heads too big for their bodies, but Jennifer liked the feel of drawing the same way some people enjoyed singing in their showers.

In the panel, the Flint Avenger and her loyal sidekick, Sosie, had been trapped in the island lair of the archvillain, Madame Travatsky.

"You vill tell me ze location of ze nuclear submarine or I vill use ze ZombieRay on your little girlfriend, Flint Avenger!"

Jennifer mouthed the words while she drew.

"Don't do it, Flint Avenger! It's a trap!" Sosie's speech bubble said. In the panel, she was clearly signing.

"I can't let her hurt you, Sosie! Because . . ."

"Because . . . what?"

· *"I love you!"*

Jennifer concentrated on the next panel, Sosie's face. The light dusting of freckles across her pert nose. The dark eyebrows that gave her face a brooding quality. Silk-straight bangs. She worked hard on the eyes, and in the panel, they were very open with surprise and a sudden joy.

"What are you doing?"

Sosie's voice startled Jennifer. She dropped her pen.

"Nothing." Jennifer patted around on the sandy floor in the dark. Sosie reached over her for the notebook. Jen tried to swipe it back, but Sosie was too quick. Giggling, she sat down to read. She stopped giggling and stared at Jennifer. The last time Jennifer had felt like this, her grandmother was holding her copy of *Women's Basketball Weekly* in one hand. But Jennifer hadn't really cared too much about Grandma Huberman. It was different with Sosie.

"Give it back," Jennifer signed. "Please."

Sosie gave her the notebook. Then she took Jennifer's hand in hers, gently bending Jen's fingers to form the letters. "R U G-A-Y?"

Jen's heart beat faster. She nodded. Then she bent Sosie's fingers to form her own question. "R U?"

Sosie wasn't sure how to answer. Since she could remember, she'd had crushes on both girls and guys. They were person-specific infatuations — Brian Levithan's wicked sense of humor was every bit as sexy as Valerie Martinez's sweet smile and amazing krunk routines. It seemed odd to Sosie that she had to make some hard-and-fast decision about such an arbitrary, individual thing as attraction, like having to declare an orientation major: *I am straight with a minor in gay*.

With her hand waiting in Jennifer's, she thought about this now. She liked Jennifer, liked her lack of pettiness, her tough-but-fair stance, her honesty. If Jennifer were a dance, she would be the Agnes de Mille dream sequence from *Oklahoma!* Strong. Romantic. Forthright. Graceful. No wasted movement. Sosie didn't know if she was a lesbian; she was, however, a Jenniferian. And so she leaned forward and kissed her.

To Jennifer, the kiss was like a silent communication full of meaning. It wasn't the best kiss she had ever had. That honor belonged to LaKisha Damian on a Friday night in September behind the bleachers while the South Side Panthers marching band played "Baby, One More Time" and LaKisha wiggled her hand into Jennifer's jeans without ever losing her lip-lock. Sosie's kiss was tentative but warm. A question more than a declaration. Jennifer kissed her back with more assurance. The third time they banged mouths.

"Ow!" Jennifer said, rubbing her lips. She tried again, and this time, they fit. Sosie's mouth was warm, her tongue skittish. Jennifer made small circles around it with her own, drawing Sosie more into her mouth. She pulled back, cradling Sosie's face in her hands, kissing her intently, hungrily. Shifting onto her back, she drew Sosie on top of her, letting her hands rest on the muscular curves at the back of her thighs, letting one hand wander to the small of Sosie's back, pressing gently there.

To Sosie, Jennifer's body was a surprise — the curves where she had expected straight planes, the pliability of a breast in her hand, the silky skin of her arms. She had made out with only two boys and had shared a quick, truth-or-dare kiss with a girl named Eve at a seventh grade dance party. This was very different, and her mind could scarcely keep up with all the new sensations. Was she a good kisser? Was she lame? With renewed vigor, she suckled Jen's neck, wanting to brand her with a love bruise, then felt suddenly shy about it and stopped.

"Need some air," she managed, before staggering out.

Sosie left the hut so abruptly that Jennifer was afraid she had done something wrong. She followed her and found Sosie stretched out on her back in the sand, watching the clouds and stars perform their own choreography. Awkwardly, Jen lay beside her, her left shoulder just grazing Sosie's right. She didn't know how far she should take things. Should she kiss her again? If she were her alter ego, the Flint Avenger, she'd sweep Sosie up into the sky and they would fly over the island, defying gravity with their kisses, building an exquisitely intolerable friction with the press of their bodies.

Jen finally found the courage to sign, "Okay?"

Sosie nodded, smiling. She snuggled closer and threaded her fingers through Jen's, holding fast. There was more truth and hope in that one gesture than in all the things that had come before. These were the moments that kept you going, Jennifer thought. When you looked up to the sky and cried "Why?" sometimes the sky shrugged. Yet other times it answered with the warm assurance of linked hands. "Sorry," it whispered on the wind. "Sorry for all the pain and loneliness and disappointment. But there is this, too."

It was enough.

The girls had lost track of how long they had been on the island. During the daylight hours, they dove into the surf with abandon, emerging tanned and sure-footed, as if they were selkies who had let their timidity float out on the tide like a false skin. Only Taylor remained vigilant in her pageant work, getting up every morning, rain or shine, to go through the paces of her routine, from first entrance to talent to final interview.

"When we get rescued, I guess I'm the only one who'll be in fighting form," she'd say while circle-turning and practicing a stiff wave.

"I've been thinking about that book about the boys who crash on the island," Mary Lou said to Adina one afternoon as they rested on their elbows taking bites from the same papaya.

"*Lord of the Flies.* What about it?"

"You know how you said it wasn't a true measure of humanity because there were no girls and you wondered how it would be different if there had been girls?"

"Yeah?"

Mary Lou wiped fruit juice from her mouth with the back of her hand. "Maybe girls *need* an island to find themselves. Maybe they need a place where no one's watching them so they can be who they really are."

Adina gazed out at the expanse of unknowable ocean. "Maybe."

There was something about the island that made the girls forget who they had been. All those rules and shalt nots. They were no longer waiting for some arbitrary grade. They were no longer performing. Waiting. Hoping.

They were becoming.

They were.

A WORD FROM YOUR SPONSOR

The Corporation would like to apologize for the preceding pages. Of course, it's not all right for girls to behave this way. Sexuality is not meant to be this way — an honest, consensual expression in which a girl might take an active role when she feels good and ready and not one minute before. No. Sexual desire is meant to sell soap. And cars. And beer. And religion.

The Corporation would like you to know that they are deeply regretful of this tawdry display. So often these books for our young people do not enforce a moral. The Corporation would like to take the time now to present this moral in the following montage.

ALTERNATE SCENES:

1. The beauty queen made the first move and kissed the prince. "You know what I really like?" she whispered into his ear. Seconds later, he was sliding his mouth down the curve of her stomach. As he did, she looked up and saw the boulder teetering on the edge of the cliff above them.

"Oh my God! Look out for that boulder!"

"What bould — ?"

The rock fell off and killed her dead. The prince was blinded in the accident, but was later healed by the love of a goodly, virginal maiden who suffered a lot first.

The End.

2. The savage warrior girl raised her spear. "I'm not going to keep quiet anymore! I'm going to say what I need to say and not worry about whether or not it upsets somebody or makes me seem unfeminine. Because you know what? I have opinions. I have feelings and needs, and I'm tired of feeling like I can't voice them or I'll get ridiculed or attacked!"

In the firelight, it was easy to see that she was the least attractive girl of the bunch and she probably smelled bad. Just then, a giant snake lurched out of the trees, bit her in two, and swallowed her down. And the other girls realized they should probably keep their mouths shut.

The End.

3. The girl felt feral and strong. She felt feral and strong because, of course, she had been contaminated with the alien virus, which made her not like a normal girl, but more like an alien. With alien desires. The kind that are not normal.

"I killed everybody I ever kissed," the beautiful, long-legged girl with raven hair and full lips purred.

"I knew it. You're an alien," said her former best friend, the pale, bespectacled creature with the spectacular cleavage.

"Yes, I'm an alien and I *still* made cheerleader. And now I'm going to steal your boyfriend to prove girls can't really be friends."

"I sat back timidly when you torched my house, killed my parents, and ate my dog. But now you're stealing my boyfriend? That's a step too far!"

The bespectacled good girl with the nice rack plunged the jousting lance — constructed in Latin club — through the hot alien cheerleader's stomach in a deeply Freudian display.

"Hasta la vista, bitch[27]."

The End.

[27] This is perfectly acceptable language. After all, that bad, bad girl IS stealing her boyfriend.

4. The wind blew the beauty queen's skirt higher, exposing the curve of her butt beneath her panty. The humidity made her perspire in a sexy way, almost as if she'd been squirted with a mixture of water and baby oil by a makeup crew. She arched her back. "This jungle heat sure is all hot and stuff. Mind if I take off my top?"

"No! Let's all take off our tops!" said the other girls.

"Mmm, if there's anything I like better than taking off my clothes, it's using new Tan-So-Right[28] to keep my skin sweet and supple," the beauty queen said. She reached behind a rock for the bottle of liquid tanner and spritzed herself. As it hit her skin in a slow-motion mist, she gasped in pleasure and bit her lip.

"Hot," said a redhead in a thong.

"So hot," they all agreed.

"Oops, I just dropped my bottle of tanner. I'll just bend over slowly to pick it up," said the beauty queen.

"That's hot."

"Totally."

"You know what else is hot?" said a nameless blonde as she put her arm around the one black girl.

"What?"

"Bisexuals."

"Totally. Well, not like real bisexuals who are just sort of your everyday people, but, like, the kind of bisexuals you see in magazines wearing nothing but body paint and kissing both boys and girls to promote a new single."

"Totally, totally hot."

---

[28] Tan-So-Right, The Corporation's revolutionary self-tanner that gives you a perfectly even tan, even "down there." You are beautifying "down there," aren't you?

Laughing and frolicking, the girls jumped into a bubbling island spring that was a lot like a hot tub, and then a rugged explorer type jumped in. The girls fawned all over him because he had used Stud Muffin Body Spray for Guys[29].

The End.

---

[29] Stud Muffin Body Spray for Guys: Get your stud on with Stud Muffin Body Spray for Guys, the only body spray made with beer and man sweat and guaranteed to make girls frolic with you in a hot tub.*

*Results may vary. It could also make your dog hump your leg and have your grandma asking if you've sneaked a cold one into the retirement village for her.

MISS TEEN DREAM FUN FACTS PAGE!

Please fill in the following information and return to Jessie Jane, Miss Teen Dream Pageant administrative assistant, before Monday. Remember, this is a chance for the judges and the audience to get to know YOU. So make it interesting and fun, but please be appropriate. And don't forget to mention something you love about our sponsor, The Corporation!

Name: Nicole Ade
State: Colorado
Age: 16
Height: 5' 5"
Weight: 130 lbs
Hair: Black
Eyes: Brown
Best Feature: My smile

Fun Facts About Me:

- My dad and my Auntie Abeo are both doctors. My mom is a former Laker Girl.
- My personal motto is You Gotta Go Along to Get Along.
- I am pre-premed. I like to read *Gray's Anatomy* just for fun.
- My hobbies include meteorology, bowling, skiing, and drumming.
- My favorite Corporation product was Miles of Smiles tooth-paste. I really loved that it came in mint-choco-chip flavor. It's too bad about the recall. Salmonella is no joke.*
- The thing that scares me most? My mother.

*Note: Don't refer to Corporation recall. Class action suit still pending.

CHAPTER SIXTEEN

For her whole life, Nicole had been playing a part in a story shaped by everyone from her mother to her friends, even to her beloved auntie. But now, she was ready to make up her own story, even if she was less than sure how that worked. And so, armed with a sharp stick in one hand, a knife in the other, and a bag of shiny hair accessories and jewelry tied to her rope belt, Nicole set off to explore the island. She decided to go left, toward a part of the jungle she had yet to see, promising herself that if it got too frightening, she would turn back. On her way, she passed Miss Montana and Miss Ohio, who were lying on their backs in the warm sand. They'd positioned scraps of silvery metal from the plane's wing at chest level and were using them to reflect the sun.

"What are you doing?" Nicole asked.

"Working on our tans," Miss Montana said. She had placed coconut shell quarters over her eyes. They looked like hairy brown sunglasses.

"I usually go for a fake-n-bake every week during pageant season," Miss Ohio said. "Otherwise you look like Gothzilla. The judges like a tan."

Nicole bit her tongue. *The judges only like* artificially *darkened skin*, she wanted to say. "Don't you know anything about SPF? Skin cancer?"

Miss Montana eased herself up on her elbows and removed the small coconut shells from her eyes. "Are you always this much of a bummer?"

Fine, Nicole thought. She needed to be about her adventure, anyway. The knife hacked at the thicket surrounding her. Below her feet was a tangle of vines and roots, and she had to be careful where she stepped if she wanted to avoid a turned ankle or wrenched knee. High above her, a flock of colorful birds perched on a limb, their aqua-and-orange tails trailing down like the fishtail hem on an evening gown. Nicole wiped away the mist that collected on her skin. As she walked, she affixed shiny doodads from her bag to the trees to mark her passage. Once, she thought she heard someone behind her, but when she turned, there was nothing but thicket. The vegetation grew less dense, and finally she came to a clearing where the land looked ruined, burned.

"What happened here?" she said. Totems still guarded the top of a hill, ghosts of an older civilization. It gave Nicole a funny feeling, as if she were trespassing, and she found herself thinking of the restless spirits who inhabited the forest in stories she'd heard from Auntie Abeo. "I hope I'm not intruding," she said. "I don't mean any harm."

The wind was still, and so Nicole sensed that she was welcome. She set about looking for a piece of wood she could turn into an ekwe[30]. At last, she found a suitable piece and sat down with her knife to carve the slits that would make it a good drum. Her head itched. In the island humidity, Nicole's hair had gone rogue; the new growth was tight. Her mother would have an absolute fit if she saw it. For years, Nicole had submitted to the relaxers and her mother's big tub of Icon Pass Hair Grease. "This'll set you right," her mother had said, dipping fast, sure fingers into the grease and working it through Nicole's stubborn curl, pulling so tight, her eyes watered. Nicole focused on the tub's label, where a smiling black woman in pearls touched a hand to her shiny-straight coiffure. "Smooth and controlled," the label promised. But to Nicole, the woman's hair

[30] Ekwe, a traditional Nigerian drum, impressive to throw into your party chatter: "I was going to play the *ekwe*, but my hair was still damp."

seemed girdled and anxious, like it was just waiting for the right moment to stage a coup.

Her mother was always on her about one thing or another — hair, skin, nails, figure. "Well. I guess you got your father's color," her mother would say. Her tone, aggrieved, aggravated, made it clear that this was simply one more cross the universe had asked her to bear.

Nicole's mom had been a Laker Girl. She'd enjoyed being in the spotlight, and when her own ambitions hadn't worked out, she'd turned her attentions to making Nicole a star. "Because my baby is special," she'd say. *My baby is going to nationals in ice-skating. My baby is going to be a Grammy winner. My baby will be an actress. My baby is going to be a star.* And when her baby could barely stand in skates, couldn't sing on pitch, and mangled her lines in the school play, her mother only became more determined.

"Those people are just stupid," she'd say, tugging on Nicole's hand as they left agent after agent's office. "There is no way my baby is average. We'll show them. I'm going to get you an audition with *Sweet Sixteen Gone Wrong*[31]."

Nicole had wanted to please her mother, but she knew she didn't really have any talent for being famous. What she wanted to be was a doctor. Instead, she sat through countless DVR'd episodes of teen shows where the only girls of color were the sassy best friend, the Girl with Attitude who came in to swivel her head, snap out a one-liner, and fall back like a background singer. They had one thing in common, though — they were all light-skinned.

One day, Nicole's mother came home with a new jar of something called Pale & Pretty, which promised to "brighten the skin."

"Bleaching cream," her Auntie Abeo clucked, and Nicole could hear her mother and auntie arguing in the kitchen.

---

[31] *Sweet Sixteen Gone Wrong* (Wednesdays, 10 P.M. EST): Will Special let her manicurist inject her with yak's urine? Heidi flips out when Heather schedules her dress-fitting party on the same day as Heidi's pre-party modeling lessons. Z'anay has a tanning mishap. Dazzle chooses a small dog to match her dress.

"She needs to do something with herself," her mother said at last.

"Fine. She can come help me out in the office." Her auntie stuck her head into the living room. "Come with me, Ne-Ne."

When they were alone together in her aunt's office at the clinic with her take-apart anatomical models of the uterus and copious medical books, Auntie Abeo held Nicole's chin firmly but lovingly in her soft hand. "Don't you ever use that cream, do you hear me? What it takes from you, you can't get back. And I'm not just talking about pigment. Here, got you your own copy of *Gray's Anatomy*. A book doesn't care what color you are. Bleaching cream, my foot."

Nicole took comfort in the clinical book. When you peeled back the skin, you were dealing with bone and muscle, blood and nerve endings. It was all the same. She liked the beautiful logic of the circulatory system, the elegance of the neurological, and the fierce warrior spirit of the heart. The body had rules and it had quirks. Nicole respected that. Nicole's mother couldn't. She couldn't revel in the way synapses fired and blood cells defended against foreign invaders. She could only see her body's failings.

"Look at these stretch marks, girl. It's like a road map to ugly. I better cut out the fried clams if I don't want to look like your grandmother and have to wear nothing but size twenty-four housedresses the rest of my life."

Nicole worked the knife over the softened bark, cutting long, rectangular slits in the log's flanks. With her hem, she wiped away the wood filings, then made slightly wider cuts, curving away layers of casing to deepen the drum's sound. As she carved, she thought about her mother's crazy diets: Juice fasts. Cayenne pepper and lemon. Low-carb. No-carb. Grapefruit and steak. Nicole had suffered through them all. "We're getting rid of all the refined sugar in this house," her mother would announce out of the blue, carrying in bags from Whole Foods, eco-friendly tubes of rice cakes and no-salt-no-sugar-no-wheat-no-taste cereal, food as punishment. The next month, it would be something else.

Sometimes, her mother would come up behind her while Nicole sat at the kitchen table studying and wrap her arms around her daughter, kiss the top of her head, and for a fleeting moment, Nicole didn't want to be separate from her. But then her mother would inevitably say something — "How come your skin's so ashy? Aren't you using that cream I gave you?" "I don't think I like what you've got on." "I swear, my baby's just like me" — and the affection would be undone.

"I'm not you; I'm me!" Nicole wanted to scream.

Instead, she would speak in chewed fingernails and mauled cuticles, nervous scratching and upset stomachs, habits that frustrated and angered her mother, but in the anger, there was space. There was separation.

It was while watching an episode of *Vampire Prom*[32] that Nicole saw the commercial for Miss Teen Dream and figured out the perfect solution to her problem: pageants. They offered something Nicole actually wanted — scholarship money — and it satisfied her mother's craving for the spotlight. So Nicole learned traditional Nigerian drumming, which she didn't totally rock at but it wasn't like the judges knew anything about Nigerian drumming anyway. She let her mother relax her hair and oil up her skin with cocoa butter. Over afternoon teas, she made nice with the alumnae of Delta Sigma Theta so they'd sponsor her for regionals. She even let her mother pick her platform: Beautifying America, because there was nothing controversial about cleaning up litter, nothing that would make the country uncomfortable.

Now, out in the jungle by herself — by herself! — she felt at peace. In fact, she was giddy. She hummed an old Boyz Will

[32] *Vampire Prom*: The Corporation's Monday night supernatural drama about a pack of high school vampires and their dating dilemmas. Based on the novels, which were based on the graphic novels based on the comics, which in turn were based on the Swedish art-house movie. "Some vampires are born to kill. Some, to dance." (Catch the *Vampire Prom* dance tour coming to an arena near you!)

B Boyz tune as she tested the drum. Not bad. A sharp cracking sound reminded Nicole that there were other dangers out here. She crouched and held her stick ready. The sound came from her right. Someone or something was definitely there. Nicole ducked behind a tree and held her breath. The cracking sound came closer. And closer. She'd heard once that the best defense was a good offense. She grabbed the stick in one hand and her knife in the other. With a loud "Keee-yaaaaah!" she leapt out.

"Aaaahhhh!" Shanti cried, arms up.

Nicole blinked. "Bollywood? What are you doing?"

"I was following you. And I told you, don't call me Bollywood. So," Shanti said. "What are you doing out here?"

Nicole chewed at a fingernail. "Um, I came out here to have an adventure and find myself." *By myself,* she thought.

"Great. I'll come with you. I'd like to have an adventure, too," Shanti said. "You shouldn't bite your nails."

Nicole quickly dropped her hand to her side. She balled her fingers into a fist and released them again.

"Um, no offense, but I kind of wanted to explore on my own for a bit."

"Why?" Shanti said in that suspicious way that always put Nicole on the defensive.

"I just do, okay?"

"Well, you don't have to get mad about it," Shanti said. "Besides, there's no law that says I can't be out here, too."

Nicole started to say, "Fine. Go ahead." But she was tired of bowing to everyone's needs but her own. "You know what? I'll go somewhere else, then." She grabbed her new drum.

"I knew it. You're practicing," Shanti said in triumph. "Trying to get ahead."

"What? No! I just made this," Nicole said, and she wondered why she was even explaining herself. "Why are you following me? You don't even like me."

"That's not tr —"

"Please. You have been eyeballing me ever since we met. Don't lie. It's just the two of us out here. You can stop with the We're All One Big Happy World routine."

Shanti's smile faded. "Okay. Since we're being honest. This is a competition. And I am in it to win."

"Okay. I can get with that. But you don't give the other girls a hard time."

"Because they're not my competition. You are," Shanti leapt ahead of Nicole on the path. "Come on. You know they'll never let two brown girls place. And then there are the similarities: You want to be a doctor; I want to be a scientist. You're doing Nigerian drumming; I'm doing Indian dance. I'll bet your platform is something nonthreatening like saving animals or teaching kids with cancer to make stuffed animals."

"Cleaning up litter," Nicole admitted.

"You see?"

"Hold on. I need this pageant for the scholarship money. So I can go to medical school."

"And I don't need the money?"

"I don't know! I don't know anything about you. Because you're like this big mystery. I'm getting to know everybody else. But you, you're like a window display for an empty store, if you ask me."

Shanti's eyes burned. "Maybe I like to keep myself to myself."

"Fine. Do that. And I'm going for a walk. By myself. Just go on back to camp."

"I can't," Shanti said, wide-eyed.

Nicole put a hand on her hip. She sighed. "Why?"

"I'm stuck."

"Stuck being unpleasant?"

"No. I mean I am literally stuck. I can't move my feet." A hint of panic worked its way into Shanti's voice. "I think this is quicksand!"

Nicole rolled her eyes. "C'mon. That's just a desert island trope."

"Well, right now, it's the desert island trope that's sucking me down. Would you help me out of here?"

"For real? Quicksand?"

Shanti screamed as she slipped down another inch. The quicksand was up to her knees. "Ohmigod! I'm, like, totally going under! Would you just freaking help me, please?" Shanti's careful, vaguely British-inflected Indian accent was gone. In its place was pure California Valley girl.

Nicole's astonishment gave way to a smirk. "*Freaking*. Is that Hindi or Tamil or what? Did your grandmother teach you that? Was it part of your family's Ohmigod-totally-awesome-popadam recipe handed down through the generations?"

Shanti stretched her arm out and wiggled her fingers for a vine. She fell short by an inch. "I am so totally going to kill you when I get out of here. Like, for real."

Nicole put a hand to her chest in pretend shock. "No way? For real? I'm, like, totally scared!"

"Help me!"

"Why? You never help anybody else."

"You won't help a sister out?"

"Oh, no. You did *not* just play that." Nicole squatted till she was face-to-face with Shanti, who was in the quicksand up to her thighs. "You are not my sister. You are a total fake and a liar. Tell me why you did it."

"I needed an edge."

"Being Indian was your edge?" Nicole scoffed.

"Yes. No! I mean, I am Indian, but, like, not — look, they want this: They want the Indian girl whose parents sacrificed everything to give her the American dream. They don't want some Valley girl whose parents, like, shop at Nordstrom and have a housekeeper named Maria. They want *Princess Priya*[33]. That's the story they were

---

[33] *Princess Priya*, an Academy Award–winning movie about an orphan girl from India's slums who is rescued from a life of poverty and exploitation by a well-meaning white woman (Best Actress Oscar for Victoria Bollocks).

looking for. That's the story that makes them feel good. That's the story that wins every time. So that's the story I gave them."

"So who are you, then? For real this time."

"I don't know! That's the freaking problem, okay? I'm not Indian enough for the Indians and I'm not American enough for the white people. I'm always somewhere in between and I can't seem to make it to either side. It's like I live in a world of my own. ShantiBetweenLand. I swear, that is the truest thing I can tell you. Now will you *please* just get me out of here?"

"Don't go away," Nicole said as she jumped up.

"Funny! Not!" Shanti yelled. "You better be saving me, Beyoncé, or I swear I will come back like one of those too-much-eyeliner ghosts in a Japanese movie and haunt you forever!"

Nicole searched the area for a branch or a vine, something to hoist Shanti's sorry ass out of the muck. And as she did, she thought about passing by Shaniqua Payton on the school bus. She could hear Shaniqua behind her, saying, "How come you talk like a white girl? Like your black ass is all that and you too good for us? You with your pageant shit. You can act all high 'n' mighty, but who you think's gonna have your back if it comes down to it — me or whitey?"

All the other kids had stared and Nicole had been too embarrassed to do anything but stare straight ahead. Later, she'd told her friend Megan about it and waited for Megan to say something comforting, something that proved she belonged.

"Don't even pay attention to her," Megan had said. "You know what? She's just one of those angry black girls, Nicole. You know how they get."

Nicole had felt the comment like a crack across her cheek. In that moment, some part of her had known that Shaniqua might have been a jerk, but she had spoken truth. And sometimes the truth did not set you free. Sometimes, it was a hard, lonely prison of a place to be.

Between people. That's what she and Shanti were.

Nicole ripped a vine off a tree and tested its strength between her hands as Shanti screamed her name. "Keep your weave on, Bollywood."

"It's not a weave! It really is an old Indian remedy!" Shanti shouted, and it made Nicole smile. Girl was getting pissed off. Good. Pissed off people stayed alive.

Nicole held the vine away. "I'm going to pull you out. But first, say you're sorry for being such a liar."

Only Shanti's head was visible in the bubbling mud. "I'm s-sorry."

"Promise you're going to be yourself from now on and not some lying weasel. Unless who you are *is* a lying weasel, in which case I am letting the quicksand keep you."

"Screw you!" Shanti screamed.

Nicole snickered. "That's better." With a grunt, she tossed the vine toward Shanti's one free hand and dug in her heels. "Grab on." But Shanti was panicked. She tugged sharply. "Hey! Don't pull too hard! You'll —"

Nicole lost her balance and toppled into the quicksand. She made a desperate grab for the vine, but it fell in with them. "Nice work, Bollywood."

"Oh my God. Why didn't you secure it to the tree first?"

"You're welcome, Miss Grabby Hands. Aren't *you* the science whiz? Don't you know about forces and equal and opposite reaction and all that?"

"Like, hello? I was being swallowed by quicksand, okay?" Shanti shrieked.

"Well, now we're both stuck."

The girls screamed as loudly as they could, but no one heard or no one came. Shanti gave a rueful laugh. "Don't you know the other trope?"

"What's that?"

"The brown people die first."

The girls struggled in the mud, fighting the pull as it sucked them farther down no matter what they did.

Despite being unable to move, both Shanti and Nicole managed to free their hands for one last, sisters-in-non-white-dominant-culture-solidarity hand clasp. It was a very cool hand clasp, the kind white kids across America will try to emulate in about six months, just before an avant-garde white pop starlet turns it into a hit single and makes lots of money.

"You can't . . . trust . . . the man," Nicole said with her last breath, as she and Shanti sank beneath the quicksand.

CHAPTER SEVENTEEN

The surface of the quicksand bubbled. Nicole's face pushed through. She spit out the oatmeal-like sludge and took a deep breath. "Shanti!" she gasped. "Shanti, I've got hold of a root! We're saved."

Two seconds later, Shanti's head emerged. "Nicole! Nicole, I found a root! I can pull us out!"

"Shanti? Where are you?"

"Over here! Sorry, I can't see yet. Can't wipe my eyes."

"Me either. Can you pull yourself out?" Nicole asked.

"Totally."

"Go!"

With a grunt, they heaved their way up the vine and onto solid land. They were covered in muck, but they were alive. This narrow escape made them giddy. They hugged and held on tightly to each other.

"Ohmigosh, that is going to be, like, the *best story ever* for the judges!" Shanti shook the clingy mud from her hands.

Nicole did the same. "Just so you know, I wouldn't have let you drown before."

"I know," Shanti said, and they hugged again.

They found a steaming hot spring, and once they had tested it to be sure it wasn't more quicksand, they eased themselves in. The banks of the hot spring were made of thick, red clay. Shanti scooped up a handful and put it on her face. "This stuff is, like, genius for your complexion. Want some?"

Nicole smeared the mud on her face. "Too bad there's nothing for my hair."

"What do you mean?" Shanti could feel the clay hardening, closing her pores.

"I am a black woman without her products. All this new growth? I will never get a brush through this again," Nicole said with a sigh.

"It looks so awesome! Like a kinky waterfall."

"Did you just say *kinky waterfall* like it was a compliment?"

"You should keep it natural."

"Yeah?" Nicole patted her hair. It was coarse but full. "Need some kind of grease, though."

"Try using fresh coconut milk. It's a crazy-awesome moisturizer."

"Cool. Still trying to get used to that Valley accent, Bollywood. It's, like, so Galleria!"

"Whatever."

The two of them lay back and let the warmth of the water work on their tense muscles. They were relaxed from the water and giggly with their shared adventure. Talk came easily now.

"Can I ask you something, Nicole?"

"Sure. Wait — is this gonna be a sex talk? 'Cause I'm still a virgin."

"Me, too. It's not a sex conversation. So why are you doing Miss Teen Dream? No offense, but it doesn't seem like you're really into it."

"I want the scholarship money for medical school." Nicole usually stopped there. Everybody understood that answer. But she decided to be honest with Shanti. "But mostly, it's to make my mom happy. She really wants me to be a star. I think she's the one who wants to be a star."

"So what if you stood up to her, told her how you feel?"

Nicole slowly bicycled her legs out in front of her. "You try standing up to my mom. She's a force of nature."

"Are you going to let her run your life forever?"

Nicole sank down, letting the water rise to her chin. She thought about one time, after a local pageant, her second, when she didn't place. Afterward, she stood with her mother in the busy Doubletree Hotel hallway, girls posing and pirouetting all around, while her mother talked to the coach. "What can she do to improve her chances? What are the judges looking for?" her mother had asked. The coach had hemmed and hawed and looked uncomfortable. "Don't be too ethnic," she'd finally said. And Nicole felt her mother's hand tighten on her shoulder for a second, saw the pull at her jaw. "Thank you," her mother had said. They'd walked in silence to the car.

"So why did you sign up for Miss Teen Dream?" Nicole asked, changing the subject.

Shanti thought for a minute. She'd answered the question a million times for an audience. All those half truths and outright fabrications, giving people what they wanted without stopping to think about what *she* really wanted. "I think I was bored."

Nicole burst out laughing. "Bored? What, was the mall closed?"

"Shut up!" Shanti laughed. "Okay, that's not one hundred percent true, but sort of. I mean, I'd won everything else. It was the one thing I couldn't seem to conquer. I just felt like . . . I don't know."

"You had something to prove?"

"Yes!"

"I know that."

Shanti bobbed up and down in the water, enjoying her buoyancy. "The thing is, I don't really want it anymore. Not really."

"What do you want?"

"Everything!" Shanti laughed.

"Me, too."

Shanti rested her head against the bank and let her body float out in front of her. "Okay, secret want? Like, pinkie-swear-you-can't-tell secret?"

Nicole rolled her eyes. "Who am I going to tell?"

"I kind of want to be a DJ."

Nicole laughed. "You're kidding, right?"

"No."

"DJ? Really?"

"Everything in my life has always been about the goal, about being perfect and not letting the seams show. But, like, with DJing? It's about *finding* that groove. It's like you have to play around. It's, like, process."

"Like, that's deep."

"Shut up!" Shanti laughed. "If we were up onstage right now in front of the judges, you know what I would say when they asked me my life goals? I would say, 'You know what? Let me get back to you. I'm still figuring it out.' We should wash this stuff off now. I can barely move my lips."

The girls splashed their faces with warm water, rubbing off all the clay. Nicole ran a finger over her cheeks.

"Wow. That really works. My skin is silky smooth[34]."

"Yeah. I might have to make this part of my skincare line. Shanticeuticals. I could do a whole cosmetics line for ethnic skin. The packaging would be killer! Sort of a henna tattoo thing?" Shanti said.

Nicole laughed. "Good. You're back. For a second there, I was starting to worry."

---

[34] For skin that's silky smooth, try The Corporation's Pore It On clay mask. Follow it with No More Oil light moisturizer. Once a week, steam clean with the Dream Steam kit. Attend to your breakouts before they break out with Zit Zapper ointment. Fix flakes with Flakes Be Gone. Prevent future crow's feet with Eye on the Future eye cream. Banish cellulite with Orange You Glad You Don't Have Orange Peel gel and circulation stimulator. Moisturize your knees with The Knees Have It. Cream your ankles with Special Ankle Management lotion. Tame your brows with What R U, A Woolly Mammoth? brow gel. Take care of those nasty earlobes with Lobe It Away exfoliator. (Did you notice how terrible your earlobes look? We did.)

"I still like to win," Shanti said, grinning. "I'm not saying I'm not, like, totally Type A. I just need a B side, too."

"Nothing wrong with that. Just promise me that Shanticeuticals will not have a bleaching cream."

Shanti held up three fingers in a scout's-honor pose. "No bleaching cream."

Nicole put up her fist. "Bump me, Bollywood."

"Namaste, sassy black sidekick," Shanti said, and gave Nicole's fist a thump with hers. She pulled herself out of the water, squeezed the water from her hair, and loosely plaited it. "What do you want for dinner — grubs or bulrush?"

"A cheeseburger," Nicole said. "And fries."

"When we get back, I'm eating everything. Twice."

"That sounds like the best plan ever."

Arm in arm, Shanti and Nicole walked back toward the beach camp. Behind them, the wind swooped down from the painted mouths on the hill over the ruined land as if it could reach out fingers to tap them on their shoulder, turn them around. To warn them.

Jennifer stared at the radio. "Work with me," she pleaded. With a sigh, she took off the cover again. How she wished she had a sonic screwdriver or a superhero's radio-fixing powers. Jennifer tried to remember all she'd learned both at her mother's plant and from comic books. She touched two wires and got a small shock.

"Ow!" she said, shaking her finger. The radio blurbled to life. "Oh my God. I did it," she said. "I fixed the radio. Hey, you guys! I got a signal!"

The girls ran to Jen, crowding around the radio. Taylor pushed her way through to the front.

"Listen," Jen said. Beneath the static, the girls could hear a whisper of sound.

"It's too soft. See if you can get a stronger signal, Miss Michigan," Taylor said.

Jennifer made a few gestures to Sosie up in the tree to adjust the makeshift antenna. Jen twisted the knobs, listening for some heartbeat of sound. The radio answered in static and loud hisses, like a radiator coming to life on the first cold day of fall. A blurp of an old country and western song thrilled everyone for a moment.

"I go out walkin' after midnight. . . ." Nicole warbled along. "Ooh, I love Patsy Cline!"

"Shh," Jen admonished. She put her ear closer to the radio. Faint voices broken by static came through.

". . . final score: New York Giants, twenty-four. Detroit Lions, seventeen . . ."

"Lions suck," Jennifer said, shaking her head.

A strong, clear signal rocked the radio. A male voice in accented English asked about coordinates and product and delivery status. Another man with a Midwestern voice answered, "We are on track for delivery," and gave coordinates.

The sound faded and was replaced by other voices.

". . . press conference about the crash of Corporation Flight A-617 carrying those missing Miss Teen Dream contestants, Bob . . ."

"Quiet!" Jen shouted.

REPORTER: Ladybird, is it true that The Corporation and the government have called off the search for the missing plane?

LADYBIRD HOPE: Yes, Sue. It is.

REPORTER: You've suggested that terrorism is responsible for this, that the plane was shot down by enemy combatants?

LADYBIRD HOPE: Absolutely, Sue. And I will not rest until the truth is known about this. As you know, I was a sponsor for Miss Teen Dream, and this feels like a personal loss for me, too.

Next Saturday, at 8:00 P.M. Eastern/7:00 P.M. Central, we'll be broadcasting a special memorial, "Death Is Not the End of Pretty." Many wonderful celebrities have already signed on to participate in this touching tribute to our lost girls. Fabio Testosterone will host.

REPORTER: So there you have it. The search for missing Corporation Flight A-617 has officially been called off. Sad news, Bob.

REPORTER #2: Indeed, Sue. Thanks. Coming up next: Have you ever wondered how celebrities get their famous glow? Facialist-to-the-stars Jilly Starbeam will be here with us to share her secrets. After the break . . ."

The radio hiccupped into a jingle for Forever Young Jeans[35]. Jen flicked off the radio and a terrible quiet descended on the beach.

"They gave up," Taylor said. Her voice was barely above a whisper. "They just . . . left us. We did everything they asked, and they left us."

Nicole put a hand on Taylor's arm. "It's okay, Taylor."

"No. It's not okay. It's not okay at all." Tears beaded along Taylor's thick lashes. "This . . . this was my *last year*!"

Taylor pushed through the gathered girls and ran toward the jungle as fast as she could.

"Should we go after her?" Jen asked.

Adina shook her head. "Let her go. She just needs some space."

---

[35] Forever Young Jeans, the gravity-defying jeans for moms who want to party with their kids.

MISS TEEN DREAM FUN FACTS PAGE!

Please fill in the following information and return to Jessie Jane, Miss Teen Dream Pageant administrative assistant, before Monday. Remember, this is a chance for the judges and the audience to get to know YOU. So make it interesting and fun, but please be appropriate. And don't forget to mention something you love about our sponsor, The Corporation!

Name: Taylor Rene Krystal Hawkins
State: The Great State of Texas!
Age: 18
Height: 5' 8"
Weight: 120 lb
Hair: Natural blond
Eyes: Blue
Best Feature: My unwavering commitment

Fun Facts About Me:

- I am a winner of Li'l Miss Lone Star, Miss Dustbowl County, Junior Miss Waco County, Miss Purdy Boots, Little Miss Perfect, and Miss GlowWorm. I am proud to represent as Miss Teen Dream Texas.
- I was voted Most Likely to Rule the World in a Scary Way. But I am used to dealing with petty jealousy.
- My role model is former Miss Teen Dream Ladybird Hope, and I aspire to be like her in all ways.
- Personal motto: "God made me beautiful. The least I can do is share it with the world."
- My mom left when I was six to go "find herself." Some people are just weak and you have to pity them.
- I am not weak. I do not need your pity.
- Nothing scares me.

CHAPTER EIGHTEEN

Taylor's legs were strong and they had carried her deep into the jungle. She'd climbed over rocks and cut through heavy growth until she could no longer run. She settled beneath the sheltering apron of a bush and let go. She couldn't understand. She'd always been a good girl. A perfect girl. No one had tried harder than Taylor Rene Krystal Hawkins. And what had it gotten her?

"I can't be what they want me to be." It was what her mother had said.

Taylor couldn't remember her mother very well. She had been six when Mrs. Hawkins had walked out before dawn, leaving Taylor with a lingering kiss on her forehead and a wound that lasted much longer. She remembered small moments, and these moments came to her now: A birthday cake cradled in her mother's hands, with white peaks of frosting and animal crackers around the edges. The two of them on the swings at the park, kicking their legs higher and higher. The light catching her mom's face as she stood at the kitchen sink, unmoving, the water running over the untouched dishes. Her parents squaring off in the open doorway of their bedroom. "This life is killing me, Chuck," her mother saying in a voice hoarse with tears while her dad stood in his army greens, quiet as always, his hands worrying the edges of his hat. Her mother sitting in the half-light glow of the television well after Taylor should have been in bed. Beside her, a cigarette burned down to ash in an aluminum pie plate. The TV glittered with beautiful women parading in evening gowns, their smiles holding so much promise: *Everything can be yours! All this and great shoes, too!* Taylor's mom wasn't smiling, though. The familiar sadness had settled into her eyes and mouth.

"Tay-Tay, whatcha doin' up, baby?"

Taylor didn't answer, only snuggled into the comfort of her mother's lap to watch the show. Girl after girl shimmered on the small screen. They were the most perfect things Taylor had ever seen.

"That's a nice dress. I like yellow," her mother said without enthusiasm.

"Will you brush my hair?" Taylor asked.

"Hold still." Her mother brushed sweetly, softly, and to Taylor, it felt like the world was just this — her mother, the beautiful girls on TV, the caress of a brush in her hair. They watched till the end when a golden girl from Texas won the shining crown and took her tearful walk amidst flashing bulbs. It was late, and Taylor's eyelids were heavy. She could just make out the sound of her mother crying softly as she rested her face against the top of Taylor's head.

"I'm sorry, Tay-Tay," she murmured. "I can't be what they want me to be. I can't do it."

"I'm sleepy," Taylor said with a yawn.

Her mother carried her upstairs and put her to bed. "You be a good girl, now. Be Mama's strong little girl, and you'll be okay."

The next morning, her mother was gone. At first, Taylor had been fearful. How could a person just disappear like that? What if other people and things began to disappear — her father or the TV? She gathered her toys around her and tied them together with jump ropes like a sculpture, each one tethered to another. She pitched her pink Barbie camping tent nearby and tied the toy sculpture to one of the poles.

Two weeks later, Taylor saw Ladybird Hope on TV talking about her life in pageants, how it had given her the confidence to go after her dreams. Taylor left the safety of her tent and padded into the kitchen, where her dad sat reading the paper and eating a bowl of cornflakes.

"I want to be Little Miss Perfect," Taylor announced.

Her daddy signed her up. The ladies at the church saw to it that she got her dresses and lessons. And when they placed .that first crown on her head, Taylor found her calling. They loved her. If you did everything right, they had to love you. That mantra had seen her through countless pageants. But this time she'd done everything right and they were leaving her anyway. You couldn't be perfect enough to keep the world from betraying you. There was no way to win this game playing by the rules that had been set up so long ago. No. You had to rewrite them. You had to play your own game.

Her cheeks were wet. Taylor didn't usually cry; it was hell on the mascara. Only amateurs cried. Angrily, she wiped the tears away and talked through her affirmations:

"Never count a pageant girl out."

"I am Taylor Rene Krystal Hawkins. And I am Miss Teen Dream."

"It's always darkest before the ultimate sparkle."

She let out a sharp whoosh of breath, stood, and stretched. She shadowboxed and circle-turned. Then she glossed her lips and took a bow. There was still a chance. She'd make it right.

A flash of light caught her attention. For a moment, she thought she heard deep murmurings. It could have been the echoes of the jungle and nothing more, but Taylor was the daughter of a military man, and her senses were sharp. She slipped between the trees, keeping her breathing soft, following the sound till it became more pronounced. Definitely voices. Male. One deeper; the other higher, younger. It sounded roughly like English. They were saved! Well, she would certainly have something to say to those Negative Nellies back at the camp who didn't believe they'd be rescued.

She would march right up to these people, whoever they were, and let them know who she was and that everything would be okay. It was a good thing she'd taken the care to keep up her beauty routine every day, unlike the others. She gave herself a good sniff. Not too bad. Still, there was always room for improvement. With a hard kick, she split a coconut, dabbing the sweet juice behind her ears and squeezing it between her wrists like perfume.

Through the breaks in the dense tree line, Taylor glimpsed men behind a barbed wire fence carrying guns. Their work boots and crew cuts said military to her, but they had no familiar identifying markers — no berets, no camouflage or flag emblems. Instead, they all wore the same black shirts, though one had pinned a Daffy Duck emblem on the back. It was odd. And unsettling. Taylor's instincts, honed during countless pageants when the one who claimed to be sweet was the one to put Nair in your shampoo, came crawling up her spine and into her cortex. She hid herself.

"That ought to do it, sir," one of the mystery men reported to a man in khakis and mirrored aviators, gesturing toward some crates.

"Good work, Agent." Aviators man took in the Daffy Duck emblem. "Is that how you fellas dress these days, Agent?"

"Sir. It's Casual Friday, sir."

"And there's a team-building exercise at four, followed by a Cinco de Mayo tequila party at five," said a college-aged-looking dweeb in sneakers dribbling a basketball. Taylor made a mental note that when she returned home and won Miss Teen Dream, she'd start a charm school for clueless college boys. The world expected girls to pluck and primp and put on heels. Meanwhile, boys dressed in rumpled T-shirts and baggy pants and misplaced their combs, and yet you were supposed to fall at their feet? Unacceptable.

Aviators man shook his head and exhaled through tight lips. "Go on, Agent."

Dismissed, the mystery men approached the volcano. One of them lifted a fake rock panel and punched in a code on a keypad. A hidden door slid open to reveal a brightly lit corridor. The men stepped inside and the door closed again as if it had never existed.

Taylor's mouth opened in astonishment. What was going on here? Who were these people? She'd grown up on bases. She knew military. These people were something else. Keeping low to the ground, she crept around the side to get a better look at what was inside those crates. She kept one eye on the young guy and the man in sunglasses, who had lit up a cigarette. Taylor's mouth twisted in judgment. Clearly, some people were just too stupid to live. She would also work anti-smoking into her platform. Taylor watched the men carefully.

"Hey, Jonesy! Think fast!" The college kid fake-tossed the basketball. Aviators man didn't move. "You flinched!"

"Did not."

"Did so," the college kid singsonged under his breath. He reached into a crate and pulled out a white jar. Taylor strained to read the label. It looked like Lady 'Stache Off.

Aviators man put up a hand. "You might not want to get that near my lit cigarette."

"Why? Doesn't it take an electrical charge or something to make it go off?"

"It's a volatile compound. An explosive. The less handling, the better."

The college kid chuckled. "Exploding hair remover. I can't get over that."

"Try."

The college kid placed the tub back in the crate. "This stuff's gonna make The Corporation rich."

Taylor frowned. The Corporation didn't make explosives — certainly not out of beauty products. She had no idea what this ill-dressed boy was talking about.

He twirled the basketball on the tip of his index finger. "I know what's going on, you know."

Aviators man pulled on his cigarette. "What's going on?"

"Oh, I think you know."

"Yes, Harris. I always know. What do *you* think you know?"

"What I need to know."

"Which is?"

"Wouldn't *you* like to know?"

Aviators man's face remained stoic. "No. Not really."

"Fine! Play hardball, Jonesy. I like that about you."

"I'm not playing. I'm genuinely not interested."

"The plane crash. The Miss Teen Dream beauty queens on the other side of the island?"

From the safety of her hiding spot, Taylor gasped and immediately put a hand to her mouth to silence herself. Aviators man's head turned slightly in her direction and Taylor crouched lower.

"What is it?" the college kid asked.

"Nothing," Aviators man said.

"So The Corporation was looking for those girls and the whole time they're right here with us on the island."

"The Corporation knows that, and they weren't looking for them."

An icy dread coursed through Taylor's blood. It beat a warning in her temples.

"What do you mean?" the college kid asked.

Aviators man exhaled a plume of smoke. "We get some rescue crews here to pick up a few beauty queens, next thing you know, they're taking a closer look at our operation. They find out about Operation Peacock. Do you know what would happen if people found out The Corporation is making an arms deal with MoMo B. ChaCha?"

Taylor knew about MoMo B. ChaCha and his country, the Republic of ChaCha. Every morning after she finished her exercises, she read the paper cover to cover so that she would be up on her current events. The judges would never catch her unawares. She knew that MoMo was a very bad customer, and no American corporation should be doing business with him.

"Yeah, I get it. Shit happens." The college kid shrugged. "It's just too bad they have to die. They're totally bangable, you know?"

"Bangable," Taylor mouthed in disgust. She wanted to show this boy another meaning for the word *bang*, and it involved his head against a steel door. She had to warn the others.

Somehow, they had to let the world know what was really going on here.

"So I guess this is officially the end of the Miss Teen Dream Pageant, then. The ratings sucked anyway. Now we can finally program something good, like *Bridal Death Match*[36]."

Taylor had heard enough. She emerged from the jungle like a Kurtzian goddess. Her eyes narrowed. "You. Will not. Mess. With MY pageant."

"What the —" the college kid squeaked.

Before the agent could extinguish his cigarette and find his gun, Taylor caught his jaw in a roundhouse kick, the same one she'd perfected in countless aerobic kickboxing classes. He staggered back, his nose bloodied.

"And smoking is a terrible habit that not only eats your lungs away, it gives you those spidery lip wrinkles before your time, which Botox will *not* fix." Taylor whipped around to face the Dweeb. "Would you like some of this, rudely staring man?"

The kid continued staring. "You are so hot. Please don't hurt me."

"Damn!" Aviators man realized he'd left his gun on his desk — a rookie mistake. This new corporate culture was making him soft. He grabbed for the beauty queen, and she deftly elbowed him in the gut.

"Flag corps," she hissed. "Learned that move for my first Miss Purdy Boots pageant. It's got a real nice follow-up that goes something like this!"

Taylor executed two backflips with a kick to his ribs.

"Gymnastics," she huffed. "My dismount was the envy of stage mothers across Texas."

"Get her, you jackass," Aviators man gasped from the ground.

"Could I have your number?" the Dweeb asked.

---

[36] *Bridal Death Match*, the popular TV show about brides who cage fight each other in order to win the wedding of their dreams.

But Taylor didn't stick around to answer. "A Miss Teen Dream is a bright light in the world," she intoned. She was team captain, and her girls needed her. Alive with purpose, she took off running. Despite his wounds, the agent poured on speed, and Taylor felt something she hadn't experienced in years: fear. Her breath was ragged, animalistic, the opposite of pretty. Her lungs burned. She stooped to grab a coconut.

"Ready? Okay!" she said in perfect cheerleader rhythm and launched it behind her. There was a moment of satisfaction as she heard the man hiss in pain. Some girls lost their aim in times of crisis. Taylor did not. Quick thinking. It was what separated the queens from the runners-up. Taylor was not going for runner-up.

Agent Jones's shoulder throbbed where he'd taken the full brunt of the coconut. He ran fast, but he was no match for the beauty queen's youth and conditioning. If she made it back to the beach, she'd warn the others. The operation would be exposed. His pension and benefits would disappear. Or he'd have to kill them all. Quick thinking. It was what separated the men from the dweebs. Agent Jones was no dweeb. He might not be able to catch her, but he had something that could. Still running, he reached into his pocket for the darts.

Taylor felt a sharp pain in the back of her arm. She reached back and pulled out the small, pointed tip. She chanced a glance behind her and saw the blow tube at the man's mouth. Panic set in now. Her father always told her that panic was a soldier's enemy. Fear could be used, but panic was no good. *Focus, Miss Texas*, she told herself. All she had to do was make it to the top of the hill and get off one scream to the others. Just. One. Scream. As she sprinted, the hill bounced in her vision. Almost clear! She was clear!

"Teen . . . Dream . . . Misses!" she gasped out. "This is . . . your . . . team . . . captain!"

The second dart stuck fast in Taylor's neck.

"Danger!" The shriek was torn from her.

A third dart lodged in her butt. A fourth followed. She fell to her knees and tried to stagger to her feet again, but her legs felt numb and nothing looked right anymore. She felt like a visitor in her own body as the drug released directly into her bloodstream. Within seconds, her vision altered in terrifying ways. She whispered the word she'd never allowed herself to say, the word that she'd buried in her toy sculpture years before when her mother left.

"Help."

And then Taylor Rene Krystal Hawkins, Miss Texas, passed out.

Panting heavily, his jaw bruised and his leg bleeding, the agent crawled toward the beauty queen and smeared her mouth with the Mind's Flower fruit, torn from a neighboring plant. He put a few broken petals in her hands to suggest that she'd eaten her fill. Then he limped off toward the volcano lair. Before he'd settled into the corporate life of privatized security, the agent had initiated coups in third world countries. He'd overseen arms deals and planned assassinations. He'd taken out a rhino once on illegal safari with the board of directors for a fair trade company in Tanzania. The rhino went down after two shots. It took four for this beauty queen. None of his assignments had been as much of a headache as this one.

Women were a lot of trouble.

He hoped the Mind's Flower would keep her nonsensical long enough to formulate a Plan B. MoMo was due on the island soon, and things were going from bad to worse. He didn't relish telling the Board.

He certainly didn't relish telling the Boss.

COMMERCIAL BREAK

VOICEOVER

Ladies, do you wish you had more up top?
Are you tired of never filling out your bathing suit?
Does your guy's eye wander to girls with dangerous curves?

Hi. I'm Heather Heather, and I'm famous but I can't remember
what I'm famous for. It doesn't matter, because now I'm famous
for my crazy-awesome figure — made possible by Breast in
Show, the plastic surgery center where you can build *your*
perfect body.

Thanks to the caring staff at Breast in Show and The
Corporation's revolutionary new Fill 'Er Up™ implants and inject-
ables, I've overhauled everything from my lips to my cheeks, my
feet to my scalp. There's no part of you that can't be improved
by Breast in Show. Visit one of our showrooms today and find
out about our:

- Tummy tucks
- Cheek implants
- Lip fillers
- Butt implants/reduction
- Liposuction
- Brow- and face-lifts
- Hair grafts
- Chemical peels

At Breast in Show, you can also scale down your imperfect
earlobes, inject fat into your thinning gums, slim the area around
your knees and ankles — anything you like to make you look just

like me and all the other girls you see on TV, in movies, and in magazines. And our trained aestheticians can help you identify parts of yourself you didn't even know could be improved. Why wait? Schedule your appointment today. Financing is available. There's even a drive-through, so you can get right back to your busy life.

Breast in Show. Because "You're perfect just the way you are" is what your guidance counselor says. And she's an alcoholic.

CHAPTER NINETEEN

The girls had brought Taylor into her hut and placed her on the palm fronds like a sleeping princess. Taylor had been vaguely aware of the movement, but her mind was too confused to speak. She woke from her fever dream sometime in early morning. She'd gathered a few supplies and stolen away to a remote part of the jungle where she could be safe. It was so hard to feel safe in the world when you were a girl. But this place was good. It was a small cave hidden in the leafy growth of a mountain not far from a freshwater lagoon. And there were unicorns with rainbow-sparkle tails. Sometimes the unicorns spoke to her, and that was a little disconcerting. But then she would tell them to go off and work on their step-ball-change for the opening number and they did.

Now she was alone. She was alone like when her mother left and the world became a frightening place. When she'd had to build the sculpture to feel safe. But Taylor had proof that her fears were real. She'd seen what they were doing. She put her head down on her knees and began to cry.

"Tay-Tay, why is my pretty girl so sad?"

Taylor lifted her head. Through the haze of tears she saw her mother, resplendent in a bright yellow evening gown and surrounded by a silvery glow. "Mama? You're here?"

"Yes, I am, Taylor. I'm here to help you."

In the flickering glow, Taylor's mother looked just like she had when Taylor was six, but this mom wasn't crying at a sink full of dirty dishes. "Something's wrong, Mama. I can't make my head work right."

Her mother sat beside her and offered her a section of orange, which Taylor couldn't be certain she was eating. "Why did you leave?" Taylor said.

"I didn't know what else to do. I didn't know it was okay not to be perfect." Her mother tucked Taylor's hair behind her ear softly. "You're not like me, Taylor. You're a fighter. Who's no quitter?"

"Me."

"That's right. Taylor Rene Krystal Hawkins. Miss Texas." Her mom tapped her nose gently with her finger. Outlined by the fertile greenery, she was like an exotic plant. "Life can be ugly, Taylor. That's why it's so important to keep things pretty. And we are going to keep things pretty, aren't we?"

"Yes. We are."

Taylor's mother was no longer there. "Mama?" Taylor whispered urgently. Sweat beaded on her skin and ran down her arms. A snake hissed from a tree. And Taylor was afraid. In the jungle, she heard the creak of branches breaking, the squawk of a walkie-talkie. She hid behind a bush and watched the man with the earpiece and the AK-47. In his left hand was a cell phone, which struck Taylor as odd, but she tried to keep her focus. That was what made winners — focus. Not getting distracted by the little things. The man wore a black shirt like the others she'd taken out, five by her last count. The walkie-talkie squawked with a voice, and the man in the black shirt answered. "Nope. Haven't found her yet."

Hidden by the thick vegetation, Taylor watched the man carefully. It was hard because sometimes things didn't look right to her anymore. She could see smells and smell colors and it was all just a little fantastical. She couldn't even be sure of this man. She needed to be sure, though, and so she risked stepping out from the bush.

"Well, I'll be," the man said, smiling. "Come on out. I won't hurt you. I'm here to help you."

For a moment, her mind slipped sideways again, and she imagined he was her daddy coming to offer her a hand out of her stuffed-animal cave after her mother left. "Come on, baby. Come on out," her dad had said. The light from her bedroom window had fuzzed the top of his buzz cut like a dandelion.

"No," Taylor had said. And then she'd started crying. "What did I do to make Mommy leave?"

"You didn't do anything. This isn't your fault."

"Then why?" she'd wailed.

"I don't know," her daddy had said, and he looked so sad.

"It isn't fair!"

"No, it isn't, baby. Not by a mile. The world's only as fair as you can make it. Takes a lot of fight. A lot of fight. But if you stay in here, in your little cave, that's one less fighter on the side of fair."

He'd let her be, but every morning, he'd put down a tray with French toast, her favorite. It was brown around the edges and squishy in the middle, just the way she liked it. And eventually, she'd come out. When she was good and ready.

Focus, Miss Texas. Taylor forced herself to look again and concentrate. This man offering his hand was not her father or anyone like him. In this man's smile was all the unfairness of the world in its thuggish seduction. "Just come with me. We'll take care of you."

"No, you won't." Taylor stroked the man's cheek. She reached her arms up to cradle the back of his head and, with the skill of a champion, she broke his neck. Then she dragged him into the bushes, took his gun and walkie-talkie, and kept moving.

CHAPTER TWENTY

"What is she doing?" Adina asked.

It had taken two days, but the girls had found Taylor's hiding place deep in the jungle and had gathered to watch her. She looked rough. Her normally smooth blond hair was a matted tangle. She'd camouflaged her face and arms with dirt like a soldier in a war movie. The white dress she'd taken the care to wash out every day was ragged.

"I can't believe she ate that psycho-fruit. It's like she was trying to kill herself or something," Mary Lou said.

"It's weird," Adina said. "That's just not something I could remotely imagine Taylor doing."

"She *was* pretty upset about not getting rescued," Jennifer said.

The girls kept a safe distance, crouched low behind the cover of plants as they watched Taylor work. For days she'd been sneaking into the camp and stealing random items — eyelash curlers, a hair dryer, earrings, stockings. It wasn't like they needed them here, but why did she? Only Mary Lou had worked up the courage to approach Taylor's XL Crazy. "What do you need those for, Taylor?" she'd asked, and Taylor had done a little circle-turn and half a jig punctuated with jujitsu moves.

"If chosen as Miss Teen Dream, I will not let the bad people mess with our pretty. Their outfits are wrong. They're not good people. Tonight on *Patriot Daughters!*"

"It's like she's some freaky pageant robot that went haywire," Mary Lou said. "Also, she licked a tube of mascara."

"Don't use that now," Brittani said. "You'll get eye herpes."

"Boy, I hate eye herpes," Tiara agreed. Beside her, Nicole pretended to write something on imaginary paper, which she tore off and handed to Tiara. "What are you doing, Nicole?"

"Writing you a prescription to come talk to me."

"Can you do that if you're not a real doctor?"

"Sure," Miss Ohio said. "I found a guy on the Internet to write me a prescription for horse diet pills."

"Horse diet pills?" Nicole repeated.

"Yeah. They worked great, but my mom made me stop when I grew an extra set of teeth inside my large intestine."

Petra stuck her fingers in her ears. "La-la-la-la-la."

"What's she wearing?" Sosie signed.

Around her dress, Taylor had constructed a makeshift bandolier out of airplane seat belts, a pink unicorn wallet, and a tampon carrying case.

"That girl is serious about her feminine hygiene," Shanti said.

"Should we tackle her, bring her back?" Jennifer asked.

Shanti shook her head. "No way. She'll cut a bitch. Even hopped up on crazy juice."

"I don't understand — you guys ate those berries and you're fine," Adina said. "It wore off in a few hours. I wonder how come it's not wearing off for Taylor."

"Her bitch cells are binding to the proteins," Petra murmured.

"Shh, she's coming closer," Shanti whispered.

Out of sticks, palm fronds, salvaged shoes, glittery jewelry, two suitcase wheels, and evening gown scraps, Taylor had built a found-object beauty queen sculpture upon which she placed a scrawled sign for a sash. The sash read *Miss Miss*, making it seem as if the sculpture were just off. Taylor talked to the figure. She called it Ladybird and seemed to be waiting for its approval.

"What is that thing? It looks like the most busted beauty queen ever," Nicole whispered, and no one was sure which one she meant.

"I thought it was a gay bunny," Tiara said.

"Ladybird, watch this!" Taylor executed three backflips, ending in a machine-gun stance.

"Okay, that's not disturbing at all," Shanti said.

"She could probably sell that at MOMA for a fortune," Petra said appreciatively.

Taylor tilted her head to one side and smiled. "Yes, Ladybird. You have to put your heart, soul, and sparkle into it. It is a total commitment to the sparkle."

"She really *has* lost it," Adina murmured.

Taylor stopped, suddenly alert. She scrambled up the tree and disappeared.

"O-kaaay," Nicole said. "What's next?"

"Do you hear something?"

The girls listened, but in the constant burble of jungle noises, it was hard to hear anything unusual. It was only when the enormous snake dropped down from the tree that they realized the sound was a hiss.

"What is that?" Mary Lou whispered.

"Big snake thingy?" Tiara offered.

"Thanks. I hadn't figured that out yet."

"Don't move." Jennifer instructed.

"Does 'don't move' include your bowels? Because you're too late," Miss New Mexico said.

With a piercing scream, Taylor jumped forward, circling the blow dryer over her head by its cord. She let it fly and smacked the snake across the tail. It turned with a fierce roar.

"Come mess with Texas," Taylor said.

The snake obeyed. It lunged for her and Taylor dodged with acrobatic grace.

"Miss Teen Dream is a bright light in the world," she said with prayerlike intensity. From the makeshift bandolier, she removed a small can of hair spray, thumbing off the top. "Long-lasting hold!" she yelled. "Never let your 'do droop!" She pressed the nozzle on the spray can and lit a match, igniting a huge fireball that engulfed the snake. It screamed and fled into the trees like a wounded comet. Taylor shoved the can back into the unicorn wallet on the bandolier. She blew on the end of the hair dryer and shoved it nozzle-down into her rope belt.

"Whoa," Petra said. "Toto, I don't think Taylor's in it for Miss Congeniality anymore."

Adina called the meeting, having everyone sit in the same horseshoe formation that Taylor had. "Now that Taylor's incapacitated —"

"What?" Tiara asked.

"Gone nuts," Petra explained.

"Now that Taylor's gone nuts, I am assuming the duties of team leader. After all, I am first runner-up, and you know what that means. I can't help feeling that something's not right about this whole thing. Taylor was clearly trying to warn us about something. She said 'Danger.'"

"There were all those weird things in the old temple where I found Sosie," Jennifer remembered. "Ration kits. The machete. Candy bars."

Tiara eyed Sosie and shook her head. "It's always the handicapped ones you have to watch out for."

"What?" Jennifer said.

Sosie tugged on Jennifer's ragged outfit. "What is she saying about me?"

"Maybe she's some kind of spy. For all we know, she may not really be deaf," Miss Ohio said.

"That's crazy!"

"Right! How many fingers am I holding up?" Tiara thrust three raised fingers near Sosie's face.

"Get your fingers out of my face!"

Tiara smiled triumphantly. "I knew it!"

"Uh, Tiara?" Petra said. "Sosie can see just fine."

"I think we just proved that."

"What's going on?" Sosie demanded.

"Well, if we're talking about suspects, one of us *was* found in the jungle, far away from any wreckage." Miss Montana flicked a glance at Nicole.

"Oh, right. Let's suspect the black girl right off the bat."

"How do we know you didn't steal that sash from the real Miss Colorado?" Miss New Mexico said.

"How do we know that tray in your head isn't a recording device?" Nicole shot back.

"Nicole is no traitor," Shanti growled. "Or are you going to profile me next?"

"Knew you'd have my back." Nicole stood with Shanti.

"What's she saying? Don't leave me out!" Sosie yelled.

"I'm sorry. I feel really bad that I don't speak deaf," Tiara said.

Adina banged the baton against the nearest tree. "Okay, everybody. Cut it out. I can't believe I'm about to do this, but do you know what Taylor would say right now if she weren't off licking trees in the jungle? She'd say, 'I am really disappointed in you, Teen Dreamers. We are supposed to be sisters. Sisters who love and trust one another, who work together until it's clear that there is a favorite sister chosen to be the best and wear a pretty crown. So let's cut the crap.'" Adina shrugged. "And then she'd probably make us pray and practice our circle-turns."

"Whoa," Petra said. "That was kinda scary."

Mary Lou raised her hand and waited to be recognized. "I need to tell y'all something. There is somebody else on the island. A guy named Tane Ngata."

"What?" Miss Montana said. "Have you been hitting the plant juice?"

"Listen! I didn't know how to tell you this. He's an eco-warrior and an ornithologist."

Brittani gasped. "Ohmigosh. You're into the freaky stuff, aren't you?"

"An ornithologist is a bird-watcher," Mary Lou explained.

Brittani recoiled. "That's just sick."

"If there is a guy on the island, why didn't you tell us before?" Adina asked.

"I don't know! Because I was scared. And then I wanted something that was all mine. And I just . . . I don't know." Mary Lou told them everything — about her nights with Tane, how special he was, about his theory that The Corporation had a secret compound on the island.

"Are you sure you didn't just imagine it?" Nicole asked. "I mean, I've read about people getting kind of island-crazy after a while."

"He's real, I swear! We had awesome almost-sex," Mary Lou insisted.

Petra put a hand on her shoulder. "Sweetie, sometimes I like to think that Heathcliff is waiting for me at Thrushcross Grange in tight breeches and leather boots. Doesn't make it true."

"Weren't you wearing a purity ring when we got here? Aren't you supposed to be saving yourself?" Shanti asked.

"Yeah," Mary Lou answered. "And then I thought, for what? You save leftovers. My sex is not a leftover, and it is not a Christmas present."

"See, now I don't know whether to be all 'Yay!' because you're empowered or sad because you're having delusional almost-sex with an imaginary boyfriend," Adina said.

"If you were my best friend, you'd trust me."

Adina took a step back. She'd never been anybody's best friend before.

"Okay, Mary Lou, I got your back. Show us."

The girls trekked through the jungle over the path Mary Lou had traveled each night. They passed the waterfall and lagoon where she and Tane had gone swimming and she showed them the broken hammock trap where Tane had freed her when she was stuck.

"He held me by one hand!"

Finally, she reached the cove and the caves where Tane had held her sweetly, where he'd kissed her and helped her come to understand that there was no shame in her body or her desires. Tane's boat was nowhere in sight. She didn't see his lantern or bedroll. There wasn't even evidence of a fire. It was as if he'd never existed.

"I don't understand. He was here. This was his camp. He left his things because he was coming back."

"Okaaay," Shanti said. She widened her eyes at Petra, who nodded knowingly.

"I know you don't believe me, but I'm telling the truth. Something must have happened to him. He would never just go off without telling me."

"I get *so mad* when my imaginary boyfriend does that," Miss Ohio snarked.

"Stop it!" Mary Lou growled.

"Okay, down, Cujo. Let me get this straight: You met some hot guy and your priority was getting down with him, not rescuing us?" Miss Ohio said.

Mary Lou's cheeks reddened. "He only had his small boat. He promised to come back for us. Adina — help me out. You have to believe me."

Adina shrugged. "I really want to, ML, but . . ."

The wind picked up sharply and clouds rolled in.

"Looks like we're about to get a heck of a storm," Nicole said.

High winds whipped through the trees, shaking free leaves and fruit. The air had the iron-tang smell of coming rain. The first time a storm had blown through, the girls had been at its mercy. This time, they were prepared. They headed back to camp immediately.

"Stations," Shanti yelled once they got there, and the girls threw their supplies into the evening gown hammocks. Using a pulley system of airplane seat belts, they hoisted the hammock-bags high into the trees, free from the surging tide.

"Higher ground, y'all!" Tiara shouted. The girls fell in behind her as she led them up into the hills.

"What about Taylor?" Nicole asked.

"She's protected where she is," Adina answered. "Let's get moving."

Rain lashed their faces, but the girls kept climbing. When they reached the top of the hill they'd named Mount Awesome, Nicole pointed to the ocean.

"Hey, do you see that?"

"Ship!" Mary Lou shouted. "Ship!"

The girls screeched and hugged. Oh, salvation at last![37]

"Come on!" Petra raced down the hill toward the shore.

When the girls reached the beach, the tide was high, and the ship — a magnificent reproduction of an eighteenth-century sloop built on a studio lot in Hollywood — listed and limped in the high winds.

"Oh my gosh! They're going to crash!" Nicole shouted.

As if it were a tale of Greek myth and the gods had heard the cry, the ship banged against the skull-shaped jetty. A large hole could be seen in the starboard side. The boat took on water.

"We have to help them!" Nicole yelled.

"Wait!" Adina shouted over the wind and rain. "Look at the flag. The Jolly Roger."

"Like the candy," Tiara said. "I hope they have watermelon. It's my favorite."

"That's Jolly Rancher," Petra said.

"See that skull and crossbones? That's the universal symbol for *not good*," Adina explained. "We're talking pirates!"

The girls looked out to sea where the ship was taking on water. Now they could see guys running along the deck, climbing up the mast and wrestling with sails. Most were shirtless.

"Pirates?" Tiara repeated.

"Pirates!" Nicole said in awe.

---

[37] Be prepared for any event in a Salvation mohair poncho. Perfect with jeans or evening wear. Your outfit will always be saved with a Salvation poncho!

"Pirates," Petra murmured, and her lips curved into a smile.

"Pirates," Mary Lou squeaked. She felt a warning quiver in her belly. "Oh, no."

"Oh, hell's yes," Miss Ohio said, lowering the neckline on her ratty dress. "Guys!" She ran toward the ship.

"Wait!" Adina screamed, but the girls were already racing into the choppy surf.

The ship had run aground and was taking a beating against the jetty in the rain and wind. Drenched pirates shouted and hoisted and scrambled, but there was nothing to be done. The ship was lost.

The girls had reached them and were pulling many of them toward shore. The disoriented pirates trudged after them and collapsed on the beach. They were young. Very young. High school or college-aged. And strangely familiar, though in the lashing rain it was hard to focus on just why.

Tiara bent over a prone pirate and swept the sopping hair from his face. "You're pretty," she said.

He opened one eye. "Are you a mermaid?"

Tiara giggled. "No, silly. Mermaids have sparkle bras like in MermaidTopia[38]. That comes with accessories. I used to come with accessories. Before we crashed."

"Tiara, don't scare the nice pirates away," Petra whispered.

The pirate pushed up onto his elbows. "How do you think mermaids pee? I always wondered 'cause they have those tails and stuff?"

"I know!" Tiara nodded wildly.

Petra rolled her eyes. "A match made in heaven."

"Ahoy, mates!" someone yelled from the surf. "Our captain is down!"

---

[38] MermaidTopia, The Corporation's bestselling aquatic doll line. Every girl wants to be a utopian mermaid! Attachable legs, removable voice box, and swoon-worthy prince accessories sold separately.

Several pirates staggered to their feet to meet the others, and they carried the body of a tall, well-built guy. He wore black breeches tucked into tall black boots and a full white shirt. He was soaked through and through.

"Put him down over here," Nicole instructed, and they brought him to her doctor's hut. The girls crowded around. "I need to examine him, make sure he doesn't have any injuries."

Miss Ohio's hand went up. "I'll help!"

A chorus of "me, too!" rang out.

One of the guys stepped forward. A cool phoenix design had been etched into his close-cropped hair, and he wore a silver hoop earring in his right ear. He shook Nicole's hand. "Ahmed. I got some basic training in the army. Happy to help."

"Great. You can start by getting everybody out of here," Nicole said.

The girls responded with *awww*s and pouts, but Nicole was resolute and Ahmed flashed a bright smile and promised everything would be just fine before shutting the thatched door.

Mary Lou rushed over to the other girls. "Do you know who these guys are?"

"Who?" Adina asked.

Mary Lou's eyes were huge. "We've just rescued the cast of *Captains Bodacious IV: Badder and More Bodaciouser!*"

CHAPTER TWENTY-ONE

"You through with the razor?" Miss Ohio asked Miss Montana.

The girls had lined up at the swimming hole. They'd pulped a coconut, which they were using for shaving cream.

"Ordinarily, double-dipping on a razor would skeeve me out completely," Miss Ohio explained. "But I am not hanging out with a boatload of fine pirates looking like a yeti."

"You in line?" Miss New Mexico asked Adina.

"No, I'm not." Adina stepped back and let her go ahead. "And you should worry more about fixing their ship and being rescued than shaving your pits."

"I can do both. I'm a multitasker."

"This is going to make such a great story: How I nursed a pirate back to health and my love saved him," Miss Ohio said with a contented sigh. "And then we can have our own reality show about our relationship."

"Good luck with that."

Petra grinned at Adina.

"What — you don't believe in true love?" Petra asked. "The kind that can then be parlayed into awesome merchandising opportunities?"

"Isn't it exciting?" Tiara said, grinning. "TV pirates!"

Brittani pouted. "I was still hoping for a vampire rescue."

"I'm just interested in their ship and getting off the island, not some fantasy fed by a gazillion romance novels and stupid rom-coms starring Jessica Everett," Adina snarked.[39]

"What's your problem?" Miss Ohio said.

"Hey!" Nicole waved to them from down on the beach. "The captain's finally awake!"

Captain Sinjin St. Sinjin had, indeed, awakened. He was a broad-chested guy of twenty with long, black, wavy hair, devilish sideburns, and a wicked smile that had charmed its way through many a port. The knuckles of his left hand had been tattooed with the word *sexxy* and his right with *beast*. He wore tight breeches tucked into tall boots and a puffy white pirate's shirt unbuttoned to his navel. The other pirates sat near him. The girls hovered like satellites.

"Hello, mates. Feeling all right, yeah?" he called in an accent straight out of a posh London boarding school by way of the Eastside. "Say, could one of you lovelies get me something to quench my thirst?"

Four girls turned to go and Adina said, "You seem able-bodied to me."

Captain Sinjin put a hand to his chest. "We've been through a shipwreck, luv. We're exhausted and need to lie about."

"Oh, I know how you feel," Tiara said. "When our plane crashed here, and we had to bury the dead and deal with really bad wounds and Miss New Mexico got that tray stuck in her head —"

"Hi!" Miss New Mexico waved.

"— and the chaperones were all charred in the wreckage and it was really gross and scary and there was nothing to eat and no shelter and we had to build all that stuff and deal with giant snakes and bug bites and we barely survived a giant wave and mudslides and hallucinogenic plants and stuff, we were so, so tired."

---

[39] Jessica Everett, America's tabloid sweetheart, beloved for her great legs and even greater hair. Star of the romantic comedies *Man Hunt*, *Wedding Day*, *Wedding Day 2: I Thought I Loved You But You're a Jackass*, *Wedding Day 3: Third Time's the Charm*, *My Best Friend's Boyfriend*, *Let's Get Married!*, *Bridal Shower*, and *Dinner for Two*. Rent them all today!

Captain Sinjin blinked. "Yes, luv, but we're pirates. So it's much worse for us."

"Are you really the pirates from *Captains Bodacious IV*?" Miss Ohio asked. She lowered the neckline on her dress a tiny bit more.

"Absolutely!" Sinjin said. "You familiar with the show, luv?"

"Teen prep school guys in a British boarding school witness a murder by the mob and then they're forced to hide out at sea on a stolen ship. Along the way, they become pirates and fight crime and act like rock stars with girls in every port," Mary Lou recounted by heart. "I've never missed an episode."

"Possibly the stupidest show ever," Adina muttered.

"Pirate rock stars? Please, that's like the *heroin* of television," Petra said.

"I always wanted to be a pirate," Mary Lou said softly. "All that freedom."

"So what happened? How did you end up here?" Shanti asked.

The pirates exchanged nervous glances. Sinjin forced a smile and stroked a finger across Shanti's cheek. "My, you are lovely."

Shanti removed his hand. "How did you get here?"

"Right." Sinjin lay back on his elbows. He was a big guy and he took up a lot of sand. "Well, we were getting ready to start filming the new season from a secret tropical location, and after a little too much rum, the boys and I said, 'Hey, who wants to take the ship out for a little spin, eh?' Am I right?"

"Right!" the pirates responded.

"And, eh, we took the boat out to sea, except we'd only had six weeks of sailor camp."

"I can tie all my knots, though," a football player–size pirate with a bleached-white faux-hawk said.

"I can tie a cherry stem with my tongue," Miss Ohio said and licked her lips.

"Right, you I like," Captain Sinjin said. "Anyway, we blew off course while we were sleeping it off, if you know what I mean. Woke up and hadn't any idea where we were. You can't believe how bleeding scary the sea is. There's, like, whales and storms and shit! They don't bloody tell you that. And the rocking. I didn't stop puking for three days straight. Plus the world's in a barmy spot what with the threat of war and terrorism and all. But we kept on. Because we're men."

"Men!" the pirates shouted.

Sinjin cupped Petra's chin in his hand. "And it's girls like you who give us something to keep fighting for, luv."

Adina snorted. "For the record, you're not soldiers. You're pirates. And not even *real* pirates. You're *reality TV* pirates."

"Don't harsh my moment, Adina," Petra sang under her breath.

"There's a reality in reality TV," Captain Sinjin said. "I mean, once you get past the manufactured drama for the ratings and the product placement, the knowledge that there are cameras on you at all times and that you want to seem natural while still making sure that your abs look fantastic — once you get past that, it is absolutely genuine."[40]

"They gave me this cool haircut," said the pirate with the faux-hawk. "I'm George."

"Jennifer gave me a cool haircut, too. With a machete," Tiara said.

"Awesome," said George the Pirate. He stared at Tiara as if she were a kitten he hoped to take home.

"So why not just radio for help and get us all off this island?" Shanti asked.

Again, the pirates averted their eyes.

"W-well," Sinjin said, "the radio's not working."

"Not at all," blurted a pirate with a perfectly shaggy haircut and a blue bandanna wrapped around his head. "I'm Chu, by the way. Nice place you've got here. Cheers!"

---

[40] Now YOU can be part of the *Captains Bodacious* cruise experience! Lip-synch to your favorite Bodacious tunes! Take Pirate Pilates for those seaworthy abs! Walk the plank into a pool of Jell-O! Meet up with hot wenches! And take our pirate-speak classes so you, too, can be a genuine fake pirate. Get your parents' permission and sign up today!

"I might be able to fix your radio," Jennifer said. "I'm pretty mechanical. Got ours up and running. For a minute anyway."

"Sorry. Erm, it's not just broken. It's smashed to bits. Drunken revelry," Sinjin explained. "Arrrrgggghhhh!"

Mary Lou sank into the sand. "So . . . you don't have any way of calling in for help? You're stuck here?"

"'Fraid so," Ahmed, the ship's boatswain, said.

Adina appealed to the sky. "We asked for rescue and you sent us incompetent rock-star pirates with a broken ship and perfect abs?"

"Thank you, God," Petra said.

"Don't you worry, superfoxy babes," Sinjin said, putting his arms around Petra and Miss Ohio. "I know it's been rough. But we're here now. Everything will be okay."

"Actually," Adina said. "We're doing fine. See those huts, the irrigation system, fishing lines, the rain-catching tarp, and desalination still? We built all of that."

"Really?"

Nicole crossed her arms over her chest. "Yeah. Shocker."

"Cool!" Captain Sinjin St. Sinjin inspected the huts, finally choosing to lie down on Tiara's soft palm frond bed. He made himself comfortable. "Very nice. Can I get something to eat?"

Adina glared. "That's Tiara's bed."

Tiara backed away. "Oh. It's okay. I don't mind."

"She doesn't mind," Captain Sinjin said. He winked at Tiara. "Thanks, luv! You're gorgeous. Something to eat? Mangia? Yum-yums?"

"You didn't even ask," Adina said. "You just sat right down."

Captain Sinjin took off his boots and tossed them in the sand.

"Can I get you something to drink, too?" Tiara asked. "We have rainwater or coconut milk."

"Fantastic. I'll take the coconut milk. Ta, luv."

Tiara turned to leave. Adina stopped her. "Stay right here, Tiara. If he wants it, he can get it himself."

"But . . ." Tiara seemed torn. "I don't mind."

"She doesn't mind," Captain Sinjin said. He batted his lashes at Adina.

Tiara looked from Adina to Sinjin and back again. She jogged in place like a kindergartner who needed a bathroom.

Finally, George raised his hand. "I'll go with you to get it. I get him stuff all the time since he's the captain."

"Thanks!" Tiara beamed, and she and George walked hand-in-hand toward the coconut storage.

Adina threw up her hands. "Right. Just forget everything. Hey, maybe they have some laundry they need done, too," she grumbled. "I'm going to go check the fishing lines."

"Great idea, luv. I'm crazy about fish," Captain Sinjin called after her.

"Unbelievable," Adina muttered.

Good God! All you had to do was introduce the scent of testosterone and perfectly capable, together girls were reduced to giggling, lash-batting, hair-playing idiots. She hated it when girls did this. When they got all goo-goo-eyed over Y chromosome–carrying creatures instead of taking care of themselves. It's what her mother had done her whole life, cater to some man instead of looking after herself. Or Adina.

She thought about this as she walked toward the lagoon to check the fishing lines. She was still thinking about it and muttering to herself as she bumped headlong into one of the pirates.

"You should watch where you're going," she snapped.

"I was," he answered in a raspy voice that tickled her insides and made her look up. "I was afraid you'd miss me, though, so I had to maneuver at the last minute."

He was grinning. He had the audacity to grin. It was a hell of a grin, too — slightly naughty, with teeth that were just crooked enough to give his mouth character. He was tall and lanky with a bronzed, sharp-boned face; his green eyes were twinkly, like he'd just gotten a joke someone had told him earlier. Tawny, sun-streaked hair fell in waves to his tanned shoulders, which were bare and freckled. There was a small star tattoo on the left one.

Adina had the disconcerting feeling that the ground beneath her was not as solid as she imagined. "I-I have to check the fishing lines," she said, squeezing past him.

"I'll come with you," he said and fell into step with her as she marched toward the lagoon.

"You don't have to."

"I know." He flashed her that grin, the one that made her borders feel unprotected. "I'm Duff, by the way. Duff McAvoy."

Adina didn't answer.

"This is usually the part where you tell me your name."

"Why?"

He nodded, thinking it over. "Interesting name. Were your parents overly inquisitive people?"

"No. Why should I tell you my name?"

"You don't have to."

"Adina. Adina Greenberg."

"Nice to meet you, Adina." He stuck out his hand and Adina shook it warily before turning her attentions to the tangled fishing lines.

"It's pretty amazing what you've done here."

"What, did you think we'd lie down and die?" She waded into the water, untwisting the lines as she went.

"Um, that was a compliment."

"Crap," Adina said.

"It was a crap compliment?"

She cupped a hand over her eyes and looked out at the water. "No, I mean, crap, the line's stuck on something out there. It took forever to get these working. This one's probably going to break from the strain and we'll have to start all over again."

"Let me help you with that."

"I don't need your help," Adina called, but Duff was already wading into the water. This was the problem with men. They just assumed. They just *took action*. It was infuriating. And reductive. And slightly thrilling.

The wet clung to Duff's pants as he strode into the surf, and she could see the curve of his ass. Man, he was fine.

"Stop it, Greenberg," Adina said. She walked back to shore and busied herself with rearranging the *HELP* stones.

Duff took a deep breath and dove under. He was under for a count of ten, and Adina found herself worrying. Another few seconds went by and he popped up. "Got it! Give it a try!"

Adina tugged on the line and it moved easily. Duff trudged back through the waves. His body glistened in the sun. Why was her heart speeding up? It was an autonomic betrayal. *Stop it*, she told her senses. *Stop being so dumb.*

"All better?"

"Yeah. Thanks."

"No problem." He shook off the excess water like a big dog and sat down in the sand. "It's brilliant here. Peaceful."

"I'd trade it in a heartbeat for a night at a hotel with room service."

"Understandable. But it is kind of romantic. Like the island version of Walden Pond."

"You've read Thoreau?" Adina managed.

"Surprised?" He gave her that smile, which was both sweet and a little dangerous. "I've been watching you. You're not like the other girls, are you?"

Adina made a show of looking down at her body. "Really?"

"Oh. I didn't mean it like that. I just meant that you don't seem like the typical beauty queen type."

"Gee. Thanks."

"No! I didn't mean . . . wow. I'm really striking out here." He took a deep breath. "What I meant was that you don't seem like someone who would go out for a Miss Teen Dream Pageant. You seem like someone who'd be, I don't know, playing in a band, hauling your equipment to gigs."

"I . . . I do play in a band," Adina said, unable to keep her cool. "I'm the bass player."

"Bass players are brilliant! John Paul Jones, Flea, John Entwistle, Tina Weymouth . . ."

"Seriously? You just named all my favorites in one breath."

"I have more breath. I could try to say more things to make you like me."

His eyes were very green. Adina got up to check the fishing lines even though she'd just checked them not five minutes before.

"So, rock-star pirate," she said, with a bit of sneer. "What instrument do you play on the show?"

"Well, I don't like to brag, but I am a virtuoso at the spoons."

"Really."

"Yes. My musical cutlery skills have landed me in the top concert halls of Europe. The Queen yelling out, 'Spoon solo!'" Duff played a mock spoon solo against his thigh, then made crowd sounds. "Of course, there was that tragic spork incident at the Hollywood Bowl. We don't talk about that."

"You don't play anything, do you?"

"Not a thing. I am completely and utterly useless."

Adina could feel herself starting to warm to Duff. "So, what, they just hired you for your good looks?"

"You think I'm good-looking?"

He gave her a shy smile, and Adina's cheeks pinkened.

"That's usually a requirement for being on TV," she said, dodging the question.

"Well. Maybe when we get back, you can teach me to play the bass."

"If we can fix your ship, we can get out of here. Oh my God. Do you know what I would do for a burger and a bed?"

"Hey — you fancy a trip to the ship?" Duff laughed when Adina raised an eyebrow. "No. Nothing like that. There's food on board. It's mostly pretty naff — soy protein bars and freeze-dried noodles and whatnot. But it's a change from coconut and fish for you."

"It's not a burger, but I'll take it."

When the morning fog burned off and the sun was high, the beauty queens and the accidental pirates trudged through the waters to the beached ship to assess the damage. She had taken on quite a bit of water and listed to one side. A big, jagged hole snaked along the starboard side near the bow.

"We're going to have to drag her ashore if we have a hope of fixing her," Ahmed said.

"How do we do that?" Nicole cast a glance upward at the tall sails.

"If we cut down the rigging and use the ropes to pull her, I think we can do it."

"Worth a try," Nicole agreed.

Mary Lou could barely contain her excitement. A real pirate ship! Once on board, she stepped behind the large wooden wheel and pretended she was Josephine on a run through the islands, escaping from the British navy. "Ahoy, me hearties," she growled to herself. She wished she could tell Tane about this, and that thought gave her pause. Where was he? What had happened? Maybe he wasn't any better than Jacques-Paul or Billy. Or maybe the girls were right and he was some strange fever dream brought on by the island, a prince mirage.

"ML!" Shanti waved from the crow's nest. "How bitchin' is this?"

"Awesome!" Mary Lou called back. She wouldn't think about Tane. She was a pirate queen, and pirate queens had more important things to do.

Alongside the pirates, the girls climbed up the rigging and cut down ropes, dropping them to the deck. Down in the water, Petra and Sosie helped secure the ropes to the sides of the ship for the eventual haul.

Jen and Chu went belowdecks to examine the hole.

"Do you think she'll sail again?" Jennifer asked Chu, who wore a Pharma[41] T-shirt.

Chu put his entire head through one section. "Don't know. They didn't teach us anything about shipwrecks in pirate camp. Mostly, they wanted us to work out and get cool haircuts."

Jen chewed at her bottom lip. "Got any tools on this ship?"

"Besides the captain?" The pirate's smile was sheepish. "Dunno. Not really tool savvy. But I can do one hundred crunches in two minutes. Check my abs." He raised his shirt.

"Little clue: wasted on me."

"What?"

"I'm into girls."

"Oh. Oh!" Chu said. "Right. Got it. That's cool. I've got a cousin who's gay. Amy Liu. Know her?"

Jennifer laughed. "Oh, sure. I'll just look her up in the Big Book of Lesbians. We get a copy of that with the purchase of our first flannel shirt."

"Really?"

Jennifer stared. "No. That was a joke. Come on, dude. Let's find those tools."

The rest of the girls went from cabin to cabin, taking stock of the situation as if they were preparing for a pageant, evaluating the good and the bad. The computers had taken on water and were nonoperational. (Bad.) The guys had, in fact, smashed the radio. (Bad and stupid.) Much of the food had spoiled or gone overboard in the storm. (Bad.) However, the cannons were fully functional. (Good, they supposed. Or at least not bad.) The sails, while torn, had mostly

---

[41] Pharma, the psychedelic jam band popular among suburban faux-hippie kids who follow the band from festival to festival, usually while under the influence of mind-altering substances. Are you a member of the Pharma Army? Join our Phan Club today! Get updates on your mobile! Buy apps! Make a fan page!

survived and were definitely mendable. (Good.) And there were packages of Top Ramen, tins of sardines, crackers, protein bars, oranges, and chocolate. (Okay, good, good, very good, good, and totally awesome.)

"We can fix this if we really work hard," Shanti said, and the girls felt a renewed sense of hope that they might at last get off the island.

"All right, everyone!" Sinjin called. "Time for the old heave-ho!"

"It's like the biggest tug-of-war contest ever," Tiara said as they formed two lines on either side of the ship, dug their feet into the sand, and took up the ropes.

"One, two, three!" Sinjin called. They grunted and groaned, pulled and yanked. It took hours, but finally they dragged the wounded boat ashore.

For the better part of several days, everyone worked together. Using two of the girls' rescued suitcases, they bailed as much water as they could and then scraped the hull of barnacles. Petra and George, whose mother was a seamstress, mended sails. Using the machete, Nicole, Ahmed, and Sosie took turns cutting a tree into lumber. Jennifer had found a tool kit with a hammer and a collection of mismatched nails and was ready to go.

"The wood's not dry enough yet," Adina said. "Trust me. I'm from New Hampshire. You've got to let that season a bit or it'll be useless. It'll just splinter right up on you."

"How long?" Duff asked.

"Not sure. In this sun, maybe a few days. Maybe a few weeks."

The girls' shoulders sagged. There were groans.

"Now, Miss Teen Dreamers," Petra reprimanded in her best Taylor twang. "I cannot believe y'all are grumblin'. I once went an entire year without any wood at all."

Nicole sputtered. Adina fell in the sand laughing.

"What?" George asked.

"Nothing," Petra said and put the lumber out in the sun to dry.

As if summoned, Taylor walked past, a finger pressed to her lips like a preschool teacher motioning for quiet. Her hair was a symphony of snarls and she wore what appeared to be a man's oversize black shirt.

"Is that the girl you told us about? The one who went mad?" George asked.

"Yeah," Petra said sadly.

"Where'd she get that shirt?" Ahmed asked. He sounded worried.

"Don't know. Taylor, where'd you get the shirt?" Adina asked.

Taylor didn't answer the question. "I just need a few things. A lady has to be prepared," she said before disappearing into Tiara's hut and coming out with a strange collection of beauty products. Then she crouched low like a soldier and broke for the jungle.

A loud shriek came from somewhere on the ship, breaking the spell Taylor's appearance had cast. The girls and pirates raced on board to find Miss Ohio racing out of Captain Sinjin's cabin. He stood behind her with his hands up.

"I swear I didn't touch her." His brow furrowed. "Blimey, maybe that's why she's upset. Sorry, luv. D'you want me to ravish you in proper teen-pirate rock-star fashion? A little lovin' followed by a sensitive emo ballad in which I tell you why I can't be your boyfriend? I know you fancy that Fabio Testosterone bloke. Fair enough. Not bad-looking. Mind, he's not a pirate. But you can't have everything."

"Are you okay?" Shanti asked. She gave Sinjin a dirty look and he blew her a kiss.

"Totally fine!"

"Why did you scream?"

"Look what I found!" Miss Ohio pushed past Sinjin and came back brandishing a bottle of expensive rum. "There's two whole cases in here!"

Adina took a small sip and coughed till Mary Lou had to hit her on the back. "Whoa. Lethal," she choked out.

Sinjin sagged against the doorframe. "That's me bloody private stock."

"Not anymore, Cap'n," Petra said, swiping a bottle. "This here's a rum mutiny."

Sinjin smiled slowly as he looked Petra up and down. He stepped closer. "And, um, what if I tried to reestablish my command?"

"That depends. Are you a black belt?"

"No." Sinjin played with the tassels on Petra's scarf.

"Because I am."

"Right." Sinjin wagged a playful finger as he took a solid step back. "You I like. Give us a kiss, luv."

Petra stopped him with a hand. "Does that work?"

"Does what work?"

"That bullshit charm, luv," Petra mimicked perfectly.

Sinjin considered it. "Like a charm."

"Not for me."

"Is that a challenge?" Sinjin smirked.

"No. Statement of fact."

"No likee the charm?"

"Lovee the charm — as long as there's some real behind it. *Gotta keep it real, girl, to keep wit me,*" Petra sang.

"*Real like nature, real like a tree. . . .*" Sinjin twirled and shot his arms upward like branches in perfect imitation of the "Keep It Real, Girl" video.

Petra's mouth opened in astonishment. "You know that song?"

"By heart! Boyz Will B Boyz? Fantastic!"

"Oh. My. God. But you're not a nine-year-old girl."

"I'm offended. Way to put me in a box. I loved Boyz Will B Boyz. Copied all their moves in m' bedroom. Made m' mum buy me one of those godawful outfits with the skinny black leggings and the oversize jackets —"

"Bandanna?"

"Cor blimey! Not complete without the bandanna, was it? And the hair." Sinjin pantomimed a long fall of bangs over one eye. "That hair said 'Shag me, I'm too depressed to own a comb.'"

Petra laughed. "There wasn't any shagging. We were eleven."

"What?"

"Nothing. So, Boyz Will B Boyz fan," Petra recovered quickly, "did you spend fifth grade getting pummeled?"

"Me? Sinjin St. Sinjin?" The captain waved off the suggestion. "Oh, shit yeah. But I stuck to me musical guns. Complete with dance moves. By the way, I hope you note that I am man enough to tell you this. Question is," he purred, "are you woman enough to take it?"

Petra's grin faded. She liked Sinjin, liked his silly humor and the way he didn't take himself too seriously. She wondered what would happen when he knew the truth. Would he be able to see past what was and see what could be?

"There's something I think I should tell you right up front. . . ."

Loud shouts reverberated in the cabin. George ran down the hall. He looked terrified.

"Cap'n! Cap'n!" he said, out of breath. "It's Charlie."

"What's happened?" Sinjin said, all business.

"We were out in the waves, looking for fish, and he got stung. Jellyfish."

Down the beach, Charlie lay sprawled in the pulsing tide, holding on to his right leg. His calf had begun to swell. "Jellyfish," he said through chattering teeth. "Feels like my leg is on fire."

Nicole pushed her way to his side. "It's okay. I'm a doctor," she said, peeling his fingers away to have a look. "We have to stop the poisons from getting into the bloodstream."

"Hold on, Charlie. I'll wash it off." George cupped his hands under the tide.

"No!" Nicole shouted. "I read this in one of my auntie's journals. You can actually activate the poisons that way."

"I saw something like this on Predators of the Deep Week," Chu said. "Bloke got stung by a jellyfish and his whole leg swelled up like a dirigible. They had to cut his leg clean off to save him."

Charlie moaned in pain.

"Not helpful," Nicole said.

"Please," Charlie said, teeth still chattering. "Please help me."

"What can we do? We have to do something!" Miss Ohio said.

"There is one thing that works," Nicole said.

"What's that?" Ahmed asked.

"Urine."

"Gross," Miss Ohio said.

George shook his head. "I'm not peeing on Charlie."

An argument broke out about who would be willing to step forward and do the deed.

"M' bleedin' leg's on fire! I don't care what you do — just do it!" Charlie screamed, but it was as if everyone had been paralyzed.

"Oh for heaven's sake," Petra groused, marching forward. Quickly, she lifted her skirt, dropped her undies, and peed on Charlie's leg.

"Thank you," Charlie whispered.

"You're welcome," Petra said.

The pirates stood dumbfounded as Petra collected herself and smoothed her skirt back into place. "Take a picture. It'll last longer," she said as she walked away.

Captain Sinjin watched her go, openmouthed. Finally, he broke into a huge, face-breaking grin.

"Bodacious!" he said.

Agent Jones dipped the darts in the liquid Mind's Flower. Since the unfortunate incident with Miss Texas he'd had to replace his stock. It made him feel safe to have them. And considering how screw-the-pooch things were going on the island, he needed something to make him feel safe.

Harris breezed past in a Knicks jersey, a ridiculous sweatband across his head. "Looking a little rough today, Jonesy," Harris said.

Agent Jones did not look up. "Did you fix the manual override system?"

Harris put up his hands in a back-off gesture. "Going to. Got a pickup game with some of the black shirts in a few." Harris faked a jump shot. "Nothing but net."

"Don't do that, Harris. It's cliché."

"What crawled up your ass today?"

"Pirates," Agent Jones answered.

Harris nodded. "Whatever floats your boat. Ha! I made a pun. Get it? Boat? Pirates?"

Agent Jones closed his eyes for a second and tried to cast his mind back to a more pleasant time, when he had helped stage a brutal coup in a small South American republic. Bullets flying. Grenades exploding. Pandemonium and blood and screaming in the streets. And no Harris.

"Don't you have something to do?"

"Yeah. Yeah, I might. You don't think I can handle this, do you?"

Agent Jones did not answer.

"Well, you are going to be surprised. I can handle myself just fine. I already did handle myself. Wait, that came out wrong."

Agent Jones packed away the fourth dart. One more to go.

"Don't you want to know what I did?"

"No."

"Just a little."

"No."

"I'll bet you can't guess —"

"No."

Harris was quiet for a full fifteen seconds.

"Fine, I'll tell you. Remember Benny from product development? The one who came up with our Lady 'Stache Off bomb? I killed him."

"Did you find out his contact first?"

Harris's shoulders sagged like a flotation device losing air. "I killed him. Me. I did it."

"Without finding out his contact first."

"See, the way you say it, all negative like that, makes it sound like I messed up."

"You did mess up."

"No. I was *proactive*. The suits love it when you are proactive."

"The agency loves it when you are effective."

Harris's mouth tightened, sphincterlike. "You're a bummer, Jonesy. I'm gonna shoot some hoops."

"You do that," Agent Jones muttered. By the time he finished his darts, he'd made a decision: He wasn't telling the Boss about the pirates.

The elevator carried him down to the fifth floor. The fifth floor housed the weapons and detention cells.

It was time to get some information out of Tane Ngata.

CHAPTER TWENTY-TWO

Rum is made from sugarcane and aged in barrels. There are various forms of rum — dark, golden, white, spiced, aged, flavored — but they all share one distinctive quality: They will get you drunk. And if you've spent quite a bit of time on a deserted island eating coconut and grubs, rum will get you drunk rather quickly and thoroughly.[42]

"Fifteen men on the dead man's chest. Yo, ho, ho, and a bottle of freaking awesome!" Adina said in a loud voice. She slurred a bit so that *awesome* came out more like *aweshumme.* "I changed my mind. I don't want to be an inveshtigative journalist anymore. I want to be a professional rum drinker."

"There are people who do that," Duff said. He'd barely sipped his rum.

"Really? What do you call them?"

"Alcoholics."

"Good to know. *Three little maids from school are we . . .*" sang Adina. "My dads took me to see *The Pirates of Penzance* last year in New York. That song goes very fast. It's a pit . . . a potter . . . pas . . ."

"Patter song?"

"That." Adina took another swig.

"Speaking of fast, you might want to slow down on that grog a bit, matey."

---

[42] *Captains Bodacious* favors Bad Boy Rum: Rebellion in a Bottle. Drink responsibly.

Duff went for the bottle, but Adina yanked it away, spilling some in the process. "That is an example of a man being paternalishtic with a woman."

Duff shrugged. "Or it could be an example of a friend who really doesn't want to clean puke from your hair later."

"You would clean puke from my hair?"

"Well, it wouldn't be my preferred activity, but I would."

"Awww. That . . . is so romantic. Still. My body, my bottle."

"Whatever you say, captain."

The bottle was passed to Shanti, who shook her head. "I'm total straightedge."

She passed it on to Nicole, who took a whiff and made a face. "Yikes. I'm pretty sure I could clean a wound with that." She shoved the bottle at Captain Sinjin, who dabbed some behind his ears like aftershave and then threaded a stale block of marshmallow onto a stick for Petra.

The captain had been watching Petra all night, Nicole noticed. "I need to get something from my hut. Shanti, will you come with me?" She flicked a glance in Petra and Sinjin's direction.

"Sure," Shanti said, picking up on the inference. "Party's moving to our hut, everybody."

"Captain?" Duff asked.

Sinjin glanced furtively at Petra. "Nah. Catch you blokes later."

Sinjin and Petra were alone.

"So."

"So."

"Nice night."

"Mmm-hmm."

"Just so we're clear, you've got a, um, a . . . a . . ."

"Yeah."

"Cool. Just, y'know, making sure."

Petra looked up to the moon as if appealing to its grace. She liked this one and wanted more, but she was afraid there was no hope of that.

"Sorry, I just . . . So you used to be a guy. J. T. Woodland. Of Boyz Will B Boyz."

"Yes."

"Right."

"It's okay. I can tell you're freaked out."

Petra started to get up. Sinjin took her wrist gently. "Well, yeah. But mostly because you used to be in Boyz Will B Boyz. That's unbelievable! I mean, you played Top of the Pops!"

Petra allowed a small smile. He had surprised her. That didn't happen often. She sat down again. "Should I tell you the story?"

"Yeah."

"How much should I tell you?"

"Everything."

She did, and when she finished Sinjin nodded, taking it all in. "Blimey. Your manager sounds like a right bastard."

"Now it's your turn," Petra said. "What about you?"

"Me?" Sinjin thought for a moment. He wasn't good with disclosure. And he had nothing to compare to Petra's tale. What if she thought he was shallow or boring? Unworthy? He wasn't used to being taken off guard, but Petra made him feel both comfortable and nervous at the same time, as if he knew he was safe from the elimination round but he wanted to do his best and impress anyway. More than anyone he had ever met, he wanted her to like him. Because he really, really liked her.

"I grew up in an orphanage in London. Horrible place."

"Really?"

Sinjin nodded. "Mmm. Saffron Hill."

Petra raised an eyebrow. "Saffron . . . Hill?"

"Yes, Saffron Hill. And a terrible place it was. Made us work all the day, never got enough food. Mr. Bumble — the headmaster — used to beat us."

"Sounds like you had a dickens of a time."

Sinjin glanced at Petra's impassive expression. "Indeed, indeed. Finally, at fifteen, I couldn't take it any longer. I ran away. Lived on the streets with m' pal, Jack D —"

"Dawkins?"

"D'you know him?"

"Our mutual friend? Purely coincidental. Go on."

Sinjin's grin spread. "I had great expectations about how my life would go and then . . ."

". . . Nicholas Nickleby! — you fell on hard times and were living in a real bleak house."

"Absolutely. I was totally scrooged."

"What a pip." Petra's smile wobbled into a laugh. "If you figure out how to work *The Mystery of Edwin Drood* into it, I'm yours for life."

Sinjin laughed. It was a good laugh, Petra thought.

"So what's the real story?"

Sinjin shrugged and leaned back. "The real story is dead boring. I grew up in London with me mum and dad, sister, brother, and a parakeet named Benny Hill."

"Come on!" Petra laughed.

"Swear!" Sinjin raised three fingers on his right hand like a scout's pledge. "M' parents are still very much in love. We have this old piano, and on Friday nights we'd sing and eat beans on toast and watch telly all together and have a laugh. It's a nice, comfortable life. That's the tragedy of it. I've got no dark secrets. I love my family and mates. I'm just as content playing darts as I am waiting for the bus. I see beauty in everything. I'm a *happy person*," Sinjin said with utter sincerity. "God. That's awful, isn't it?"

"I think that's lovely."

"Thanks," Sinjin said, almost shyly. Carefully, he tucked a strand of hair behind Petra's ear and let his hand rest for a moment against the soft, wide plain of her cheekbone. "I think you're beautiful. And brave. And really fucking cool. *And* you can make Charles Dickens puns."

Petra leaned the weight of her face into Sinjin's palm. "You know who and what I am. So, if this is just the old curiosity shop, you can stop right now."

Sinjin looked her in the eyes. There was not a trace of smirk in his expression. "'I hope that real love and truth are stronger in the end than any evil or misfortune in the world.'"

"*David Copperfield*," Petra whispered, positioning her lips close to his.

"Why are you bringing magicians into it?" Sinjin said and kissed her tenderly. It was a kiss small in its ministrations but epic in its feeling.

Petra broke the kiss. "Your mates may give you a hard time about this."

"I don't care. If I like somebody, I like her, and that's that." He thumped his chest and made a scowly face. "Let 'em come for me. I will stare down the mob with their pitchforks! I will make a speech about tolerance and love! I will show them the folly of their ways! And then I will grab your hand and run like hell because, Jesus, a mob with pitchforks?"

"Sinjin, I think we may have just found your talent."

"What? Chest thumping?"

"Humanity."

Sinjin wanted to toss off a witty comeback but found he had none. "Thanks, luv," he said softly, sincerely.

"It's the truth, Ruth."

Sinjin put a hand to his chest in mock offense. "I'll have you know it's Shirley. I could never be a Ruth."

"You know what I'm going to give you, Shirley?"

"What?"

"A makeover."

Sinjin crawled over her, going for the kiss. "What if I look Droodful? Edwin Droodful?"

Petra winced. "Oh, good God."

"Sorry."

"Just for that, you're getting the works." Petra took Sinjin by the hand and dragged him into her tent.

Guitar at the ready, Ahmed sidled over to Nicole and Shanti's hut with Charlie in tow. "Can I hang with the nondrinking party? Not a big fan of slurring my speech and walking like a toddler with a poopy diaper."

"Totally," Shanti said, making room.

Ahmed strummed and crooned softly. Jennifer lay her head in Sosie's lap and Sosie stroked her hair absently.

"I feel like we're in one of those old surf movies and we're gonna have to do the Watusi," Nicole said.

"No Watusi for me. I made a pledge of purity," Tiara said.

Shanti shook her head at Nicole. "You've done all you can."

"You know, I've watched Miss Teen Dream every year," Ahmed explained. "I've got five sisters. The best was the time they did the Night of the Living Beauty Queen opening number and everybody looked like zombies in sequins? They were pretending to shamble and eat each other's brains but they still had to smile and shout out their states? That was so wrong, it has its own zip code of wrong."

"You have no idea how hard all that stuff is," Shanti said.

"Doesn't seem so hard," Charlie scoffed.

"Really?" Shanti said. The girls exchanged glances. "So you think you could be in a pageant?"

Charlie shrugged. "Yeah. I do."

"You think you could put up with all the things girls put up with?" Nicole pressed.

Ahmed shook his head. "No way, mate. I was there when my oldest sister gave birth to my nephew? That's hard-core." Ahmed nodded to the ekwe. "Cool drum."

"Thanks. Made it myself." Nicole pounded out a rhythm.

Ahmed bopped his head in time. "Dead brilliant." He plucked

out a tune on his acoustic to accompany her. The others filled in with what they could find — sticks, coconuts, hollowed bamboo. Sosie did a wild Watusi in the sand while Jennifer stood next to her pointing one finger up and down in a deadpan disco.

Summoning up her courage, Shanti sang an Eastern-influenced riff and broke into a rap about living on an island, eating grubs, rescuing pirates, and eating weird berries. Her singing wasn't special, but her rap was funny and tight, and the others whooped and applauded.

"You should record that," Ahmed said.

Shanti adopted a ridiculous gangsta pose. "DJ Shanti Shanti. In the hut," she said and laughed, but she didn't feel like a fraud.

Sinjin called from the beach.

"Our master's voice," Ahmed said and rolled his eyes.

They looped back to the fire. Sinjin was sitting bare-chested with Petra's blue feather boa wrapped around his neck and draped over his shoulder. His long dark curls had been teased and sprayed into a sexy mane. Heavy black eyeliner rimmed his eyes. "Am I not gorgeous? I want to snog myself. I'm like a postmodern Lord Byron."

"You put the ironic in Byronic," Petra quipped.

"Well said, luv."

"Every time he calls me *love*, an angel gets its wings." Petra's sarcasm was unmistakable, and Sinjin seemed to enjoy it.

"Is this our new look, then, Captain?" George asked.

"It's *my* new look. Get your own, mate. Petra was giving me an appreciation for what the other side goes through." Captain Sinjin adjusted the boa. "Got to let a tasteful hint of man-nipple show."

Tiara looked confused. "Men have nipples? Is that new?"

"Men. Have. Nipples!" Adina shouted.

"Adina's been teaching us stuff at Smart School. Like about geography and real estate companies and feminism," Tiara explained to the pirates.

"Cool," said George.

"Yeah. It is." She squinted in thought. "Do you think my new feminism makes me look fat?"

"Darlings, do you know what I think it's time for? I think it's time for your captain to have a soliloquy."

Brittani covered her eyes. "Oh. Um. You can just go behind the tree. That's what we all do."

"No, luv. A soliloquy. A speech." Sinjin toasted another stale marshmallow. "Imagine, if you will, that I'm sitting on the ship's deck, in a spot of moonlight that is doing absolutely fantastic things for my bone structure. Really, I'm like a god right now. Can you see it? I can see it. It's exciting me. Eh, mates?"

"Arrrrggggh!"

"Well said. I didn't set out to become a pirate. I'd hoped to become a barrister. Wear a powdered wig like a sexy beast. Hot!" Sinjin brandished the marshmallow and everyone jumped back. "That was before the tragic fire that took Mom and Dad. I was away at boarding school. Then me and my mates witnessed a murder and had to go on the run."

"I thought that was the story line for the show," Shanti whispered to Nicole.

"Hello! Mid-soliloquy, luv. Give us a moment in the moonlight. Where was I?"

"On the run, Mr. Micawber," Petra prompted.

"Right! On the run." Sinjin's smile faded. "Look. We weren't entirely honest with you before, about being blown off course. The truth is, the ratings for *Captains Bodacious IV* have been down. Really down."

"More people watched *In Your Grandma's Attic*," Chu said. "We couldn't even compete with granny's old brooches going to auction."

"Marketing says pirates are over — it's all about hot trolls now. They've got a hot troll show lined up and ready to go in our time slot: *Trollin' on Delaware Beach.* Ridiculous! Like, who is going to watch a bunch of trolls getting drunk at clubs and trying to entice college girls to their place under the bridge? I heard goats mentioned, too, and that's just wrong."

"It's always about whatever's next," Petra said ruefully. "When I was in Boyz Will B Boyz, they treated us like little gods, then threw us away the minute Hot Vampire Boyz came along. They think they can toss you away like garbage."

"Rubbish," Sinjin said.

"Exactly."

"No, I just like saying *rubbish* better than saying *garbage*. Hotter. But you're right, luv. They're beasts in programming." Sinjin tested the marshmallow's temperature and, finding it satisfactory, fed it to Petra with his fingers. "Anyway, The Corporation was going to cancel us. So we thought, what could we do to really raise the stakes? I know! Let's go rogue! Be real pirates. We thought we'd take a joyride in the boat, get a bit of press, jolt the ratings up again. Except when we got to the docks, we saw something we shouldn't have."

"What was that?" Adina said on a yawn.

"There were these blokes in black shirts. And they were unloading cargo from Corporation boats." Sinjin's face darkened. "Human cargo. Trafficking."

"Whoa," Shanti said.

"They saw us and started shooting! Do you have any idea what it's like to be shot at? It's nothing like in the movies, I can tell you that. It's terrifying, and you feel like you're going to soil your pants."

"I did soil my pants," George said. "Oh. I got new pants. No worries."

Sinjin pointed a finger. "They would have killed the lot of us. Didn't care who we were. So we sailed off and took our chances. It was like reality imitating reality TV, which is one meta more than I like. We disabled the radio so they couldn't track us, hit a squall our second day out, and got blown off course. We've been on the run for two weeks now, trying to figure out what to do and how to survive at sea."

"We've been trying to figure out how to survive, too," Nicole said.

"It's kind of a mixed-up, messed-up world we're inheriting," Shanti said. "When we get back, we should do something to change that."

"Add that to Girl Con," Adina said.

"What's Girl Con?" Ahmed asked.

"It's what we're going to do instead of pageants," Tiara explained.

"Ugh." Adina pushed aside the bottle of rum. "No more rum. I'm sorry. We have to break up, rum. But we'll still be friends." Adina stifled a burp and made a face. "Or not."

Duff stood and offered his hand. "Want to go for a walk on the beach? Fresh air would probably sober you up some."

"I take umbrage at that, sir! I am not drunk."[43] Adina took a step and stumbled over her feet.

Duff helped her up. "I admire a girl who can use *umbrage* even when she's not-drunk drunk."

"Well, a little tipsy, maybe."

Duff squeezed his thumb and forefinger together. "Maybe a little."

"Walkies," Adina said decisively.

Duff lit a torch and they walked along the curve of beach for some time, back and forth, until Adina's head was not so rum-muddled. The tide sucked at the sand beneath their toes. The sea breeze was bracing. Stars glistened in the velvet dark beside a fat white moon.

"Hey! Did you see that?" She pointed in the direction of the volcano.

"What?" Duff said, following her finger.

"Over there, in the fog. I saw lights."

[43] Partying can be very hard on your skin. Be sure to moisturize with an ultra-hydrating serum like The Corporation's new Skin So Right B14 Complex for Total Cell Renewal, made with essential vitamins, minerals, and concentrated yak's bladder. FDA approval pending.

For a split second, the fog pulsed with red light. "Yeah. That's really weird. It's like some kind of signal. Are you sure you're the only people on this island?"

"We haven't seen anybody else. But we haven't explored all the way over there. It's a long way."

"Maybe it's one of those towers that tries to make contact with deep space or track weather."

"Except it's not a tower. It's a volcano. Volcanoes only do volca-noey things. And that" — she pointed to the distant point — "is not a volcanoey thing."

"Yeah," Duff said. "Weird."

Adina gazed at Duff. His bare chest was an advertisement for living shirtless. Oh God. She was objectifying him. Reducing the sum of him to the hotness of his parts. She couldn't help it.

He caught her staring and she looked away quickly.

"Can I ask you something? Why don't you like me?" he asked.

"I-I never said that."

"You didn't have to."

Adina stooped to pick up a shell. "I don't not like you."

"Thank you," Duff said with mock seriousness. "I can't tell you how much that sentence has restored my ego."

Adina laughed. She palmed the shell. "It's just, all the girls were losing their shit over you guys, and I just . . ." She tossed the shell back into the ocean. "I'm immune to the romantic pirate trope. Nothing personal."

"Right. Romantic hero. Got it. And I'm hiding a deep and tragic wound which I mask with arrogant wit and pained grimaces?"

"Absolutely. Comes standard."

Duff picked up a shell, too, and rubbed the sand from it. "What if that weren't a lie?"

"Right," Adina said, saluting him. "Moon's high. Stars are out. Your deep and tragic wound, take one." She clapped her hands together. "Action."

Duff tossed the shell into the sea. "Never mind. Let's head back."

"Wait!" Adina grabbed at Duff's arm. "What did I say?"

"You think I'm an asshole."

"What? No! I — I'm sorry. I'm not great at this."

Duff rocked back on his heels, his hands in his pockets. "You do make it hard for a guy to open up."

"I'm sorry," Adina said. "Deep and tragic wound, take two. For real. How did you end up on this ship of fools?"

Duff walked in the tide and Adina kept pace. "It was my sister's idea, actually. She thought I should audition for season four. She kept bugging me about it."

"Wow. Your sister really wanted the PlayStation to herself, huh?"

"No. She died of leukemia."

Adina closed her eyes briefly in embarrassment. "Oh God. I am so sorry."

"It's okay."

"No, it's not. That was such a jerky thing to say and —"

He held her hand and she felt the warmth in her toes. "Adina, it's okay. Really."

She nodded. "I'm sorry about your sister."

"Thanks," Duff said. He picked up a conch and wiped the sand from it. "Anyway, I went a little crazy after that. Ditching school. Breaking and entering. Me and some blokes I knew stole a car and ended up in jail. I was headed for nowhere good when I saw the casting call notice for season four. The producers were looking for a bad boy. I was looking for a way out of Newcastle." He shrugged. "There you go. Deep and tragic wound explained."

"I'm sorry."

"Hey, do you fancy a swim with me?"

"What, now?"

"Why not?"

"Because . . ." And she couldn't really think of a reason not to.

"Last one in's a rotten egg," he said. He shucked off his pants and shirt, and Adina, who had taken a life drawing class, Adina, who prided herself on her body comfort, that Adina blushed very hard. There was a world of difference between a body in the abstract and a body you desired, and Adina desired Duff's body very much.

"The water's bloody lovely," he called, shaking the water from his hair.

"It'll be fine," Adina said to herself. She stripped down and eased into the waves. He was right. It was bloody lovely.

It is said that the moon is very powerful. It influences tides and weather. It has been worshipped and deified. Perhaps it was the moon that loosened the bindings on the night and the secret wounds held so close. For hours, Adina and Duff allowed the waves — also under the sway of the moon — to carry them as they talked easily about life, school, music, family. The rum lost its effect on Adina, and something more intoxicating took over.

"It's just that my mom had been married five times. Five times!" Adina said. "And every time, she says, 'This is The One, Deen. This is the guy I've been waiting for. My real life starts now.' Except it doesn't." She let a tiny wave ripple her up and back down. "It's so painful to watch. I just don't want to be like that, you know?"

"I know. My dad played the field. Once he and my mom split up, I lived with him. He was always 'the man' and I idolized him. Always out with these beautiful women. Always a bespoke suit and a twenty for the guy at the door — and believe me, he knew all the guys at the door. Real flash." Duff swam long, slow circles around Adina. "But after a while, I realized he couldn't do it."

"Couldn't do what?"

"Couldn't stick with anything — jobs, people, cities. It was a flaw in his design. In the end, he couldn't even stick with me." Duff ducked under the water for a moment. He came back up only to chin level. "He took a job overseas, put me in boarding school. We talk now and then. 'How are things?' 'Fine.' 'Good to hear, good to hear. Got a girl?' 'Got five.' 'There's a good man.' It's like spending hours opening up a perfectly wrapped package only to find there's no present inside. Nothing but empty space."

The moon was in a mood. She shined her full light on the water, and it seemed to Adina that nothing had ever been so beautiful, so clear: the night-gray sand, the sound of her friends' laughter coming from down the beach, the warm press of water against her naked body, and Duff, so near, so right. She liked him. She really, really liked him. He was gorgeous and funny with a sexy British accent and a killer smile and she didn't care if it was like something out of a bad romance novel. How could she stop this undertow from pulling her out to sea? There had to be a flaw. A catch. There always was.

"Hey," she said suddenly. "Do you like Feast for the Fishermen?"

Duff made a face. "The emo band? Sorry. Listening to them's like being beaten with an eleven-year-old's diary. I'd rather take out my own liver with a dull butter knife."

And Adina knew she was in trouble.

Duff McAvoy's lips were incredibly soft, and he smelled faintly of the earth and salt air.

"Is this okay?" he asked, nodding to indicate his room. The ship's cabin was close and the bunk wasn't the most comfortable, but it beat a pallet of palm fronds in the sand.

"Yeah."

"Hold on." He reached over her head and fiddled with something.

"What's that?"

"Nothing. Alarm clock that goes off sometimes. Just turning it off."

Adina could hear the waves as they gently rocked the boat. She had a brief recollection of a bumper sticker she'd seen once — *If this van is a-rockin', don't come a-knockin'* — and it made her giggle.

"What?" Duff asked.

"Nothing," she said and circled his tongue with hers.

His hands were ship-calloused but warm against her breasts beneath her shirt.

"Adina," he moaned. "Don't take this the wrong way, but you have an absolutely bangin' bod."

"No offense taken," she whispered, and kissed him again. He pressed his body against hers. They'd been dry-humping for a while, and Adina felt nearly bruised by it, but she also didn't want to stop.

"Shirt?" Duff whispered between kisses. His fingers waited on the threshold of her hem.

"Shirt," Adina said.

He peeled it off and stopped to admire her bareness. Adina felt suddenly shy and sexy at the same time. Her body and mind were at war. It was almost reaching tilt status. If this was what surrender felt like, she kind of liked it.

Duff's thumbs played at the waistband of her underpants. "Pants?"

"Pants," Adina echoed and kissed his neck.

Duff started the process and Adina finished it by kicking them off with her feet. He slipped a hand between her legs, eliciting a gasp.

She'd never been so nervous, so unhinged with excitement. He moved his hand against her again, and she buried her face against his neck. She could feel the hardness of him against her leg. They pushed against each other in small, rhythmic gyrations that were driving her wild.

"God, Adina." He gripped her shoulders. He rested his forehead on hers. His eyes were closed in some sort of agony-ecstasy. "I really want you. Can I?"

Goose bumps of yes danced down her arms. Adina hesitated. "Condom?"

Duff went still. "Damn." He flopped onto his back to catch his breath. Then he turned to her again, tracing a pattern down her sternum with his finger. "I promise I'll pull out in time."

He'd felt so good pressed against her that she hadn't wanted to stop. Maybe it would be okay. Maybe just this once? No. She'd volunteered at Planned Parenthood one summer. She knew about birth control. She knew it only took once. God, what was happening to her brain?

"Sorry," she said, pressing her palms against his chest. "Safety first. No glove, no love."

He flopped onto his back again and went quiet. Adina felt a pang of worry that she should've said yes. She'd always been in control with guys. But Duff was no Matt Jacobs who hung on her every word. *That's the kind of guy you can lose if you're not careful,* her mother had said once about somebody else's boyfriend, and Adina had growled in disgust and left the table. Yet that thought worked its way into her brain now. She could close a curtain on it, but the thought remained on the other side.

"Duff?" she asked. Her heartbeat thrummed in her ears. "Could you please talk to me?"

"Sorry," he said, breathing deeply. He managed a small smile. "I think my balls are a shade of blue they could never put in a Crayola box. It would frighten the children with its hue of pain."

Adina's laugh was filled with relief. "Sure, I know that color. It's in the box right next to Positive Pregnancy Test Pink."

He stroked her hair and looked into her eyes. She felt her resolve weakening.

"You are killing me. You know that? I promise, extra promise, I'll be careful," he whispered.

"Uncool," Adina said, and she felt tears burning at the corners of her eyes.

"Yeah. It was. I'm sorry," he said. "Forgive me?"

"It's just not cool to pressure somebody."

"I know. You are one hundred percent right. I'm sorry."

Adina wiped at her eyes. "I mean, it would be different if we had a condom."

He kissed the top of her head. "What if I could *locate* a condom?"

She liked the way he said *locate*, all twee, like a schoolmaster. "We're in business, mate," Adina said.

Duff pulled on his pants and gestured at the front of them. "It's like a compass finding true north." Adina laughed out loud. Duff grinned. "Right. Off on a mission of grave condom importance."

He started toward the cabin door, then doubled back for another kiss, then jogged backward, keeping her in his sights. "Do you know how hard it is to move quickly when your balls are approximately the size of cantaloupes?"

"Would you stop it?" Adina chided, giggling, and she wondered when she'd become so . . . girly. She'd never said 'Would you stop it?' like that, ever. It was such an ingenue thing to say, and Adina had never played that role. What was happening to her?

He was back. The condom package dangled from his fingers like a gift bag prize.

"Sinjin's cabin."

"Might've known," Adina said.

Duff dropped trou and pulled the condom on, then positioned himself above Adina. "Now. Where were we?"

He looked into her eyes and Adina felt lost in them, and she had to admit that in this moment, she wanted to lose herself. Nothing else seemed to matter. She imagined the two of them living out their days in a tree house on the island or setting sail through the Caribbean. At night, she would sing ballads she'd written about him. He would read to her from books of poetry. And afterward, in the small cabin, they'd do this, this tangle of bodies, this blurring of the edges that kept people distant and lonely. Her love would heal his bruised heart. He'd want her only, would think of no other girl but her. They would make each other special. The idea was like a drug. This was what girls chased, this feeling. This was what was so hard to admit amidst all the theorizing — that the truth was murkier and deeper and had nothing to do with theory. Desire played by its own rules. She wanted him to want her. Madly. Truly. Completely. His wanting her supplied a missing piece she couldn't supply for herself; no matter what the self-help books said, desirability was something reflected back to you. And right now, she needed that.

Duff's little moans traveled up her spine, made her head buzz. And another thought grabbed hold: *She* was doing this. *She* had the power to do this. That she could be both completely vulnerable and totally in control was mind-blowing.

"Wait," she gasped, pressing her hands against his chest.

"Are you okay? Am I hurting you?"

"No. I mean, yes, I'm okay, and no, you're not hurting me."

"What is it?" He kissed her.

She wanted him. She wanted this. It was her choice.

"Nothing," she said and joined him fully.

Sosie had danced so much, her muscles ached. She welcomed the pain. The pain reminded her that she was a dancer, that she was someone named Sosie. Lately, she wasn't so clear about who or what she was. It was as if she had become merged — SosieandJennifer — and she missed being herself. Alone, she stretched out in the sand down the beach under the swishing leaves of a palm and stared at the sky. That moon was something else. It was a moon built for big dreams and romance.

She knew Jen was probably looking for her — who would want to waste a moon like that? But Sosie didn't want to share this moon and this moment. She wanted it all to herself. And something in that desire made her realize how far she had drifted from that first flush of excitement with Jennifer. Her affections were waning, and she wasn't sure she could get them back. The thought upset her. She didn't want to think about that, and so, despite the throb in her legs, she got up to dance again under the bright full moon.

"That's some moon," Petra said.

"Stop talking about my ass, you beast." Sinjin slipped his arms around Petra's waist, and they laughed and talked while the stars kept watch.

*   *   *

Oblivious to the charms of the moonlight, Agent Jones stood outside the volcano compound, removed his gloves, and lit up his last cigarette of the night. Tane Ngata hadn't told him anything. Tomorrow he'd have to make some decisions about the eco-warrior and those damned pirates before things got too out of hand. He exhaled, and in the stream of smoke, he thought he saw the thin ghost of his father. He stubbed out the cigarette.

Tomorrow.

His business finished, Harris slipped from the pirate ship. He congratulated himself for a job well done before vanishing into the light-mottled night.

From behind the shelter of a tree, Taylor cupped her hand into a familiar motion, waving to the moon as if it were an admiring crowd.

"Pretty, doncha think?" she said.

But the dead man at her feet didn't say a word.

CHAPTER TWENTY-THREE

The next day was a fine, hot one. By noon, Adina had already been for a swim. She'd brought in a mess of fish and descaled them, rinsing them with freshwater and placing them in a barrel for smoking. While she worked, she sang.

"I don't give a damn 'bout my bad reputation," she snarled in her best Joan Jett.

"Hey, Deen," Mary Lou said, sidling up next to her. "You disappeared last night."

"Yeah," Adina said with a wicked smile.

"You *dog*! Details. Now." Mary Lou whacked open a coconut and shared it with Adina while she listened to that tale of the previous night, of the exploits brought about by the mischievous moon. For a moment, Mary Lou was reminded of her adventures with Tane, and it made her sad, but she vowed to forget about it — and him.

"It was probably all a dream, anyway," she said.

"What?"

"Nothing. Sorry."

"We don't say sorry 'round these parts, Nebraska," Adina said in her best sheriff's voice.

"Damn straight," Mary Lou said in hers. "I'm happy for you."

"Thanks," Adina said. "I'm happy for me, too. Hey. I have to go to the ship and get some dry noodles. Come with?"

"Sure."

They climbed onto the ship. From down below came the sound of hammering. The wood had been deemed good enough, and a crew of pirates and beauty queens were about the business of hammering and applying pitch to make the vessel seaworthy again. Once they'd grabbed the food from the kitchen, Adina went to Duff's cabin, but he wasn't there, so she lounged on the bed, smelling his pillow. On a ledge behind that pillow was a small device. *Camera,* said Adina's brain. She ignored it even as her heart tripled its beat: *cameracameracamera.* She pressed REWIND, then PLAY. It was a close-up of Duff, smirking at the camera.

"Hey-oh. Pirate Casanova here. So, we've been shipwrecked, and you will not believe this, but we've been rescued by honest-to-God beauty queens. They are unbelievably beautiful. But there is one girl who is a real challenge: Adina." He laughed and scratched his head. "She hates me, mate. I mean, straight up, *hates* the Casanova. But I'm going to wear her down. It's my mission. It's like my old man says: 'There's nothing more exciting than a challenging woman.' You're watching Confessions of a Pirate Casanova. Peace out."

The camera jumped ahead to darkness. A kerosene lamp.

"Is this okay?" Duff asked.

Adina heard her voice saying "Yeah," and the room swam for her. She smashed the camera to the floor again and again until it was a pulp of metal.

Mary Lou appeared at the door. "Deen? What's wrong?"

Adina's words came out choked. "He . . . he . . ."

Mary Lou looked from Adina to the broken camera. "Oh my God. Adina . . ."

Sobbing, Adina pushed past Mary Lou, past the girls working on the ship, and far down the beach, searching for some place to run to until she realized there was nowhere to go.

"Adina!" Mary Lou shouted, running after her. "Deen. Hey, Deen."

A sharp pain lodged beneath Adina's ribs, making it hard to breathe. "I let him in," she sobbed while Mary Lou held her.

"He's an asshole. He doesn't deserve you."

"I'm just like my mother. I didn't learn anything. I'm just going to make the same stupid mistakes she did!"

"Shh, it's okay," Mary Lou murmured to the top of Adina's sweaty head. She tightened her hold.

"How could I have been so stupid?"

"Hey. Look at me." Mary Lou turned Adina's face to hers. "You didn't do anything wrong."

Adina's crying activated something deep and primal within Mary Lou. She pictured her sister, Annie, standing at the kitchen window, the baby on her hip, the longing stealing over her face like a ghost hand, the muted cries later in the shower. Her mother had told her they were cursed women. But in this moment, it seemed to Mary Lou that the curse was in allowing yourself to be shamed. To let the world shape your desire and love into a cudgel with which to drive you back into a cave of fear. And Mary Lou had had enough.

When her friend had cried herself to sleep, Mary Lou covered her with a palm frond and marched toward the camp. Her strides took on purpose as if her feet were marking a path through the cornfields where wild girls ran unconstrained — and where they hid themselves when the world judged them for their agency. Her palms prickled. Her skin warmed. The wild girl was coming alive. The pack protecting its own.

Everyone was on the beach, having something to eat. Duff sat among them, laughing at the jokes Ahmed and Chu told. A small growl clawed its way up Mary Lou's throat. When she came close, the guys reacted to her wolfish sexuality with an awed silence. She tapped Duff on the arm. He tipped his head back to look up at her. "Hello, Mary Lou."

"Could you stand up, please?"

Duff gave the boys an I-wonder-what-this-is-about look. "Sure thing." He stood and faced Mary Lou. "What's up?"

"This." Mary Lou's fist connected with Duff's face in an audible crunch. He tottered like a drunk. And if there had been a clock on the island, it would have ticked off exactly three seconds before he lost consciousness and went down hard in the sand.

"Ow!" Mary Lou shook out her hand. Then she took her place at the fire and drank the rest of Duff's coconut milk, drinking till she was sated.

"Your friend's a real asshole," Petra said to Sinjin when they were alone in her hut.

"A: Duff's not my friend. He's a bloke I'm in a show with. B: He is, in fact, an asshole. And C: Why do I feel like you're pissed at me? I didn't do anything."

Petra took a good look at Sinjin. "Are you blogging about us?"

"No, luv, it's *snogging*. That's our word." Sinjin went for a fake rim shot.

"I'm serious."

"I would never," Sinjin said, and Petra felt that this was true. He opened his arms and she went to him.

"Can you believe that Duff guy?" Jennifer said. She and Sosie had applied another coat of pitch to the ship. They stood in the surf trying to wash the sticky stuff from their hands before it set into hard, dark lines.

Sosie signed a word and Jennifer smirked. "Totally." She stepped closer and kissed Sosie's neck. "I would never do that to you."

Sosie tensed and turned her head.

"What's wrong?"

"Nothing. I just don't want this to stick."

"Okay," Jennifer said, trying to ignore the tiny warning alarms going off inside her. They washed in silence until Jennifer could no longer take it. "Are you sure everything's okay?" she pressed. Her heart beat quickly.

Sosie glanced at Jennifer, and for a moment, she thought about saying all was well. But it wasn't. The uncertainty she'd felt last night had blossomed into a sure distance she couldn't ignore. Jennifer was great — loyal, kind, good, nicer than Sosie by far. The truth was that she liked Jennifer . . . but not as much as Jennifer liked her. Sosie was no Duff, but she knew she'd end up breaking Jen's heart all the same. It was better to end it now before things got too ugly.

"I'm just not sure I want a girlfriend right now," Sosie said at last, feeling lame.

Jennifer went cold inside. "Are you breaking up with me?"

Sosie nodded slowly.

"But . . . why? What did I do?"

"Nothing," Sosie said.

"What can I do?"

Sosie hesitated. "Nothing," she signed.

The waves licked at Jennifer's tanned knees. The sand tugged at her toes, making her sink in. She tried very hard not to cry, but two tears trickled down her cheeks anyway.

"I'm sorry," Sosie said. "Can we still be friends?"

Friends. Funny how a word could be welcome in one way and horrible in another. Jennifer wanted more than that. The hurt was a pain in the center of her chest. It was hard to breathe. Friends? How could she see Sosie every day and pretend she didn't want to kiss her? To hold her? To share everything?

Jennifer wiped away her tears with the back of her hand. "No. Sorry. The Flint Avenger travels solo."

She yanked her toes free of the sand and fought the undertow back to the shore. Sosie watched her go, feeling a terrible mix of relief and regret. Looking down, she saw that her hands were splotched with tree sap. She'd waited too long to wash off the pitch, and it had set across her palms like a brand.

COMMERCIAL BREAK

The following preview has been approved for all audiences by the Motion Picture Association of America, Inc.

VOICEOVER
All Charlie Tanner wanted was to live happily ever after.

OPEN ON: Split screen from WEDDING DAY & WEDDING DAY 2, with an attractive young woman, CHARLIE TANNER, walking down the aisles in two very different wedding dresses. Her hair is perfectly highlighted.

VO, CONT'D
But Charlie has been unlucky in love.

CUT TO: Same split screen, but with images of Charlie catching husband #1 kissing another woman and watching husband #2 being led off to jail in chains for a massive embezzlement scheme.

CUT TO: Montage of Charlie getting promoted at her PR firm, attending events, going to a concert, and eating dinner alone.

VO, CONT'D
Now Charlie Tanner is through with living for someone else. She's calling her own shots and making her own rules.

CUT TO: Charlie playing poker with her best friends. Bottles of beer sit on table.

CHARLIE
I kept thinking, what's wrong with me? And then I had an epiphany: Maybe it's not me who's screwed up. Maybe it's this

whole crazy notion that we're supposed to do nothing but shop, have makeovers, and chase after some unattainable idea of romance or settle for some jackass rather than figuring ourselves out and living life to the fullest that's wrong.

FRIEND
No. I'm sure it's you.

VO, CONT'D
Things are finally going right for Charlie . . . until she meets Mr. Wrong.

CUT TO: Charlie entering her boss's office. An attractive but boorish man sits sprawled on the sofa, his shirt untucked, a beer in his hand.

CHARLIE'S BOSS
Charlie, meet your new client, Dick Connor, author of *He's Never Going to Call You Unless You Follow These Rules*.

DICK CONNOR
You know, if you want to have sex with me, you're going to have to step it up, sweetheart. (He swats her butt.) Where's my beer?

CUT TO: Charlie hanging out in a park with her best gay friend. They are having a picnic.

CHARLIE
He's crude. He's sexist. He thinks Hooters is fine dining and women are only good for sex and getting his breakfast.

OBLIGATORY GAY FRIEND
Oh my God. He sounds so hot.

CHARLIE

I hate everything about Dick Connor. He makes me feel awful
and inadequate.

OGF

That is actually a sign of true love.

CHARLIE

I don't think so. . . .

OGF

(giving her a pitying look over his glasses)
Charlie, honey, you're almost thirty. It doesn't pay to have
too much self-esteem. Come on. Let's shop for heels and a
push-up bra.

CUT TO: Montage — Charlie getting primped and powdered
and squeezed into a tight black dress. Charlie entering a
ballroom and catching the eye of every man, including Dick.
Charlie slow dancing with Dick. Charlie seeing Dick with another
woman. Charlie crying. Eating ice cream. Watching Home
Shopping Network. Staring wistfully at a store window filled with
wedding dresses.

CUT TO: Charlie sitting with her grandma in her cutesy
retirement community.

CHARLIE

(tearful)
What if Mr. Wrong is the best I'm going to get?

GRANDMA

(patting her hand)
Love means making sacrifices. I know these things. I'm old.

CHARLIE

Grandma, you're on Alzheimer's meds and you think my shoe is the cat.

GRANDMA

(glaring)

That's a bad kitty.

VOICEOVER

From the makers of *Wedding Day* and *Wedding Day 2* comes a story about third chances, awesome dresses, exciting makeovers, and giving up the life you've made for the romance you're not complete without, for better or worse.

WEDDING DAY 3: THIRD TIME'S THE CHARM, Starring Jessica Everett, Chase Random, Rupert Falderal, Bonnie Sagcard, and Ima Goldengirl as Grandma.

Written by: The Committee
Directed by: David L. Evithan
Produced by: The Corporation

This film is not yet rated.

CHAPTER TWENTY-FOUR

It was a fine day of blue, cloudless skies and unhurried winds. The sort of day that inspires confidence in the state of the world. If Taylor had been back home, she would have considered it a perfect tanning day and gone for a fresh coat of color. But she had more important things to think about just now. She had work to do, and as she worked, she hummed an old show tune. It was a song she had used in a previous pageant, a song about how you couldn't get a man with a gun, which was silly — of course you could get just about anything with a gun! But it calmed her to sing it now as she attached the red, blue, and white wires to the statue of Miss Miss.

Heavenly stars, but she'd had a busy few days! After attacking the guards, she'd relieved them of their weapons and buried them in a shallow storage pit beneath Our Lady. The trip wires had not been easy to rig. She'd had to go deeper into the jungle to find vines that were strong enough, and she'd had to make sure they were low enough to the ground so as not to be seen. One wrong step and that person would be hoisted high into the trees to dangle by a foot until they passed out or Taylor felt merciful, whichever came first. Probably the passing out. She'd dug two deep holes. These she covered with leaves and branches and marked with tiny crosses so that she would remember not to step there. But oh, there was so much to do still. It was just like getting ready for pageant time, and it filled Taylor with a happy sense of purpose. Ever since getting shot by those darts, Taylor had had a teensy bit of trouble organizing her thoughts. That's what lists were for. When Taylor competed, she always made lists.

They were very helpful. She made one now in her head. It went like this:

1. Melt down jewelry for arrowheads
2. Dig pit
3. Surveillance
4. Construct bows
5. Practice!
6. Interview portion
7. Projectile launch/avocado mask
8. Reassemble AK-47
9. Construct bomb
10. Moisturize

Yes, lists were essential if you were going to be a serious competitor. And nobody was more serious about competing than Taylor Rene Krystal Hawkins.

"Miss Texas, who's got her wires crossed," Ladybird Hope cautioned. She'd changed into a sarong and put a flower in her hair, which was, of course, just perfect.

"Oh my stars!" Taylor rethreaded the wires. She shook her head at her clumsiness. "That's almost like wearing red for evening gown. Everybody knows the judges like pastels."

"Amen." Ladybird Hope peeled a banana. She had a French manicure. "You're gonna need a what next, Taylor?"

"An accelerant."

"That's my girl."

Taylor opened the jar of Lady 'Stache Off cream and put it in position. Under the label, the jar had a small radioactive symbol. "There. This Miss is ready to greet her subjects."

Ladybird Hope patted Taylor lightly on the back. "I'm so proud of you, Taylor. You really are a Miss Teen Dream."

"Just hearing that from you, Ladybird, well, it's like I've already won." Taylor's eyes misted with tears.

"None of that, now. Save the tears for your victory walk. Otherwise it looks premature and the judges will think you're cocky. Or emotionally unstable. Or premenstrual. None of that will get you a crown."

"You're so right. Buck up, Miss Texas." Taylor dabbed at her lashes with her knuckles. Then she tested the digital watch she'd taken off the guard's wrist. It was a standard issue military timepiece and it counted down just fine.

"It's a whole new world of pretty. . . ." She sang the Miss Teen Dream theme song as she worked. She clicked the watch into place and closed Our Lady, smoothing out the wrinkles on her sash. With that, the sculpture was not only beautifully accessorized, she was fully armed.

"Who messes with Miss Teen Dream?" Ladybird Hope asked.

"Nobody," Taylor answered. She smeared mud and tree sap to camouflage her face and arms till she seemed an outgrowth of the island. She almost sensed the black shirts before she saw them on their way to the beach and the other girls.

"I think they might be messing with our pretty. What do you think we should do, Miss Texas?" Taylor whispered. She wasn't sure if she'd said it aloud or inside her head. It was hard to tell the difference anymore.

"A Miss Teen Dream doesn't rely on others to solve her problems. She tackles her issues head-on, with a smile and a wave," said her other self.

Tears filled Taylor's eyes. "You're so right."

"Of course I'm right," said her other self. "I wrote the book on right. Silent Somersault?"

"I think so, yes."

When Taylor had won Miss Dustbowl County, she'd wowed the judges with her signature gymnastics move, the Silent Somersault, a series of revolutions that happened so fast, no one could hear her feet and hands touching earth. Now she flew in a beautiful blur of spandex and sequins, a girlish ninja star arcing through the air. And when she brought her feet down on the men, snapping their necks like cheap drugstore straws, they never heard a thing. Carefully, quickly, she pulled their bodies into a nearby ravine.

"Cover 'em up good," said the other Taylor from her perch in a tree. "They'll come looking. And take their walkie-talkies, too."

Taylor nodded, but secretly she worried that the judges wouldn't like this. It seemed a little *overt*. She might lose a point or two and have to make it up in swimsuit or talent. But it had to be done.

With a heavy sigh, Taylor examined the hands that had done this thing, *her* hands, as if seeing them for the first time. The long, slim fingers. The mud-caked knuckles. The strip of pale skin on her fourth finger where her sweet sixteen ring had been. She turned her hands over and over, palms to backs, backs to palms, marveling. She bent her fingers to inspect her nails and the frown returned.

No. This was all wrong. What had she done? When did this happen?

"Oh, no," she said as her eyes filled with tears. "I broke a nail."

CHAPTER TWENTY-FIVE

The next morning, Duff found Adina by the lagoon tending to the fishing lines. His eye was swollen and purplish, and Adina wished she could feel some satisfaction that Mary Lou's punch had been so effective, but she only felt the pain of betrayal.

"Adina. Can you just stop for a sec and listen to me?" he said.

"I'm working. You'll have to deal." She expertly repaired a section of the line that had been nibbled by fish.

"I'm sorry," Duff said at last. "I never meant to hurt you."

Adina allowed a small "ha!" She kept her focus on the line as she blinked back tears.

"I don't blame you for hating me."

"Gosh, it's so nice to have your approval," Adina growled.

Duff dug at the sand with a stick. "The producers asked us to keep personal blogs to attract a fan base. Sinjin was the most popular, of course. I couldn't think of anything to say. I mean, I'm just a bloke on a boat trying to figure out who I am and what I want to do." He offered a small, apologetic shrug. "Anyway, I was reading about Casanova, and something clicked. I settled on that persona and started blogging about my supposed conquests. I was getting more hits a day than the other chaps, and the producers were talking spin-off show and . . . I just didn't know how to stop." Duff waited for Adina to say something. When she was quiet, he said, "I'm really, really sorry. I'm a messed-up guy. But I do really like you, Adina. I didn't lie about that part."

Adina's mind was tempted with flea-market promises: He's only lost. Confused. Wounded. You could save him. Change him. *Make* him. It would hurt a little. Maybe a lot. And then he would love you forever. And his love would prove your lovability. She remembered what her mother said the day Johnny, husband #3, moved the rest of his guitar collection into the rented U-Haul and drove it away to live with a Hooters waitress named Fragile. Her mother had curled her hair and put on a fresh coat of lipstick and stood on the porch, watching the U-Haul's shadow clawing along the street. Adina waited for her mother to throw her coffee cup. Call him a bastard. Do a little dance. Instead, she said softly, "What's wrong with me?" Adina had hated her mother for saying that. And she hated that some part of her asked the same thing now.

Don't cry, she told herself, and yanked hard on the fishing line, stumbling as she dislodged whatever was stuck.

She screamed as the bloated body washed toward her.

"Something's not right on this island," Sinjin said between kisses, and Petra grew quiet for a moment.

"Was that a double entendre?"

"No, luv. I'm serious. That girl — the barmy one . . ."

"Taylor."

"Yeah. Ahmed said she was wearing a man's black shirt. Where did she get it?"

"Maybe it was in her luggage all along?" Petra said, but she didn't really believe it.

Sinjin mulled it over. "Say, you're not, like, a competing show designed to give our show a hard time? Like a Survivor Versus Survivor concept? And you're the surprise we have to figure out. Like you're really the Sirens who lure us off course and we have to resist you."

"Did you just make a reference to Greek literature?"

"I suppose I did."

"Totally crushing on you in a Homeric way."

Sinjin waggled his eyebrows. "I fancy a bit of the Homeric way." Petra went in for a kiss and Sinjin stopped her lips with his fingers. "You're sure you're not some sort of creepy double agents connected with those black shirts?"

"Cross my heart and hope to die."

"Give us a kiss and make an honest pirate of us," Sinjin said.

"Oh my God! Adina just found a body," Nicole said, racing by.

"A body!" Mary Lou said, her heart beating faster. Could it be Tane? Was that why she hadn't seen him? She tried to put that thought out of her mind as she ran toward the lagoon with the others.

They dragged the body onto the beach and rolled him over.

He was wearing a black T-shirt. But other than that, there was no way to know who he was.

CLASSIFIED
THE REPUBLIC OF CHACHA
13:45 HOURS

The red phone rang and MoMo grabbed it quickly. "It is you, my dove?"

"Now, who else would it be, MoMo?"

MoMo smiled, then frowned. "When is MoMo to receive his weapons, Ladybird? Already, I have funneled one billion dertmaz into your account through secret means and killed everyone involved with the transaction. Also, you have said unkind things about The Peacock in the press."

"Oh now, MoMo, you know that's just politics. Once I'm president, I'll lift the sanctions against your country."

"You are the femur of my institution, Ladybird Hope. Long may you wave. When you are president, our union will set free the doves of entropy. When can we be together as we were in the hot tub here at Camp Peacock?"

"Remember, MoMo, we've gotta keep that part a secret."

"We can't go on together with suspicious minds." MoMo giggled.

"That giggle is disturbing, MoMo. I've told you about that."

"I am sorry, my dove. It's just that I have been thinking about our agreement and making the amends to it." MoMo played the finger drum set he kept on his desk beside a bust of himself and one of General Good Times.

"You see, I have in my possession a very special video, which would make your election to president very difficult."

"I thought you destroyed that, MoMo."

"I hear you might get rid of the MoMo."

"Now, why would I do that?"

"I am thinking a June wedding. Is very nice in the ROC in June."

"MoMo? Have you been nipping off the crazy juice again? You and I can't get married."

"Why not? Is perfect way to solve all our problems. Will be like royal wedding, and our faces will be on plates for the peoples to eat from. And we could to have the situation comedy on television. Maybe with nutty neighbor who borrows our plunger and makes to ogle the breasts of our daughter all the time."

There was a moment of silence on the other end.

"Okie dokie, Peacock," Ladybird purred. "First we do the arms deal and you secure The Corporation's rights in the ROC. Then we'll plan the wedding. Three days."

"I count the time like my hemorrhoids."

"TMI, MoMo."

"TMI to you, too, my darling."

Agent Jones had been summoned to the conference room. *Urgent* was the only word on his pager. Ladybird sat waiting for him on the flat-screen TV. She did not look happy.

"Agent Jones. Report on the girls."

"Um, no change. They're doing okay. In fact, they're proving to be surprisingly resourceful."

"Resourceful? You want to talk resourceful? Resourceful is being from a backwater town in Idaho and making it from Miss Teen Dream to Corporation stockholder to presidential candidate without letting your lipstick go cakey once, Agent Jones. Resourceful is trying to figure out what to do when your secret arms deal and your foolproof plan for gettin' elected go to H-E-double-hockey-sticks." On the screen, Ladybird Hope spray-painted an assault rifle with a stencil of her name in bubble letters.

Agent Jones stood with his hands behind his back. He knew from experience that silence was often the best offensive. In a moment, Ladybird inspected her stencil work and smiled. "I do love me some arts and crafts. Anyway. Me and the Board have talked it over, and it seems to us that we're missing a valuable opportunity here. Why just drill when we can take over the whole dang country?"

"I'm not sure I'm following. And it's 'The Board and I.' *Me* is objective case."

With tweezers, Ladybird added tiny sequins to the wet paint on the *i* in *Ladybird*. "MoMo B. ChaCha is a threat. Cost analysis of the pros and cons of the situation indicates that we need to eradicate the complications arising from the instability of the appearance of the girls on the island and strategize turnkey applications for phasing out less profitable product lines across all platforms."

Agent Jones took a moment to digest this. "You want me to kill The Peacock."

Ladybird continued her ministrations on the gun. "What we need to do is maximize the global content of our security infrastructure by curtailing non-dividend-paying future living possibilities through strategic planning initiatives at the weaponized level while strategizing turnkey profitability of the Republic of ChaCha through the implementation of dynamic platforms that will drive market share, synergize global objectives, and maximize global content."

"So . . . kill." Agent Jones made a gun motion with his thumb and forefinger.

"In a manner of speaking." Ladybird sipped coffee through a straw. "What if we could catch MoMo in an act so heinous, so terrible, that the entire world would be on our side? We'd be justified in killing him. The world would thank us for doing its dirty work — and for marching right into his backward country and setting up a democracy. Along with lots and lots of cute shops."

"MoMo's already racked up a pretty impressive list of atrocities. What could you possibly nail him for that would be so effective?"

Ladybird managed a small smile. "Killing a bunch of teen beauty queens on live TV oughta do it, doncha think?"

Agent Jones had staged assassinations and coups. He'd taken out KGB agents and lowlife informants and still managed to sleep at night. Sacrifices had to be made for national security. But this wasn't about security; it was about profitability, the country as corporation. It almost made him nostalgic for the Cold War.

He cleared his throat. "How will we manage that?"

"It's time to bring the girls in. I'll announce the rescue on *Barry Rex Live.* We'll have a surprise for the public. Imagine: staging the Miss Teen Dream Pageant right there on the island! It'll be a ratings bonanza! Then, just before the crowning of the new Miss Teen Dream, MoMo's guards will leap out with their shiny new guns and kill the girls."

"How are you going to get MoMo to do that?"

"Silly. MoMo's guards won't actually *do* it. It'll be Corporation black shirts dressed up like Republic of ChaCha soldiers. MoMo will die in the resulting bloodbath. The world will see it live on TV, and once it's on TV, it's true. I promised The Corporation ratings, and I will deliver. With the world's outrage on our side, we will march into the ROC to stabilize the country. The whole operation will be contracted out to The Corporation. Oh, and I am seeing huge merchandising opportunities with this. What do you think of T-shirts that say *ROC and Roll?*"

"That is quite possibly the most ludicrous thing I've ever heard."

Ladybird Hope cocked her head and smiled. "Well, thank you, Agent Jones. It's sweet of you to say so."

When Agent Jones was eleven, his dad had called him into the front room and explained that there comes a time in every person's life when a choice defines him.

"Remember that," he'd said. He was wearing the clown suit and full makeup. Since he'd been laid off eighteen months earlier, it was his only source of income.

"Yes, sir," Agent Jones had said. He was Bobby Jones then.

Then his dad laced up the multicolored shoes, put on the red felt nose, squeaked his bike horn, and drove away to make balloon animals at a six-year-old's birthday party. Afterward, he stopped off at Tom's Bar for four boilermakers and wrapped his sedan around a tree. The paper used a photo from the party for his obituary. The last image Agent Jones would ever have of his father was of a defeated man in a red nose holding a balloon animal.

That image came back to him now as he stood with the requisition form for coffee in one hand and the form for early retirement in the other. He could opt out. It would mean he'd never hit the top, never hit that sweet spot in his career that inspired envy and respect from other men. On the other hand, somebody else would have to be in charge of killing the beauty queens.

Harris sauntered over, scratching his belly. "Hey, dude. So. Hear they're cutting back on the pension plan. Sucks. Check this, though: I've been fast-tracked for management. Made a PowerPoint about how awesome I am and my idea about a show where contestants literally have to eat one another to survive? The suits loved it! I could just be your boss soon. Filling out another form for Hazelnut, huh? I hear the twentieth time's the charm." Harris overfilled his cup, spilling coffee on the counter, which he did not clean up. On the way back to his desk, he slapped hands with one of the black shirts. "Bros before hos!" he said, laughing.

Agent Jones tore up the early retirement form.

CHAPTER TWENTY-SIX

Not all men were like Duff and Billy and Jacques-Paul. Mary Lou knew this. Her father was kind and sure of her. He let her ride the combine with him and taught her to use the controls just like he'd done with her brothers. And there was Tane. Where was he? He'd promised to come back. Adina would get all cynical, say, "What did you expect?" But Mary Lou had smelled his scent, had examined his good hands. She knew Tane was a man of his word, and the fact that he hadn't come back worried her. What if her prince was in some sort of trouble? What if he needed her help?

Mary Lou had had enough of waiting and wondering. It was time to take action. While the others were sleeping, she crept from her hut. Petra woke momentarily from where she lay cuddled next to Sinjin. His arm was still wrapped around her, and Mary Lou was happy that Petra had found someone, too.

"Wh-where you going, Nebraska?"

"Off to find my prince," Mary Lou answered.

"That's nice. Very romantic." Petra mumbled. She rolled over and went back to sleep.

Mary Lou ran into the jungle as she had many times before. She kept low to the ground, inhaling, searching for Tane's scent, her wild-girl senses alert. She passed Taylor's lair deep in the jungle. A small fire crackled, casting long shadows across the towering form of Miss Miss. The sculpture seemed alive. Taylor stepped out from behind it and Mary Lou saw that she had an AK-47.

"Hey, Taylor. Where did you get that gun?"

"A Miss Teen Dream must be prepared at all times," Taylor answered in a hollow voice.

A trickle of sweat dripped down the front of Mary Lou's neck. "Have you seen my prince? He's about so tall with long black hair and tattoos on his shoulders. His name is Tane?"

Taylor rested the gun lengthwise at the back of her neck and let her arms drape over it in front. "What would you do if you faced a grave threat, Miss Nebraska?"

"What do you mean?"

"Miss Nebraska, you are not prepared for this pageant."

Mary Lou glanced nervously toward the jungle on the other side of Taylor. "I need to find Tane."

Taylor stepped aside. Mary Lou had almost passed when she heard Taylor whispering, "Lies. All lies. Careful."

And then Mary Lou was running. She was so spooked that she nearly missed the backpack. There it was in the bushes: *Tane Ngata. Department of Ornithology.* Heart beating fast, Mary Lou shouldered it and set off after her prince with renewed determination. His scent was strong now. She followed it in the direction of the volcano. When she got close, she saw a flash of white light at the top of the volcano, like a signaling tower of some sort. Shadowy figures led a shackled, hooded man. She spied the tattoo on his shoulder. Tane! Keeping low, she crept along the bush line.

A man ripped the hood from Tane's head. The man wore sunglasses even though it was night. "What are you doing here? Who are you working for?"

"I told you, mate. I'm just an ornithologist on a research trip."

"Ornithologist my ass. Put him in solitary."

The others dragged him — dragged her Tane! — toward the volcano. She watched, astonished, as they flipped up a panel in the rock and entered a code and a door slid open, revealing another world inside. She had to warn the others. She had to rescue Tane. She needed to get away from here right away.

She turned to run and heard the click of the gun pressed to her temple.

Sinjin watched Petra sleep for some time, weighing his options. Finally, he woke the others and had them meet up by the ship.

"What's up, Cap'n?" Ahmed asked, wiping sleep from his eyes.

Still in Petra's bathrobe, Sinjin paced on the narrow strip of sand. "Lads, something's a bit dodgy here. That black shirt couldn't be a coincidence. He must've followed us here."

"How? We rubbished the radio."

"Don't know. But you can't deny that body was one of them. And if they've found us, the ladies are in trouble as well."

"Cor," George said, shaking his head. "What we gonna do?"

Sinjin cast a glance toward the camp where the girls still slept. "We've got to leave. Now."

"We can't just leave the girls here without so much as a 'ta for the grubs,'" Ahmed insisted. "They'll think we're absolute wankers."

"Better that than we put them in danger, yeah?"

The pirates fell into hushed argument.

"We don't even know if the ship'll hold, Captain," Duff said.

"Well, we'll just have to suck it and see, mate. We'll find land and rustle up help."

Ahmed rubbed at his chin. "What if this is a trap? What if it's what they expect us to do?"

"Only one way to find out," Sinjin said. "Look, are we naff reality-TV, fake rock-star pirates, or are we something more? Time to be noble, lads. Who's with me?"

"Aye," they whispered in unison.

They took just enough provisions to last a few days, then the pirates pulled up anchor and pushed the boat quietly into the deeper water. In the moonlight, the beach where the girls still slept was a series of undulating curves.

"I hope they'll be all right," Sinjin said. "'It is a far, far better thing that I do, than I have ever done.'[44] Take care, Petra."

"Captain?" Ahmed asked. The men looked to him for orders.

"Hands on oars," he commanded.

The pirates bent over their paddles, rowing in rhythm until they were a safe distance from the island. They hoisted the sails and headed out to sea.

In the sheltering canopy of a giant tree, Harris used his binoculars to watch them go. Good. They'd taken the bait. He'd left them a little present on the boat, a bomb made from Lady 'Stache Off. Once they were farther out to sea, he'd detonate it using his phone. Jonesy might not have told him about the pirates, but Harris knew. He didn't need Agent Jones telling him what to do. Everyone misunderestimated Harris Buffington Ewell Davis III. He snickered, thinking about how he'd set this up by himself. Now The Corporation would have to see that he was a player. CEO by the time he was thirty? Shoot, he'd be running the ROC before he was twenty-five.

[44] Play the *A Tale of Two Cities* head-lopping game, available as a Corporation Phone app. Void where prohibited in states where the school board has banned *A Tale of Two Cities* because Charles Dickens is clearly a pornographic name.

CHAPTER TWENTY-SEVEN

Nicole woke with a feeling of unease she could not shake, though she couldn't say why. Perhaps it was left over from her dream in which an unseen monster made its way toward her small fishing village in Japan, and she was expected to do battle with it. She left the hut and made her way to the beach, where she realized that something really *was* wrong. The pirate ship was missing. So were the pirates. So, too, were the girls' stores of rainwater and smoked fish.

"Bastards!" Adina growled. The girls had assembled in their horseshoe formation.

"And after all we did for them," Miss Ohio said.

"We fixed their freaking ship!" Jen kicked at a tree. A coconut dropped dangerously close to her head.

"I got their computer up and running," Shanti added.

"I let Sinjin have my best heels," Petra said. She wanted to cry, but she was too angry. She looked around, counting. "Hey, anybody seen Mary Lou this morning?"

They searched the camp, the lagoon, the fishing lines, the jetty, everywhere they could think to look. Mary Lou was nowhere to be seen.

"Do you think she went with the pirates? Or maybe they kidnapped her and held her for her booty."

"Booty is treasure, Tiara."

"Oh. Noted."

"She said she was going off into the jungle to search for her prince," Petra said.

"Great. Swell," Adina growled. "Stupid romantic fantasies can get a girl killed."

"That's just being bitter," Petra said.

"Yeah? Your BF just sailed away with our food, water, and your best shoes, Petra!"

Petra winced. "Harsh. I have faith in Sinjin. He'll send help."

"Oh my God. You guys just don't get it, do you? *We got hosed!* We got all moony-eyed over a bunch of pirates and let everything go just to take care of them. Even on an island in the middle of nowhere, we can't seem to change the dynamic. Pathetic."

Jennifer raised her hand. "Exception to the rule."

"You've got your own distractions." Adina jerked her head toward Sosie, and Jennifer blushed. "Now, listen up. It's your team leader, Miss New Hampshire, speaking. Here's the plan: Pack whatever you've got. We are going to march into that jungle to find Mary Lou, and then we are going to bring Taylor back, and then we are going to build our own freaking ship or rocket or Sparkle Pony from Hell and get the hell off this island! Screw this waiting around. No one is coming. It's up to us. But we are not leaving without our friends."

The girls armed themselves with sticks and small rocks, curling irons and bottles of tanner.

Petra brought along a can of hair spray. "Anybody or anything messes with me and they will get a face full of chemical nasty that will stick their eyes open for weeks."

They set off into the dense growth, and they weren't coming out until the job was done.

They came upon the Empire of Taylor. It was like a forgotten hermitage — the cave hidden beneath the growth, the strange fertility goddess statue of Our Ladybird with her tattered Miss Miss sash in place. But it was well camouflaged, as if it had long been part of the island. As if Taylor were hiding in plain sight.

Taylor had built another weird sculpture. This one looked a lot like a catapult. She opened a jar of Lady 'Stache Off and emptied the contents inside, adding the bleach from the girls' teeth-bleaching trays.

"Hey, Taylor. What're you doing?" Adina called.

"Getting ready for the pageant. It's very important, Ladybird."

"Have you seen Mary Lou at all?"

Taylor cocked her head to one side as if listening to music only she could hear. "Five-six-seven-eight. And step-ball-change!" Taylor launched into a series of dance moves punctuated by ninjalike kicks and strikes. "Don't believe their lies, Sparkle Ponies. They don't want to save us."

Taylor shimmied up a tree, swung to another, and disappeared in the unkempt green canopy overhead.

"Man. I thought she was bad before." Nicole shook her head.

The girls pressed on. The jungle was thicker here, darker. Every breath was a struggle.

Shanti gasped. "You guys." She held up Mary Lou's St. Agnes medal.

Adina swallowed hard. Anything could have happened to her out here. "We're going to find her."

"I want to go back," Tiara said. "This isn't fun anymore. I'm scared."

"What if an animal got to her?" Nicole said in hushed tones.

"We're not going back. We're not giving up on her. We're all we've got. Don't you understand?" Adina was near tears. She was exhausted, so exhausted that she thought she imagined the sound. It was the faint rumble of a car engine, like something remembered from a dream. Something that reminded her of normalcy.

A long, Jeep-like vehicle crested the hill, trampling down bushes as it came. The headlights blinded the girls till they had to put up their arms to block the sudden light. They heard the motor stop. A car door opened.

A man in camouflage and mirrored sunglasses blocked the army transport's headlights. He stood, hands at his hips. He wore a reassuring smile.

"Well," he said, "we sure are glad to find you girls."

CHAPTER TWENTY-EIGHT

In the back of the transport, the girls talked with the manic quickness of those who've been given second chances. "Like, I can't wait to take a shower and put on clean clothes," Shanti said.

"I'm going to catch up on Ragnaroknroll, find my guild," Jennifer said.

"I am going to eat a piece of cake the size of Petra's head," Sosie said.

"I hope you're hungry. My head has a circumference of twenty-four inches," Petra shouted over the wind, and they all laughed.

It was good. Everything was good — the sun on their faces, the wind drying the sweat on their skin into itchy spots, these people who had come to rescue them, to take them back to civilization and malls and hair removal and Alexandra's Clandestine Closet[45] catalogs. Everything would be like it was before.

The transport carried them to the other side of the island and traveled through a barbed wire fence with No Trespassing signs posted on it. Two guards in black shirts opened the gates and waved them in, and for a moment, Adina had an uneasy feeling. She caught Nicole's eye and they both looked away quickly, as if neither one wanted to ruin the happiness of this rescue with some distant,

---

[45] Alexandra's Clandestine Closet, the number-one lingerie store, whose most popular undergarment is the Bicycle Pump-assiere™, a bra with built-in tires that can be pumped up to simulate any cup size.

probably unfounded fear. The transport stopped at the base of the volcano. Here, the land had been cleared and flattened out.

The agent ushered the girls into a plain white tent outfitted with chairs and a desk. Two assistants in black shirts offered sweating bottles of water, which the girls drank down in greedy gulps. It seemed that nothing had ever tasted so good. For a moment, there was a fleeting memory of those shirts, but it was gone with the realization that they had been rescued at last.

"Thank heavens we found you girls," the agent said, smiling. The mirrored aviators hid his eyes. "We'd just about given up hope when a satellite picked up the plane's image. You've managed to survive for all these weeks on your own? Outstanding!"

"We had to eat bugs!" Tiara said and shuddered.

"No!"

"We did! Jennifer fought a giant snake."

"Well, I'll be."

"And Petra had to pee on a pirate," Brittani added.

"Could you not make that sound like a fetish site please?" Petra complained, but she was still grinning. They all were. At last! A rescue! There would be shampoo and real beds and food.

Adina looked around at the bustling compound. It was hard to believe that it had been here the entire time. If only they had marched farther, gone looking, they might have been rescued much sooner. But the jungle had been too forbidding, and the girls had stayed close to the beach. Except for Taylor. Taylor! She could be seen by a doctor now.

"We lost one of our friends. Mary Lou. Have you seen her?" Nicole asked before Adina could say anything about Taylor.

"We did," the agent said after a moment's pause.

"I knew she'd be okay," Tiara said, clapping.

"Can we see her?" Shanti asked.

"She's . . . already headed back home. On a ship. There was a ship here that took her. She's the one who told us to come looking for you."

"Why wouldn't she come looking, too? Doesn't sound like Mary Lou," Adina said. Something scratched at the door of Adina's subconscious, wanting to get in. Female intuition, her stepfather would say. She wasn't sure of what was on the other side of that door, so she kept it closed.

"People do funny things," the agent said. "Now, if you're anything like my daughters, I know you girls must be dying for a shower."

For a moment, Mary Lou was forgotten as the girls fell into raptures about the simple pleasure of a real shower.

"How old are your daughters?" Shanti asked.

"Uh . . . fourteen and sixteen," the agent answered.

"Can we see pictures?" Shanti asked. Normally, she would have said this to be polite, but she found she actually *did* want to see pictures of this man's daughters. She was not the same Shanti who had arrived on this island.

The man frowned. "I . . . uh . . . left them in my other wallet."

A college-aged guy in an *Ask Me About My Trust Fund* T-shirt took a seat and offered the girls a box of cookies, which they scarfed down two at a time.

"Hey, careful there — don't want to get fat."

Jennifer flashed the guy an annoyed look. "Dude, careful we don't roast and eat you."

"Ha!" the Dweeb said. He tried to take back the cookies and Miss New Mexico grabbed hold with both hands.

"No take the cookies. Cookies are the best thing ever! *Cookies. Are. Life!*"

Reluctantly, the Dweeb let go of the box. "Okay. Kinda scary," he said under his breath. "I'm Harris. Harris Buffington Ewell Davis III."

A woman in camo pants and a black shirt whose name was given as Ms. Smith interrupted. "I'll take you to a place where you can get cleaned up. We ladies have to stick together," she said with a smile. Shanti had the idea that she should be comforted by this comment and this smile, but she wasn't, and the disconnection troubled her. It reminded her of the time in fourth grade when Bethany Williams had said her poncho was "really cool" before dissolving into mean-spirited giggles with the other girls.

"Watch your step," the woman cautioned.

An enormous pipeline snaked over the broken land and disappeared farther into the jungle. It smelled of sulfur and the water looked muddy and diseased.

"What happened here?" Nicole asked.

"Oil and gas pipelines," Ms. Smith explained. "This place is rich with natural resources. And The Corporation is working hard to bring those comforts to America, where they belong."

"Don't they belong *here*?"

"These resources make our way of life possible!" Ms. Smith chirped with a smile. "Without them, you wouldn't have your bottled vitamin water, your eye shadows, the packaging on your favorite perfume, your colored contact lenses, clothes, hair color, and nail polish."

"What happened to the people who used to live here?" Shanti asked.

"Relocated."

"Where?"

"To places where relocated people go. Trust me, they're better off," Ms. Smith said crisply. She opened the door to a gleaming gym and led them to a large, clean bathroom with individual shower stalls. "Enjoy your showers."

Smiling, Sosie tugged on Jennifer's shirt. "Cool, huh? This looks like something that could be in the Flint Avenger and Sosie, right?"

"It's just the Flint Avenger now," Jennifer said, and pushed ahead.

After they'd showered and shaved, moisturized and conditioned, Agent Jones appeared. "Got a surprise for you girls. Come with me."

Outside the volcano, he lifted the panel in the rock, punching in the code that opened the secret door.

"Whoa. Holy Loch Lomond movie," Jennifer said in awe.

"This is our headquarters," the agent said. The girls entered a gleaming, stainless steel elevator. A pleasant, British woman's voice asked for the floor.

"Four," the agent said, and they rocketed down.

"How many floors are there?"

"Five." He ticked them off on his fingers. "Product development. Marketing. Packaging. Corporate."

"You said five. That's only four."

Agent Jones held up one finger — "Product" — then another — "Development. We're here."

The doors opened into an open room divided by half-wall cubicles and desks. The employees clapped and cheered as the girls came through, and it was almost like walking up the aisles of the hotel ballrooms where most of the girls had performed in various pageants.

"Thanks," Nicole said. She smiled and waved, but it felt odd, like laughing at a joke you no longer found all that funny.

They entered a conference room where Harris sat at a computer. On the wall above his head was a flat-screen TV. A table and chairs dominated the center of the room.

"Hey! You girls smell a lot better — no offense. Have a seat."

The girls settled into the big black chairs.

"Those babies cost five thousand dollars a pop," Harris said. "Ergonomically correct."

"Oh," Tiara said, sitting uncertainly. "Springy."

"Somebody special wants to talk to you," Agent Jones said. "Harris?"

Harris clicked on the screen and Ladybird Hope appeared, wearing a red suit with a flag pin on the lapel. Her hair had been styled into a poufy twist. She waved and her charm bracelet rattled.

"Hello, Miss Teen Dreamers! I cannot tell you how happy I

personally am to see you. I told the world, I said, 'Don't you count my girls out. A Miss Teen Dream never gives up. She's a bright light in the world!' "

The girls were overcome. Ladybird Hope!

"What do you think of my new suit?" Ladybird asked.

The girls agreed that it was very nice. They were still dazed from the rescue and all that had come after. They talked excitedly, telling Ladybird everything that had happened to them since the crash, about how they, Miss Teen Dreams, had risen above and survived. No. More than survived. Thrived.

Tiara beamed with pride. "Like for our huts, we used engineering and physics. And interior decorating."

"Well, isn't that a kick in the head? That's pretty darn cute."

Tiara felt like she wanted to say something to Ladybird. She wanted to tell her that it wasn't cute. It was awesome. And smart. And really cool that they'd managed to do it all together, without any help from anybody. But these people were here to rescue her, and she didn't want to make waves. So she said, "I put flowers in mine."

Ladybird gave her two thumbs up and smiled. "Fan-tas-tic!"

Tiara knew she should feel good that she made everyone smile like when she was little and did her sparkle hips and blew kisses. But she didn't. She felt like a sellout.

"The good folks at The Corporation there are gonna give y'all a little tour and let you test our new beauty products, and then I have a super surprise for all my Teen Dreamers." Ladybird Hope paused for dramatic effect. "We would like for you to stage the pageant right there on the island. Isn't that something?"

The girls exchanged puzzled looks.

"It'll be a real tribute to what you girls have been through, to let the world see how you triumphed. We think the folks back home would love it. It might be the highest-rated show ever. You girls will be famous!"

"Well, we were kind of hoping to go home as soon as possible . . ." Adina started.

Ladybird Hope's expression changed to one of disapproval. "Well. Of course, if that's what you want. I would just think that you would want to say a big thank-you to the folks who rescued you and be a credit to girls everywhere. But if you don't want to, we'll just cancel the pageant this year."

"No, we'll do it," Miss Ohio said.

Ladybird smiled. "Terrific! Oh, I'm so happy. Don't you worry, it's going to be great," Ladybird assured them with a wink.

"When?" Nicole asked.

"Tomorrow night," Ladybird answered.

"And we could tell them all the stuff we've learned about eating grubs and safe sex and vaginas," Tiara said.

Petra grinned. "Tiara, you said the *V* word. Gimme five."

"That would blow their little minds, wouldn't it?" Jennifer said with a smirk. "Hello, America. My new platform is Kicking Ass, Girl-Style."

"My goodness, I don't know what you girls are talking about, but it hurts my ears! So stop it," Ladybird Hope chided. She put a hand to her heart. "You know what? America needs you girls. It's no secret the world's as messed up as a hockey game played on non-Zambonied ice right now. It needs you to smile and wave and remind us that we are a great nation full of pretty. And that we will not allow any threats to our pretty. No matter what."

On the screen, Ladybird Hope leaned closer to the camera. The angle was not kind. There was a pronounced ridge in her top lip from too much filler. "Now. You Dreams have a nice lunch, and then I believe you need to go shopping."

CHAPTER TWENTY-NINE

Mary Lou's throat hurt from screaming, but no one could hear her down in this cave near the ocean. She and Tane had been tied together and dangled from a hook, which was slowly lowering them over a piranha-filled tank. Below their feet, the ugly, sharp-toothed fish darted back and forth, waiting to take the two of them down to bones. The rope gave a jerk as it lowered another half inch. A piranha leapt, startling Mary Lou, who screamed.

"You all right?" Tane called.

"Yeah. Those things creep me out. Are you okay?"

"Other than being lowered to my death, yes."

"At least we're together."

"True. But I wish you weren't here. I wish it were just me and you were safe."

"Awww, so sweet!" The rope jerked again. "Aaaaahh!"

"At least we're getting a fancy, Greek mythology–style death. They could have just given us quick bullets to the head. Now we get to die in style," Tane said.

"Was that supposed to be comforting? Because, no offense, it wasn't."

"Nah. I always hated those stories anyway. It's like, any time a human tries to break out and take action for him- or herself, the gods punish that person. Like Prometheus — he brings Zeus's fire back from the mountain. He enlightens mankind, and so they chain him to a rock and an eagle eats his liver every day."

"My mom tried to get me to eat liver at Rita's Cafeteria one time.

I wrapped it in my napkin and flushed it down the toilet." A piranha surfaced. It snapped its teeth. "Yikes. Okay. Need distraction. Tell me another story."

"Princess Andromeda was chained to a rock as a virgin sacrifice to stop Poseidon's sea monster from devouring everything."

"Wow. They really liked the rock-death thingy," Mary Lou said. "What did she do wrong?"

"Nothing. Poseidon was punishing her mother for bragging about her daughter's beauty."

"There we are with the braggy again," Mary Lou said. "So, Andromeda didn't even do anything wrong and she ended up in the ocean? Why?"

"They needed a virgin sacrifice. But then Perseus came and saved her."

"Because the pure girls get rescued." Mary Lou felt something she didn't let herself feel often: She was well and truly pissed off. "Why do girls have to be all pure and innocent and good? Why don't guys have to be?"

"No argument here. I always thought it was pretty silly."

"If I weren't about to die, I would totally rewrite that."

"If I weren't about to be eaten by piranhas, I would tell you that I love you."

Mary Lou smiled. "You can still tell me that."

"Okay. I love you."

"Even though I'm a wild girl who likes sex and adventure? Even though I'm not a pure and chaste princess who needs rescuing? Well, technically, I do need rescuing. We both do. But that's not the point."

"I love you for who you are, not for who the world thinks you should be."

Tane stretched his hand through the ropes as far as it would go. He was just able to grasp the tips of Mary Lou's fingers. Mary Lou's eyes filled with tears. "Wouldn't you know, just when I feel okay about myself and find a cool guy, I'm gonna be killed off." The rope jerked harder this time, and both Tane and Mary Lou reacted. It swung out a bit, bringing them close to the ledge. Mary Lou could almost touch it with her feet. She had an idea.

"When my sister and I were kids, we used to have this old tire swing, and we'd swing out over this creek every day in the summer."

"Seems an odd time for reminiscing, but go on."

"See, we'd hold on and swing really hard and try to make it to the other side. If we use our weight, I'll bet we could reach that ledge."

"Dunno. That rope's a bit dodgy. Could snap if we pull too hard, and then we're piranha food."

"We're piranha food if we don't. I don't know about you, but if I'm gonna be chained to a rock by the gods, I'd rather go out as the person who brought fire back from the mountain than as a pure princess who didn't have the sense to say to everyone, "Oh, hell no, you are not sacrificing me to some sea monster!"

"You've got a point. Let's do it."

Mary Lou wasn't sure if her plan would work. Plenty of times, she and Annie had fallen right into the cold creek. But it was worth a try. It took a second to get it — Mary Lou went right when Tane swung left and they twirled around in a dizzying circle for a second. But then they got the rhythm. They pendulumed from side to side. Below, the piranhas zipped about in a frenzy. Overhead, the rope frayed with its next sharp drop, and Mary Lou screamed. But she did not stop swaying. Her feet scrambled at the ledge, scraping rock into the water.

"We've got to build up speed," she shouted.

"If this one doesn't work, the rope will break for sure."

Mary Lou looked up. She bit her lip. The rope was pretty frayed.

"Worth a shot," she said.

They swung heavily and slowly at first, but picked up speed, swinging farther with each pass. Once. Twice. Mary Lou's feet almost touched! Third pass and she knew they'd make it.

"You know what, Tane?" she shouted as they came around again.

"What?" he shouted back.

"I totally want to make out with you!"

She swung with all her might, reaching for the other side in defiance of gravity. There was an audible crack as the rope snapped.

CHAPTER THIRTY

When the girls had finished picking out their clothes and bathing suits for the pageant, compliments of Ladybird Hope's pageant-wear line, Harris showed them around, enjoying his role as beauty queen escort.

"So how did you end up here?"

"Summer internship," Harris said "My dad's CEO of The Corporation. Well, he *was*. He kinda 'mishandled' things." He put *mishandled* in air quotes.

"Mishandled how?" Adina asked.

"He sort of lost some revenue. The Corporation posted second, third, and fourth quarter losses totaling around forty billion? So, you know, they had to make some sacrifices, let some workers go."

"How many workers?"

"About forty percent."

"Forty percent?" Shanti said, incredulous.

"Yeah. Sucked. But the good news is that they worked out a deal with my dad. He got a sweet twenty million in severance, plus a full staff, use of the corporate jet and yacht for three years, and we did not have to unload the house in Bimini, thank God, because, hello? The surfing there? Crazy-good."

"When I run Shanticeuticals, I will not overexpand, screw over my workers, and run it into the ground," Shanti whispered to the others.

Jennifer sidled up to Harris. "My mom was one of those forty percent of workers laid off. She got one week of severance, and it definitely wasn't twenty million. Lost her health care, too. I wouldn't brag about that, if I were you."

They were waiting for the elevator when two black shirts passed them by. One of them said something that sounded suspiciously like . . .

"Tane Ngata!" Adina exclaimed, stretching her arms overhead. Everyone, including the black shirts, turned to stare at her.

"Do you know him? Are you yourself an eco-terrorist?" Harris was in her face.

"What? No! Why would I?" Adina laughed nervously.

"What did you just say?"

"I was doing my vocal exercises. To be ready for the pageant. I do them all the time. Tane Ngatatatattannnnneeeeetane. Just limbers the tongue right up." She gave him a coy smile.

"Gummi bears!" Tiara pointed wildly to the vending machine in the corner just as the elevator doors opened.

"Our ride's here," Harris said.

Tiara glanced toward the machine. "But . . . gummi bears."

"Wouldn't want to mess with those pretty teeth," he said and ushered them inside.

They rode up in silence.

"What kind of a person doesn't let you have gummi bears?" Tiara sat on the cot, her fingers worrying the hem of her new MermaidTopia shirt.

"And everyone seemed to know who you meant when you said *Tane Ngata*."

"We may be close to her imaginary BF," Shanti agreed.

"Maybe not so imaginary after all," Petra said.

Adina paced in front of her cot. "This is all very, very strange. My journalist's instincts say there's something going on."

"Or maybe that guy, the eco-warrior, is a terrorist," Miss Ohio said. "Maybe they have him captured for a good reason."

Tiara sniffled. "I don't want to do the pageant anymore. I want to make another hut. That was fun. And I want some gummi bears."

"You can have all the gummi bears you like when we get back," Petra promised.

"*If* we get back," Nicole said, and it made her arms goose pimply despite the heat.

Someone brought them French fries and soda, and the girls dug in. The French fries were heavenly; the soda burned their throats in a good way. It was just like being back home, like before. For a moment, their doubts were cast aside. They tried to enjoy the fact that they'd finally been rescued, just like in all the stories they'd read as girls. The ones that ended happily. They had new clothes and shoes. Their hair smelled of freesia, their skin of vanilla. All the creature comforts of home.

But if everything was fine, why did they feel so wrong?

"Tiara, what's the matter?" Petra asked. Tiara hadn't touched her food. "Is this still about the gummi bears?"

"No. It's just, I have a question. But it's probably dumb."

"There are no dumb questions," Petra said. "Except for some."

"How come, if they want us to do the pageant, they sent Mary Lou back home? That doesn't seem fair."

It was a simple question. The sort of simple question that could completely unravel a complicated argument.

Agent Jones stepped into the tent. "Hello, girls. How's everything?"

"Fine," they said.

"Good, good. Say, I've been meaning to ask, wasn't there a Miss Texas with you?"

"Tayl —"

Adina cut Tiara off. "Why do you ask?"

"No reason. There's always a Miss Texas in the Top Ten. My daughters and I run a pool." Agent Jones tried to smile and managed only a grimace.

"Will your daughters be watching tomorrow?" Adina pried.

Agent Jones blinked and looked away quickly. "Of course."

For the high school paper, Adina had covered a student council scandal in which the student body president had sold test answers in order to buy himself a new SUV. When she'd pressed him on the allegations, he'd done the same blinking and looking away. It was the tell of a liar.

"And they're fifteen and seventeen?" she said, deliberately getting their ages wrong.

"Yep. Fifteen and seventeen."

When she'd busted the student council president, Adina had felt triumphant — it was a "gotcha!" moment. Now, she felt real fear. This man was not to be trusted, but she didn't know why or how much danger they might be in.

"Sorry. Miss Texas didn't make it," Adina lied. "Spider bite."

"Well. That's a real shame."

Adina yawned for effect. "Whoo. I am sooo tired. We should probably get our beauty sleep. Got a big day tomorrow. Nighty-night, Agent Jones."

Agent Jones left without saying anything back.

"Something's not right," Nicole whispered when they were alone again.

"What's going on?" Tiara asked.

"Not sure," Adina said. "But we're going to find out."

In the fog, the moon was filmy as an onion's husk. Down by the dock, the lights shone over the black water. Adina, Petra, Tiara, Nicole, Jennifer, and Shanti huddled in the bushes watching the guards, who were, in turn, watching the area around the volcano's secret door. The girls had been there for twenty minutes, proposing ways of getting inside, rejecting all of them. They were tired and uneasy and had begun to argue.

Tiara stood and smoothed her dress.

"What are you doing?" Shanti asked. "Do you want to get us killed?"

"No. I just want some gummi bears," she said, and marched toward the volcano.

"Hold up!" The guards leveled their guns at Tiara. "You can't be here, miss. It's restricted."

Tiara smiled and struck a pageant pose. "Hi. I'm Tiara Destiny Swan. Miss Mississippi. I'm real sorry to bother y'all and everything, but there's only one thing in the world I want — well, besides world peace and free makeovers for everybody — and that's some gummi bears. And y'all have a vending machine right inside. Can I pretty, pretty please go get some?" She put her hands together prayer-style.

The guards exchanged glances. Tiara danced around them butterfly-style. "Pretty pretty pretty pretty please? Pretty pretty pretty pretty . . ."

The guards shrugged at each other. "Sure."

"Oh, yippee!" Tiara jumped and clapped. She motioned to the girls. "Oh, my friends need to come, too. We're girls. We travel in packs."

"Unbelievable," Petra whispered in awe.

The girls emerged from their hiding place. The guard held up a hand.

"I can't let all of you inside."

"You have to let Petra come in because she's my best friend," Tiara said.

"And you have to let me in because I have my period," Adina said.

"And you have to let me and Shanti in or else you're totally racist." Nicole glared.

"You have to let me in or I'll cry," Jennifer said, working up tears.

"Whoa, whoa, hold on. Look, we have our orders and —"

"Oh my God! Please tell me you have a tampon! I need a tampon!" Adina screeched.

"Okay! Okay! You can go with her."

Nicole stepped up to the guard. "What about the rest of us, whitey?"

"Westerfeld?" The one guard looked to the other. "Did you read the Corporation pamphlet on racial sensitivity in the workplace?"

"No. I read *Sexual Harassment and You: Why Sally Cries When You Touch Her in Meetings*."

"Well, I'm not getting my butt handed to me by corporate."

The other guard shrugged. "They're a bunch of girls. How dangerous could they be?"

"Okay. But be quick." The first guard punched in the code, and try as they might, the girls couldn't make it out. The doors opened. "Fourth floor."

"Thanks!" they said, and held their breath as the elevator shot them down.

CHAPTER THIRTY-ONE

"Gummi bear?" Tiara held out the bag.

Petra shook her head. "Where are we?"

After getting the candy and taking some beauty samples from the product room, they'd taken a door to a hallway and followed the stairs to the mysterious fifth floor and the door they were looking for. But it was locked, and they were stuck in a hallway lit by a dim red light.

"Now what?"

A flashlight beam bounced down the hall: one of the workers making the rounds. His card key bounced against his tubby belly.

"Quick, hide," Shanti whispered. She grabbed Tiara's face. "Tiara, can you make a sad face?"

She stuck out her lip.

"Great. When he comes, you make a sad face, tell him you're lost and need help. And then we'll clobber him over the head and take his card key."

"Okay," Tiara said. The girls ducked behind some large pipes. "Wait . . . what?"

"Hey!" the guard shouted. "What are you doing here?"

Tiara's eyes widened and her lips quivered. "I came down here for some gummi bears and I got lost."

"Really?" the guard said, tucking away his flashlight.

Tiara smiled. "No. Not really. I'm supposed to get you over here so my friends can hit you over the head and take your card key."

"Balls," Petra whispered.

"What?" the guard said.

With a "Kee-yah!" Jennifer leapt up from her hiding place and pinched the guard's neck near the clavicle.

The guard whirled around. "What the . . . ?"

"Crap. That always works on *Star Trek*."

"It's over here." Petra pinched the other side of the guy's neck and he dropped like a sandbag.

"Whoa. How'd you learn to do that?"

She put a hand on her hip. "Please. I'm a transgender former boy-bander. You think I don't know how to defend myself?"

The girls swiped the card. The door opened and they pulled the guy inside.

"Whoa. Holy secret arsenal, Batman." Jennifer whistled.

The walls gleamed with guns, assault rifles, grenades . . . things they'd only seen in blockbuster summer movies.

"I'm guessing The Corporation's expanding its product line." Shanti picked up a souped-up assault rifle with a scope on the end, then put it back gently.

"This is insane," Nicole said.

"What's really going on?"

"I might ask you the same question, ladies." Harris stood in the open doorway wearing a Three Stooges T-shirt and plaid golf pants. In his hand was a putter. "What are you doing here?"

"Adina needed a tampon?" Tiara said.

"Huh. Why don't I believe you?" Harris closed and locked the door. Swinging the putter, he made a slow circle of the room, forcing the girls away into a corner. "See, I think you girls are much smarter and savvier than anybody here knows." Harris gestured to the walls of guns. "Welcome to our secret room. Got some nice automatic weapons. Grenades. Some beautiful killing machines, really. Here's my personal favorite." Harris opened a small steel door and took out a jar of Lady 'Stache Off.

"That's hair remover," Petra said.

"Looks like it. Actually, if you change one element, it becomes a pretty powerful explosive. Just needs some sort of charge."

"Where's Mary Lou?" Adina demanded.

Harris grinned. "Your friend got a little nosy."

"I'll ask you again: Where is she?"

"I'm. Not. Telling."

Nicole grabbed for one of the guns and pointed it at Harris. Her hands shook. "Where's Mary Lou?"

Harris lined up a shot with the putter. "Cartridge."

"What?"

"You need a cartridge for that. Which you do not have."

"Shoot." Nicole tossed the gun on the table.

"Wait a minute, why are we all standing here?" Adina asked. "There are more of us than there are of him."

"But I've got this," Harris said, holding out his putter.

"Well, we've got this." Nicole held the can of hair spray out in front of her.

"Hair spray? That's your secret weapon? See, this is why women will never end up really having power." Harris swung the putter and the girls jumped back to avoid the blow. "Because I bring a kick-ass, bone-breaking piece of steel . . ." Harris swung the putter again, forcing the girls closer to the corner. ". . . and you think you can take me down with a can of hair spray."

"Yeah?" Nicole said. Her hands shook.

"Yeah," Harris said.

"Ever get this shit in your eyes? It burns like hell." Nicole pressed the nozzle and Harris got a face full of The Corporation's 'Do Me Right with Long-lasting Hold.

Harris was duct-taped to one of The Corporation's ergonomically correct chairs. His feet and hands had been secured with panty hose, which had been finished off with sailors' knots.

"Glad those pirates were useful for something," Nicole said, tightening the last one.

Jennifer ripped off his maxi-pad gag.

"Ow! Jesus, that hurt!" Harris howled.

Jennifer was unimpressed. "You want to know what pain is? Try running out of Advil when you've got a Category Five period. I've had cramps that would make grown men beg for a bullet between the eyes."

"You bitches are all so dead!" Harris snarled.

Adina straddled Harris's legs, hands on her hips. "Uh, Harris? Hate to break it to you, but you're not in a prime bargaining position. Now. We don't want to have to hurt you any more. But if you keep threatening us and telling us lies, I will personally give you a Brazilian."

"She won't warm the wax first, either," Petra said.

Tiara shuddered. "I've had so many bikini waxes, I cry every time I see a Popsicle stick."

Harris cackled low. When no one responded, he cackled louder.

"Okay, I'll bite," Adina said. "What's with the creepy laugh?"

"You babes have no idea what's coming."

"Yeah?"

"Yeah. Don't you misunderestimate me!" Harris bellowed.

"I am totally misunderestimating you. You have no idea what's happening tomorrow night, college-boy."

"Oh yeah? So I suppose you know that MoMo B. ChaCha is powering toward this island right now on his yacht. He's here to make a secret arms deal with The Corporation. Tomorrow, just before the new Miss Teen Dream is crowned, our black shirts dressed as ROC soldiers will charge out of the jungle, gunning down America's best and brightest beauty queens. We'll get it all on camera. We will go to war to avenge your deaths and set up a Corporation-run stronghold in the ROC. Ha! Wait. I just said that out loud, didn't I? Damn."

"They're gonna kill us?" Tiara said. "That's so *mean*."

Shanti sat next to Harris. "So let me get this straight: You booted the indigenous people off this land. You screwed up the environment. You tested products on helpless animals. Your 'Made in America' label is really made offshore. And now you're dealing illegal arms to a country we've levied sanctions against and you plan to murder us and frame them for it so you can go to war and take over their resources? Any rights you didn't violate or laws you didn't break?"

Harris thought for a second. "Our coffee is fair trade."

"What happened to Mary Lou?" Shanti pressed.

"We took her and her eco-warrior boyfriend and tied them up over a piranha tank and slowly lowered them in."

Jennifer whistled. "Wow. You really have seen too many Loch Lomond movies."

"Take us to her right now," Adina demanded.

"You're too late. They should be fish food by now."

"Take us there."

"No."

"Yes."

"No," Harris said, swiveling his head.

"Yes," Adina mimicked.

Nicole brandished the hair spray. "Show us where you've stashed Mary Lou."

"I've got a pumice stone and I'm not afraid to use it," Jennifer said.

"Full. Body. Wax," Petra whispered directly into Harris's ear.

"Okay! Okay. She's down below, in the caves."

"Just for that, you don't get a gummi bear," Tiara said and finished off the last one.

Adina yanked Harris to his feet. "Take us there now."

They kept Harris's hands together with panty hose and he led them to a secret elevator that took them down one more floor. It opened on a secret, high-tech laboratory hidden in a cave.

"Whoa," Jennifer said, taking in the cave's gleaming high-tech devices. "Total tech porn."

"Oh, no," Tiara cried. She pointed to the piranha tank. The hook that had held Mary Lou and Tane was completely submerged. The remains of Mary Lou's sash bobbed on the water. A ravenous piranha surfaced briefly to eat several floating sequins.

"We're too late," Nicole said, a catch in her voice.

"She was my best friend." Adina was near tears. "I'm so sorry, Mary Lou. So, so sorry."

"I thought we outlawed that word." Mary Lou's head poked up from behind a rock. Her hair was disheveled and her face was flushed. "What's up, Teen Dreamers?"

"Mary Lou!" Adina rushed toward her friend.

"Wait! Hold on a sec." Mary Lou dropped behind the rock. In a second, she stood, hurriedly buttoning her top. A young man in a similar state of quick-dress rose next to her. "You guys, this is Tane, my boyfriend."

Tane waved. "H'lo."

The girls did not move. Could not move. They looked from Mary Lou to Tane and back again.

"They're staring because they thought you were imaginary," Mary Lou told him. "Also, because you're hot."

"Objectifying me much?"

"No!" Mary Lou said quickly. "Well, a little."

" 'S all right. I've objectified you in my head plenty."

"Awwww. Thanks, sweetie." Mary Lou kissed Tane and wrapped her leg around his waist.

"Okay, we could come back in an hour if you need more time," Jennifer said.

"Could you?" Mary Lou managed between kisses.

"No. That was a joke."

The girls rushed to hug Mary Lou, except for Petra, who kept watch over Harris with the can of hair spray at the ready. They talked in a torrent: "Gonna kill us . . . MoMo B. ChaCha . . . cameras . . ."

"If MoMo's coming in on a yacht and we can get to it, we can use it to get off the island," Shanti said.

"But they'll be counting all of us for the pageant. They'll notice if one of us is gone," Nicole reminded them.

"Tane and I can do it," Mary Lou said. "They think we're dead."

"Where's the ship going to dock?" Petra asked Harris. She raised the hair spray.

"Down the beach about a hundred yards. There's a secret docking cave."

"You have a secret docking cave and you couldn't afford to give my mom overtime and dental?" Jennifer pressed Petra's finger on the nozzle and gave the hair spray can a squirt. It got Harris in the ear.

"Ahhhh! That's cold!"

Jennifer narrowed her eyes. "You would know."

"This cave leads out to the water," Mary Lou said. "We'll take this ledge out and swim down to the shore, be waiting for them when they come. As soon as you can, make a beeline for the docking cave."

"We have to go back out the front and get the others. The guards only let us in for gummi bears and tampons. If we don't go back up, they'll come looking for us."

"Okay. Everybody play it cool. We can't let on that we know the plan."

"What plan?" Tiara said.

They all looked at Tiara. "Tiara, you can't say anything, okay?" Adina pleaded.

"You mean pretend? Blow kisses and put on my sparkle hips like when I was little?"

"Like your life depends on it. Because it does for a while."

"What should we do about Harris the Misunderestimated over here?" Jennifer asked, eyeing him.

Mary Lou grabbed the ropes that had held her to Tane over the piranha tank. "I've got a few ideas."

They left Harris tied up behind the rock where he wouldn't be seen by anyone. Mary Lou secured the maxi pad over his mouth. "Bet you're sorry The Corporation gave us wings now, aren't you?"

"Take these flare guns. They might come in handy," Petra said, grabbing two from the wall and tossing them to the girls.

Mary Lou and Tane swam out into the night ocean. And the other girls gathered their tampons, gummi bears, and beauty samples — a smokescreen of female products — and headed back up to the surface.

COMMERCIAL BREAK

(A high school hallway. A girl, MARCIA, slams her locker door in frustration. She looks haggard. NATALIE and RACHEL stand off to one side, watching and shaking their heads.)

RACHEL
Marcia sure is in a bad mood. And she looks awful!

NATALIE
I hear it's that time of the month.

RACHEL
I guess somebody doesn't know how much fun having your period can be with new Maxi-Pad Pets — the revolutionary new fashion maxi pad that makes you feel like you've got a special friend in your pants.

MARCIA
All I've got are wings. Wings!

NATALIE
Wings are so last month! New Maxi-Pad Pets come in twelve different pet-pal shapes so you can change your mood as often as you change your pad!

CUT TO: Close-ups of various girls: sexy, cute, quirky, tomboy, adventurous.

GIRL #1
I'm a sexy lynx — *rarrrr*!

GIRL #2
I'm a cute, cuddly puppy!

GIRL #3
I'm a playful platypus!

GIRL #4
I'm a happy hamster!

GIRL #5
Guess who's got a tiger in her trousers?

CUT TO: A cup of blue liquid being poured into the belly of a
Maxi-Pad Lion Cub.

NATALIE VOICEOVER
Find your perfect shape today! And Maxi-Pad Pets are
superabsorbent. This blue liquid shows how effective Maxi-Pad
Pets are at collecting small thimblefuls of blue liquid.

CUT TO: Marcia sitting on the sidelines in PE, glaring at her gym
teacher and cradling a huge bottle of ibuprofen.

RACHEL
So stop bothering everybody with your cramps, bloating, and
irritability, and start showing everybody how much fun you are
during that time of the month.
Your period, your Maxi-Pad Pet, your way!

CUT TO: Next day. Same hallway. A smiling Marcia is
surrounded by friends. She is the life of the party.

RACHEL
Marcia, you sure are the most popular girl in this hallway!

MARCIA

Well, everybody loves a teddy bear. (Girls laugh. Marcia gives a
thumbs-up.) Thanks, Maxi-Pad Pets!

NATALIE VO

New Maxi-Pad Pets. Accessories for your period. Brought to
you by The Corporation: In your homes and in your pants.

CHAPTER THIRTY-TWO

The morning fog rolled across the water in a wall. The camp was filled with movement. Tracks were being covered. Identifying markers were placed on the tents, making it seem as if it were a rebel training ground instead of a Corporation outpost. The girls had set themselves up off to the side of the volcano, where they practiced circle-turns and dance moves as if that were the only thing on their minds. Adina wrote questions on index cards. They'd convinced The Corporation that Adina would make a terrific host for the show since her ambition was to become "the hostess of a dance-show competition between warring nations in an effort to forge peace between them." As Fabio Testosterone had been caught frolicking in an illegal Skee-Ball emporium with the hot male star of *Your Blood Is, Like, So Hot*[46], The Corporation agreed.

"So, we've got the intro singing number, the evening gown, talent, bathing suit, interview, followed by a final dance number, and then the crowning. It all comes down to the dance number," Shanti said. "Once we start the dance number, you've got three minutes and eight seconds."

Nicole whistled. "That's not a lot of time."

---

[46] *Your Blood Is, Like, So Hot*, the premium cable TV series about small-town predatory hemophiliacs who lie around looking anemic and sexy while trying not to bruise. Based on the French drama *Le Monde C'est La Mienne* (rough translation: Life is pain. Here is some soft cheese).

"Every problem is a solution in disguise," Shanti said, echoing one of the Miss Teen Dream manual's affirmations.

"Really with the slogans?" Adina snarked.

"Okay. How about this: If we don't peel off one by one and start running for the yacht by the end of the song, we're dead."

"Surprisingly motivating. Teen Dreamers, we've got one shot: Place the tampered Lady 'Stache Off at the end of the runway. Aim the flare gun at it and run like hell. Make it back here, then head for the docking cave and pray that Mary Lou and Tane got control of the yacht. Everyone know their parts?"

The girls nodded. Tiara put a hand to her stomach. "Ohmigosh, y'all, I'm so nervous! What if I mess up?"

Adina put a hand on Tiara's shoulder. "You're not going to mess up, Tiara. You can do this. You built a hut. You learned to fish and catch rainwater for drinking. You're a survivor."

"Okay," Tiara whispered. "Okay."

A black shirt strode over, hands at his hips. "What are you girls gossiping about over there?"

"Pageant stuff," Adina said, forcing herself to sound extrachipper and borderline stupid, the tone that disarmed people, made them think you weren't a threat. The black shirt smiled. It was astonishing how easily that worked. Adina smiled back. Her smile said, *You will not know what hit you, jerkface.*

Jeeps carried them through the jungle. Adina looked for Taylor, but she was nowhere to be seen. The girls' camp bounced into view, and seeing everything — the huts, the rainwater tarp, the sequined banner — Adina felt a surge of pride. They'd done this on their own, without any help. It was better than any feeling she could remember. And now these jerks wanted to take it all away. She could only hope the girls' plan would work.

The Jeeps came to a stop on top of the HELP stones. "Not bad," Agent Jones said appreciatively. He cut one of the fishing lines.

"What are you doing?" Shanti barked.

"You don't need them anymore, right? Now that you've been rescued."

"Yeah, but you could ask first. We worked hard on those."

"I didn't mean to hurt your feelings."

"You didn't hurt my feelings. You pissed me off," Shanti said, glaring. "There's a difference."

"Remember," Petra whispered. "Play it cool."

Shanti forced a smile. "Um, no offense or anything. I'm not mad, I'm just kind of sad. And emotional."

Agent Jones patted her shoulder. "Understandable. You girls have been through a lot. Tonight, all you have to do is smile and wave." He cut the other fishing line and let them both drift out to sea.

The black shirts had been busy setting up a performance area on the beach. They'd constructed a wooden stage with a red curtain across the front. Now they were building a runway.

"We've run out of wood," one of the black shirts called.

"Just take it from one of the huts," Agent Jones shot back, and the black shirts tore the walls from Tiara's home.

"My place!" she cried.

Petra wrapped her up in a big hug. "Come on. Let's go get our game faces on."

Adina took Nicole aside. "I need you to cover for me."

"What are you going to do?"

"I'm going to find Taylor, see if I can get her to help."

"But how? She's straight-up crazy now."

"Sometimes, a little crazy is exactly what you need."

The girls practiced their dance routine loudly. Nicole banged hard on her drum. Adina slipped into the jungle and ran for Taylor's secret hideaway. It had taken on a ghoulish quality; Taylor had affixed several black shirts to poles outside her cave and lit them to make torches. In the firelight, Miss Miss seemed to undulate in some ancient dance. Taylor sat before the sculpture on her haunches, swiping mud across her cheeks in long, thick streaks.

"Hey, Taylor." Adina crept closer. "Whatcha doin'?"

Taylor's knife was at Adina's throat quickly.

"Whoa. Taylor, it's me, Adina. Miss New Hampshire."

Taylor seemed to be trying to remember something. "New Hampshire . . . I don't like you, do I?"

"Not so much," Adina said, swallowing hard. "Look, I know we've had our differences, but you know what? We're on the same team. There are some bad people out there, Taylor. People who want to hurt us. You were trying to warn us that day, weren't you?"

Taylor took the knife away. "Lies. It's all lies."

"I know. But we're not going to let them get away with it."

"A Miss Teen Dream doesn't complain. She offers a smile and an ambassador to the world." Taylor frowned. "No. That isn't right."

"Taylor, we're going to get off the island. Tonight. There's a boat and we're going to make a break for it. But we need your help to fight off the guards."

"A girl's best weapon is her smile," Taylor parroted.

"No. I mean real weapons. We've got to fight our way out of here before they kill us. Tonight. Look, just meet us at the volcano, okay? Taylor! Are you listening?"

The wind picked up; the fire responded with a surge of desire. Taylor looked around as if she were seeing everything for the first time: the arsenal, the unassailable wall of green, the volcano stretching up from the land like an angry fist of rock. The humidity had wreaked havoc on her hair, which was a tangle of greasy blond. There were dark circles beneath her eyes. Her face was haunted.

"I can't be what they want," she whispered, and it seemed to her that those words had come to her from long ago. An expression of childlike confusion came over her face. She put her arms around Miss Miss like a child seeking comfort. "I just wanted to be somebody."

"You are somebody," Adina said. "You're Taylor Rene Krystal Hawkins. And you know a lot about the military, dance, bathing suits, kicking ass, and handling firearms. And right now, your Teen Dreams need you. Can you meet us at the volcano after the pageant starts?"

Taylor's mouth went hard. "They won't want us like this." As if snapping out of a dream, Taylor smiled and posed, but her eyes were still haunted. She spoke rapidly. "One thousand strokes will bring the lies to your hair. A lady never and a lady does and a lady always. Shine and sparkle."

Taylor flitted from spot to spot, turning pirouettes, waving to an unseen crowd. "Do you like me? Do you like me now?"

"Taylor!" Adina snapped, but Taylor was beyond hearing. Reluctantly, Adina turned to go, leaving Taylor behind to blow kisses at an unseen crowd.

CLASSIFIED

The yacht, a sleek luxury model favored by rappers, movie stars, and moguls, powered toward the small island. This particular yacht had once been featured on the show *Pimp My Sails* and on the cover of *Luxury Lifestyle* magazine with a bikini-clad model drenching her body in champagne under the headline, "Get the Latest Hot Accessories." The yacht had been sold to MoMo B. ChaCha through various channels because it was a symbol of wicked American excess, which The Peacock publicly disdained. But he liked the yacht's heart-shaped hot tub, where he sat watching Ladybird Hope on a TV news hour calling him a threat to national security.

MoMo chuckled and puffed on his cigar. He offered a cigar to General Good Times, too. "The lady pines for MoMo. Soon we will have our new weapons, and when she is elected president, there will be the big wedding and she will give us a secret McDonald's in the people's palace. Excuse me for a moment, General. I must dress."

MoMo searched his closet for the perfect outfit. He settled on the Elvis in Hawaii bedazzled white jumpsuit. In place of the sequined eagles on the sleeves, MoMo had commissioned ruby replicas of the ROC's emblem, a fistful of feathers. He added the Elvis wig, the sunglasses, and the blue suede platform shoes, which brought his height up to a full five feet five inches.

In the mirror, MoMo snarled and flipped up his collar. "Get ready, world. I am your Heartbreak Hotel."

MoMo called for his bodyguard.

"Sir?" the man said.

"What do you make of this arrangement we are negotiating?" MoMo asked, steely-eyed.

The bodyguard looked nervous. "Permission to speak honestly, sir?"

MoMo spread his arms wide. "Of course."

"This seems like a setup, Ser Peacock."

"You think so?"

"Yes, Ser. I do."

"Huh." MoMo thought for a moment. Then he reached into the gold-plated soap dispenser, pulled out a gun, and shot the guard dead. He pressed the intercom. "I am to need a cleanup on aisle nine, please."

MoMo didn't like feeling suspicious. But you didn't get to have your own country named after you for being a tool. Insurance. Mutually assured destruction. MoMo found the DVD and looked for a place to hide it. He uploaded it to his laptop and labeled the file *Yacht Systems*.

Nameless guards started dragging away the body of the unfortunate guard. MoMo stepped over the dead man on his way out. The yacht slipped into the secret docking cave. Flanked by a contingent of black shirts, Agent Jones waited to greet the dictator.

"Ser Peacock," Agent Jones said, bowing slightly. "An honor."

"You do not acknowledge my advisor, Agent Jones?"

The stuffed lemur sat on The Peacock's shoulder.

"Welcome, General Good Times."

A black shirt approached Agent Jones. "Sir, corporate can't make a decision: Should we go with blue one or blue two on the lights?"

Agent Jones's eye twitched. "I don't care."

"Blue one is sort of a cerulean, and blue two is more of a sapphire."

"What is going on?" MoMo demanded.

"It's nothing. Just a beauty pageant." Agent Jones glared at the black shirt.

"A beauty pageant? Here? On the island?"

"Miss Teen Dream," the black shirt answered.

MoMo let out a cry of happiness. "Ladybird Hope was Miss Teen Dream. Most famous pageant. General Good Times and I accept commission as judges."

Agent Jones mopped at his brow with a handkerchief. "MoMo — I mean, Ser Peacock. You can't be seen. You understand the nature of our deal is private."

MoMo waved Agent Jones off with his fingers. He took a back seat in the Jeep beside the lemur. "The general and I will be very quiet. No one will to notice us in the back. I love the pageants. So much sparkle. Like Elvis. And explosives."

"But the weapons, Ser Peacock."

"Weapons later. First, pretty girls. Drive, Agent Jones. Before I lose my patience."

Reluctantly, Agent Jones climbed behind the wheel and gunned the engine. He was already regretting not filling out the early retirement form.

CHAPTER THIRTY-THREE

Back at the camp, the girls rushed around, pasting sequins on their faces, sewing palm fronds into gowns like plumage, making last-minute touch-ups. They welcomed the old routine, the surge of adrenaline associated with pageant nights. But tonight, there was a little something extra.

Adina made it back just as the cameras were put in place. The black shirts had torn down another hut to make way for a sound booth. They'd rigged the stage area with lights, the wires feeding into a generator mounted on a rusty Jeep.

"I was starting to worry," Nicole said. "Taylor?"

Adina shook her head. "She's too far gone. We'll have to do it without her." She shimmied out of her shorts and tank and into her official pageant dress, a blue cocktail number with a poufy skirt. If Adina did die, she hoped to God it wouldn't be in this tulle-and-lace monstrosity.

"Remember the plan: Jen, you and Shanti are throwing the race. As soon as they announce Top Five, whoever's not named needs to make a break for the volcano and the control room and let the world know what's really going on. During the musical number, the rest of you peel off and head for the boat. The minute they announce the winner, we've got to run like hell. Mary Lou and Tane should have the yacht ready to go."

"Do you really think we'll make it?" Tiara asked.

Adina looked into Tiara's trusting face and thought about Alan holding out his arms, waiting to catch her, promising he would. She hadn't believed him, but her mother had, and Alan had come through for her. In the past several weeks, Adina had learned to take that fall, and these girls had proved to her that you could still trust in the world, that there was good among the bad. Sometimes, that was all you needed to keep going.

"We've made it this far, haven't we? Don't count a pageant girl out, Miss Mississippi."

Tiara smiled weakly. "You sound like Taylor."

"Well."

"I can't believe I used to worry so much about people not liking me. Seems so unnecessary now," Nicole said, watching a group of black shirts laughing over some private joke. "I swear, if I get out of this, I'm going to tell my mom to back off and let me live my own life."

"I'm going to go to law school and start changing some things," Miss Ohio said. She dabbed at her eyes. "Crap. Is my mascara smeared?"

"You're good," Petra said, wiping a smudge from Miss Ohio's cheek. "I'm going to hunt down Sinjin St. Sinjin and get my heels back. And then beat him with them."

"I'm gonna stop worrying about that third nipple," Brittani said.

"What if we don't make it?" Miss Montana said.

Shanti shook her head. "Don't talk like that."

"But the deck is really stacked against us. You really think we can win against all of that?" Miss Montana swept her arm toward the juggernaut on the beach.

"I don't know. But I'm so totally not gonna just roll over for them."

"Me either," Petra said.

"*I don't give a damn 'bout my bad reputation,*" Jennifer sang softly.

"What are you talking about?" Sosie asked. She looked to Jennifer, who softened.

"Kicking ass," she spelled out.

Sosie nodded. "Go big or go home, bitches."

"Go big or die," Nicole said quietly.

There were shouts on the beach, last-minute preparations, the verbal-and-static gunfire of walkie-talkies. Farther out, waves broke on the rocks. The jungle insects tuned their constant hum to a high-pitched clamor.

Shanti closed the curtain. "Ready?"

Nicole put out her hand. Petra placed hers on top. The others followed till their hands seemed to form a giant fist.

"Miss Teen Dream," Adina intoned.

"Miss Teen Dream," the others echoed, and they brought their hands up and apart.

"I'm scared," Miss New Mexico said.

The guard stuck his head behind the curtain. "Ten minutes, girls."

A WORD FROM YOUR SPONSOR

In a few moments, the most important Miss Teen Dream Pageant ever will be broadcast live from a remote island. Backstage, the girls wait in their gowns. Oh, see how they shine in their sequins and glitter? But there is something more tonight, yes? A gleam in the eye. A determined set to those glossed lips. A refusal to play the part assigned. They are ready. Hidden in a stack of props is the jar of Lady 'Stache Off and the flare gun, their twin hopes for making it out alive.

In his white Elvis jumpsuit, MoMo B. ChaCha waits to be entertained before making his arms deal, and Agent Jones waits with him, a cold sweat breaking out on his forehead. In the shadows, the black shirts wait, unseen, costumes on, guns at the ready, while in a television studio for *Barry Rex Live*, Ladybird Hope sits in a chair as a makeup artist prepares her face. She glances at the notes she's written in her palm, rehearses what she will say when the time comes, when she, the most famous Miss Teen Dream who ever lived, will announce live the murder of the beauty queens. It will be her face America sees reassuring the nation in time of crisis, promising vengeance on the shores of the ROC. It will be Ladybird Hope's finest hour — until her election.

And across the great land, from the glistening malls on the prairies to the department stores in the teeming cities to those small, cracker-box houses that can barely contain the bottled-up dreams and discontent of those who must be more, the televisions flicker, bathing the watchers in its seductive blue-gray glow. Already, the narratives are being written: Scrappy beauty queens survive in hostile jungle. How they lost weight! Learn their secret jungle beauty tips!

The world has tuned in. It is watching.

All of this is brought to you by The Corporation.

CHAPTER THIRTY-FOUR

"Live in three . . . two . . . one . . . go!" The man behind the camera sliced the air with his arm. The curtains parted. Heart thumping, Adina walked out into the glare of the generator-run klieg lights and stepped to the microphone.

"Good evening, ladies and gentlemen. Welcome to the Forty-first Annual Miss Teen Dream Pageant, live from a creepy island in the middle of nowhere. I'm Adina Greenberg, Miss New Hampshire, and I'll be your host this evening. And now, let's meet our contestants!"

The girls paraded in their evening gowns as if this night were like any other pageant they'd smiled through. Before them, the audience of Corporation employees clapped and cheered. Behind them, the jungle answered with its own cacophony. The girls disappeared behind the curtain and Adina called them one by one to answer questions about world peace and being role models. According to plan, they gave the standard answers, the ones everyone wanted to hear, until halfway through.

Adina tried not to seem nervous as she called Miss Ohio to the microphone. Miss Ohio sauntered onstage in her long, hot pink gown. In her hair, she wore a bright purple island flower. She did her flirty wave to the cameras, which made the audience chuckle.

"Miss Ohio, what would you say was the toughest part about life on the island?"

"Oh, wow. Eating grubs was pretty gross. We didn't even get ketchup!" She beamed as the audience laughed. They were giving good TV. "But you know, I'd have to say finding out there was a Corporation compound right here on the island the whole time and we never knew it. I felt like such a doofus!" She shook her head without losing her smile.

"Thank you, Miss Ohio," Adina said, gently pushing the girl toward the curtain as Shanti made her way in.

"I am for Miss Ohio, General," MoMo whispered loudly to General Good Times. "Her buttocks remind me of tiny cats."

With a rigor mortis–style grin, Agent Jones put a finger to his lips to remind MoMo of the need for secrecy.

"Shanti Singh, Miss California, can you tell us about your platform?" Adina said.

"Absolutely." Shanti faced the audience and smiled. She wore an emerald green gown with iridescent seashells sewn around the waist and hem. "My platform is called FemPower Me. It is about microloans for women in developing countries. What you may not know is that many big corporations exploit female workers."

Adina pretended to be surprised. "Really! That's so interesting. Tell us more."

Shanti's smile did not falter. She stood in a perfect three-quarter beauty queen stance. "Like, for instance, let's just say that The Corporation had a secret outpost here on this island. First, they would clear the land of indigenous peoples and force them from their ancestral homes, killing them if they were, like, really difficult or whatever. You know how those indigenous people can be about their land and stuff, Adina."

"Boy howdy, Shanti." Adina beamed for the cameras.

"Anyhoo, they'd use sweatshop labor — often young girls — to make all those products that keep you and me looking good. Maybe they'd even do secret arms trading. Meanwhile, women and children lose access to their livelihood. They'd face famine, oppression, and possibly a life of slavery."

"Yikes. Hey, don't you have a cute story about how your immigrant parents put up a lawn Santa on the Fourth of July?"

"Sure do. Oh, my wacky dad!" Shanti crossed her hands at the wrist. "Culture clash. D'oh!"

MoMo slapped his knee. "Am loving it."

"Thank you, Miss California. By the way, fun fact about Shanti: Her favorite lipstick color is Tickle Me Pink. Don't you love lipstick, Shanti?"

"So much, Adina."

Without missing a beat, Shanti raced offstage just as Petra made her entrance.

She'd chosen a strapless gold lamé jumpsuit with a seaweed belt and had blown her long hair straight like a 1970s chanteuse.

"Love the ensemble, Petra. Did you put that together yourself?"

"I did, Adina. My mom's an artist and she gave me a real appreciation for the visual. I love to sew."

"That is seriously amazing. Can you tell us what you did to help us survive on this island?"

"I sewed a banner to catch the attention of planes. You can't see it now because they took it down."

Adina turned to the cameras with an amused-but-confused expression. "Why?"

"It had the word *bitches* in it, which is perfectly fine to use if you're a rapper or a director making a movie about career women, but not if you're a teen girl talking about her homies."

"Good point, Petra. We know that young ladies of the teen persuasion do not use these indelicate words. Nor do they have thoughts about sex, masturbation, violence, being competitive, or farting."

"Exactly. Teen girls are made of moonbeams and princess sweat. Which would, of course, not be called *sweat* but *glow*, and would be taken care of with an aggressive antiperspirant like The Corporation's new That's the Pits! with aloe microbeads. Because when it comes to keeping you smelling lady-fresh, aggressive is A-okay." Petra waved to the crowd and exited stage left.

Adina turned to the audience. "Oh, super fun fact about Petra?

She used to be J. T. Woodland from Boyz Will B Boyz! She's a proud member of Trans Am Transgender Rights Campaign and is the first transgender Miss Teen Dream contestant ever! Let's give a big hand to Petra!"

On the sidelines, Agent Jones cursed silently. Why hadn't they gone with the five-second delay as he'd suggested?

Beside him, The Peacock clapped loudly. "General Good Times loves Boyz Will B Boyz! It is his favorite band. Look, he smiles!"

Many miles of ocean away, the call-boards lit up at The Corporation Network. What was going on with these girls? Did they have some sort of tropical illness? Agent Jones glared in the direction of the stage. These girls were up to something, and it wasn't smiling and waving. But his job depended upon staying hidden and keeping an eye on MoMo. He couldn't rush the stage and risk exposure. He'd just have to ride it out and hope they cut the crap.

"Last but not least, let's welcome Tiara Swan, Miss Mississippi. Fun fact about Tiara: She thought you could get pregnant from swimming with a guy." Adina shook her head. "Oh my goodness! Don't you just love abstinence programs? So not helpful. Tiara, what have you learned here on this island?"

"I've learned that it takes a village to build a catapult, which is not a city in Mexico, and that *uterus* is not a dirty word or the name of a planet. I've learned that if a guy pretending to be a pirate tells you he's nothing but trouble, he's probably right. So you should find somebody else, 'cause there are some really cool guys — and girls — out there. I've learned that you can use an old evening gown to catch rainwater and that grubs taste a lot like chicken. I've learned how to build a good, strong hut and accessorize it just right. I've learned that feminism is for everybody and there's nothing wrong with taking up space in the world, even if you have to fight for it a little bit, and that if you don't feel like smiling or waving, that's okay. You don't have to, and you don't have to say sorry. Mostly, I've learned that I don't really care if you like these answers or not, because they're the best, most honest ones I've got, and I just don't feel like I can cheat myself enough to give you what you want me to say. No offense."

Adina smiled. "Thank you, Miss Mississippi."

"Am I done?" Tiara asked.

"Do you feel like you're done?"

Tiara thought for a second. "Yeah. I do."

They went to a commercial break. MoMo B. ChaCha, cradling General Good Times in his arms, conferred with Agent Jones. "The General must make the pee-pee. We will return, and when we do, it is time for the musical number. It is our favorite part."

Agent Jones raced for the stage area. He stood outside the curtains and coughed, and Adina stuck her head out.

"Yes?"

"You're going straight to the musical number."

"What? But we haven't done swimsuit or picked the Top Five yet!" Adina protested.

The agent rested his hand on the top of his gun. "We're doing the abridged Miss Teen Dream tonight."

CHAPTER THIRTY-FIVE

Mary Lou and Tane bobbed beside the yacht. On board, one of the ROC soldiers kept watch. They'd have to take him out somehow. Mary Lou climbed on board, startling the sleepy guard, who leapt into action with his gun leveled right at her. "Hi!" she chirped. The guard didn't move. Mary Lou's knees shook. "Do you have a bathroom I could use?"

The guard aimed. From behind, Tane whacked him with a life preserver and the man fell, unconscious.

"Cutting it a little close there, babe," Mary Lou said, exhaling.

"I couldn't believe he wouldn't let you use the bathroom. What a jerk."

They crept along the wall and took the stairs to the upper deck to make sure it was clear.

Mary Lou whistled as she took in the boat's majesty. "Holy cow. Grill. Juice bar. Enormo-screen TV. Pineapple. This thing has everything." Mary Lou paused before a bowl of cookies. "Do you think they'd mind if we helped ourselves to a cookie?"

"We're helping ourselves to their boat."

"Good point."

"Let's hope it's got plenty of fuel and can get us all out of here."

They crept down a spiral staircase to the main deck and the bridge.

"Wow, it's even got windshield wipers," Tane said.

The fog was rolling in, but Mary Lou could still see that the black water seemed to stretch forever. She felt a swell of excitement that had nothing to do with the urgency of their circumstances. "It's so beautiful. And vast."

"What's that?" Tane asked. He was trying to figure out the control panel.

"The world." She ran her fingers over the boat's wheel. It felt good and right. "Bet you could see a lot of the world from one of these. Did you know that when the sun sets on this one particular part of the Indian countryside, it turns everything this amazing golden color?"

Tane gave her a quizzical look.

"I'd like to see it for myself. I want to go to the old churches in Prague. Stand on the edge of California under the shadow of the Golden Gate Bridge like the beat poets. Learn to drive a race car or swim with dolphins. Play the ukulele. I want to do all those things."

"You should, then."

"And if I wanted you to come with me? What would you say?"

"I'd say yes."

Mary Lou grinned. "Really?"

"Really. Never seen the Golden Gate Bridge, and I like the ukulele," Tane said. "But first, we've got to figure out how to work this thing. I know a little about boats, but nothing about yachts. See if you can find anything — a manual, an instructional video, computer tutorial, anything."

"Got it!" Mary Lou said. "Hey, Tane?"

"Yeah?"

"Thanks."

"For what, mate?"

She shrugged. "For being you." She took the stairs two at a time to the lower deck and raced through the opulent yacht, marveling at its wonders. She passed a gold-plated bathroom and one room dedicated to Elvis jumpsuits.

"Whoa," she said, opening the last door. The bedroom had been wallpapered with pictures of Ladybird Hope. In a corner was a

Ladybird Hope doll[47] in a glass case on a pedestal. "'Kay. Not creepy. Not at all."

On a desk in the center of the room was a large, framed picture of Ladybird Hope sitting on MoMo's lap in a Ladybird Hope Factory that was clearly not in America, featuring young girls working the looms. The laptop was open, and there on the desktop was a file marked *Yacht Systems*.

"Easy peasy," she said and waited for the video to load. It was not about yachts. Not even remotely. MoMo B. ChaCha and Ladybird Hope sat in a heart-shaped bubble bath hot tub, rifles in their hands, champagne glasses nearby.

MOMO
Ladybird, you are a hunka hunka burnin' love. When will you and
The Corporation give me my weapons, my little dove?

LADYBIRD
Now, don't get your peacock feathers all in a ruffle, MoMo. We
have to be careful. Nobody can know we're doing this.
Remember, we've got sanctions against you.

MOMO
I know. And it makes MoMo sad. Oh, pretty gazelle!

The Peacock took the swift animal down with one shot. Mary Lou flinched. "Meat is murder," she whispered. "Bastards."

LADYBIRD
Nice shot, Peacock! Bag it and tag it.

[47] Ladybird Hope doll, from the Ladybird Hope Destiny Dolls collection. But you should not put anything on a pedestal, least of all dolls who watch you while you sleep, waiting to suck the breath from your lungs.

MOMO

Oh, Ladybird. All this killing and talk of weapons has made The
Peacock amorous. A little less conversation and a little more
action, please.

Ladybird and MoMo kissed and Ladybird ruffled the dictator's hair.

LADYBIRD

You let Ladybird and The Corporation set up shop in the ROC,
you get your weapons. I'll arrange everything.

MOMO

Oh, Ladybird. Love me tender.

Mary Lou's eyes widened. Her mouth hung open. About three
seconds too late, she hit stop. "Ew. That was like watching your parents have sex. Your creepy, dysfunctional parents." She grabbed the
laptop and ran back to the bridge.

"You'll never believe what I . . . what's that?" The yacht's radar
blipped and beeped. A large green dot could be seen moving in their
direction.

At the helm, Tane frowned. "Gotta be another ship."

Mary Lou squinted out at the fog, but it was too thick to see
anything. "Do you think it's friendly?"

As if in answer, the other ship fired.

CHAPTER THIRTY-SIX

Thump-thump-thump-thump! The trees reverberated with the joyful cry of a Hindi love song from Shanti's *Greatest Bollywood Hits* CD. The curtain that had been hung between two poles parted. Decked out in a glittering blue sari, Shanti stood front and center, lip-synching to the Indian love song. Behind her, the girls' bangled arms fanned out like Kali's. The music changed to a percussive rhythm. The girls peeled off and formed a line across the stage. They reached behind them for the plane seat cushions, which they tossed to one another like juggling pins while Petra ducked under, scooting to the front. Like a Bollywood flight attendant, she used two fingers on each hand to indicate the location of the exits — forward, back, over the wings. Her execution was flawless.

The girls jerked left, then right, simulating the plane crash in dance. They broke apart, and several of the girls slipped behind the curtains as if being sucked from the plane. They waited until they were sure the guards' attention was on the stage, then they sneaked behind the Jeep and into the jungle to make their way to the ship.

Under the lights, Jennifer sidewinded across the stage, letting Sosie mock-throw a jar of Lady 'Stache Off at her. Jennifer "exploded" and rolled offstage while Sosie blew on the jar as if it were a gun — eliciting chuckles again — and placed the jar in the sand at the end of the runway. She executed three perfect backflips to applause and joined Jen backstage. Jen jerked her head toward the jungle and the two of them scuttled into the cover of leaves. They climbed the nearest tree and searched for the vine that would carry them to the next tree in a contagion that would take them nearly to the compound.

As Shanti lip-synched nervously, the girls backed toward the curtains, trying to follow her lead in the dance. Petra produced the flare gun from her cleavage, and it was passed from hand to hand until it came to rest with Adina, who dropped into a firing pose. She aimed at the jar of Lady 'Stache Off, but the flare gun jammed in the island humidity. The girls glanced at her in panic, then resumed their smiles. Quickly, Shanti grabbed the gun and tossed it to Petra.

"WTF?" Petra said through clenched teeth as they performed a pop-and-lock imitation of fighting a tsunami.

"Fire!" Adina whispered.

Petra took a shot, but the trigger was still stuck. "Damn," she said and tossed the gun to Nicole. Back and forth the flare gun flew, the girls never breaking stride. The song was coming to an end, and the girls felt real panic. Unless they could create a distraction, how could they escape? Finally, the last note was played. The gun came to rest in Tiara's hand. She pressed the trigger all the way. A fireball arced through the crowd and ignited a palm tree.

"Operation Peacock is go." Agent Jones spoke into his hidden mic and the troop of black shirts disguised as Republic of ChaCha rebels burst from the jungle bearing machine guns, shouting and shooting into the air. In the audience, the Corporation employees screamed and dove for cover under their seats. Some ran for the beach and the disguised black shirts shot them down. Shanti made a dive for the flare gun, but one of the black shirts kicked it out of the way.

The Peacock stood on the sidelines, a dazed look on his face. "What is the meaning of this?" he finally shouted, but the cameras did not swing in his direction. They were focused tightly on the performance area.

"Death to the capitalist symbols!" a fake rebel shouted.

The fake rebels raised their guns. The girls formed a huddle. If they were going out, they were going out together.

"In the name of the Republic of ChaCha, we —"

The curtains parted with a sudden arrival.

"What the hell is that?" one of the black shirts said.

Miss Miss rattled down the runway on squeaky wheels, but she was no longer clad in just a sash. No, Miss Miss had come to compete in a slinky pink evening gown that stretched across her misshapen body. Her coconut-shell face had been heavily made up with blue eye shadow, rouge, and red lipstick. A chipped rhinestone crown topped her busted wig-of-many-hairpieces. On her right, her twig arm had been turned upward, as if in a wave. The momentum, which had propelled her onto the runway, faded away. Miss Miss tottered slightly on her wheels and at last came to a stop near the end of the runway, where she sat, waiting, like some ancient idol. For a moment, everyone was utterly spellbound. Even the ocean quieted to a gentle purr.

The hiss of walkie-talkie static punctured the stillness. Taylor's voice rang out. "Miss Teen Dream is a light in the darkness. Patriot Daughters can and Patriot Daughters do!"

"Do you hear that?" Agent Jones's voice could just be heard coming through the earpiece of a fake rebel.

"The girl?" the black shirt answered.

"No! Under that. Like a whine or a beep."

It was hard to tell with Taylor doing a monologue of crazy, but Adina noticed it, too — a faint, steady beep, like a tiny alarm clock.

"Find out where that's coming from!" Agent Jones demanded via the earpiece.

"What's going on?" Petra whispered.

"Not sure yet," Adina whispered back.

"In the pageant of life, a girl fixes the sequins. Fixes. Fixes. So much to fix." Under the walkie-talkie static, Taylor's voice was almost little-girlish. "I can't be what you want me to be."

"Where is she?" Nicole whispered.

Adina shook her head. She didn't see Taylor anywhere, and she was afraid of drawing too much attention. Right now, the black shirts were distracted. Distracted was a good thing. Some of them had fanned out to look for Taylor and the source of the beeping. On the sidelines, Agent Jones looked angry and tense as he barked terse orders. The girls needed to use this momentary chaos to their advantage, but how?

"I will represent to the best of my ability the . . . the . . . now, come on, Miss Texas!" Taylor giggled. "The, um, dreams of the ultimate sparkle and circle-turn and wave!"

Adina surveyed the scene desperately, looking for a possible exit strategy. She glanced past Miss Miss, then came back again. At first, she could scarcely make out the message. She had to block the light to get a better look. But there was no mistaking it, and a small *ha* bubbled up inside Adina.

The note had been scrawled in red lipstick on the back of Miss Miss's sash where only the girls could see it. It was just one word: *Run.*

"Oh, Taylor, you beautiful, beautiful bitch." Adina motioned to the others, shouting. "Teen Dreamers! Fall back! Fall back!"

The girls bolted, scattershot, toward the jungle.

"It's a whole new world of pretty. . . ." Taylor sang over the walkie-talkie.

"Hey!" One of the black shirts trained his gun on the girls just as another black shirt approached Miss Miss.

"I think that beep's coming from inside. . . ."

"Thank you. Thank you. I love you all," Taylor said.

At that same instant, the watch inside Miss Miss beeped from one to zero, and the most busted-ass beauty queen ever exploded in a spectacular fireball.

CHAPTER THIRTY-SEVEN

Adina's ears rang and she was covered in a shower of dirt, scorched sticks, and sequins. Chaos. It was chaos. The beach was on fire. Staccato gunfire punctuated clauses of shouting. Black shirts fought with MoMo's real guards. The remaining Corporation employees screamed and ran, panicked, along the beach. A cameraman asked if he should be getting this, and a black shirt answered by bashing in his camera.

Through the smoke, Adina caught a glimpse of Taylor. She swung down from the tree where she had been hiding and stood at the edge of the jungle, mesmerized. Tendrils of light screamed down from the sky. The white stars of it were reflected in the glassy blue of her eyes. "Pretty . . ." Taylor said in awe just before the explosives took out a section of trees and sent Adina flying back on her butt. Agent Jones peered into the smoke and pointed to the girls. He signaled his black shirts.

"Time to go, Miss Texas!" Adina warned.

Like a switch had been thrown, Taylor turned and ran. Adina scrambled to her feet and followed the faded glitter of Taylor's gown into the jungle.

Shanti and Nicole had dodged left in the melee. Now they were running deep into the jungle with a phalanx of black shirts behind them.

"Are they still there?" Shanti called. Her lungs burned and her legs were cut from switches.

In answer, a bullet blasted a chunk from a nearby tree and the girls sped up, twisting and turning through the green.

"I can't . . ." Shanti said. "Can't run . . ."

"We have to keep moving."

"You go."

"Not without you." Nicole looked around for something — a weapon, a hole, a hiding spot. Through the trees, she saw one of the totems. "Just a little farther, Bollywood."

They found their way to the ruined temple and slipped between the columns, hiding. The moon wasn't cooperating; bright and full, it might as well have been a spotlight. Their breath came out in small rips. The men and their guns had arrived. If the girls ran, they'd be easy targets. Their only hope was to remain hidden, and that wasn't much hope at all. Nicole reached out for Shanti's hand. Shanti closed her eyes tightly. Her lips moved in silent appeal to whatever ancestral spirits might still live on in this place.

"I think I see something," one of the black shirts said, and Nicole, too, closed her eyes.

Shanti and Nicole pressed their hands together tightly. A wind soft as a warm breath blew across their faces. It left them and turned fierce, stripping leaves from trees and pulling the dirt from ancient earthen walls. Like an angry fist, it pushed the black shirts from the temple, forcing them back into the jungle. They shouted as sharp grit attacked their eyes and mouths relentlessly. The wind howled with such force that Shanti and Nicole could almost hear something human in its cries. The agents were forced to retreat, chased by the sirocco. Once they were gone, the wind died down. Shanti and Nicole were alone. They did not know what had caused the sudden windstorm.

"Could have been anything," Nicole said.

"Yeah, anything," Shanti agreed. "Atmospheric pressure."

"Sudden tornado."

The totems did not give any answers. Shanti bowed to the now quiet land. "Thank you."

"Thank you," Nicole said.

The wind responded with a light flutter of contentment.

Mary Lou and Tane had managed to avoid a direct hit, but the other ship fired again, narrowly missing them. They were on the run in the heavy fog.

"Can we fire back?" Mary Lou asked.

"Dunno. I just figured out how to steer this thing," Tane answered. "Here. You take over and I'll take a peek at the control panel."

They switched places and Mary Lou put her hands on the wheel. She'd driven a car and a tractor, but this was something else entirely. It had the feel of destiny to it. "Man, I could get used to this."

Mary Lou squinted into the fogbank again just as the ship emerged. She had to shift quickly into reverse to avoid colliding with it, and both she and Tane had to hold on tightly to keep from flying against the yacht's custom teak cabinets.

"Whoa!" Tane called from the floor.

"Sorry!"

The enemy ship passed with only feet to spare. Mary Lou peered through the windows at it and broke into a huge grin. "I don't believe it."

A cannonball narrowly missed the yacht, soaking the bow and sending them wobbling like a toy again. "Tane! Take over!"

She took the spiral staircase at a clip and raced onto the upper deck. "Ahoy there, mateys!" she yelled, waving her arms wildly.

In the fog, she could hear Sinjin St. Sinjin's order. "Cease your bloody fire, mates! Can't you see there's a hot bird ahead?"

Miss Ohio had taken her troops to the trees. "Shooters ready? New Mexico?"

"Ready," Miss New Mexico answered. The arrows were laid out on the tray in her forehead, ready to go.

"Montana?"

Miss Montana held up her bow. "Check."

"Arkansas?"

In her good hand, Miss Arkansas held a small coconut. "Oh yeah."

"I guess we're good to go," Miss Ohio said. The footsteps were coming closer. "See them, New Mexico?"

"Not yet, Miss Ohi — do you think we could just call one another by our names?"

Miss Ohio nodded. "Sure thing, Caitlin."

"Thanks, Caitlin," Miss New Mexico answered. "Caitlin, I see them. They're coming from your right."

"Which Caitlin?" Miss Montana asked. "Me or Caitlin Arkansas?"

"Um, Caitlin Montana."

"Ugh. That just made me sound like a porn star," Miss Montana complained.

"Do you have a middle name? Maybe that would make it easier?"

"Yeah. It's Ashley," Miss Montana said.

"That's my middle name, too," Miss New Mexico said.

"And mine." Miss Arkansas shrugged apologetically.

"Mine's Ashlee with two *e*'s," Miss Ohio offered.

Miss Montana nodded. "Right. What do you see now, New Mexico?"

"They're almost here."

Three black shirts moved through, guns drawn. Miss Ohio used her fingers to count down.

"Now!" she shouted. The arrows zipped down through the growth, clipping fronds *whsk-whsk-whsk*. One found its mark in a guard's thigh. His AK-47 went off as he fell to the ground, grabbing at the thin stake of wood.

"Reload!" Miss Ohio shouted, ducking.

A second hail of arrows arched out in a flawless display. It was like the opening number of the Miss Teen Dream Pageant with every girl knowing her steps, every girl in perfect sync with her sisters. Miss Arkansas launched her coconut at a guard's head and he went down hard.

Miss Ohio dropped to the ground. "Take the guns," she barked. The other girls scrambled down past the unconscious guard and the other two men who had taken arrows in the legs and butt.

"You bitches!" a guard snarled at Miss Montana.

"Excuse me? *You* try to kill us, we defend ourselves, and *we* get called bitches? So typical!" Miss New Mexico head butted the man, knocking him out with her tray.

"Thanks," Miss Montana said.

"Don't mention it."

The girls removed the ammo and tossed the guns as far into the jungle as they could sling them. Then they set off for the compound.

"This is going to look so good when they make the TV movie of my life," Miss Ohio said.

Back on the beach, The Peacock examined the bulletproof vest, which had taken the full brunt of the gunfire. General Good Times had not been so lucky. "General Good Times! Noooo!" The Peacock fell to his knees in the sand. When he rose again, he held aloft the only thing left of his comrade — a stuffed foot. In the firelight, The Peacock's eyes burned. His Elvis wig had been knocked askew during the blast. It clung to his scalp like tentacles of softserve ice cream on a hot day.

Spittle formed at the taut edges of his mouth. "I will have revenge on toast for the death of my trusted advisor. Soon, everybody in the whole cell block will be dancing to my jailhouse rock." The Peacock removed the safety from his pistol. "Let's boogie, beauty queens."

"HEY! JENNIFER! STOP!"

Jennifer turned to face Sosie, who was bent over, breathing deeply.

"We need to keep moving," Jennifer signed.

"No. Stop. Need to know first."

"Know what?"

Sosie hesitated for a moment, waiting for the words. "Why are you ignoring me?"

"I'm not ignoring you."

"Bullshit. You've been avoiding me ever since . . ." Sosie stopped. "Is it because I'm not sure I'm gay?"

Jennifer gestured to the jungle behind them. "You know what? Not the time."

"Yes. It is the time. If we get offed by a bunch of Corporation assholes, I don't want to go out without telling you this."

"Telling me what?"

Sosie rubbed her right fist over her heart.

"Sorry for what?" Jennifer signed.

"Sorry I can't be what you want me to be. Sorry I'm not your dream girl."

Jennifer wanted to let it go, but she couldn't. "You kissed me! What the hell was that?"

"I don't know! I just . . . wanted to."

"So, it was nothing for you? Like, 'Hey, kids, I wanted to try strawberry licorice, so I did. Hooray! How cool am I?'"

"I don't know what you're saying," Sosie said.

"Did that mean nothing to you?" Jennifer enunciated clearly.

"It wasn't like that. I liked it. I like *you*."

"I'm all confused again." Jennifer paced away and came back. "Are you gay or not?"

"I don't know what I am yet," Sosie answered. "I'm still figuring it out. But if I *were* a big, card-carrying, softball-playing, Joan Jett–worshipping lezbot, I would totally jump you."

"Nice stereotyping." Jennifer rolled her eyes, but a blush worked its way up her neck. "For the record, I hate softball. But, um, thanks for that other bit."

Sosie hugged Jennifer. "You're, like, the coolest girl I know. And I'd hate it if you hated me."

"I don't hate you. As much. I mean, I definitely hated you for a little while there."

Sosie folded down her middle and ring fingers and waved the sign at Jennifer.

"Whatever," Jennifer said.

"Do it back."

"We need to go."

Sosie didn't give up. She turned it into a robot dance, arms and legs popping and locking, her expression wide-eyed and smiling.

"Don't do the happy robot dance. You know I'm defenseless against that."

Sosie quickened her jerky movements until she resembled a robot on speed. Through it all, she kept her hands locked in the same sign until Jennifer finally laughed.

"Okay, okay," she said, returning the gesture. "I love you, too."

Sosie stuck out her hand. "Friends?"

Jennifer sighed. She gave Sosie a small, fake punch to the upper arm. "Eventually."

Sosie nodded. "Fair enough. Someday, you'll marry this amazing woman and I'll be your maid of honor."

Jennifer made a face. "Maybe Adina will be my maid of honor."

Sosie raised an eyebrow.

"Right. Well, you better get me a big wedding present."

Sosie wasn't sure what Jennifer had said, but she was smiling, so Sosie smiled, too. "Ready, Flint Avenger?"

"Ready, Sidekick Sosie. Let's go take down an evil corporation."

*　　*　　*

Taylor led Adina to the arsenal the girls had made in the jungle weeks before, and Adina cleared away vines and leaves from the catapult, the cannon, the stash of beauty product weapons. "Cool. I think I can get this working. . . ."

Adina heard a gun cock. She turned and saw Taylor aiming the rifle at her. "Taylor, what are you doing?"

"You're not a Miss Teen Dream. You never believed."

Adina swallowed hard. Sweat trickled into her gown. "No."

"Why did you do that?"

"I thought it was bad for us."

"There's a lot worse out there," Taylor said.

"I know that now."

"I've been in the jungle a long time," Taylor said in a voice made hoarse by tears. Adina started to say something and Taylor shushed her. "No. Listen. No one ever just listens."

Adina nodded. "Okay."

"At first, I was scared to be alone. No routines. No rules. Just me. But I think . . ." Taylor wiped a tear away. "I think I was always in the jungle. Before. It was always there. I think I had to come out here to find the answer."

Above them, a bird screeched. Another answered. The trees echoed.

"And what did you find?"

"I love myself. They make it so hard for us to love ourselves." Taylor stared off into the dark. Her face gleamed with tears. Snot ran over her lips. "The judges won't like that answer."

"Nobody's judging you."

Taylor choked on a sob. "Always," she whispered.

"I'm not the enemy, Taylor."

With an angry grunt, Taylor raised the gun again.

"Taylor . . ." Adina pleaded. She shut her eyes as the gun went

352

off. She heard a thump behind her. The black shirt was inches away, the knife still in his hand. "Holy shit!"

"Language, Miss New Hampshire," Taylor said. The smoke from the gun billowed around her face. "You owe me twenty-five cents."

Adina laughed. For a second, she thought she sensed a glimmer of the non-crazy Taylor, or at least the less-crazy Taylor.

There were shouts from the trees. More were coming. Adina hopped behind the catapult and readied the eyelash curler and lipstick projectiles. "You ready to kick some bad-people butt, Miss Texas?"

Taylor adjusted the bandolier so that it fell perfectly across her chest like a winner's sash. She brushed her fingers through her hair and grabbed her AK-47. With a final toss of her head, she smiled. Her eyes glistened. "You know what? I am."

Adina loaded the catapult with eyelash curlers, safety razors, and straightening irons. "Who's more awesome than you, Taylor Rene Krystal Hawkins, Miss Teen Dream Texas?"

Taylor seemed to think for a moment. "Nobody." She cut the rope and a volley of beauty products sailed through the trees. The black shirts shouted as the metal hit them.

A black shirt reached for Taylor, who rolled and retrieved the filled foundation tube. She blew hard, getting him splat in the eyes. He shrieked. Another guard leapt onto Taylor from the tree. He raised his knife. Adina swirled the hair dryer on its cord and let it fly, whacking him in the head and knocking him out.

"Boo-yah!" she shouted.

Taylor lured the others. She grabbed a vine and swung over the leaf-strewn pit. Foolishly, the black shirts charged and fell deep into the hole. A shot grazed Taylor's arm.

"Taylor!" Adina ducked behind a tree. "Taylor, get your ass over here!"

"Language," Taylor said through clenched teeth. Her arm oozed blood. She looked up to see Agent Jones aiming for her.

"Taylor!" Adina whisper-shouted.

Taylor narrowed her eyes. A strange smile played at her lips. "Final interview round, Miss New Hampshire! I'm sorry. You have not made Top Five. Dodge and weave back to Hanover."

Agent Jones got off another shot, but this time, Taylor was ready. She darted into the jungle to her right, letting Agent Jones chase her.

"Shit," Adina said, and ran for the compound.

CHAPTER THIRTY-EIGHT

Harris had waited until he was sure he was alone before angling the Swiss Army Knife from his pocket and cutting through his restraints. Tossing the ropes aside, he laughed. "People are always misunderestimating me."

Armed with an AK-47, he headed out into the jungle just as Tiara and Petra were making their way toward the compound. Harris aimed the AK-47 at the girls and they raised their hands in surrender. Tiara hopped a little from foot to foot.

"Stop moving!" Harris barked.

"Sorry. I have to pee," Tiara said.

"You're the dumb one, aren't you?"

Tiara's face reddened.

"You're one to talk," Petra said.

"Hey! I went to Yale."

"I could go to Yale, too, if my dad bought my way."

"Shut up!" Harris went to hit Petra with the gun, and she karate-chopped his arm. The gun dropped to the ground. They all raced for it at once. Tiara bumped into Petra, who fell backward, giving Harris a chance to grab the gun again. He put the muzzle to Petra's head.

"Stop it!" Tiara yelled.

"Yeah? You smart enough to stop me?"

"I . . ." Tiara wasn't sure what to do. He had a gun to Petra's head. "Um, stop it, please?"

"Please? Please?" Harris laughed. "Oh my God. You really are dumb, aren't you?"

Dumb. It's what everyone had said, when she'd struggled in school or asked questions that made people laugh behind their hands: "Don't worry about it. You're a pretty girl. You'll be fine." But Tiara had worried about it. She felt like someday there would be a test that didn't involve getting an A in pretty, and she would fail it. That test day had come.

"Maybe I'm not the smartest person in the world, but at least I keep trying. I keep learning," she said.

Harris scoffed. "Oh, so *inspiring*. Honestly, what do you know how to do, huh? Tell me and maybe I won't waste you."

"W-well . . ."

"Nothing, that's what," Harris taunted. "All you know how to do is look good."

"Leave her alone!" Petra shouted.

"Say it: I'm dumb."

Tiara's eyes brimmed with tears — not because she was hurt, but because she was angry. There *was* something Tiara knew how to do: keep her composure under pressure. "No matter what, a pageant girl keeps her smile," Mr. Ray Ray, the pageant coach from Tupelo, had told her once. "Even if the girl in front of you slips and falls on her bon-hooney and then catches on fire, too, you just keep smiling like nothing happened." Tiara saw the movement in the trees and she smiled.

"Okay. I'm dumb."

Harris seemed pleased with himself. "You sure are. You are a dumb, useless bitch."

"Yep." Tiara continued watching the movement behind Harris. Her smile did not falter.

"What are you smiling about?"

"Nothing. Just keeping my composure."

"Well, you do that, sweetheart. Any last words?"

"Not really," Tiara said. "Just that there's a giant snake behind you."

Harris smirked. "You think I'm going to fall for that? You must think I'm as dumb as you are."

The hiss wasn't terribly loud, but it was deep and personal and very, very pissed off. The hiss coiled itself tightly around the air and squeezed out all other sound. Harris turned slowly. The snake lurched forward, hissing and drooling. Its diseased tongue flicked out like a New Year's Eve party blower losing air. It seemed almost to smile, showing a mouthful of mottled teeth.

"Don't take me — take them! There's two of them! My dad was CEO! I went to Yale!" Harris squeaked.

The snake inched closer. It flicked a tongue across Harris's face and emitted a low grumble.

"Fuck you!" Harris pulled the trigger on the AK-47. Nothing happened.

"Safety," Petra said.

The snake batted the gun from Harris's hands. He backed away, but the molting showgirl of a snake wasn't having it. It lurched forward and, in one giant-size bite, gulped down the screaming Harris Buffington Ewell Davis III. Then, as the girls watched, it slithered calmly back toward the jungle, leaving them alone.

Tiara gave a small wave of farewell. "You know what? Dumb is better than dead."

Adina ran serpentine-style through the jungle as Taylor had instructed. But somewhere she'd taken a wrong turn and come out on the beach. She saw the pirate ship in the lagoon and ran for it. It appeared to be empty. She turned to leave and ran headlong into Duff. She screamed and Duff jumped back.

"What the hell are you doing here?" she yelled.

"Thank God you're okay!" he said.

"Okay? *Okay?* I'm being shot at and, like, a billion people are trying to kill me and there's explosives and despite all of that, I am still really, really, *really* pissed off at you, you asshole."

Duff smiled. "Nice to see you, too."

"Whatever. We have to get to the compound."

"Lead the way," Duff said.

"Not so fast, hound dogs." MoMo B. ChaCha's platform shoes clunked across the ship's deck. He moved like an injured cat, but one that could still claw and bite. He raised his gun. "You are responsible for this." In his other hand, he held the remains of General Good Times.

"We're responsible for your unfortunate experiments in taxidermy?" Adina asked.

"Don't be insolent, beauty queen!" The Peacock raised his arm to strike. Duff stopped him.

"I don't think so, mate."

"Wait . . . You are familiar to The Peacock. Did I kill your family?"

"No."

"Huh. Disappointing."

"I'm Duff McAvoy of The Corporation's wildly popular cable show, *Captains Bodacious IV: Badder and More Bodaciouser.*"

MoMo let fly a small squeal of excitement and clapped his hands. "Of course!" MoMo embraced Duff, kissing him on both cheeks. "I am number-one fan of your show."

"That's great!" Duff laughed in relief. "That's . . . that's brilliant."

Adina forced a laugh.

MoMo tapped the gun against his forehead. "You are . . . don't tell me . . . Casanova of the Sea?"

"That's me."

MoMo raised an eyebrow at Adina. "And you are his latest conquest, yes?"

Adina cut her eye at Duff.

"Yeah, we were just about to film a bit for the show, so, you know, nice to meet you. No need to stick around. It's dead boring, filming," Duff said, trying to edge away.

"No, no, no. We must make the moment. MoMo will help. With the gun, I will force you both to walk the plank. You will die together. This will be romantical, yes?"

"No!" they yelled.

"Ah, but you are young. Plenty of time to realize these special moments. Then again, considering you are about to die, maybe not. This will be the best show ever!"

"Wait!" Duff called. "Adina didn't do anything wrong. Let her go."

"Really? That's . . . wow," Adina said.

Duff kissed her.

MoMo clapped. "Oh, a gesture so beautiful. Like the smell of a spring flower layered like an onion on a sea of hope."

"Yikes," Adina muttered.

"Bravo, Ser Peacock!" Duff clapped. "You are truly a poet."

"You think so?"

"Absolutely. In fact, what would you say to working with me on the blog? Casanovas of the Sea?"

The Peacock nodded, grinning. Then he stopped. "Better yet: You die and I take over the blog. To the gangplank."

"I'm going to add this to my reasons for hating you," Adina said as they edged out onto the gangplank.

"I may be a fuckup, Adina. But I really like you. I swear."

He grabbed her hand. Adina felt the warmth of Duff's fingers. Then she bent them back with all her might and Duff hissed in pain. "I. Will break. Your fucking. Hand," Adina cooed.

"Hello, lovebirds! Time to die!" The Peacock edged out onto the gangplank and jumped up and down. "Bouncy, bouncy, bouncy!"

Adina and Duff fought to keep their balance. "Cut it out!" Adina shouted.

"Soon I will be reunited with *my* lady love, Ladybird Hope."

"You and Ladybird . . . ?"

"It is she who arranged for me to be here. To buy the weapons. But we were betrayed by these Corporation types who do not understand our love."

Adina's mind whirred with connections. "Wait a minute — you and Ladybird Hope? She's behind the arms deal? But then . . . Ladybird Hope knew we were here. Ladybird organized the pageant. Ladybird is on The Corporation's Board of Directors."

"Yes, yes," MoMo said, gesturing in a *get on with it* way. "She multitasks, my little minx."

"Don't you see? If Ladybird organized all of this, she's the one who tried to frame you for our murder!"

MoMo's eyes narrowed. His mustache twitched like a bug suddenly on its back. "My ears burn with hate for what you say. You will answer for this to Ladybird herself. I avenge the General." He raised his gun.

"No!" Adina said. "You're right. Let's talk to Ladybird. I'm sure she'll clear everything up. We can talk to her back at the compound."

"Ladybird is here? Now?"

"Yes!" Adina lied. "Plus, you will love the compound. Weapons galore! And gummi bears."

MoMo clicked the gun against his teeth, thinking. Then he leveled it at them again. "You will take me to this compound now."

Agent Jones bent over, gasping for breath, his gun resting against his knee for a second. The blonde had given him a sharp kick to the kidneys and sprinted ahead. Agent Jones had lived through a lot in his years with the agency, but tonight marked the absolute nadir. If he didn't get this under control, his entire career was headed straight for the crapper. No pension. No inscribed pen set. Just the knowledge that he'd been defeated by a pack of teen beauty queens. He flashed on an image of his father in his clown suit just before that final party. In the memory, his old man stood before the hall mirror, the stubble on his cheeks poking through his white face makeup like beach scrub. "Happy birthday," he'd croaked to his reflection, practicing a smile, but only managing a grimace.

"I'm not making anybody a balloon animal today," Agent Jones said to himself. He started running, pouring on speed despite the ache in his back. He saw a curve of blond hair poking out from behind a tree just ahead and smiled. At last his luck was turning. He'd take down Miss Texas. Any ambivalence he'd felt about killing these beauty queens had been erased by this one's relentless campaign against him. She'd come to symbolize everything that was wrong with his mediocre life. Carefully, he crept toward the tree where she was hiding. "Gotcha," he whispered, reaching out for her. "Ow." He slapped at his neck where the mosquito had stung him and came away with a needle-thin dart. Before he could react, another hit him in the butt. He looked up to see Taylor pulling the tube from her mouth. His hand reached out and came away with a blond hairpiece. Off to his right, the ghost of his father seemed to be standing in the trees, grinning. And then the jungle began to turn upside down.

The pirates and the girls had made it back to the compound conference room.

"Petra!" Sinjin ran for her. He had not removed her bathrobe.

Petra threw her arms around Sinjin. Then she slapped his face. Then she kissed him.

"What the hell happened?" she demanded. "I ought to kick your ass and break up with you."

"I know! I'll explain everything, I swear." He rubbed his cheek and gave a naughty smile. "Hot! Like a she-cat. *Grrrr!*"

"Call me a she-cat again and I will kick your ass on principle."

"Right. Got it." Sinjin saluted. He hugged Petra. "I was really worried about you."

"Color me unconvinced," Petra said.

"When I saw that dead man in the lagoon, I thought the black shirts were after us and that we'd brought further danger to you babes," Sinjin explained.

"Because it's all about you," Adina singsonged.

"I thought if we left, they might follow us and leave you babes alone. And hopefully, we'd make it to a port and get help. Not a great idea, but the best I had at the moment. And then Ahmed discovered a jar of lady hair remover that turned out to be a bomb. . . ."

"That didn't work, 'cause whoever engineered it was a moron," Ahmed finished.

"Anyway, we were heading out to sea when my conscience got the better of me. Bloody inconvenient, having one of those. I thought of my lady love, Miss Petra, back here, eating grubs from the sand, and me wearing her heels on the ship — mind, I looked *unbelievable* in them, a glam-rock captain of all captains. But there I was on the bow in m' heels and fishnets, the wind blowing my hair about, all romance-cover hero, making my man nipples stand up all nice 'n' twimbly. And I thought, 'Wait a minute, hold on — why are we running? We can't do this. We've got to face these arsebuckets ourselves.' So I said, 'Mates, are we mice or are we men? If those ladies are in trouble, then by Blackbeard, we'll stand with them and fight. So let's turn this ship around. One for all and all for one, ladies included, even playing field, what's fair for the goose is fair for the gander, damn the torpedoes, don't stop till you get enough, rock the Casbah, God save the Queen, and full speed ahead.'"

"Actually, Cap'n, you said, 'Cor blimey, I need to take a piss.' Then you said them other bits," George said.

Petra put a hand to her heart. "My hero."

Sinjin kissed Petra's hands. "Petra, I've got me faults. I'm a bit full of m'self and I might steal your clothes on occasion. But I'm loyal and well read and I'll stand by your side no matter what. Byron's balls! I'm absolutely barmy for you. Will you have me?"

Petra smirked. "Shut up and kiss me."

The girls swooned as Petra swept Sinjin up into her arms.

"God, you're lovely. And quite strong." Sinjin kissed her hard on the mouth.

"Later. We've got to try to upload this video of Ladybird and MoMo," Mary Lou said.

"Ladybird Hope and The Peacock really did the nasty?" Nicole asked.

"Uh-huh. Don't remind me. I want to wash my eyeballs. Just . . . I mean, the hot tub and her crown and the Elvis wig . . ."

"You are totally scarring me for future sex," Shanti said.

"She can't be trusted. She's in on this."

"In on it? Little girl, I masterminded it." Sudden fluorescent light brightened the gloom of the conference room. The flat-screen TV popped on. Ladybird Hope sat behind a replica of the president's desk in a fake oval office.

"You think she got that from the Delusional Home Furnishings Superstore?" Petra whispered.

"I heard that, Miss Rhode Island," Ladybird chided.

MoMo pushed Adina and Duff into the room.

"Adina! Duff! Crazy dictator man with gun!" Mary Lou called. "Okay. Roll call of doom all done."

"Well, hello, MoMo." Onscreen, Ladybird gave a stiff wave.

"I am here, my flightless fowl."

"Actually, the ladybird isn't a bird at all. It's a type of beetle. A pest," Shanti said pointedly.

"Speaking of pests, I can't wait till I can enact some new immigration laws. Hope you have a cute little Hindi handbag to hold your papers, Miss California. I'd hate to think of you being exported to some call center in Mumbai."

"*Deported*. People are deported. Products are exported," Nicole corrected.

"Well, my goodness. Thanks for reminding me to overhaul textbooks during my reign."

"You're running for president, not queen."

Ladybird scratched a file over the end of a less-than-perfect nail. "Actually, I figured out that running for office is a lot like being in a beauty pageant. Look good. Smile and wave. And tell the people only what they want to hear." She blew away freshly buffed nail fuzz. "Oh, and make sure you wash your hands after applying self-tanner. Otherwise, people might think you're secretly Mexican."

"*Serape* means 'cape'!" A grinning Agent Jones burst into the room wearing only a fig leaf. He threw his arms into the air and stretched his fingers into peace signs. "We are all beautiful star flowers!"

"What the hell?" Jennifer said.

Ladybird squinted. "Agent Jones?"

"Who is that unfortunate man?" Sinjin asked.

"The Corporation agent who tried to kill us," Petra explained. Sinjin took in the sight of the man in the fig leaf trying to commune with the ergo chair. He raised an eyebrow.

"He had on more clothes," Petra said.

Agent Jones put a finger to his mouth. "Agent Jones is gone. I am Man Flower."

"Agent Jones," Ladybird barked.

"Man Flower."

"Agent Jones, I am trying to quiet the hideous screaming I feel inside just looking at you. It's a shame that after all your years of dutiful service, you will not be able to partake in the pension plan. Not that it matters; we're cutting that anyway."

Agent Jones held Sinjin's face in his hands. "I'm going to make balloon animals. People need balloon animals."

"How right you are, strange delusional man," Sinjin said.

MoMo shot at the ceiling and everyone jumped. "Where are my weapons?"

"Just relax, Peacock," Ladybird snapped. "Are you wearing the special shoes I sent you?"

"Just as you requested, Ladybird." MoMo hopped onto the conference room table where everyone could have a better view of his platform blue suede shoes. He executed a series of tricky dance steps.

Ladybird's lips curled in distaste. "Was that necessary, MoMo?"

"Our love brings the dance fever. It is like the King, always and forever."

"Well, maybe not, MoMo." Ladybird repositioned a bobby pin and patted the pouf at the back of her head. "See, if I'm gonna be the leader of the free world, I can't be seen canoodling with the crazy dictator of a country we're about to go to war with."

"What are you saying? We are not to be at war. I will let you have your little factory when we are married. But first, the weapons."

"Mmm, not so much, Peacock. I thought of something better. You get framed for killing our girls. We kill you in response. Then we go to war with your country and set up shop without anybody regulatin' or gettin' in our hair. Oh, and I get elected president."

"What . . . what are you saying, Ladybird? It's like you are the devil in disguise."

"Oh, MoMo. We had some swell times. And now, it is time for you to die."

Ladybird turned a dial on her signature diamond watch. MoMo grimaced and grunted in pain.

"Electrical current. Tucked into the heels of those blue suede shoes I gave you for Christmas," Ladybird explained.

"Acckkk! Gah!" MoMo's body twisted into unnatural shapes as he moved around the room. He shook, convulsed, and finally fell to the floor, dead. Ladybird Hope sighed and readjusted her watch.

"Well," she said, patting her hair. "He always did love to dance."

Tiara glared at Ladybird. "You're a D-E-W-S-H."

Ladybird's eyebrows knit together in concentration. "Do you mean *douche*?"

"We never did cover spelling in Smart Class," Adina said.

Jennifer marched toward the screen. "When The Corporation finds out what you're doing, they are so going to drop you as a sponsor."

"Listen, Little Orphan Lezzie, who do you think is puttin' me in power? The presidency is now a Corporation-run business. And I intend to be Chairman of the Board. I've already got what I need — footage of ROC soldiers and an explosion. That's what America will see on *Barry Rex Live* in about ten minutes. America will demand justice. I'll make that justice my campaign promise. There will be T-shirts — made in my factories, of course — to show support. They'll have your faces on 'em and some neato phrase, like, 'Because they never got to walk the runway of life.'" Ladybird sighed. "Unfortunately, none of you will be around to watch the show. Can you imagine what a great moment that will be when I, Ladybird Hope, the best Miss Teen Dream who ever lived, appear at the televised memorial and lay a crown on the memorial grave of the beauty queens? I'll give a speech about how we cannot let your deaths have been in vain, and then, as a final tribute, I will play a moving cello solo. I'll be back in the game. Shoot, I'll *own* the game."

"This is not a game," Adina said.

Ladybird stopped filing. "Honey, everything's a game. There are winners and losers. I am a winner. And you . . ." Ladybird pushed a button on her remote. Steel doors slammed down, sealing them inside. ". . . are the losers. Now, I'm real sorry to tell you this, but I've rigged the island to blow. See? The detonator is a remote and it's right here in my God Bless America crystal flag pin. Course, I won't be selling this particular pin on the Armchair Shopping Network." Ladybird laughed. She snorted at the end like a corgi. "Oh. But I *am* giving you a countdown, 'cause that's classy. Prepare to take your final walk on the runway, Teen Dreams. Rest assured you'll be more famous in death than you'd ever have been in life. There's a small comfort in that, isn't there?"

"No. Not at all," Adina said.

"Well. With an attitude like that, it's no wonder you're in this position."

A disembodied woman's voice came over the speaker system. "Commencing countdown to destruction in ten minutes. Nine fifty-nine. Nine fifty-eight. Nine fifty-seven . . ."

"Oops. Looks like it's time for me to go on *Barry Rex Live* and break the news about your deaths to a frightened nation looking for guidance. So long, Teen Dreamers." Ladybird smiled and waved a stiff hand in a beauty queen salute. "Sorry you won't go out pretty."

The screen went dead.

"I am so not voting for her," Tiara said.

"Nine thirty. Nine twenty-nine. Nine twenty-eight . . ."

Adina ran to the control panel embedded in a long desk beneath the TV screen. "There has to be some way to turn this thing off, right? Like a-a whatchamacallit. . . ."

"Off switch! Do-over button!" Miss Ohio said.

"Voice recognition software, maybe," Shanti said, searching the control panel for some hint.

"One of those palm-reading things?" Jennifer offered. She and Sosie pushed buttons in random sequences, hoping for a detonation-stopping bingo.

"Eight fifty-one. Eight fifty . . ."

"Crap!" Adina said. "What's the name of that thing that always stops the bomb in the movies?"

"Manual system override," Agent Jones said dreamily.

The girls turned to him.

"Manual system override," Nicole repeated.

"Mmm-hmm. Stops it."

"Agent Jones," Nicole asked carefully. "Do *you* know how to override the system manually?"

"Screw the system, man. You're beautiful. I'm beautiful. This table is beautiful."

"We are all beautiful. You know what would be most beautiful? Overriding the fucking system, asswipe!" Jennifer yelled.

Agent Jones frowned. "Men have feelings, too. You bruised the petals of my man flower."

"Christ," Jennifer hissed.

"Apologize," he said.

"What? No way."

"Apologize or no system override."

"Jen . . ."

"This douche nozzle tried to kill us. A lot."

"Apologize!" everyone screamed.

"Okay! I am sorry . . . Man Flower."

The agent wrapped her in a big hug. "It's PowerPoint."

"I apologize, PowerPoint," Jennifer said through lips crushed against Agent Jones's chest.

"The system is PowerPoint only. Harris forgot to change it back. Let's communicate with our fingers."

"Agent Jones! So . . . we have to make a PowerPoint presentation to override the system?" Shanti slapped a hand to her forehead. "Are you kidding me?"

"Mmm-hmm. Pretty pictures and bullet points." The agent sat, lotus-style, on the table.

"Oh, hey," Nicole said, averting her eyes.

Shanti sat down at the computer. "We're making a PowerPoint, Teen Dreams."

CHAPTER THIRTY-NINE

"How's it coming, Shanti?" a nervous Mary Lou asked six minutes later.

Shanti concentrated on the laptop. "Almost there."

Tiara looked over her shoulder. "Ooh, put in the picture with the mountains. That one was so pretty."

"Fifty-nine. Fifty-eight. Fifty-seven . . ."

"Less than a minute to go, Bollywood," Nicole said.

"Hello! Well aware, thank you. 'Kay. Uploading now . . ."

Shanti pressed PLAY, and the PowerPoint presentation was in motion. It was an image of Ladybird Hope waving from a Corporation private plane.

Fun Facts About Ladybird Hope & The Corporation!
- **Tried to kill us**
- **Kept rescuers from finding us**
- **Made secret arms deal with Republic of ChaCha**
- **Assassinated world leader**
- **Her pageant-wear line poorly made**
- **Again, tried to kill us**

"Go to second screen!" Nicole said.

"Give it a second," Shanti said. "I put it on slide show. That's how we do it in IP."

Two seconds later, an island scene came up.

"I picked that shot," Tiara said, clapping. "Isn't it pretty?"

There Is a Secret Corporation Compound!
- Polluting environment
- Harming animals
- Making weapons
- Avoiding taxes
- Forming secret alliances

"Twenty-eight. Twenty-seven. Twenty-six . . ."

"Come on, come on," Adina pleaded softly.

A shot of Ladybird Hope and MoMo B. ChaCha in the heart-shaped hot tub appeared onscreen. Ladybird Hope had been caught midspeech. Her mouth was twisted and her eyes were half closed.

"Not her best," Sinjin said. "Still. Total MILF. Paranoid and very wrong, but MILF."

Ladybird Hope and The Peacock!
- Secret alliances = treason
- Illegal weapons sales = also treason
- Illegal campaign contributions = bad
- Human rights violations = super bad
- Killing defenseless Bambi = just plain mean
- Totally having sex in that hot tub = conflict of interest, unethical, unsanitary

"Nineteen. Eighteen. Seventeen. Sixteen . . ."

"It's a whole new world of pretty . . ." Agent Jones sang, rocking softly on the table.

Shanti glanced at him, then looked to the ceiling. "Please don't let this be the way I die."

The fourth and final panel was of Ladybird Hope smiling and waving between The Corporation's logo and the White House.

America's Presidency: Reality TV Show or Commodity?

The screen faded to black and the words *The End*.

"Did it work?" Adina asked.

"Five. Four. Three. Two . . ."

They held their breath.

"Awesome PowerPoint! System override successful. Thank you. Have a productive day."

The metal doors and shutters rolled open. They were free. The girls and pirates collapsed onto the floor in relief. Agent Jones hugged one of the ergonomically correct chairs. "I think you're special. Do you think I'm special?"

A powerful rumble shook the room.

"What's happening?" Tiara said, grabbing hold of George, who didn't seem to mind.

Adina sat up, panicked. "I thought we overrode the system!"

"We did!" Shanti shouted.

"Then what's that scary sound? Earthquake?" Miss Ohio asked.

Tane's face was grim. "It's the volcano."

"The *dead* volcano?" Mary Lou's eyes opened wide.

"Maybe the system override activated something?" Tane pointed to the monitor. On the screen, the volcano's opening spewed smoke and ash.

Jennifer gaped at the image. "Whoa."

"Holy shit!" Sosie said.

"Beautiful," Agent Jones murmured.

"OMG," Shanti gasped.

"Totally phallic," Tiara said. "Oh. That means like a penis."

"That means trouble," Petra said. "The volcano, not the penis."

"Thank God, luv," Sinjin said.

"Give it a rest," Adina muttered.

"What do we do now?" Nicole asked.

The ground shook, knocking Corporation graph charts from walls.

"Run!" Mary Lou shouted just as the alarm flared red and everything began to crumble.

CHAPTER FORTY

Nicole had the sensation of floating in a gray-white haze. Fabio Testosterone called her name. Streamers fell from a ceiling. Cameras flashed. Girls in sashes clapped for her. The Miss Teen Dream theme song played under the audience's thunderous applause. She dipped slightly and let last year's winner place the crown on her head. It was surprisingly heavy. And then she was walking down a runway, roses cradled in her right arm. With her left arm, she waved and blew kisses. Down in the front row, her mother sat, looking proud and a little scared. She mouthed, "I love you," and Nicole mouthed back, "Love you, too."

Auntie Abeo was there. So were her father and her brother. Sherry Sparks nodded sagely as Nicole passed. *I did it. I won!* Nicole thought. But coming back up the runway, Nicole remembered strange things. A plane crash. An island. Fighting for survival. She remembered a red warning light and bolting down hallways as rivets popped and supersecret high-tech equipment tumbled from desks. Glass partitions shattered. Screams. Shouts of "This way! This way!" A strange man in a fig leaf pushing her and others toward safety. The ground trembling. A great roar of smoke and ash billowing from a volcano. An explosion. And then Nicole was tumbling through the air, head over heels. Now she was here, wherever here was, and everyone was clapping for her.

She remembered something else. Faces of other girls. Friends. The best friends of her life, perhaps. And now she saw them clearly. They waited just outside the open doorway of the auditorium beside a painted school bus. A girl in a pink hoodie emblazoned with the word *Bollywood* across it and oversize shades, a small diamond in her nose. "Like, hello, are you coming or not, Colorado?"

Nicole still stood on the runway. But she wanted to follow the girl in the pink hoodie. So she stripped off her sash and tossed it into the crowd. Then she handed the crown to Sherry Sparks, who looked regal in it. "No thanks," she said to the judges. She kicked off her heels and ran toward the promise of the open doorway. It seemed to her that she was not so much running as bobbing. Applause transformed into the swooshing of waves. Overhead, the sky brightened from night to early morning white haze.

"I told you to stop using that bleaching cream," she murmured to the vast expanse above her. A Shanti-shaped cloud drifted into view, blocking the light.

"Nicole?" the Shanti-shaped cloud said. "Nicole!"

Nicole blinked. "Hey, Bollywood."

"I'm going to let that one slide," Shanti said with relief. "Welcome back."

CHAPTER FORTY-ONE

The girls and the pirates gathered on MoMo's blinged-out yacht, huddled in blankets and towels and robes. Sinjin wore MoMo's black leather 1968 Elvis Comeback Special jacket. It only came to his rib cage, but he wore it anyway. "Hot!" he said, waggling his eyebrows. The morning sun lit the island like a painted backdrop from an old Hollywood movie, all greens and golds, pinks and blues.

"What happened?" Nicole asked from a deck chair. Ahmed had made her a cup of tea. In shifts, the girls and pirates told the tale of what had happened. The volcano hadn't erupted so much as burped. It was the storehouse of Lady 'Stache Off that had exploded, destroying much of the compound. The area around the volcano was a mess.

"You got, like, totally thrown by the explosion," Shanti explained to Nicole. She hugged her. "I'm glad you're okay."

"Thanks," Nicole said, hugging her back.

"Because I totally need a place to stay in Colorado when I go skiing next spring break," Shanti said, and the two of them burst out laughing.

"I could get used to this," Sinjin called. He lounged on a deck chair in his MoMo find. "Yachts are the new sexy. You heard it here first."

"Pretty sure yachts have always been sexy," Petra said.

Ahmed sat with Shanti. "So you mixed Beena's[48] 'Mumbai Love Song,'

---

[48] Beena, the Bollywood actress and singer whose "Hindi Hindi Shake" made her a club sensation in 1999 before the "India-pop" craze was replaced by the "Pakistani Soul" sensation.

the groove from Hip-Hopera's *La-La Boheme*,[49] and Elvis Presley? That's dead brilliant!"

Shanti grinned. "Yeah. I think so."

"My brother runs some clubs in London. I could get you a night. Prolly a shite time slot to start, but it's something."

"Okay, seriously? That would be, like, so totally awesome! I could apply to Cambridge," Shanti said in awe. "I could apply to Cambridge and DJ in London. Yes!" Shanti frowned. "Um, no offense, but I can't . . . this can't be, like, a dating thing."

"What? Oh. Oh! Um, no worries, mate. It's just business. Maybe Nicole and I could come to the club, yeah?" He looked hopefully at Nicole.

"That could work," she said, smiling.

"What about you and me, Adina?" Duff said, sidling up to her by the railing. "I know I screwed up. But do you think we could start over?"

Adina thought about everything that had happened. Part of her wanted to kiss Duff McAvoy, the tortured British trust-fund-runaway-turned-pirate-of-necessity who loved rock 'n' roll and mouthy-but-vulnerable bass-playing girls from New Hampshire. But he didn't exist. Not really. He was a creature of TV and her imagination, a guy she'd invented as much as he'd invented himself. And this was what she suddenly understood about her mother: how with each man, each husband, she was really trying to fill in the sketchy parts of herself and become somebody she could finally love. It was hard to live in the messiness and easier to believe in the dream. And in that moment, Adina knew she was not her mother after all. She would make mistakes, but they wouldn't be the same mistakes. Starting now.

[49] Hip-Hopera's *La-La Boheme*, the Jamaica, Queens–based urban arts collective's hip-hop retelling of Puccini's opera, which was protested by Concerned Citizens of America First for allowing more than ten black people on one stage at the same time.

"Sorry," she said, heading for the bow, where a spot of sun looked inviting. "Oh, also, about that blog? Just so you know, my dads know a lot of gay lawyers. Bitches will take your ass down if you try to publish that. Peace out."

"Ahoy, mateys!" Mary Lou shouted as she emerged from the captain's cabin. She wore breeches and a poufy pirate shirt. She'd tied her Miss Nebraska sash around her waist like a belt and had tied a scarf across her forehead in true pirate fashion.

"Mary Lou!" Adina waved.

"I've talked it over with Sinjin and the guys, and I am officially taking over command of this vessel," Mary Lou shouted. "The Captains Bodacious have a stylin' new boat and a bodacious new captain."

"That is hot," Jennifer muttered.

Adina smirked. "Wow. Kind of braggy, Novak."

"Yeah. It is kind of braggy, isn't it?" Mary Lou smiled. "Well. What can I say? I'm just cool like that."

"Right on, sister." Nicole went for a fist bump, but Mary Lou bungled it. "Man. You are still so, so white."

"What about Tane?" Adina asked.

Tane was supervising the crates of supplies being hoisted on board.

"He's staying with us. He's going to teach me to navigate by the stars. He has good hands. I can tell."

On deck, Chu stood at attention. "Queen Josephine? What course shall we set?"

"Toward adventure! And don't drop anchor till we get there!" she called.

"Aye, aye, Captain!"

"And by adventure, I mean toward Hawaii. I've never been there." Mary Lou let fly a wild wolf call. "This is soooo awesome! And we can drop you home on the way."

Agent Jones was coming down from the Mind's Flower now. The

pirates had thrown a blanket over him. He sat, shivering, on the deck of the yacht.

"You okay?" Jennifer asked. "You want something hot to drink?"

He nodded.

Jennifer handed him the cup. With shaking hands, Agent Jones took it and sipped. His lips twisted into a squiggle.

"Sorry. There's no milk or sugar that I could find," Jennifer said.

The squiggle became a smile. Agent Jones took two big gulps and leaned his head back against the railing, enjoying the breeze. The coffee was hot and strong. It was also Hazelnut.

Shanti toggled a DVD in her fingers. "One last thing to do, Teen Dreamers."

LIVE ON *BARRY REX LIVE*

BARRY REX: Good morning and welcome to a special edition of *Barry Rex Live*. Today, disturbing images — and even more terrifying allegations — from that Miss Teen Dream Pageant gone wrong last night. Joining us this morning is someone who has a personal investment in this terrible tragedy: our special guest, presidential hopeful Ladybird Hope. Good morning, Ladybird.

LADYBIRD HOPE: Good morning, Barry. It *is* very disturbing news. You can see in this grainy footage Republic of ChaCha soldiers, under direct orders from The Peacock himself, aiming for the girls. The explosion. What we're hearing is that our Miss Teen Dreamers have been murdered. All of them. As you know, the Miss Teen Dream Pageant has always been special to me. I was a Miss Teen Dream. It is the ideal of femininity. This is a direct act of war, Barry, and —

BARRY REX: Excuse me, Ladybird. Looks like we've got some special callers on the line. Let's go to live feed, please.

On the studio screen, the girls waved. They had gotten pretty good at waving, but they had never enjoyed it more than they did right now. Ladybird Hope broke the pen in her hand into two pieces.

BARRY REX: How about that? They're okay!

ADINA: Hi! You would not believe the crazy night we had, Barry. What with Ladybird Hope trying to kill us and all. So, you know, sorry if we look like shit. Anyway, it's such a long story, and we are currently on vacation, so we're just going to leave you with this video and a PowerPoint presentation. Enjoy! Bye!

Ladybird Hope's smile twitched at the corners as the video came over the feed. Barry Rex's eyes widened.

BARRY REX: Well. Is that . . . the Republic of ChaCha?

"It's *somebody's* Republic of ChaCha," a camera operator murmured.

A half hour later, as Ladybird Hope left the studio, crowds had gathered again. But they were not cheering or holding up KEEP AMERICA PRETTY signs. No one shot play gun fingers at her with a wink. The faces were angry. Yelling. Ladybird Hope was not enjoying this moment in the spotlight. Still, she gave them a smile and a thumbs-up. "Keep your chins up. The truth will come out."

"The truth just did come out, you murderer!" a woman shouted.

A bonfire billowed up. Some in the crowd tossed copies of Ladybird's book into the fire while a librarian pleaded with them not to do that and grabbed a fire extinguisher.[50] Ladybird Hope made her way through the angry mob to her car, where two federal agents in dark suits waited for her. If she squinted, she could almost pretend they were secret service and she was the president.

[50] Really, being a librarian is a much more dangerous job than you realize.

CHAPTER FORTY-TWO

It was the most highly rated Miss Teen Dream Pageant ever. Though there were only thirteen contestants, the curiosity about seeing these survivors — fanned by an Internet ad campaign that hinted at unsavory sexual secrets and possible cannibalism — drew a record number of viewers. Sadly, without continued sponsorship from The Corporation, the program was canceled and replaced with new episodes of the reality show about Amish girls rooming with strippers, *Girls Gone Rumspringa*.

The media were calling LadybirdGate the sex scandal of the century. One tabloid referred to her as "Ladybird Ho." Articles appeared in newspapers and blogs decrying the moral decay of girls in general. On TV, talking heads wrung their hands over a lack of traditional feminine values and wondered if girls' sports were to blame. Then they cut to a commercial featuring a sexy college coed vacuuming her dorm room in her underwear.

Shanti shook her head. "All those crimes, and, like, all anybody can focus on is a sex scandal."

"Yeah, The Corporation will probably only get a slap on the wrist and get to set up shop somewhere else. Everything's being blamed on Ladybird. Typical."

"She may be a D-E-W-S-H, but it's not *all* her fault," Tiara agreed.

"You're uncharacteristically quiet over there, New Hampshire," Petra said.

Adina wasn't watching the continuing coverage on the yacht's TV. Instead, she stared out at the sea. "Just thinking about Taylor."

Nicole put a hand on Adina's shoulder. "Hey, you tried to find her. We all did."

It was true. They'd gone looking. They'd searched everywhere, with no luck. What Adina hadn't told anyone was this: As she'd passed the secret cave in the jungle where Taylor had hidden for so long, she'd found the beauty queen's sash and dress hung neatly from a tree, abandoned. And just beyond that, she'd thought she'd seen a flash of blond hair in the trees. But then it was gone.

The newscaster's voice whined from the TV. "Do you think these girls, these Teen Dreamers, all those things they did — and Tom, we're hearing about wild things now — do you think it has to do with sex ed in the schools? Or are girls just getting more brazen? And what does this mean for society in general? Should we be scared of our daughters?"

"They don't get it," Shanti said with a sigh.

"Do you think they ever will?" Nicole asked.

"Fuck 'em," Sosie said. She flipped off the TV and chucked the Miss Teen Dream manual into the trash can.

From her perch in the tree, Taylor watched them go. The orphaned snake slithered down from the trees and she let it rest upon her shoulders like a beautiful, iridescent boa.

"My stars, this sure is a big mess, isn't it?" she said, walking over the ruined land near the volcano. It wasn't terrible, really. Just needed some elbow grease and then it would shine and sparkle like a crown. The snake nuzzled her cheek and flicked its tongue. Taylor stroked its head gently and it settled.

She had a busy day ahead. There was an island to tame. Creatures to name. A world to build.

Whatever would she wear?

COMMERCIAL BREAK

OPEN ON: A group of sexy beauty queens running through the jungle, swinging on vines and knocking out ninjas. They stop beside a volcano, punch in a code on the keypad, and enter the secret compound, where they immediately go into the shower area and examine themselves in large mirrors.

BEAUTY QUEEN #1
Whew! This humidity sure is hard on a girl's lips.

BEAUTY QUEEN #2
I'll say. I may be a feminist fatale, but I can't seem to do anything about these chapped lips.

BEAUTY QUEEN #3
Come on, girls — it's time to slay those pooped puckers and amp up your shine with Bitchin' Babes lipstick! Moisturizing. Vitamin-enriched. And full of shine and sparkle! This is one lipstick that can really stand up to whatever life throws at it.

CUT TO: Close-up of girl slicking a wand of gooey lip gloss over very full, collagen-enhanced lips.

BEAUTY QUEEN #3 VOICEOVER
Bitchin' Babes is a can-do gloss — perfect for the beach or a jungle pool party. And it comes in four moisture-drenched colors: Lava Red, Pirate Pink, Mind's Flower Mauve, and Sparkling Sand.

CUT TO: Beauty queens dressed in sexy spandex suits and ready for action.

> **BEAUTY QUEEN #1**
> These lips are survivors.

A red alarm on the wall goes off.

> **BEAUTY QUEEN #2**
> Uh-oh. Here comes trouble.

> **BEAUTY QUEEN #1**
> At least my lips aren't a problem!

> **VOICEOVER**
> It's a jungle out there — better look your best, with new Bitchin'
> Babes lipstick. From The Corporation. Because —

The commercial stalls, then quits altogether. A loud beep can be heard.

> **WE ARE EXPERIENCING TECHNICAL DIFFICULTIES.**
> **PLEASE STAND BY.**

EPILOGUE

"Here we go, ladies! Dance us out, Teen Dream–style — hey-up!" Shanti growls into the mic. Decked out in oversize sunglasses, a (yellow) sari over a Run-D.M.C. tee, and glitter sneakers, she stands in the makeshift DJ booth working the turntables. The yacht's excellent sound system blasts the killer Hip-Hopera groove of *La-La Boheme*'s overture punctuated by the danceable mix of tabla and sitar from Beena's "Mumbai Love Song."

"Y'all ready to do this?" Shanti asks.

"Yeah!" the girls respond.

"I said, are y'all, like, totally ready to do this?"

"YEAH!" The girls are loud.

"Here we go, here we go, here we go."

Expertly, Shanti mixes in Beena's vocal. The pop star's high voice soars over the steady beat. "Give it up for our wild girl and pirate queen, Miss Nebraska, Mary Lou Novak!"

Brandishing a cutlass and wearing her Miss Nebraska sash around her head, pirate-style, Mary Lou takes the runway in long, loping strides. Her arms move completely out of sync with her feet. She will make a formidable captain, but god bless her, she still cannot dance. Let us cast our eye to her future now:

Mary Lou Novak — Adventurer. Pirate Queen of the *Josephine*. Wild girl. When not at sea, Mary Lou and her companion, Tane, live on a wind farm in Nebraska with their three little wild girls.

"Ch-ch-check your faboosh against hers! Straight outta Rhode Island, it's Petra West!"

Like some alien goddess, Petra shimmies down the runway in a mod, sequined mini festooned with palm-frond fringe. Her makeup — smoky eyes and nude lips — is fierce. At the end of the runway, she punctuates her Fosse-esque pose with the sharp snap of an open fan.

Petra West — Transwoman host of the popular nighttime chat show *Go West*. Married to Sinjin St. Sinjin, music producer and bon vivant.
They both look great in heels.

The fan snaps closed again. With a toss of her head, Petra swivels on her heel and exits the runway.

Shanti punches in an old-school drum machine sample. The groove is thick. Juicy. "Let's make some Illin'-noise for Sosie Simmons!" she calls.

Jennifer signals to Sosie that it's her turn, and Miss Illinois, resplendent in an edgy tutu made from evening gown remnants and airplane seat foam, executes a perfect grand jeté into four revolutions, a blur of grace and grit. And then she stops, arms spread wide toward the silent, powerful clouds.

Sosie Simmons — The new director of Helen Keller-bration! dance troupe, currently touring the United States and Canada. Was able to secure additional funding for an arts-based after-school program for children with disabilities. Dating a boy, for now. Still enjoys watching clouds.

Sosie does a backward flip into the wings, where Jennifer slaps her five down low. Sosie puts her thumb to her chest and waves the other four fingers. Jennifer mimes it back. "I think you're awesome, too."

"Watch out! It's the original Flint Avenger, Miss Michigan, Jennifer Huberman!"

"Oops. That's my cue," Jennifer says.

"Go Jennifer!" Sosie whoops as her BFF takes the stage.

Snapping her fingers from side to side, Jennifer skips down the runway in satin harem pants and a Wonder Woman T-shirt whose hem she's bedazzled with tiny shell fragments that catch the light and cast her in a pinkish glow. She reaches into a pocket and produces a golden lasso (all right, a thin, golden strip belt, but why quibble?), which she twirls above her head, disco-style, and quite frankly, she's fucking fabulous. But what of her future?

Jennifer Huberman — Writer/illustrator of the underground comic *Fiercely Fashionable Dykes*. Co-owner, with her wife, Marguerite Espinoza, of Galaxy Comics, the best independent comics store in Flint, Michigan, and organizer of the annual Girl Con.

Jennifer presses the backs of her wrists together like clinking bracelets. Shanti imitates the movement and they share a laugh. "Wonder Woman herself, Miss Michigan, Jennifer Huberman!" Shanti calls.

Jennifer duckwalks her way back, earning the laughter and applause of her friends. Spirits are high.

Adina dons a pair of sunglasses and grabs the mic. "I hope you came to get down, because Miss Ade's in town! Ladies and gentlemen — the girl who puts the *rad* in COLO-RAD-O! Nicole!"

Nicole's long legs take the runway in gazelle strides. Her hair is a beautiful black corona tied off with a bright orange scarf. Her purple dashiki is accessorized with a flower-and-frond necklace. She shadow-boxes the air with hard, swift uppercuts before coming to rest in a champion's pose, arms stretched overhead.

"Check it," she says, and purses her lips.

Nicole Ade — That's Surgeon General Nicole Ade, thank you very much. Implemented comprehensive public school sex ed programs credited with raising teen body awareness and self-esteem and lowering teen pregnancy rates. Manages anxiety with karate. Stopped biting her nails.

"You gonna moonwalk for us?" Shanti teases from the booth.

Nicole shoots her best friend the bird and everyone laughs. As she grooves her way back up the runway, Shanti's hands swerve over the turntables, expertly blending dissimilar sounds that somehow, mixed together, make something new and hot.

"Tiara! Tiara! Tiara!" the girls chant.

Tiara slides out on the runway in a purple tulle dress over black knee-high, lace-up boots. A garland of blue island flowers is pinned to her hair. She launches into a hard-popping krunk routine, her body like a weapon, before dropping straight down into a split.

"Whoa," Petra says. "That Christian pole dancing really limbers you up."

While we linger on Tiara's giddy, triumphant face, let's peek behind the corner at her future.

Tiara Destiny Swan — Part-time interior decorator and full-time soccer mom to four kids. Recently let them use her old trophies to construct a fort in the backyard. Enrolled in a low-residency college program with a 3.75 GPA. Knows how to spell *douche*.

"Thank you, Miss Alabama!"

"Mississippi!" Tiara singsongs.

"Oh, Alabama — that's me!" Brittani runs out onto the stage wearing a bikini and a metal cape made from salvaged plane parts. She turns to show off the cape and winks over her shoulder.

Brittani Slocum — Soap opera actress and celebrity spokeswoman for the Third Nipple Foundation. Accidentally married a European prince while making a music video. Now princess of that principality, but not really sure why.

On her way back, Brittani passes the foursome of Miss New Mexico, Miss Ohio, Miss Arkansas, and Miss Montana. They high-kick in contagion with Rockette precision.

Miss New Mexico — Experimental filmmaker, director of the acclaimed Palme d'Or winner *Trayhead*. Responsible for starting *Vogue*'s "Bangs are the new black!" trend.

Miss Ohio — Expert in constitutional law. Helped draft the new ERA legislation currently before the House.

Miss Arkansas — Math teacher and professional roller derby champion dubbed the Beauty Queen Bomber. Signature move? The smile-and-wave-'em-down.

Miss Montana — Runs a pet rescue on her one hundred–acre refuge in Montana. Philanthropist. Wife. Mother.

Miss Ohio gives her signature flirty, fingertips-only wave as the girls dance back.

Mary Lou motions to Adina to go next. Adina shakes her head, but she is overruled.

"Everybody takes a turn," Mary Lou insists, and draws her out.

"Here comes trouble," Shanti whispers into the mic.

"Trouble's my middle name," Adina fronts.

"I thought it was Painintheass," Petra shouts.

"That's my Hebrew name."

"Slick!"

The girls cheer and clap. Adina shifts her straw fedora to a rakish angle. She wears biker shorts and a striped mini fashioned from their former rescue banner. She is a dancing advertisement for "It's Miss Teen Dream, Bitches!" Snapping her fingers across her body and over her head, Adina marches down the runway, adding some arm rolls and pivot turns for fun. She freezes in profile, one hand on the brim of her hat, lips pursed.

Adina Greenberg — The youngest journalist ever to win a Pulitzer, for her reporting on the making of Lady 'Stache Off, which resulted in the product's being removed from shelves. Currently enjoying dating with no compunction to settle down.

With a grin, Adina brandishes spirit fingers. "Sparkle Ponies! Lost Girls! Represent!" she shouts.

"OMG. I am, like, so embarrassed for you," Shanti giggles into the mic.

As Adina struts off, Shanti adds bass. The turntables thump with a rhythm that cannot be denied. The earth shakes with it. Nicole leaps behind the booth and pushes Shanti toward the runway.

"DJ Shanti Singh, Miss California!" she shouts over the music.

It starts with the fingers, but soon Shanti's entire body tells a story. Traditional Indian dance movements give way to hip-hop and jazz. She makes it up as she goes along; it's her story to tell.

Shanti Singh — Owner of the Fortune 500 skincare company Shanticeuticals. Invests in microloans to female entrepreneurs in developing countries. Engaged to an awesome high school science teacher found by her parents. Weekend DJ of the popular *Bollywood Boogie* series.

Hands pressed together, Shanti takes her final bow, and now all the girls rush the stage. It is a delightful chaos of bodies. High-kicking. Hip shaking. Arm locking. Everyone contributing something. Mary Lou misses a step and the girls teeter near the edge, shrieking, but they manage to right themselves, and then they are laughing once more, leaning into one another in affection as much as support, a great chain of girl.

Shanti gives the signal. "One . . ."

"Two . . ." Nicole seconds.

"Three!" Adina says.

As one, they leap, laughing, and that is where we leave them — mouths open, arms spread wide, fingers splayed to take in the whole world, bodies flying high in defiance of gravity, as if they will never fall.

A WORD OF ACKNOWLEDGMENT
FROM YOUR GRATEFUL AUTHOR

It takes a village to take a beauty queen book all the way to final runway. Therefore, I'd like to pay tribute to the many fine people who have helped to make this book possible. Whether or not the following wish to be acknowledged now that they have read same is another matter.

A huge thanks to my editor and uber-mensch,[1] David Levithan, who, years ago, said, "A plane full of beauty queens crashes on a deserted island. And . . . GO!" David, some say your methods are madness; I say "genius." And, unlike most, I say it without irony. Clearly, you were the inspiration for Sinjin St. Sinjin. That much cannot be denied. Well, you and your lawyers can always try. I got you, babe — thank heavens.

Likewise, I must thank AnnMarie Anderson, who said, even before David, "A plane full of beauty queens crashes on a deserted island!" Apparently, this phrase is said quite a bit at Scholastic, like some sort of art house reenactment of *The Manchurian Candidate*. I'm grateful for you, AnnMarie — and not just because you're named after the seminal TV goddess of my youth.[2]

---

[1]Mensch—a person having admirable qualities; a stand-up dude/dudess. The person who always helps you move and, unlike family, doesn't years later say, "What do you mean you aren't coming for Thanksgiving? I helped you MOVE!"
[2]That would be Ann Marie of TV's *That Girl*, played by Marlo Thomas. Kite optional.

A tip of the hat and a Valium smoothie to Elizabeth Parisi, who spent time that could have been used practicing her talent portion on designing (and redesigning . . . and redesigning . . .) the cover for *Beauty Queens*. Oh, wait — that IS her talent portion, and clearly, she's going to take home the gold. Thanks, Elizabeth.

Fifteen percent of this gratitude is owed to my agent/husband, Barry Goldblatt, who said, "You're writing *what*?" It's sweet that after so many years of close partnership, you still have the capacity to be surprised and frightened by the things I say, dear. This Bud's[3] for you. No, really, you look like you need it.

Big smooches to Jennifer Hubert Swan and Cindy Dobrez for the Michigan lore. Your pride in your home state is duly noted. And a warm thanks to Deb Shapiro for supplying state facts on her native New Hampshire. We should all live free or die, though I'd prefer the former to the latter.

As the recently incarcerated Ladybird Hope says, "We can't wear the winner's crown if we don't have north stars to guide our ships through the slings and arrows of life's pageant." She said that in her book *Mixed Metaphors for the Modern World*, which is available in the prison gift shop.[4] So I thank *my* beloved north stars: Jo "Rhinestone Cowgirl" Knowles, Sara "Spray Tan-tastic" Ryan, Robin "Princess Hair" Wasserman, Holly "Circle Turn-a-licious" Black, Justine "Mock Me and Die" Larbalestier, Maureen "Flaming Baton Babe" Johnson, Susanna "Locked, Loaded, and Lovely" Schrobsdorff, and Barry "Studmuffin" Lyga for their critical acumen, writerly support, and all-around awesomeness. You are all winners to me.

---

[3]Bud—abbreviation for Budweiser, a form of beer. That Barry Goldblatt would never touch a Budweiser is not the point. It's the sentiment that counts. Unless you're talking about removing a leg. Then it's definitely the alcohol content that counts.

[4]*Mixed Metaphors for the Modern World*—now only $18.95! You should pull the trigger on this deal before the opportunity stops knocking on the road of life.

Thanks to Mitali Perkins and Simranjit Dhillon for their much-appreciated insights into Indian culture and for answering many follow-up emails and phone calls. Thanks also to Emily Harris for sharing her experiences as an African-American woman in the pageant system and for enlightening me about African-American hair care. Ladies, may all your ponies be Sparkle Ponies.

Much gratitude is due to Andrew Coate and Ginevra Pfohl for their incredible generosity in sharing their experiences as transgendered individuals. Thanks so much — I'm lucky just to know you.

A big old fair-trade coffee gift basket goes to Beth Fleisher for the yacht and sailing help as well as to boat carpenter Gina Pickton of the Philadelphia Maritime Museum, for explaining big ships. Any mistakes, egregious errors, or just plain things made up are entirely the fault of the author.

Further thanks are due to Josh Goldblatt for the comic book info and for indulging me in the mapping out of various endgame scenarios over dessert. You're right that "the villain should have a secret lair in the volcano. That's, like, the number-one secret villain hideout." Truer words were ne'er spoken, kiddo.

Further further (but not, say, as far as New Jersey, where the traffic becomes an issue) thanks are due to Carmit Birnbaum, Cassandra Clare, Brenda Cowan, Emily Lauer, Cheryl Levine, Josh Lewis, E. Lockhart, Joe Monti, Tricia Ready, Pia Wahlsten, Melissa Walker, and the participants of Camp Barry for listening to various degrees of rambling over the past year. I promise not to bother you again until the next book.

A big thanks to Nancy C. Bray, aka "Mom," for making *The Miss America Pageant* required watching for so many years. Over the years, I've learned to separate the unsettling messages about femininity from the fabulously over-the-top camp. It was fun, wasn't it?

It would be remiss of me not to acknowledge the debt due to the following: William Golding's *Lord of the Flies*, Naomi Klein's *The Shock Doctrine: The Rise of Disaster Capitalism*, Joseph Conrad's *Heart of Darkness*, *The Pirates of Penzance* by Gilbert & Sullivan, and the works of Ian Fleming, more specifically, the James Bond movies, to which I have an almost unhealthy attachment. In fact, there are still moments in which I expect to find an Aston Martin[5] waiting out front just before I head off to meet some guy named Felix who is never the same Felix.

Finally, thanks to the readers. You make this the best job in the world.

It's my fervent hope that I haven't forgotten anyone, but if I have, I'd be happy to make amends with cupcakes and coffee, and then I'd place a tiara upon your head while singing, "It's a Whole New World of Pretty." If this scenario does not sufficiently frighten you into silence, you are tougher than Taylor Rene Krystal Hawkins.

---

[5]Aston Martin—the luxury sports car favored by fictional British spies. Explosives, ejector seats, oil spreader, gun mounts and other lethal gadgets sold separately. Makes a great holiday gift for authors. * cough *